Accounts of Furlasia: Kunklestick's Prophecy
By M.P.VanderLoon

For Mom

Acknowledgements

Writing a book is no easy feat, it takes hard work, patience, dedication and motivation. I had always dreamed of being a writer but there is no guarantee I would've followed through on my goals if it weren't for a few select people.

For starters, I'd like to thank my husband Derek VanderLoon, who patiently listened to me babble on about my made up fantasy world despite not being a fan of fiction himself. Also he helped turn my rough draft map into a thing of beauty so I am grateful for that as well.

One of my closest friends and biggest supporters is Joshua VanSluyters. He had my back from day one, his words of encouragement helped give me the motivation I needed to push through the process and actually follow my dreams. It's hard to say if I would've finished this book without him in my corner.

My book editor, Adam Leavens, helped me take my story which had its fair share of errors in its original couple drafts and turn it into something magical. He helped guide my words in a way that would best connect with readers and helped me sound smarter. For an amateur author, that is invaluable.

The cover art was designed by user betibup33 at Thebookcoverdesigner.com. Her artwork for the cover is truly amazing and really helped my book pop.

Even though she is not around to see me finish my goals, I will always be grateful to my dearly departed mother for the life lessons she imparted onto me during her life.

Terria
Hills of Edmere
Morlay
Roo
Rangmar
Jordoon
Cristol
Cristol Lake
Ecglides
Tordenth Forest
Arlen Bog
Frand
Berloth Forest
Neverous
Hark Mountains
Solorian
Furlasia

Prologue

Furlasia was a land of beauty and wonders, yet at the same time no place for the faint of heart. A vast land of many different climates and terrains, one minute you were in an immense forest with trees so tall you can hardly see the sky, and the next, frigid temperatures threaten to kill you. There was no compromising with the land. Here lay a great city where the buildings were made of the most beautiful polished stones that had ever been seen. The city was called Terria, and it was one of the most prominent and important cities in all of Furlasia. Terrians, as they were called, are a diverse people of many different pigments and personalities. About the only trait they all shared was their pointy elongated ears, and an unusual love for drama. No Terrian seemed to mind their own business. If someone was having a bit of a spat, it didn't take long for everyone to know about it.

Terria was a brimming city full of shops, taverns, almost anything you could imagine, this city had. And more than just its shops and landmarks this city had cutting edge technology that none other in Furlasia had. The Vanguard army was armed with unique weapons not yet seen outside the gates of Terria called *Beacons*. These were powerful rifles that projected tiny beams of light that scorched anything they hit. Because of the power and the danger they posed, the use of them was permitted solely to the Vanguards. Technology so deadly could not be trusted in the hands of civilians who so often acted on emotions rather than logic. They were a tricky weapon to manufacture. Only a few knew how.

If you traveled into the grimiest part of town — in the center of the city — where the air smelled of soot, and the ground was stained black, you would find a blacksmith. He was a curious fellow, very private and not particularly good at speaking. An old injury had left him with a bit of a lisp, yet his strange mannerisms and unkempt appearance did little to deter his customers — his products spoke volumes even if he could not. It was he and he alone who had discovered the crystals in the mines to the west. And though no one knows for sure how he came up with the design, one day he created a weapon so impressive the King knew his army had to have it. Since then, *Beacons* had become the official weapon of the Vanguard army.

This mild-mannered and strange blacksmith went by the name Falker Squarelef. His only employee was his son, Septus, whom he had adopted at a young age. Septus was twenty-four years old and had long, nappy, rust-colored hair that hung at shoulder length. His eyes were bluish green, his skin freckled and pale. He was not regarded as the most attractive guy; most girls his age avoided him like the plague. He often dressed in loose, baggy clothes that had holes caused by burns from working in the shop, his overwhelming appearance of poverty contributed greatly to the loner status he had acquired.

"Hash you shorted out all the nuts and bolts?" Falker asked with a lisp, yet stern voice. He sat at a soot-covered, unstable desk wearing large bifocals and examining a piece of paper. Each time he attempted to follow the paper with his finger the desk would wobble to one side or the other.

"I'm nearly finished," Septus yelled from a distant room where he was hard at work patiently sorting out various size bolts and nuts that had been tossed in a wooden crate after being forged. As he picked through the crate he would put the bolts and nuts in their own separate boxes.

"I was hoping to go out with some of my friends as soon as I'm finished here if that's all right."

"I don't *she* anything wrong with that. Where are you *guysh* going to be?" Falker asked as he cluttered around the shop occasionally bumping into something and knocking it to the floor with a clang.

"We were going to go and search the woods for trinkets left behind by travelers. I found some pretty nice ones last time we went out," Septus replied with a pause. There were only a few more pieces left to be sorted. He was excited to get out of the shop. It was hot and stank of burnt metal.

"Well keep an eye out for ramite. I could use *shome* for a table I'm building for the kitchen. It's not been fun eating on the floor *shinsh* that last one broke in an apparent *accshident*." Falker said with a suspicious tone. He had known the table breaking was no accident; Septus had been fooling around with some friends and as usual, the home was the causality. They both had decided to pretend each other believed the lie in this instance.

Septus wore a grin on his face as he sorted out the last of the bolts. His mind wandered to the day the table was broken. He and Emlin had been goofing around the house with swords when his sword had struck the table and broke it in half. You could say one thing about Falker: he made *very* good swords. "I'm finished," Septus exclaimed with a smile. "I'm outta here." He grabbed his coat and made his way to the door.

"Be home in time for *shupper*," Falker said as he eyed the parchment he had lain across the desk; on it he had a poorly drawn design for the new table he planned to build. The door closed and Falker smiled to himself as he stared at the plans. *That boy is so much like me it's almost uncanny,* he thought to himself. He smiled and went back to his designs.

The air was chilly and moist as Septus made his way through the city towards the main gates. Since the days of the undead, a large gate had been constructed that surrounded the entire city. Citizens coming and going had to pass through the gates and let the guards know why they were leaving and when they planned to return. Septus always liked to be secretive so his answers were always vague but he never had any problems with the guards. He approached the gates and two guards began to pull them open.

"I'd ask where you're going, but you lie every time anyways. Be back before dark. That's all I ask," said Harold, a large guard wearing a heavy silver armor with red crescent moons chiseled into its arms and legs and a full moon on the breastplate. The armor had been designed to have the same appearance as Terria's flag; a black full moon with two red crescent moons on either side of it.

"Why, Harold, I would never lie to you," Septus said with a mischievous smirk. He hadn't realized he was that bad at lying, but apparently the jig was up. Lucky for him, Harold was a pretty relaxed guard, those he regularly saw he barely questioned. Still, he couldn't help but wonder exactly at what point Harold had realized he wasn't going hunting for trinkets, he had always brought at least one back to prove what he had been doing. Perhaps it was the poorly hidden sword he attempted to hide under his coat. Septus waved at the two guards as he walked through the gate, they gave a subtle nod and proceeded to push the gates shut.

The walk through the woods was peaceful; being outside the city, even little annoyances like the constantly pestering bugs seemed like blessings. As nice a city as Terria was, it easily could smother you with how busy it was. As you got further away, the smell of burnt metal became less noticeable; instead, you were greeted with the euphoric smell of grass and pollens from the plants. Loud voices and music were replaced by the chirping of insects and the grunting of the various animals in the trees. Septus stopped in front of a very old tree and looked around. A crunching sound in the dried fallen leaves warned that someone or something was near.

"What took you so long?" Septus called out. From behind a cluster of thorn covered bushes, stepped Princess Emlin. She looked as gorgeous as ever with rosy cheeks and long brown hair. Her soft green eyes could almost convince you she was an angel. However, Emlin was not a typical princess, she took more comfort in hunting than tea sessions. Her clothing was tattered like that of a poverty-stricken maid or a street dweller, a disguise that helped her sneak out of the city gates regularly. No one cared if a filthy street bum left or if they even came back, but a Princess was another matter. If she wanted to leave Terria she was always to do so with an armored escort.

"You just got here yourself," Emlin gingerly replied.

"Good point. So are you ready to have an adventure?" Septus asked confidently. He didn't tiptoe around her and coddle to her feelings; he treated her as an equal, not as royalty which was what made her first become fond of him.

"Lead the way." She leaned in close and gave him a kiss on the lips. As she pulled away, Septus displayed a smug grin.

In one of the surrounding trees; a red furless primate called an Oekie hung from a branch by its sharply pointed tail. As he saw the kiss, he turned away and started jumping and swinging between trees. Zewop was his name, and he was the King's unofficial pet and personal spy. As he reached Nasliegh Keep, he started climbing the bricks until he came to a stop outside a large window pane. He started knocking urgently on the glass until the window was opened by none other than King Hervott, ruler over Terria. Zewop began grunting and growling while pointing towards the forest.

King Hervott wore no crown on his head like a stereotypical King. His hair was brownish gray and hung down to his shoulders. His skin was pale from being cooped up inside so often. Today, he was wearing a silver doublet with brown diamonds sewn into its fabric, but this was pretty much his normal attire.

"Emlin is with him again, you say?" Hervott curiously asked. Zewop began jumping and grunting faster; clearly he was making an urgent point. "He did what?" Hervott furiously exclaimed.

Zewop continued his grunting and pointing until his message had been clearly conveyed. "Thank you, Zewop. As always, you've been invaluable. I must squash this before it goes any further," Hervott murmured as he turned and walked over to a basket sitting alongside his bed. He reached inside and pulled out a misshapen brown and orange fruit and handed it to Zewop who began howling in appreciation before jumping out of the window and disappearing into the forest. Hervott closed the window and turned around, marching furiously across the room towards the main door. He flung it open and called out to a guard standing at the end of the hall.

"Summon Vicham for me, please. Have him brought up here at once." Hervott demanded. The guard responded and diligently left the hall. *How could I have allowed it to go this far? With him of all people?* He shut the door in a huff of frustration, and made his way over to his custom-made chair to wait. It was over the top and a mostly hideous chair that had been hand carved with an unflatteringly dark stain—a gift for his fiftieth birthday. Every second he sat in it, he felt more infuriated, he had wanted to get rid of it years ago, but couldn't find the nerve to disregard a gift from the cities' highest religious figure, the High Mother. *I'm going to let the chefs use this chair to fuel the stove tonight—every second this sarcastic gift sits in my room, I can feel her mocking eyes.* His angry thoughts were interrupted by a stern knock on the door.

"Come in," he called out.

"You rang, sir?" Vicham asked sarcastically. He stood tall, skinny and had a darker complexion and longer ears than most in Terria, and his bald head made him appear wise, which he mostly was. Hervott stood up from the table and walked over to a picture on his wall; it was a picture of Emlin. He grabbed the side of the picture, and it moved outward revealing a small cubby in the concrete wall. He reached inside and pulled out a bracelet that had a skull being eaten by a snake on it; the bracelet was silver, and the skull had small gemstones in each eyelid. He turned and brought it to a table and set it down.

"Do you remember when we took this?" Hervott asked.

"It's not a day I could ever forget, nor will anyone. You took this as your prize on the day you conquered the necromancer Agavordis," Vicham sternly replied. He was looking at Hervott with a concerned look, *Why is he pulling this thing out* he wondered.

"On that day, when I defeated that monstrous man I took this bracelet from his wrist, I took something else from him that day as well. A small boy. A boy who I hesitated to spare, but I just couldn't live with killing him. I gave him to the blacksmith after he volunteered to raise him as his own."

"Yes, I'm aware of this."

"I spared that boy, but I have always been afraid of him. He comes from pure evil and like brown eyes or the color of your hair, I always worry that evil has been passed down to this boy. Every day I lie in my bed wondering if today is the day he starts to follow in his father's footsteps. At times, it keeps me from sleeping, the nightmare. The memories. He's not allowed to set foot in this castle, and yet I feel like he *is* in here, somehow," Hervott wore a blank, expression as he stared off. "You wouldn't believe what Zewop just told me."

"Sir, I still can't believe you think you can talk to Oekies,"Vicham said with a slight laugh. He had seen first-hand these so-called communications Hervott had with Zewop and all he ever heard was grunting and howling. Still, as silly and preposterous as it seemed, it did appear like he learned the occasional thing from this primitive communication. Communications with animals weren't entirely unheard of, but usually, only wizards possessed this ability. *So why Hervott?*

"Fair enough, my friend. I told you I was taught many years ago how to make out what they're saying. Zewop has proved to be an excellent way to see what is going on beyond our walls."

"And what is going on?"

"Emlin has taken a liking to the boy. She has been sneaking out with him almost every day. I let it go because mostly they just practice with swords and I don't mind her learning to defend herself. I've always known she loathed being a princess—she would rather hunt than curtsey. But she thinks of him as more than just a friend. She's *kissing* him now. Emlin is my *only* daughter and heir to my kingdom. I can't have her falling in love with the son of the most evil man to ever walk these lands. This relationship *must* be stopped. I need the boy to leave the city. I need him to go far enough that Emlin cannot find him." Hervott explained.

Banishing a child? Is he crazy?

"Are you sure about this? If Emlin finds out, she will never forgive you. Maybe there's another way to fix this. He's barely an adult and truthfully he hasn't given you any reason not to trust him. He hasn't done anything wrong." Hervott abruptly stood up and grabbed the bracelet giving it one last look before placing it back in its hiding spot.

"She's too young for this Vicham, she's only barely a woman. She can't protect herself, not against this kind of darkness. I'm not willing to sit around and wait any longer. The boy is wrong, everything about him is wrong. He has a sniveling way about him and every time I look at him I see nothing but evil. It's only a matter of time before what's buried deep inside him decides to crawl its way out. Do you feel comfortable just waiting for that to happen? You're like a second father to Emlin, if you care about her well-being, you *will* do this for me."

Hervott pleaded. He slowly placed his trembling hand atop Vicham's shoulder and gave it a slight squeeze.

"Alright Dwennon, I'll do it," Vicham said as he stood up from his chair and started walking towards the door. He had always found it difficult to turn his friend down, even when he knew it wasn't the right thing to do. *Friendship often does cloud the mind's judgment, not all decisions made from love are the right ones.* Hervott knew Vicham felt uneasy, but he was fine with exchanging his friend's uneasiness for his own peace of mind. As Vicham pulled open the door, he paused, *this could be exactly the turning point that ruins the boy's integrity.*

"Dwennon, what if doing this makes the boy snap? What if you are forcing him to become the monster you fear?"

"It's a chance I'm willing to take, my friend. He cannot stay; he *cannot* stay in Terria, not for even one more day."

Chapter 1

The city felt cold and empty. Apart from the usual sounds of tires grinding along the pothole infested roads and the all too frequent scream of sirens there was little sign of life. Walking down the desolate trails of concrete gave Nikalas a sense of power and authority. His tangled brown hair hung in front of his glasses causing him to brush it aside every few minutes. He maintained himself so poorly that he truly looked the part of a burnout. His outfit further confirmed this; he wore baggy black pants with a chain dangling from the pocket and a T-shirt that read *Trivium*.

Wandering the streets of Detroit alone at night was a comfort to him. Life wasn't easy for the homeless. The city was unforgiving and full of people who were just as likely to rob you as help you; there were few honest faces to be seen. Truth be told, he was only homeless by choice. He had a home — a place he could've stayed — but he had chosen to run away instead.

After the tragic disappearance of his parents when he had been thirteen, he had been sent to live with his overbearing aunt. He had barely stayed with her for a month before he had decided he couldn't tolerate it. She was a spiteful woman who enjoyed gambling more than she ought to and living with her had proved more stressful than comforting. Her ultimatum to him was the last straw. "My way or the highway," she had said. So he chose the highway. The highway, however, had led him straight to foster care. After six months in a facility, he had nearly found a new home with a young couple. But they came across as rich yuppies trying to give back some of their good fortunes. Charity? There was hardly a word Nikalas despised more than *charity*. The night before the papers were set to be signed, he climbed out the bathroom window and officially became a resident of the streets.

There were more than a few kids on the streets in situations just like his. They tended to stick together to help each other make it. At any moment, they could've found a shelter or gone back into the foster care system, but they didn't. They chose to stick with the hard life on the streets. Some of them were made stronger by it, and some *didn't* make it. Nikalas liked most of these kids, but often chose to spend his nights alone, wandering the streets, searching. He was never sure what it was, a sign maybe? A big break that miraculously would change his life? Whatever it was, he hadn't found it yet. It was nearly eight o'clock, which meant closing time at the Cottage Inn pizza place. At night, they often threw away leftover pizza and pasta. On certain nights, a young man worked who would give them to Nikalas. *It's not charity, it's survival* Nikalas would tell himself.

He started to make his way down the grim sidewalks when he noticed a couple of people trailing him from the corner of his eye. *Damn*, he thought to himself.

"Stop following me!" He yelled, annoyed. Quickly he whipped around to get a good look at his stalkers. It was Chris and Henry, two boys he had at one point teamed up with but after a falling out had decided to cut ties.

"Hey, we know where you're going, and we want in," Chris said.

"Yeah, split some of that pizza with us," Henry added.

"What are you guys talking about? What pizza, I don't have pizza," Nikalas replied. He lifted his hands and waved them in the air to further illustrate his point.

"No duh man, we can see that. But we've seen you before. We know you have a hook up at Cottage Inn," Henry replied. Nikalas laughed to himself and started to crack his knuckles as he slowly walked towards them. *Gotta fight for what's yours,* he thought. If he let them join him this time, they might try to come every time. Or worse, maybe they would beat him to getting the scraps entirely, leaving him with none.

"Oh, you think you can scare us, huh?" Chris laughed. "There's two of us Nikalas, don't be stupid."

"I've taken down four guys before, four guys that all knew what they were doing. We aren't together guys. I'm on my own, and you're on your own. Now if you try to keep following me, I'm gonna have to stop you. I still like you guys so obviously, I'd rather not," Nikalas explained as he gulped. "So are you gonna walk away willingly or am I gonna leave you on the ground whimpering?"

Before he could even get into a fighting stance, his face was already throbbing. A right hook from Chris had landed straight across his eye. He covered his face and looked at the boys furiously.

"You sucker punched me!" Nikalas cried out. That was only the beginning; the next one went straight into his gut. He fell to the ground holding his stomach and moaning in pain. Next came a barrage of legs, all hitting him in different parts. Each kick made him feel like he was going to vomit. After what felt like two whole minutes of kicks, Chris cleared his throat and hocked a loogie at Nikalas. On the ground, in the very same predicament he had threatened, Nikalas lay bruised, battered and moaning.

"Dude, you're a wuss. You always have been," Chris laughed as he gave Henry a high five. "Let's get that pizza." The boys turned around and disappeared into the night.

Getting up was hard and it hurt, but he couldn't just lay there. There was a throbbing sensation all over his face, and he could feel a headache coming on. In a staggering amount of pain, he got up to his feet and started walking to his hideout. He approached an abandoned house on a dark street full of similarly run down looking houses. Cautiously, he looked around to make sure no one was watching, then quickly got inside. Exhaustion had set in, getting beat up can do that to someone. He limped around the house and climbed the dark stairs until he found a desolate bedroom with nothing but a single mattress remaining. Despite being an old springy bed, it felt great to be embraced by its softness and warmth. He lay there, still reeling in pain and looking up. The popcorn etched ceiling often gave him escape. As he glanced at it, he couldn't help but imagine that he was looking at the night skies of a foreign land; maybe even a different world entirely. His eyes got heavy and before long he was asleep.

The dream always began the same. Nikalas stood in front of the bathroom mirror brushing his teeth and humming while he looked at himself. Gobs of toothpaste dripped down his chin and into the sink. His mother would be annoyed if he didn't take the time to wipe away the leftover toothpaste, but he was in a rush tonight. As he finished brushing and rinsing his mouth, he looked down at the toothpaste stuck to the ceramic bowl.

"Hurry up Nikalas or no book," a voice called out. He quickly shut off the light and darted down the hall to his room. Once inside, he jumped into his bed and hid under the blankets. In the distance, the footsteps signaled that his father was near. Stephen Noise stepped into the room with a book under his arm and looked around confused. The room was empty, or at least, it appeared to be.

"Hmm, I was sure I told Nikalas to get into his bed. Oh well, looks like he's not here," Stephen said smiling.

"I'm here, Dad," Nikalas whispered.

"Nikalas? I hear you, but I don't see you. Where did you go? Are you in the closet?" He quickly opened the door and pushed aside some hanging clothes. "Nope. Are you under the bed?" He bent down and got on his knees as he searched under the bed. Slowly, Nikalas uncovered himself and made his way to the edge as he looked down at his dad, still crouching. As Stephen began to sit up, Nikalas blurted out,

"Boo!" He yelled. Stephen acted as if he was scared stiff.

"Oh, my goodness! Where were you?" He asked.

"I was under the blanket," Nikalas laughed. Stephen bopped himself on the head.

"How come I never remember to check under the blanket? Oh well, you sneaky guy. Lay back down," Stephen laughed. He waited for Nikalas to tuck himself back under his blanket. "So which story do you want to hear tonight? We don't have much time before lights out."

"I want the story about the wizards fighting the giants."

"Ah yes, the one where Kunklestick greatest of all the Wizards defeated *Ingrid the Terrible* with his bare hands." With a chuckle, he opened the book he had been holding and started telling the story. He tended to get very immersed into acting out the stories. He would stand on chairs, crawl on floors, whatever made the story more exciting. There were so many stories Nikalas could've asked for, but he always seemed to want to hear about the Wizards of Furlasia.

"Boom, boom, boom. Great footsteps could be heard, and the townspeople all looked scared and started to run towards their homes. Suddenly, Kunklestick appeared with the Wizards. Armed with only their staves, they slowly approached the giant, prepared for a fight. *Ingrid The Terrible* raised his bat in the air, the spikes covering it shined bright in the sunlight. With a terrible howl, he started to swing the bat straight towards the wizards."

The obtrusive sound of a garbage truck backing ended the dream. It was a pretty familiar dream, though. He knew how it ended. Kunklestick and the Wizards defeated the giant, and all returned to peace. Happy endings like that didn't exist here, at least not for Nikalas. There was no more time for fairy tales. As he climbed out of bed, he was reminded of the events of the previous evening. His whole body was throbbing and aching, lifting his shirt revealed bruises all along his chest. Even hours after it had happened, he was still filled with embarrassment. Talking a lot of talk didn't matter if he couldn't back it up, and last night have proved just that—he couldn't back it up. Once word got out he would lose all the credit he had among the street roamers. There was only one way to remedy this: he would need to track Chris and Henry down and get revenge.

The stairs creaked as he slowly hobbled his way down them. A bright light was seeping through the cracks between the boards that covered the windows. With the sun this bright it had to be late; he quickly reached into his pocket and pulled out his cell phone to check the time.

"Eight o'clock? Shit!" he exclaimed as he darted for the door. Math class would be starting in thirty minutes and he couldn't afford another tardy. He quickly darted outside, closing the door behind him. There was still a puddle in the neighbor's yard from the rainstorm a couple of days ago. He casually walked up and started scooping water into his hair. Looking around to make sure the coast was clear, he lifted his shirt and splashed some under his arms. He leaned in to get a whiff. *Not great, but not bad either.* He quickly put his shirt back on and limped his way down the streets.

The classroom was already filling up by the time he found his seat. The bell had not yet rung; he let out a sigh of relief and pulled out his book. Math lectures were among the most boring he could imagine. Listening to his old home economics teacher explain sex was more comfortable than listening to all this talk of numbers. As usual, the lecture dragged on for what felt like hours. The bell rung signaling his freedom and he closed the book in relief.

Halfway down the hall to his next class, he suddenly felt a hand tap him on the shoulder. It was Mr. Anderson, his math teacher. "I'd like to speak with you back in the classroom if you have a minute," he said. Nikalas looked up at a nearby clock on the wall.

"Can it wait? I've barely got a minute," Nikalas replied. The last thing he wanted was yet another lecture on life from this twice divorced old geyser.

"No, come on. Follow me. I'll write a note for your next teacher." Rolling his eyes, he began to follow Mr. Anderson back to the empty classroom. Inside, Mr. Anderson closed the door and walked to his desk, leaning against it while motioning for Nikalas to take a seat.

"Nikalas, your work lately has been suffering. I know you're smarter than your grades reflect. Mind telling me what's going on?" Mr. Anderson asked.

"I've got a lot of shit going on in my life, man. What do you want from me?" Nikalas exclaimed.

"I want you to excel, but if you won't do that, I'll settle for a passing grade. Your failures reflect as poorly on me as they do on you. Maybe more so, actually. I'm supposed to be helping you understand this stuff. What can I do to help?"

"Honestly, I have more important things going on in my life to concern myself with than these stupid grades," Nikalas replied.

"What kind of things? Anything that has to do with your face? What happened to your face, Nikalas? Who did that to you?" Anderson questioned as he walked closer to get a better look at the damage. "That looks bad Nikalas."

"It's nothing, barely feel it," Nikalas replied.

"Are you gonna tell me who did that to you? Assaulting someone bears consequences," Anderson waited for a moment, staring contently at his pupil.

"I'm not telling you anything. I'm outta here. As I already said, I have another class. I'd hate to fail that one as well," he thrust himself out of the desk, knocking it over in the process and stormed to the door. For a moment, something hampered his exit. A feeling began to wash over him, a feeling of uncertainty. He slowly turned around to get another glance. Mr. Anderson was in the process of reaching down to pick up the flipped over desk. As he noticed Nikalas, he straightened back up, pausing to look at Nikalas.

"Yes? Do you have something else to add?" Mr. Anderson asked. His tone remained just as calm as ever — as if having to pick up the desk hadn't phased him. *I should apologize,* Nikalas thought to himself. But his stubbornness wouldn't let him. He shook his head *no* and exited the room.

Night had once again befallen the strained city. Clouds loomed above, and the lightning was trying to hide behind them. There was a storm coming, yet tonight the streets were more populated than the night before. The decision had been made; he was going to track down the two boys and get his revenge. There was just the small matter of finding them: it wasn't exactly a small city. Fortunately, the selection of hangout spots for the homeless was small. With any luck, they would be easy to find.

His theory had proven correct. Just as he expected they had chosen to spend this evening under the bridges. *Such a cliché.* Cautiously he approached one of the bridges being sure to keep his eyes open. Huddled around a blazing trash can were Chris and Henry, just as he had expected. As Nikalas neared, the boys looked at each other and let out a whistle. From around the corner, ten other street roamers emerged as if from thin air. *Screw that,* he quickly turned around and began walking back to where he had come from, hoping that they didn't realize it was him. From behind him, the sound of quick footsteps had changed to sound more like thumps. He was being chased. Taking the cue from the sounds, he began to sprint as fast as he could down the dark streets.

The bright lights of downtown were a welcome sign indeed. From a nearby restaurant, a crowd of people had exited.

They continued to laugh amongst each other not even noticing Nikalas running straight towards them. The crowd was at least enough to stop his pursuers. Looking back, he noticed they had stopped their chase.

"That was close," he muttered to himself. It was beginning to become abundantly clear that he was not meant to get revenge; in fact, avoiding confrontation seemed like the much more attractive option at this point. This evening certainly warranted a trip to his favorite spot in the city. Campus Park, which regarding parks had little to offer of what he traditionally had considered important to a park. There were no slides, no jungle gyms, no merry go rounds. But there was a view, a beautiful view, and an exceptional water feature. This water feature did more for him than a jungle gym ever could. It made him remember his parents, which lately was becoming harder and harder. Each trip to the waterline was like reuniting with them, even if only in spirit.

For this trip, he decided it best to stick to the well-lit streets. Best not to be caught off guard by any hooligans looking for someone to beat on. All was going well, the breeze provided a comfort, the air was dense, and it was clear the storm was nearly upon the city. In the distance, he noticed a few suspicious looking people heading towards the water line. Each of them was well hidden and wrapped in trench coats. *Nothing ominous about that,* he thought. This was a strange sight even in a city like Detroit. Keeping a safe distance, he began following them as they continued to make their way down the streets. For a brief moment he caught a glimpse of what looked like a tail hanging in the back of the coat. This only served to further his curiosity, as now he began getting brave and getting closer.

As they continued towards the waterline, Campus Park came into view. The strangers were heading straight for it. What he saw next caused him to rub his eyes in disbelief. Directly in front of the water feature was a green beam of light, it flickered and cast a green glow all around the park.

"What the what?" He whispered to himself. Loud crashes of thunder and flashes of lightning broke the silence; the strangers came to a stop and looked up towards the sky. Their faces were dark and still quite hidden, there was something hanging behind them, he was sure of it. Slowly, rain began to trickle from the skies; puddles began to form, and one of the figures said something to the others. He couldn't make out what they said, but suddenly they all turned and started walking toward the beam. Keeping low to the ground and hiding behind any object he could find, Nikalas continued to get closer.

"Hey, punk. There's no one to protect you now!" A voice yelled out in the background. Nikalas quickly turned around to see where the voice had come from. There they were again, the guys who had relentlessly chased him earlier. Their numbers appeared to have grown yet again, he now counted around twenty. In the background, the figures all had walked into the light and were nowhere to be found. The light continued to flicker — the rain passing through it caused the once solid green beam to be filled with hundreds of small black dots. Nikalas started backing toward the beam, being sure to keep his gaze fixed on the mob.

Thunder crashed once again, and the mob began darting towards him. The light from the beam was now very bright. He was standing directly in front of the beam looking at the stampede. The closer they got, the more he considered taking the gamble. He didn't know what was inside the beam, but he was sure what waited for him here. If these guys wanted, they could easily kill him. He was defenseless and outnumbered. He gulped and took a couple more steps back. Everything was green, and then there was nothing but darkness.

"What happened?" He whispered to himself.

Chapter 2

The cold dampness of rain had faded and given way to thick, muggy, humid air that almost instantly left a sticky feeling on the skin. Nikalas squinted as he looked up towards the bright sun. Glancing around, he was taken aback by the sights; there were neither buildings nor streets. Instead, he was surrounded by forest, and an impressive forest at that, the trees here loomed overhead almost like buildings, and they numbered in the thousands. The redwood forests of California had always been a dream to see. These trees looked similar, but there was something foreign about them. One thing about all this was clear: The beam had sent him *somewhere*.

"That was a portal? Awesome," he blurted out.

"Hey! Who are you?" A voice bellowed. Nikalas quickly whipped around and let out a slight scream of shock. Staring back at him was a creature that looked to be over seven feet tall with coarse, green scaled skin. The reptilian looking creature was dressed head-to-toe in roughly put together armor, and the face of a woman was painted on the breastplate. A long tail with a sharp point hung behind it, and its fingers all ended in long claws. Lying on the ground were the discarded trench coats he had seen the strangers wearing. It was *them*; these were creatures that he had seen in the night.

"Answer me, you vile being!"

"My name is Nikalas Noise. Who are you?" He asked as he slowly raised his hands in surrender. The forest was filled with loud chirps, howls, and grunts. Nothing about this land seemed welcoming—even the grass appeared hostile with its thorn-tipped ends. Here in the center of a strange, hostile land, he stood face to face with a mob of reptilian creatures. The Akordans — as they were called — all stood, hands on their swords prepared to cut him down at a moment's notice. With the portal closed, he had nowhere to run; he was trapped. Slowly, the creatures edged closer to him; they were certainly an unsettling bunch.

"You ask no questions. You get no answers. We talk, you listen." one of them stuttered, there was a long scar in front of the creature's throat. *A battle wound*? Perhaps the reason for the strange dialect.

"You're one of Hervott's spies, aren't you? Speak, or have your tongue cut out!" another yelled, drawing a sword and pointing it towards him.

"Who? I don't know who Hervott is. I followed you from the city." Nikalas replied as he cautiously backed up.

"You'll have to forgive him. He's not trained in the art of conversation. He's usually just good at gutting things that move," a calm voice said from the front of the group. Krytus slowly emerged from the front of the pack. He must've been the leader; as he walked closer, each of the Akordans stepped to the side to make room for him. He looked like the rest of them, but his shading was brown rather than green. His armor was rough and full of gashes, his presence disheartening. Nikalas felt a new sense of dread as the leader came to a stop in front of him.

"You came from the stone city?" Krytus questioned.

"Yes, I'm from the stone city. I'm a human. What exactly are you?" Nikalas asked with a quivering lip.

"We are Akordans, the mightiest species in all of Furlasia. None dares challenge us for fear of our wrath and our blades. So tell me why we should not kill you, Nikalas? He who has followed us through the crossing," Krytus asked, nodding towards his holstered sword. Nikalas glanced toward the weapon and gulped when something suddenly grabbed his attention. Krytus was carrying something, something he clearly prized. A glass box and inside a golden necklace with an inscribed medallion. He held it close as if it was a child; it must've been important.

"I'm not a threat. You all have swords and such. I have nothing. Why kill an unarmed man? I didn't even mean to end up here. I didn't know what would happen if I walked into the light," Nikalas replied. "Is that why you were in the city?" He nodded towards the glass box. Krytus pulled it closer and grunted.

"What do you know of it?" He growled.

"Nothing. It's really lovely, but I'm not sure it would look good on you," Nikalas mocked. Krytus laughed, it was an obnoxious mix between a cackle and a growl; the combination was rather unpleasant to hear.

"Human, you say?" Krytus turned and looked toward his men "He's funny. We could use such humor in Neveraus. Bind him. He comes with us," he ordered. As his men began rustling around trying to find a means to secure their guest, Krytus began making his way back to the front of the group.

"I'm not that funny," Nikalas called out as a couple of Akordans began wrapping his hands in primitively made rope. "Really, I'm actually rather boring, most people think I'm lame, you should just leave me here." The Akordans laughed as they finished securing his bonds.

"Ha ha, he is funny," one of the Akordans said as he held the rope's end and began pulling. His words of plea fell on deaf ears. With his hands bound he was slowly dragged behind his captors. Berloth forest was a strikingly large place, and made up a good portion of Furlasia. Traveling through it was inevitable, but most tried to avoid it either way. There were fouler things than Akordans wandering among the massive trees.

The journey took its toll, his wrists were beginning to rash and his legs were becoming sluggish. Their muscular nature made traveling great distances an easy feat for Akordans; poor Nikalas however was feeling the pain. Finally, after marching for three hours non-stop, Krytus came to a stop. Something in the air caught his attention; he started sniffing the air like a dog trying to track the source. Some of the others joined in, their deep breaths were so loud all other nature was tuned out. At last he held up his hand, ceasing the noise and pointed towards a tree in the distance.

"Do you smell that? Something is following us. Brutus," he turned toward one of the smaller Akordans. "Check it out." Although smaller and younger than the others, Brutus was no less brave. Often the younger Akordans were eager to prove themselves, and the senior ones didn't mind one bit: *Let the rookies take the risk* was the mentality. The young Akordan drew his blade and slowly started walking toward the tree, behind him, the rest prepared themselves. He drew closer, caution in every step. Eager and brave didn't equal stupid. With each passing step, the scent got stronger. Something was definitely nearby.

A metallic ping rang out as an arrow was let loose and bounced off Brutus' armor. With a dulled end, it wobbled through the air landing at Nikalas' feet. Before any of them could react a second one came, this time bouncing off the young Akordan's forehead. *Well, that's something*, Nikalas thought to himself.

Out of the tree, from a high branch, leaped a cat-like creature with mustard colored fur that was riddled with brown blotches. It was a Delopar named Inca, one of the toughest and keenest warriors in Furlasia. She was armed with a sword and had held it high over her head as she descended through the air. Her attack was blocked as Brutus quickly raised his weapon. The back and forth clang of sword against sword began to ring through the air as the two fought one another. Inca's attacks would almost be mesmerizing to someone who respected combat. Her moves were graceful and calculated. On the other hand, Akordan's didn't typically think a fight through; swing until you kill something, surprisingly this was almost nearly as effective.

Three more emerged from behind the tree line as the fight continued. Draxton, a suave looking man who looked as though he belonged in a salon rather than on a battlefield. Broli a large, red-bearded man with the look of a drunken Norsemen and Princess Emlin who truthfully looked more like a warrior than any of the three while being the least qualified. As she glanced the situation over, she quickly locked onto one of the Akordans holding Nikalas and let loose an arrow. Once again the arrow was wasted on the tough exterior.

"Their skin is too tough for that, dear," Draxton said with a grin of joy as he picked a target and began to engage. The skin of an Akordan acted as a natural armor; it was extremely dense, and it took quite a bit of force to puncture. Nothing but an up close and personal attack with a sword would do the trick. Still, Emlin was hardly the first person to try this, others that tried this often met a grisly demise. Luckily, she had back up, she nodded with a smile and reached for her sword. Yelling like an Amazonian warrior, she charged toward the captors and began to fight.

Wake up, wake up, wake up! Nikalas thought to himself as he closed his eyes, reaching for his arm he quickly gave himself a firm pinch. This was all too ludicrous to be real—clearly he was having another dream. No, he was lying on the ground at Campus Park after being pummeled, he was sure of it. His eyes were pressed firmly together, the sound of fighting still continued to ring in his ears. *It's just a persistent dream. Wake up, you fool.* Exhaling a deep breath, he opened his eyes to see Emlin standing inches from him.

"I said, 'Are you okay?'" She repeated. In his daze, he hadn't even heard her trying to talk. Well that, and the overwhelming stress of being in the middle of a battlefield. Wonder-struck he stared back at her before she sighed in annoyance and turned around to block an attack. She was mesmerizing, to say the least; her fighting was neither graceful nor sloppy. Clearly she had training, although she could likely use more. All that considered, though, seeing her hair flow around as she quickly engaged and deflected had him stupefied. Who were these people that had come from out of nowhere? They seemed like friends, but perhaps they just wanted to hold him hostage too.

"Throw him a weapon!" Draxton called out to Broli who was in the midst of a heated back and forth fistfight. Each time he landed a successful punch, he burst out in laughter; oddly he did the same when he got hit. If he wasn't insane, then he wasn't far off. He looked toward Draxton as he listened, then shot his attention over toward Nikalas. With his attention on Nikalas, his foe took the opportunity to land a jab on his cheek. Broli hastily turned toward his assailant and let out a mighty growl as he lifted up his left leg. The force of his kick sent the Akordan flying into another; they both crashed to the ground tripping another and creating a pile. Quickly, he reached into his belt and tossed a sword towards Nikalas' feet.

"Well, go on man! Pick it up and help," Broli yelled.

"I've never used one of these," Nikalas said as he reached down and picked it up, finally noticing that his bonds had been cut. It was deceivingly cumbersome; he nearly dropped it as he stood back up. His hands gripped the handle firmly, how hard could it be? Broli shook his head and cheerfully picked up his ax and nestled it firmly into the spine of an unsuspecting Akordan. As if falling from the sky, Inca swooped in and cut the creature's neck. She exchanged a nod of approval with Broli, and then got back to it.

As Draxton fought his rival, there was hardly a single hair out of place, but not for lack of trying. He kept his posture perfect and his swings to a minimum. Eventually, though, his target went down; they always went down. He ran his hand through his hair and smiled. The fighting raged on with everyone slaying at least one foe, apart from Nikalas, who was still preoccupied by his self-motivation. *You can do this.* Moments later, the forest went silent. He looked around to see the fighting had ended; Broli was laughing insanely as he watched Krytus scurry away from the battlefield, tail between his legs. Emlin raised her bow and aimed it at the spot that was getting smaller by the second.

"Emlin you already know that won't work. You need to use a blade; you need to get up close and personal," Inca said. "I'll get him."

"No, let him go," she said as she lowered her bow. "Let him warn the others what messing with our kind will cost them." She watched Krytus disappear into the distance for a moment. *Coward.* With the Akordan threat neutralized, all attention turned back to Nikalas, who stood still shaking and still holding the sword. As he realized he was being stared at, he dropped the sword and raised his arms.

"Come now lad, if we wanted to kill you, we would've done it by now," Broli chuckled. He and the others started to edge a little closer. Who was this stranger? He had a way about him that seemed foreign even for a land as diverse as Furlasia.

"Who are you? I've never seen you in the city before." Emlin questioned as she looked him over. "Where did you get such an outfit? Are you from the hills of Edmere?"

"Emlin look at him; he's one of the peasants of Rogthar — scummy and unkempt types they are. Best not get too close to him. They carry nanclims — very nasty and very tough to get rid of." Draxton shuddered as he continued to examine Nikalas and took a couple of steps back as he ran his hand through his hair.

"I say he looks like one of the thieves of Morlay. My village was robbed only a couple days ago. It's not even a day's walk from here. Where is the Rubix, thief? Tell me!" Inca yelled as she drew her dagger and placed it against Nikalas' throat.

"You fools, he's not from here at all," Broli laughed. Inca lowered her blade and turned toward Broli. Nikalas sighed with relief. "He's traveled here from another realm."

"What nonsense is this?" Inca laughed. "How much mead have you had today Broli?"

"How can you tell?" Emlin asked. The idea clearly didn't seem as preposterous to her as it did Inca, but, then again, the royalty were privileged to information most in Furlasia only were able to speculate about. Many had heard the rumors of traveling to different realms. To most it was just stories to tell the children, but there were those who believed.

"Just look at him, the people of Edmere are all of darker complexion. He's as pale as a corpse. The peasants of Rogthar can't even afford half the clothing that he has on. I've been there. Trust me, most walk around only a couple items shy of nude. And the boy has no cunning; if he *were* a thief of Morlay, he'd be a lousy one," Broli took a few steps closer to Nikalas and held out his hand. "Empty your pockets, boy." The man was huge, especially compared to Nikalas. He had to be close to six foot five. He promptly did as he was told. Reaching into his pockets, he grabbed a hold of the only thing he could feel. It was small, made of plastic. A cellphone, he carefully set it into the large man's hand and took a step back. Broli smiled and pompously waved the device in the air.

"What evil device is this?" Inca snarled.

"It's not evil. Although where I come from some might say it is. We use them for talking to people over a great distance. It's called a cell phone." Nikalas quietly explained. Inca shot him a look of distrust, and he looked to the ground aghast.

"Inca stop it," Emlin ordered. She quietly walked closer. "Tell us everything. How did you get here?"

Over the next few minutes, he did his best to explain the absurdity that led him to this moment. The fight with the boys, getting chased, spotting the Akordans and being held captive. Everyone seemed convinced by the story — except Inca, but it was like Delopar to be distrusting. Too many atrocities committed against them had them paranoid and suspicious of newcomers.

"Sounds like a load of fuit to me," Inca declared. "A portal that magically sends you to another world? Do we look like children?"

"It's real Inca, trust me," Emlin deadpanned. "My father will want to hear of this. We must bring him back to Terria. What is your name, stranger?" Her glare made him feel impuissant, was it her emerald green eyes, was it the way the humidity had frazzled her already curly brown hair. It was hard to say, the fact remained, she was tantalizing.

"My name is Nikalas Noise," he responded.

"I'm pleased to meet you Nikalas, "Emlin replied, she extended her hand in greeting, he paused for a moment before finally shaking it. *Perhaps he is foreign after all*, Inca thought to herself. Here, those that greeted the princess knew to kiss her hand; it was considered polite and a sign of respect. This boy did not know the customs; shaking hands was a primitive gesture. Emlin withdrew her hand, confused, and waved her hand in the air.

"Let's get a move on. We have a lot of ground to travel," she ordered. The others started to rummage the ground for supplies; Inca and Broli exchanged a few laughs as they sorted through the corpses and looked for items of use. They appeared unfazed that this pile of death was of their making. As he watched, Nikalas found it hard to feel sympathy — who knows what they had planned for him had these three not showed up. He took a deep breath and started to cough. The air was thick with the smell of decay. It had been less than thirty minutes since the battle, but the heat was intense, and the corpses were already starting to rot.

As the last of the supplies had been pillaged, the group began the long trek back to Terria. Unlike the march with the Akordans, this walk was filled with chatter, although little of it was directed toward him. Mostly, the three bantered back and forth about plans for the remainder of the day or who had fought better. He managed to learn that this merry little group had nicknamed themselves *The Protectors*. Their mission was first and foremost to find a long lost friend of Emlin's named Septus. The second mission was to keep the Akordans away from their lands and help anyone in need.

At first when she had begun her search for Septus, she had been accompanied by Falker, one of the town's blacksmiths. However, after months without so much of a trace or a clue, he decided that Septus did not want to be found, and returned to his shop. That's when she formed The Protectors. It had been almost a year since they assembled and began their cause. The search had so far been in vain.

Each of the members was unique in their way; each offered something different. Draxton, from Morlay, a royal city to the far North in Furlasia, had joined them after he had been rescued by Broli from a nearly fatal fall. His cunning personality and skill with a sword, not to mention his contacts and people he was able to barter with to get things, made him invaluable to the group.

Inca, on the other hand, was a Delopar, perhaps one of the oldest species in Furlasia. She was not charming. In fact, she was cold, ruthless and nearly unpleasant to all who met her. Once you got to know her, there was a fierce loyalty. Not only was she Emlin's best friend, she was perhaps one of the best warriors in all the land. Broli was a woodsman and a friend to Falker. He was quite strong and very skilled with an ax, but more importantly, he was a loyal friend. *The Protectors*; they seemed like a mismatched band of misfits, but together they were effective.

As they continued their journey, they entered a new region of the land called Tordenth. Tordenth forest was a vast and deep labyrinth; the trees lined up so perfectly it appeared intentional. It was ravaged by severe heat, a lack of water and was full of violent creatures that wanted food. The more he learned about this place, the more Nikalas could feel his stomach turning.

"This place sounds awful," Nikalas replied as Broli explained some of the finer details of the forest.

"It's not so bad, once you understand it. This forest is fierce, but it will make you a better and stronger person—a survivor. In some cultures, it is a rite of passage for the young boys to spend five days out here alone. If they come back, they are treated as men," Broli replied.

"And if you don't?" Nikalas asked.

"If you don't?" Broli confusingly asked.

"Come back," Nikalas replied.

"If you don't come back, it's because you're dead," Broli laughed. *Yup, I've got to get back home.* Nikalas thought. He looked over at a tree and saw a small rodent running along a patch of dirt, as it neared the trunk, a large vine grabbed the rodent and squeezed it so hard it burst.

"What the hell was that?" Nikalas exclaimed as he pointed toward the vine which was now wrapping itself back around the tree trunk. Broli turned to see what he was pointing at and let out a chuckle. *Is everything horribly funny to him?*

"Ah, that's just a june vine. They are very easy to spot and kill. I wouldn't worry about them," Broli replied. As Nikalas' stomach started to twist with the overwhelming feeling that he was about to hurl, that was when he saw it: *Nasliegh Keep.*

Fear was replaced by wonder as they edged closer to the large surrounding gate. The whole city looked like it had come straight from the pages of the books his father had read to him as a child. There was something familiar about this place, something that evoked a feeling of déjà vu. Nikalas took a deep breath and pulled in the scents — fresh bread, exotic foods and factories. It smelled like *home.*

"At last, civilization," Draxton let out a sigh of relief and ran his hand through his hair.

"Oh? Was five hours away from your precious mirrors too much for you?" Inca joked as she slapped Draxton on his butt. He ignored the motion and continued straightening his hair. As they approached the surrounding border, two gated doors started to slowly open. On the other side stood two uniformed guards.

"Princess Emlin. Welcome back," one of the guards said, bowing.

Chapter 3

Holding onto the glass box as best as he could, Krytus made his way through the forest until he reached a clearing. Massive forest suddenly gave way to a marshland that spread for miles. If you followed the correct path you could stay on land, but if you stepped too far in one direction, you stepped into muddy water filled with unknown creatures. There was heavy moisture to the air and a visible white fog so thick it seemed almost tangible. This place was known as *The Ecglides*, and it was a region of Furlasia few could travel to. The very air was poisonous to breathe. This, however, was of little concern to Akordans. Their lungs handled the fumes just fine. This was the one place in all of the land where they could escape persecution—their only sanctuary of uninterrupted peace.

Krytus began the long trudge through the Ecglides only occasionally stepping off the path into the muck. Footsteps from Akordans that had come and gone before were still visible in the patches of land. Clearly, it hadn't rained recently, which for the Ecglides was rare. Most days, clouds hovered above the Ecglides as if to shade it from the sun. Usually, the clouds brought heavy rain which eroded their tracks. The journey across the Ecglides was close to a three-hour affair. It had to be done on foot due to the treacherous nature of the ground, not to mention that no animal could breathe the air apart from *Uboroxs,* which were difficult to tame. After an agonizing walk full of close calls, Krytus finally made it to the far side of the Ecglides where he was greeted by a large bog. Less than a quarter mile from the bog sat a large mountain that extended about a mile wide.

Krytus wasted no time diving into the chilled recesses of the water, the box still firmly in his grasp. The Arlen Bog was a unique habitat that contained creatures seen nowhere else in Furlasia. As he continued to swim deeper and deeper, he found himself surrounded by the usual oddities, which for him and most Akordans weren't so much odd but rather familiar. There were many different types, some aggressive, some docile. Most didn't attempt to mess with the Akordans. In these waters, Akordans were the top of the food chain.

Krytus was an excellent swimmer—as were most Akordans—their tails moved back and forth in unison, propelling them through the water quickly. They also had the added benefit of being capable of holding their breath for an impressive ten minutes. After a rather brief swim through the bog, he emerged inside a large cave. He set the glass box onto the cold, rigid, rocky ground and pulled himself out of the water. His arrival caught the attention of a couple of nearby Akordans who were standing against the rocky walls of *Neveraus*, the unofficial home for all Akordans.

Akordans had called Neveraus home for nearly twenty years. What had started as a mere few hunched around a fire cooking fish had now become a blossoming city. The population was in the thousands, and it was full of shops, homes, and training camps. Anything you could find in Terria you could find here. There was much more to Akordans than most in Furlasia thought. They were highly intelligent and more than capable of holding their own. At the center of Neveraus stood a colossal statue carved from cave rock, it depicted *Herratia*, the mother of Akordans and their official deity. Krytus made his way through the city, giving the occasional glance and nod to his comrades until he reached a small castle that had been built at the very end of the cave. *Neveraus Hold* was not a fancy affair, but it fulfilled its purpose nicely. Outside the entrance two husky Akordans stood guard, keeping out unwanted visitors. Although for the most part, all were equal amongst the Akordans, there still had to be leadership, a hierarchy. Neveraus Hold served as a home for those deemed fit to lead.

"Welcome back, Krytus," one of them said gruffly, as he opened the door and stepped aside.

"It's good to be back. Anything interesting happened while I was gone?" Krytus asked. The other guard shook his head firmly.

"All quiet. He's still in there. Hasn't stepped out once," the guard replied. Krytus nodded in approval, and then brushed past them and stepped inside.

The lighting was tenebrous inside the hold; torches were secured to the walls yet provided little light. In the center of the main room sat a large throne designed for the future leader. Krytus was important in rank among the Akordans, but neither he nor the rest considered him the true leader. He confidently navigated the halls, taking several twists and turns, going down a flight of stairs and then a few more turns until he reached a hallway with a wooden door at the end. With no interest in knocking, he lifted the handle and pushed the door open.

The room was gloomy; flickering flames danced across the ceiling and an open wound left the air with a rank odor. Lying on a small cot in the corner was Septus, his face and left arm wrapped in primitive bandages. His breathing was slow and shallow; his wounds were taking their toll. As Krytus stepped into the room, Septus slowly turned to glance at him. Every movement caused pain, but this was important, he had waited days for Krytus to return.

"Have you found it?" He faintly whispered.

"I have," Krytus replied, holding the box over the bed for Septus to see. Filled with excitement he tried to reach for it, but a sharp pain caused him to grimace and drop his arm back onto the blanket. "Not getting any better?"

"Does it look like it? It doesn't matter; now that you have recovered the *Talisman* I should be able to heal faster," He rudely replied, the prospect of finally donning the talisman gave him a jolt of adrenaline. Just enough to get him out of bed. He quickly flung himself from the bed and walked over to a mirror that hung on the wall and looked himself over. His right eye was glazed over, leaving him only able to see from the left. He looked awful, but still a lot better than a couple of weeks ago.

"Once I heal, I want to start tracking down the next talisman. I'm sick of waiting."

"We'll get you healed. The important thing is you make good on your promise. My kind doesn't take well to false prophets," Krytus reminded. "I'll send in the healer," Krytus said calmly setting the box on a dresser next to an old leather bound book. *Not that incompetent fool,* Septus thought to himself. He had already let the healer try to help; it didn't work out so well.

"I don't want to see that imbecile, he's useless. I had to wrap my own bandages. The claws you guys have make fine movements nearly impossible. The only thing that healer can do is give me more wounds to worry about. No, thank you," Septus dismissively waved his hand. He walked over and looked at the box Krytus had set down. *What is this containment?*

"Where's the key?" He asked as he leaned in to further inspect it. The glass box was pretty basic in its appearance; it had a gold painted metal bordering the top and bottom, aside from that, it looked like basic glass. Inside, the necklace was placed on a small pedestal made especially for this piece of jewelry.

"No key, you break it open," Krytus replied. Septus quickly signaled for Krytus to leave him be. He had waited long enough for this moment. Now in his solitude, he picked up the box and gave it one last glance. *This is the moment you've been waiting for.* With all his might, he threw it to the floor. The loud crash rebounded against the rigid walls, and bits of glass bounced all over the floor creating a sharp minefield. He smiled with satisfaction and reached into the mess to retrieve the talisman that was resting still on the floor. Holding it close to his good eye, he could just make out some sort of inscription; the language was old, and had not been used for many years. *What did it matter, anyway? The power was contained in the talisman, not the writing.* Still, he couldn't help but feel nervous. What if this was a bad idea?

A few more minutes of reflection and self-negotiating and he finally decided to do it. He had waited for days in agonizing pain, — this power belonged to him. Slowly, he lifted the talisman above his head and lowered it down, letting it come to rest just below his throat. Even with his clothes on, the stone felt cold against his skin. It had been worth the risk, for a mere second later, a force of energy pulsated throughout his body. His veins felt chilled as if ice was coursing through them. Things in the room that were once blurry came back into focus. His vision had improved, the once lingering throbbing sensation in his face and arm had faded away. At last he felt like himself again.

"What a rush," he laughed to himself as he frantically began to peel the bandages from his face and arms. He stood, gazing into the mirror, mesmerized. There wasn't so much as a scar left behind. This power was unlike anything he could've imagined; it was transcendent. The talisman glistened under the faint light from the candles, and the weight that had once felt as heavy as a rock now felt light as a feather.

"Most powerful wizard in the world indeed," he whispered to himself.

Krytus stood looking at the throne, deep in thought. He had long wished to see a leader sitting atop it. He himself had sat upon it from time to time. For all intents and purposes, he *was* the ruler of Neveraus. Still, though, neither he, nor most of the others considered it to be his throne. He was merely the steward.

"You'll have your throne back soon, Mother. I promise." His words fell to the floor like tears in the night. There was no audience, no mother to hear his words, just the air between him and the throne. His placement at the foot of the throne was noticed, however. A passerby humbly approached, placing his hand firmly on Krytus' shoulder, and giving a firm squeeze.

"Surely it should be you sitting on the throne. You're the one who has helped to unify our people and bring order to Neveraus. Without you, this place would be nothing more than a cave," the Akordan respectfully said.

"I appreciate that, brother. It's been amazing what we have accomplished here. But that seat is not for me, it's not for you, it's not for any of us." He turned toward his peer and gave a firm stare.

"Who then? Who else is qualified to be our leader?"

"Mother," Krytus replied.

"Mother Herratia is dead, Krytus. You *must* accept this. It's been nearly thirty years," the Akordan retorted.

"I think I have an answer for that," a voice said in the distance. From a dark corner of the room, Septus emerged dressed in new attire. His garb was black, and behind him hung a silver and black cape. One of the last traces of *Agavordis*, he wore the uniform proud and confidently. Coming to a stop in front of the two Akordans, he looked at them both and beamed.

"At long last, the time of the Akordans has arrived," Septus said.

Chapter 4

Terria's streets were overflowing with gawkers all determined to get a glance of Nikalas as he was led by Emlin toward Nasleigh Keep. The city was far more impressive than he imagined. He had half expected to see a small town with, a few drunks, a couple of whores and a modest castle. Instead, he found himself in the middle of a sprawling city. Each feature seemed more interesting than the one before. There was an attention to detail that was remarkable, from the wide streets made up of sand colored bricks to the perfectly designed shops and homes. With each passing step, whispers from the spectators crawled into his ear and made a home.

"Look at his ears," someone said.

"Who is that?" said another. He almost felt like an object people planned on bidding on. The sensation was painful and annoying. His eyes glanced back and forth as he took in the sights, but beyond the sights of the city, the people were eye-catching as well. Almost every single person he saw had pointed ears. *Oh my God, I'm surrounded by fricken elves.* Nothing felt normal here—even the pets seemed strange. One Terrian had what looked like a black bear secured to a leash. Another was bent over giving a snack to a blue dog with a bark that sounded animatronic.

"Keep up, boy!" Inca barked while shooting him an angry glance. He quickly picked up the pace and caught back up to the group.

"What's going on?" said another voice. Nikalas' arrival was an exciting event; all the bored housewives and lonely store clerks had something to gossip about, and gossip they did. As people saw the new stranger, they would run toward one another and start whispering, pointing in his direction. After a few more minutes of gawkers and gossipers, they had finally reached the steps of Nasleigh Keep. The castle was impressive, to say the least. Two points stood high in the sky each one topped with a crescent moon facing in the opposite direction as the other. Each window was made of stained glass that contained pictures which told a story. Some bricks were gray, others were black. They alternated, giving the whole castle a very hypnotizing appearance. The whole place brought to mind modern architecture from home, but it was clear this castle was very old.

"Keep your mouth shut unless spoken to, all right? You're bound to be asked a lot of questions. My father is very suspicious of new people," Emlin explained. Her arms flailed about as she spoke, and it was kind of cute. He nodded in agreement, and followed the group up the stairs, coming to a stop at a drawbridge that had yet to be lowered. A guard in one of the windows of the castle took notice of the party of people patiently waiting and gave the signal for the bridge to be lowered. It was slow and creaked rather loudly; there was a clicking sound similar to a roller coaster chain. Beads of sweat started forming on Nikalas' forehead as the bridge continued to be lowered. Broli gave him a pat on the back and winked as the bridge came to rest against the dirt. The first step onto the wooden bridge was a nervous one, his nerves were firing, telling him to turn around and run, *All I have to do is run and find a spot to hide*, he thought. But then again, where would he go? He sighed and glanced over the bridge at the river surrounding the castle; it was like a moat but made up of crystal blue water instead.

"That's some beautiful water. Where I come from, you have to travel hundreds of miles to see water like that," he quietly whispered to Broli.

"That's no water dear boy. That's *Ricter*; you wouldn't want to take a drink from that. A very painful death awaits any who falls into that river," Draxton explained. Ricter was a bit of an odd occurrence in Furlasia. It was pure acid and although deadly and corrosive to most creatures in Furlasia, there were certain types of hard scaled fish and organisms that survived in it. They were the only fish in all the land that nobody dared trying to catch, so naturally they had gotten quite big. The river ran for miles before dumping into a sizeable lake due south of Terria. Nikalas gulped as he imagined falling in.

In grand fashion, the castle doors slowly pulled open. The décor was breathtaking. He had to stop himself from pulling out his cell phone. Inca had thought it was some kind of evil device; the last thing he needed was a bunch of paranoid guards coming at him. Crystal chandeliers hung all over the elegantly painted ceilings. The floors were lined with large stylish tiles made up of glistening rock. Along the walls various paintings were hung depicting a King, a pale woman with black hair and Emlin. They stood proudly as they posed.

The King's trusted advisor, Vicham started walking down a large staircase that stood before the throne eager to greet Emlin. One glance at Nikalas, however, and he paused and turned back around. *That was weird.* Moments later, he returned, this time making it all the way down.

"Your father is on his way down. Who is your guest?" Vicham asked as he looked Nikalas over. *And why is he dressed so foolishly*, he thought to himself.

"Vicham, this is Nikalas. We rescued him earlier from a group of Akordans that had captured him. He says he's from a land called *Michigan*," Emlin replied as she gestured to Nikalas.

"Michigan? Hmm, Michigan doesn't sound familiar. Although I don't claim to be an expert on all of Furlasia," he replied as he continued to examine Nikalas. There was an awkward silence in the air that lasted for what felt like an hour, but in truth was a mere couple minutes. The sound of a door opening upstairs, followed by the echo of footsteps ended the silent tension. From the top of the stairs near the throne, King Hervott was slowly making an intimidating and shrewd entrance. Each passing step echoed throughout the great hall, each echo causing Nikalas just a little bit more anxiety. He came to a stop next to Vicham and began studying this new visitor; he spoke no words just stared, taking in all the details he could.

"Who are you?" King Hervott finally demanded. His voice was so commanding and loud that Nikalas couldn't help but flinch. He shot Emlin a look to see if she planned on intervening, but it was clear he was on his own for this part.

"My name is Nikalas Noise," he replied. Over the next few minutes, he slowly retold the story of his arrival into Furlasia. The creatures, the portal, the rescue, all the details he could. Hervott listened to most of the story with a twisted look of suspicion and disbelief. *He's with them. He's trying to infiltrate Terria and destroy us all.* The voice in his head begged him to listen and he usually did, rarely did it seem to be wrong. He tried his best to listen, but the voice was persistent. *He wants*

Emlin; he's going to kill her. Hervott cracked a grin as the story finished and pulled Vicham to the side as they began to whisper, occasionally firing incredulous looks towards Nikalas.

"Guards take him to the dungeon!" Hervott abruptly ordered. *What the hell?* Two guards dressed head to toe in silver uniforms and holding weapons started walking towards Nikalas as commanded.

"Father, what are you doing?" Emlin questioned. "He explained everything. Did you not listen?"

"Yes, I did it was interesting, but missing a lot of truth. Until I know for sure I can believe his story, he will be treated as hostile, an ally of the enemy."

"What enemy? Why do you always feel we are at war?" Emlin groaned.

"Hey, let go of me, you fools!" Nikalas bellowed as he struggled with the two guards.

"Don't struggle, Nikalas. I'll take care of this," Emlin pleaded as she tried her best to comfort him. Even her soothing voice couldn't distract him from the fact he was being manhandled by two soldiers. His attempts to struggle were futile; he was grossly outmatched, and that he was surrounded by soldiers all prepared to kill him, he finally decided to give in. Hervott shook his head with approval and proceeded back to his quarters with Vicham following behind.

"What are you gonna do?" Inca asked a troubled looking Emlin.

"He's got to stop doing this. Treating everyone so poorly, we have no reason to doubt his story. If he was a spy wouldn't he have a fouler feel to him?" Emlin rhetorically asked.

"Honestly? He feels pretty foul to me," Inca replied harshly. Emlin scoffed at the remark and looked toward Broli.

"You're a Delopar. Your kind is always very suspicious of everyone," Draxton chimed in as he shot Inca a coquettish smile. She did her best to roll her eyes at his heinous gesture.

"The boy speaks the truth, but your father has been through a lot in his years. He's paranoid, but I'm sure you can talk reason to him. Go on now, help that poor boy get outta this predicament. Come on you lot. Let's go have a pint," Broli motioned towards the door.

"Sounds good to me. I haven't had a brew in hours," Draxton replied as they made their way to the exit.

Emlin marched promptly up the stairs and paused for a moment at the sight of the throne. It was made of a beautiful white sparkling rock that was a sight to behold, but not much to sit on. In fact, it was so uncomfortable that her father rarely sat in it. Most of the time when he allowed visitors, he simply stood next to it with his hand placed on the backside. On each side of the throne were stairs that led up to a catwalk. She took the stairs to the left and followed the catwalk until she came to her father's quarters; then burst inside without so much as a knock.

"Come in," Hervott sarcastically announced. "Very good of you to bring him here, sweetie. If he's in league with the Akordans, I think he is, we must find out what he knows quickly."

"Have you lost your mind? He's not in league with them—he was their prisoner! We rescued him from the Akordans. Krytus was holding him captive and taking him somewhere. Do you ever listen to anyone but yourself?" Emlin blurted out. This was getting to be a regular thing for him. Always paranoid, always thinking war is brewing. *It's ridiculous,* she thought to herself.

"When we came upon them Nikalas was in restraints and being dragged. Krytus was at the front holding a glass box," she added. Clearly, the mention of a box was of interest to Hervott; as soon as she uttered the word, his eyebrows perked up.

"What was in the box?" Hervott questioned. Emlin shook her head in uncertainty. He quickly turned toward Vicham, who was standing quietly listening to the two banter and gave a simple look. The look was more effective than words ever could be, it said, *Find out about the box.* Vicham nodded with understanding, and turned to exit the room.

There were two main places to hold prisoners in Terria, but the most common location was in an underground tunnel system deep within the Vanguard Keep. That's where Nikalas was, that's where the answers lay. Vicham made his way back down the steps and once again into the great hall. From there he went to the left and followed the hallways until he reached a door that was essentially a supply closet. Inside that room was a door that led into the basement dungeon. As he stepped into the supply closet, he quietly closed the door behind him and then turned and looked toward a wooden door in the floor. He lifted it up with an annoying squeak and let it come to rest against a crate full of glass bottles. Down the stairs he went, the light from above slowly fading away, leaving just the dim darkness of the dungeon.

"Hey, when am I getting outta here?" A voice called out. The tight corridors made the voice sound unreasonably loud. Vicham jumped and quickly turned to see who had said it. Wort, who was known around Terria as being a man who couldn't resist a good tonic was standing in the shadows with his face pressed firmly against the bars, an unsettled look on his face. *He's down here again?* Vicham thought to himself. *Will he ever learn?* He didn't have time to listen to the town drunk complain. Hervott wanted answers, and he intended to get them. Towards the very end of the dungeon was Nikalas sitting on a rolled up bed pad patiently twirling his thumbs.

"This must be pretty scary to you, being imprisoned like this," Vicham mumbled. Most cells in the castle dungeon were empty, but nevertheless he didn't need unwelcome ears, keeping the conversation to a whisper would be the best way to prevent gossip.

"It's not my first time, actually back home, I kinda learned to appreciate having a bed and a meal provided," Nikalas replied.

"You were imprisoned back in the city of Michigan? Why?" Vicham questioned.

"Michigan is a *state*, not a city. And mostly because I'm prone to making bad decisions. I stole food from a store once, and I wasn't very slick about it. Stupid shit, really."

"Same story as Wort down in the other cell," Vicham replied. For the next few minutes, he tried his best to develop a trust between him and Nikalas. Experience had taught him that compassion was more effective than threats.

"Did you see what Krytus was carrying? In the glass box?" Vicham finally asked.

"It was a gold necklace of some kind. They brought it back with them through the portal or whatever it was called." Nikalas replied.

"Portal works. In order to open up pathways between realms, you need to use a godly device called a *Tobin*. They're very rare and extremely difficult to come by. It sounds like the Akordans have managed to find one, and I doubt it was on their own." Finding a well-hidden weapon of the gods wasn't something Vicham thought them capable of. Akordans were warriors, not treasure seekers. No, the whole story really gave him the impression there was someone in the shadows playing the puppet master. But who? And why?

"Be patient, Nikalas. You'll be out of here soon. I promise." With that, he was off. A Tobin, a necklace, a mysterious leader uniting the Akordans, Hervott would want to hear this immediately. He quickly made his way back down the cell block. As he passed by the cell Wort occupied, he could just faintly see him lying on the floor sleeping in a puddle of liquid near his hips. *Gross,* he thought to himself. This was the fourth time in just a month Wort had been tossed down here, soon he would face banishment. Hervott had no patience for repeat offenders.

Hervott was nowhere to be found as Vicham entered the King's quarters. Their many years of friendship had afforded him the right to enter the room whenever he needed. He checked the private bath, but still no sign. Perhaps he was with Emlin. Her room was on the way to his own, so he decided it made sense to stop there next. Princess Emlin was very protective of her room, like most women she valued having a private place to call her own. One had to be invited to set foot inside, and that was a rare occasion. He took a deep breath as he stood in front of her door waiting for the courage to knock. When she was scorned, Emlin could be one of the harshest women he had ever met.

"Just knock, you fool. She's only a princess," he whispered to himself. Little self-pep talks like this were a common way to force courage. He gently knocked twice and the door flung open.

"Oh, it's you. My father sent you to speak with me?" She asked, annoyed.

"Actually Emlin, I can't find your father. I was hoping you knew where he was," Vicham calmly replied. She rolled her eyes and blew some dangling hair out of her face and pulled Vicham inside, closing the door behind him.

True to form, her room was designed to satisfy a Princess, with a large double bed too big for just one person, down blankets and pillows, and blue and pink lace dangling over the walls. These decorations had been chosen for her,but Emlin had put her own personality into the design. Where most girls would keep a mirror, she kept a sword rack with two swords mounted. On her vanity, she kept a simple hand mirror in place of a large one. Where you would usually find jewelry, she kept arrows. Next to her bed, books on war and strategy rather than stories of love and desire. About the only girly thing about her was a box of letters from Septus she hid under the bed. No one knew about this other than her, not even Inca.

"When is he going to free Nikalas?" She questioned as she plopped herself on the freshly made bed. Through the curtains, warm light cast a triangular shape onto the floor. Vicham took a step into the ray of light and held out his arm, letting the warmth hit his skin. Each small hair cast an even smaller shadow.

"Very soon, I expect. I've spoken to him and I believe he is telling the truth," he replied. She promptly stood up and walked toward him, her eyes fixed on his with intensity.

"I thought there were no more Tobins. The last one was stolen after the war. How is it possible for the Akordans to have one?" She asked. Emlin, Vicham and Hervott were the only people in Terria privileged to the knowledge of Tobins. To all others, they were nothing but a bedtime story. Before the war, Hervott had been in possession of one of these rare devices, but one day it had mysteriously disappeared.

"Well, Undr left more than one behind. We knew about the second one, but it was quite well guarded, and we didn't see any reason to worry about it," he explained. Furlasia was a land of many different religions, most of them had different beliefs, but the one element present in almost all of them was the god named Undr. He was said to be the guardian of Furlasia, put in charge by powers higher than him to keep a watchful eye on the land. To travel between the different lands, he created a device called a Tobin. Eventually, he abandoned his quest leaving the Tobins behind, hidden and guarded by ancient traps.

"Well, it seems like maybe you should've," Emlin pointed out. A light breeze brought in the smell of steel and smoke. She paused at the scent. Memories of Septus filling her head. *It's time for another search*, she thought. Vicham nodded in agreement and bowed as he backed out of her room.

King Hervott frantically rummaged through the Nasleigh Library, which was located in the east wing of the castle. The library was very old and quite large. Row upon row of books were perfectly organized by subject matter, and each subject area was then organized by either the author or date written—a chore the old woman who ran the library took quite seriously. At the moment, however, the library was unattended. He had dismissed her for lunch so that he could have privacy. Grabbing books, he would read the title, then toss them to the floor. A loud thud echoed throughout the room as the door to the library was pulled shut. He paused to see who it was. *Oh no,* he thought, *she's back already.* He drearily looked around at the mess he had made. The footsteps continued to ricochet until, from the shadows emerged Vicham. This was cause for a sigh of relief. He smirked and proceeded to continue tearing apart the shelves. The room was a disaster; it would take hours if not days to put it back in order.

"When they told me you were in the library I told them they had to be mistaken. You don't read, in fact, you've frequently told me how much it bores you, so what are you doing in here besides making a mess?" Vicham asked, reaching down to pick up a book. *Indigo* it read. He shrugged, then tossed it back down.

"Keep an eye out for Alfreda, will you, Vicham? That old lady scares me," Hervott said as he continued bouncing from shelf to shelf frantically searching.

"What are you looking for?" Vicham asked. He got no response. "Perhaps I could help." There was nothing other than the thump of books falling to the floor.

"Aha!" Hervott exclaimed as he pulled the spine of an older looking book from the shelf. It was clearly one of the libraries oldest books. The binding was falling apart, and the cover was barely held on.

"Did she hide this on purpose? Why was this so hard to find?" All the rummaging through books had exasperated him.

He carried it to a table and set it down. Titled *Accounts of Furlasia*, the book was the most important document in all of Terria. Every single piece of history involving Furlasia was contained within this worn out book. Each city kept their copy of the book, and hopefully, most had kept it in better condition than Terria had. Carefully and slowly he flipped through the pages, most were sewn into the binding, but occasionally an unattached page was found, these were entries added after the book was bound. Finally, he stopped flipping and pointed to a page.

"Come see this," he said, waving his arm urgently. Hervott never got this excited about books; this alone made it intriguing. Vicham drew close to his King.

When the man with magic arrives, the return of the Necromancer will be imminent.

"Who wrote this?" Vicham asked skeptically going over the words repeatedly. The statement was vague, but he was starting to guess the point Hervott was making.

"This is Kunklestick's prophecy. He was the only person in all of Furlasia with the gift of foresight," Hervott replied.

Now there was a name not spoken for many years. In the years before the war, the Wizards were the second most respected beings in all the land, second only to the three kings. Guardians and warriors all in one, Wizards were sought in times of great need. Kunklestick had been the sole wizard to survive the war with the necromancer Agavordis. After months of strenuous battles, the maniac Agavordis had finally been defeated. However, Kunklestick didn't believe it was over. While in a delirious state, a vision came to him, and soon after he wrote the prophecy. Was it the ramblings of a man who was tired from war or was there some truth to it? Kunklestick had proven before that he was able to see the future, so his words were written down as fact. Many, however, dismissed such a notion, claiming that Agavordis was gone for good. Vicham was a fan of the latter and didn't try to hide it.

"Okay, Dwennon. First of all, I don't think he knew what he was talking about. I mean he was over eighty even back then, at that age who knows what nonsense your mind can come up with. But let's just say he was right. That boy is about as skilled with magic as I am. You can't possibly believe he is the one referred to in the prophecy," Vicham retorted.

"It makes perfect sense Vicham. The boy just *arrived* did he not? And I think I know *exactly* what was in the box Krytus was carrying. He told you, didn't he? He told you it was a necklace, right?" Hervott stared at Vicham intently awaiting a response. Everything in him told him to lie, the whole idea was absurd. But Hervott's eager expression just made it hard to keep things secret.

"Okay, you're right. That's what he said."

"It wasn't a necklace, it was a talisman. One of the three talismans I had Kunklestick hide. It's happening again; someone is trying to gain the dark power, and they are using the Akordans to hunt down the talisman's needed," Hervott began flipping pages once again. *Agavordis' War with the Three Kings*, the page had a crude illustration of the necromancer and underneath a detailed account of what had happened as written by a local historian named Chaucey. On the next page were more illustrations, this time of the three talismans containing the power stripped from the necromancer after his defeat. There was little to argue, Hervott was making sense, which lately, seemed a rarity. Perhaps the war and doom he was always warning about wasn't as nonsensical as it seemed.

"So what do we do?" Vicham asked. His heart was starting to race at the thought of the dead walking the lands once again. The images still haunted his dreams. His mother had been turned into a servant of Agavordis. Many honorable people had had their resting place defiled by the vicious necromancer — the idea that someone would be trying to bring this chaos back into Furlasia was sickening.

"We need to talk to Nikalas, show him this picture and see if he recognizes it," Hervott replied as he started making his way to the exit. They were just a few feet away when the door was pushed open, and there stood Alfreda, the librarian with a look of horror spread across her face.

"Hervott!" She bellowed in a voice loud enough to frighten even the toughest and bravest Vanguard soldier.

Chapter 5

The halls of Neveraus hold were neither classy nor stylish. Cosmetic appeal had been the last concern for the Akordans when they had built it. Maybe one day improvements could be made, but until then it was a stark and cold place. The bricks were dark, grimy and damp from water leaking through the mountain. Septus did his best to navigate the strange place; he had never been allowed in Nasleigh Keep, so his experience with castles was rather limited. *Still, they likely aren't supposed to look like this,* he thought. After some winding stairs which led to yet another dreary hall that smelled like musky mildew he approached a poorly crafted door with a handle that lifted up. He took a deep breath and pulled up; it took some force since the handle was rusty but eventually it gave way.

Waiting not so patiently inside was a handful of Akordans, who gave him a glare of disapproval as he closed the door behind him. Just a year ago, walking into a room full of hostile Akordans would've given him cause for panic. The talisman had changed that; just one of the many things it had changed. One of the impatient Akordans grunted to make his displeasure known.

"There a problem?" Septus asked as if he was unaware of his tardiness.

"Where have you been?" Krytus demanded, taking a big step toward Septus. Septus smiled and ignored the comment as he casually walked over to the table and set down a dirty, large book. Dust fluttered about as he carelessly let it fall to the table top. *Accounts of Furlasia,* it read. The Akordans began watching intently as he flipped slowly through the pages before coming to a stop at a new chapter. *Herratia, Witch of the Hills,* beneath the title was a stunningly drawn portrait of a young woman with long black hair, jagged, coarse skin and teeth that looked capable of tearing up flesh much like a wild animal would. She was dressed in rags and behind her hung a long tail. She maintained a mostly human appearance while having a reptile quality like that of an Akordan.

"Where did you get this book?" Krytus asked as he carefully ran his hands over the picture.

"What does that matter? I have it, that's all you need to know," Septus grinned. "This book is like a recipe. This book is how we will bring her back."

The legend of Herratia was one of the most famous stories told in Furlasia. Her reign was brief at best, but the effects of her life were still felt even to this day. Few knew the full story behind her transformation, from the stunningly beautiful wife of the King to the lovely, yet *terrifying* beast she had been at the time of her death. These pages told just that story.

She had been a young priestess long ago, living in Terria and devoting every day to praying and living a life loyal to the goddess Gravi. One day, she met a young man destined to be King—Dwennon Hervott. The love story between them was as clichéd as any other. Marriage led to a baby, he took the throne, and all was going great—until it wasn't. A mysterious and powerful sickness took the life of the child, and from then on Herratia was not the same. In secret, she began experiments trying to resurrect the deceased princess. After Hervott had realized the remains of his daughter had been tampered with, anger took over him. He had had Herratia arrested, and she was to be escorted out of the city.

During the transport, a violent storm erupted causing the prisoner cart to crash; she took full advantage of the distraction - killed the guards and fled. The next time anyone had seen her, she had somehow become a hideous reptilian beast—likely the result of an experiment gone wrong.

Rumors of a witch in the mountains began to spread across the villages. Loud sounds could be heard echoing throughout the mountain range and sightings of a witch with a tail fueled stories of horror. Before long, a party of brave soldiers tracked her down—simply due to the carnage she left around the mountains. Surrounded by six ruthless men, she stood little chance. She was stabbed in numerous places before succumbing to her wounds. Her body was left in the cave she had dwelled in, but there was more to her than her killers had noticed. Underneath the ragged rags was a bump, the bump of pregnancy. From her still warm corpse emerged a creature even more heinous than she was—the very first Akordan.

"I know where she is," Septus confidently smiled.

"Where?" One of the Akordans asked.

"That's my little secret," Septus closed the book.

"How long before you honor your side of this bargain?" Krytus asked.

"I'll be honest. I have no idea how to bring her back. That's why I'm going to need to study this book. But I'm quite positive I can't do it until I have all three talismans," Septus replied. Behind the table sat a chair, an old wooden one with rough grains and the occasional splinter. He plopped himself down and looked around the room at his audience.

"Bring me those talismans. Do whatever you need to do to get them. If you have to kill, kill. If you have to torture, torture. Use whatever force you need to. There is no action that is wrong when you are doing it for your mother. This is your opportunity. Finally, after years of being mistreated and cast aside like vermin you now have the means to rise and save the woman who gave you life. Together, we can bring about a change for the Akordans. Together, we can find a way to put things right. Now, go. Hunt them down. Do not return until you have them," he cried out as the Akordans all started to make their way to the door.

There was an excitement in the air; their steps seemed more eager. The prospect of killing in the name of their mother was something any Akordan could get behind. Their dislike of Terrians and all those like them could be put on hold just this once. Septus had given them a reason to unite. Maybe he was playing them. Maybe he was one of the abusers, or perhaps he could actually be trusted. Only time would tell, but the notion was encouraging. Akordans, while being very tough were like children in a way. Angry, violent children. With their mother gone, no one could control them, they craved this control. This leadership, this bond. As the room emptied, Septus smiled to himself. *That was a pretty good speech*, he thought, *and to think I almost let that wretched King break me.*

The sparring arena was packed with excitement, hundreds of Akordans had gathered to watch a fight between Nevo, the greatest warrior amongst them, as he took on a dozen challengers. This was to be a simple contest of skill, not a fight to the death. It was located in one of the far corners of Neveraus, yet it was one of the most popular places in the city. Sparring was a great way to take out pent up rage, and it improved the soldiers' combat, so it was good all around. The arena wasn't a particularly elegant place—it didn't evoke feelings of a Roman Colosseum, it was more of a pit. A bed of jagged rocks covered the bottom so as to complicate the fights; the boundary was made up of twisted wire that had prolonged points extending every couple feet.

Nevo sat on a bench drenched in darkness and listened to the roar of the crowd. He lived for this; he felt most comfortable with his fist in someone's face. Being the younger brother of Krytus had caused him a lot of resentment. Everyone looked to his brother for advice and leadership, and Nevo had been left on the sideline, thought of only as a warrior. Ironically, combat was his favorite hobby, so the speculation wasn't far off. However, he had always felt like he had a mind for strategy that Krytus paid little attention to. He had vocally spoken out against bringing a Terrian into Neveraus but, as always, his voice was not heard. Breaking a few bones seemed about the only thing he could do to keep from going after the boy and killing him himself.

"All right, you bunch of animals, now for the moment you've all been waiting for. Keep your chits close and bet carefully, this promises to be an interesting fight. One to remember. Well, let's stop talking and get some blood pouring. Send out our challengers!" An announcer stood in the center of the arena and pointed to a side area as a horn was blown that was so loud most in the arena flinched. With loud chanting and singing the twelve challengers marched out into the arena. Each was covered in the usual battle armor; each was carrying a sword or mace. The crowd erupted with cheer as each warrior entered the arena.

Next came Nevo, and his entrance got things moving. Each Akordan that had been sitting now stood up and cheered, some growled. Either was an acceptable way to greet a warrior. His expression was deadpan as he marched calmly to the center of the pit. Every stone in the pit was loose, a wrong step could cause you to fall, a fall could be your end. Dried blood from former fights stained the ground, and the odor of decay hung in the air, but, for the most part, was not noticeable to Akordans. Once he was in the arena, he stood across from the twelve challengers looking them over. Some were large, some were small, some were larger than him. *The bigger the target was, the more unstable their walk,* he smiled to himself.

"No killing whatsoever, leave a pulse. Other than that, make 'em bleed. The last one standing is the new champion. Keep it dirty, and remember Mother is always watching. Let the carnage begin," the host yelled out. A horn blast signaled the start of the fight.

All at once the challengers charged forward, letting out a battle cry fierce enough to bring panic to even the most tenacious Akordans. Nevo turned around, belting to the far side of the pit. Taking them on all at once would be foolhardy, and he knew it. Each lunge was painful, the sharp rocks covering the floor made sure of it. Behind him the challengers pursued, hot on his heels and ready for blood. A loud booing erupted from the crowd.

"Are you gonna keep on running away like a Terrian or are you gonna fight?" The announcer asked through a hollowed metal tube; his voice echoed against the walls allowing all to hear. *I have a plan, you idiots. This oughta shut them up.* He quickly turned around and darted toward the herd. As he closed in, he lunged into the air and crashed straight into them. Two of the challengers fell onto their backs.

His claws gashed at their faces over and over, with each new swipe small pieces of flesh lodged beneath each nail. Once his opponents looked like they had been mauled by a wild beast, it was time for a change. Dual pounding. He lifted up one fist and smashed it into the face of a challenger then repeated the action to the other. Each fist took a turn greeting a face, back and forth, back and forth. His attacks were barbarous, but then again one could expect no less from an Akordan. His fist had just started feeling sore when a pair of arms wrapped around his chest and next thing he knew he was flying face first into the rocks. The stinging sensation on his face spoke volumes. *Ugh, now I'm awake. Who the hell did that?* He pulled himself to his feet just in time to get a glimpse of the curiously strong attacker.

"Saunder, Saunder, Saunder!" The crowd cheered. This Berserker of Neveraus had risen to popularity even faster than he had. There was no denying his skill, most of it due to his large size, a whopping seven and a half feet tall, all muscle. Even for Akordans, this was excessive. *Where did he come from?*

"And here's Saunder, our late challenger. Will he be the one to steal the title?" The announcer spoke as if he had just read his mind. Nevo reached to the ground searching quickly for the sharpest rock he could. He let out a loud growl and hurled one straight at Saunder. The rock smashed against his forehead and bounced back to the ground.

"How cute," Saunder laughed as he wiped the meager pain away like a booger. *Worth a shot,* Nevo thought to himself. From behind Saunder, a couple more challengers were charging, hoping to get to Nevo first. Instead, they found themselves looking up at the ceiling after Saunder's arms came straight out, clotheslining them. Then came darkness. Saunder quickly brought his feet down on each of them knocking them unconscious. The audience gasped in shock.

"This is my fight!" Saunder yelled out as he turned and looked at the remaining challengers. There were no objections.

Nevo readied himself as the Goliath neared.

"Come on," Nevo called out waving his hands in the air beckoning Saunder to hurry his pace. His taunt worked, better than he could've hoped. For such a large beast, Saunder was surprisingly fast. His shoulders bashed into Nevo knocking him back a couple of feet. Next, he spun around and brought his tail around hoping to knock Nevo down. Instead, he found himself in a position destitute of promise. Nevo let out a mighty roar and dug his claws into the muscular flesh of the tail. The muscles wrapped around his claws like gloves embracing a hand in warmth. Saunder's cry resonated throughout the arena; he grabbed Nevo pulling him closer. His breath was heinous as he sadistically grinned before bringing his forehead forward smashing against Nevo's.

It was all the remaining opponents could do, but cower on the opposite side of the arena. Nevo and Saunder continued to beat violently on each other, neither wanting to give in. There was too much at stake to let the other win. This title meant everything. Whoever held it had women and spoils whenever they wished. But more important than the prizes, was the status. Being a hierarchical society, nothing could be more important than this temporary title. The two Akordans were beginning to look like punching bags as they continued trying to best each other.

To the crowd's surprise, Nevo finally managed to corner Saunder. What followed next was nothing short of vulgar. Haymakers left and right, each one making contact. With each landed punch, it became clear Saunder's jaw was close to breaking; this didn't stop him, though. A final crack secured his victory as the jaw finally became unhinged. Nevo spat a mouthful of blood at his opponent who slumped to the ground gripped in agony, then turned his gaze to the remaining challengers. Gaping in fear at the horror they had just witnessed, they tossed their arms up in defeat. *Never surrender in the arena, fools.*

A surrender in the arena was like a dishonorable discharge. If an Akordan did this, they would be shamed by all who came near them—even the children were permitted to spit at their feet. It was reversible, however—get back in the arena and try again. Even if an Akordan tried and failed, they were at least treated as brave, but there was no greater dishonor than surrender. The crowd erupted in a cheer as Nevo walked to the center of the arena looking aggrieved. He shamelessly threw his arms in the air, basking in his victory.

The dining hall was loud with laughter and conversation as Krytus made his entrance, his presence stopped the chatter for a moment, but soon his arrival had little effect. The smell of roasted pork and ale filled the air; it was overpowering, but not in a bad way. Like most rooms in the keep, the lighting was dim, and the echo effect of the stone walls made all conversations, even whispers seem raucous. Sitting around a long wooden table were twenty Akordans, all with their mouths full of meat and a cup of ale next to their plate. Proudly sitting at the end wearing a makeshift crown of bones tied together was his brother Nevo, who looked like he had fallen down a cliff and hit every rock. Krytus paused as he looked his brother over, assessing the injuries.

"You should see the other guy," Nevo scoffed as he caught wind of the inspection.

"What happened?" Krytus asked as he motioned for one of the Akordan's sitting to the right of Nevo to vacate the chair. He sat down and began to nibble on what was left on the plate.

"Well, if you weren't so busy entertaining the Terrian, you would've remembered that today was my title challenge," Nevo replied. He took a big gulp of his ale and let out a rancid belch. "I am victorious once again."

"Barely it seems," Krytus mumbled. He continued to fork food into his mouth, washing each bite down with ale. As he set down his mug he glanced over at a couple of tomatoes in the center of the table, which stood out like a sore thumb against all the protein. Grousing, he reached across the table and grabbed them, paying little mind to the two mugs spilled in his efforts. All went silent as everyone stopped eating and stared in curiosity. The gawking eyes did little to sway his appetite, tuning out the audience he took a big bite, juice splattering one of the soldiers in the face. For a moment, the Akordan opened his mouth, preparing to protest. A stern glance from Nevo silenced him.

"I wonder about you sometimes, brother," Nevo scorned. "I'll have the cook beaten for putting such rancid food at the table." Krytus shrugged off his brother's vile comments and continued to eat.

Everyone at the table rubbed their bellies in satisfaction. A few loud burps and farts signaled that the meal had come to an end.

"What's our next move?" Nevo asked.

"Septus claims to know where she is, and how to awaken her," Krytus replied.

"Do you believe him?" Nevo grilled.

"Possibly. I feel it's worth the gamble. If he knows how to bring her back, we can finally have a fully united species. It's what we've always dreamed of," Krytus replied.

"And if he doesn't? What happens if he's just another lying piece of trash?" Nevo asked.

"We have the chefs chop him up and put in a stew with some potatoes," Krytus replied. Nevo's eyes widened at the thought. Killing Septus had been on his mind since the moment he had stepped foot into Neveraus.

"Now that's a plan I can get behind. Terrian flesh is so tasty. Especially when you slow cook them," Nevo licked his lips as he pictured it. His imagination began to run wild with the thought of how it would go down. *Here Septus, come in here. We found the last talisman. And then I sneak up and slit his throat. Mmm. Terrian stew for all.* Krytus slammed his mug on the table to snap Nevo out of his fantasy.

"I want you to gather some men and find the remaining talismans. I found the first one, but now I'm needed here. You leave at daybreak tomorrow," Krytus sternly commanded. He stood up and pushed his chair in. "This is a serious duty, not to be taken lightly. Are you capable of that?"

"Do you think of me as an imbecile? Of course I can find some stupid jewelry. Just make sure I'm not wasting my time, or

I'll hold you *and* that slime responsible," Nevo requited. As Krytus walked away, Nevo smirked, glancing around the table with glee.

"You're all coming with me," he ordered.

"I don't want to take orders from that stupid boy," one of them retorted.

"Neither do I, but you're not taking orders from him. You're taking orders from *me*," Nevo calmly replied. Normally such back talk would've resulted in a right hook to the face, but his fist was already so sore. *I'll forgive it just this once.*

"You're just issuing orders given to you by that traitor Krytus," the soldier barked. *Okay, that's it.* He quickly grabbed the mouthy Akordan by the back of his head and smashed it against the table. The force of the impact knocked the remaining cups onto their sides, spilling all the precious ale. After a couple more, he paused to look him over. His expression still didn't seem remorseful; *a few more times ought to do it.* He proceeded to repeat his motivational training until finally someone spoke up.

"That's enough Nevo. He's no good to us dead." He let go of the soldier and let his head fall to the table unconscious.

"Sorry. I got a little carried away. No one ever calls my brother a traitor. He's done more for our kind than any one of us. Don't any of you ever forget that," Nevo demanded as he shook his finger.

"Take this piece of trash back to the barracks, and find a replacement for him. We leave first thing tomorrow. Have your gear and be ready for combat," he looked around the table at the attentive faces. "You're dismissed."

Chapter 6

Nikalas lay in the darkness contemplating thoughts of home. Not the place he squatted in but home, before his parents had disappeared. Here in the dark dungeon, he could think of nothing but them. Each day without his parents had gotten easier and easier but still in times of trouble his mind went to them; surely they could've gotten him out of this. In the distance, a door flung open reverberated against the dark empty walls. He eagerly perked up feeling hopeful. The footsteps against the floor continued to clatter as they drew nearer and nearer. Could it be? Was he finally to be freed? He stood up and leaned against the bars looking into the dark.

"It seems your patience has paid off," the words came suddenly from the darkness. In the shadows stood Vicham, who had a pleased-with-himself look about himself as he twirled a ring of keys.

"I'm free?" Nikalas asked hesitantly.

"King Hervott wishes to speak with you," Vicham replied. He fumbled a bit as he tried several keys, but at last, the cage was unlocked. Freedom—or, at least he was *hoping* that's what this was. Together they walked the dark narrow corridor, their footsteps echoing the whole way. Nikalas had chosen to remain behind Vicham rather than next to him. Out of respect or fear he wasn't quite sure, although it was likely the latter. As they neared Wort's cell, he couldn't help but pause. For hours, the strange man had been his only company, and it seemed odd not to know what he looked like. Peering into the darkness of the cell, he could make out the shape of the man they called Wort.

He appeared to be sitting on the floor rocking back and forth and staring at the corner wall. His heart nearly stopped when Wort turned to acknowledge him, all he could see were glowing eyes; the strange man whispered something, but it was so faint he couldn't quite make it out.

"He's waiting for you, Nikalas. The King isn't one to enjoy waiting," Vicham said as he placed a hand on his shoulder. Nikalas shook off the strangeness of the man in the dark and continued to follow his liberator. Up the stairs and into the supply closet they emerged. The door was wide open as Vicham had left it. In the distance, the commanding voice of King Hervott ran through his ears. It seemed as though he was issuing some commands about dinner. "Don't forget the rolls," he thought he heard.

King Hervott sat on his throne looking majestic and powerful, his royal garb looked freshly pressed and cleaned as though he had changed just to speak with Nikalas. The thought was encouraging but unlikely. Vicham whispered into Nikalas' ears to *stay put* as he proceeded to take his spot next to the throne.

"Nikalas, my boy. How are you," Hervott blurted out cheerfully. Before he could even mutter a syllable he was cut off. "Sorry about that whole mess with the dungeon. Things have been quite tumultuous around here. I am always paranoid about new faces—perhaps too paranoid at times. Allow me to formally introduce myself." He stood from his throne and bowed.

"I am King Dwennon Hervott, you can address me as Your Majesty or Lord Hervott, either is fine," his whole demeanor came off as inebriated. Perhaps he had helped himself to some wine before deciding to free Nikalas.

"I was rather interested in what you said earlier about being from another world. Would you humor me in a walk? I'd like to hear your tale again," he tossed up his hands in innocence. "This time I promise not to doubt you."

"To be honest, Your Majesty," Nikalas replied. "I'd rather just get back home."

"I understand. Walk with me; we'll talk all about it," Hervott said, but with a clear undertone that Nikalas understood it was an order, rather than a suggestion. Nikalas took a deep breath and nodded his agreement. Up the stairs toward the throne he climbed, and then proceeded to follow the King and Vicham up to the surrounding catwalk. From up here, the view of the great hall was quite breathtaking.

The walk to the King's quarters was a brief one, probably by design; he didn't look fond of walking. As they stopped in front of the door, Hervott stepped to the side, making room for Vicham to come around and push the door open. *That was lazy,* Nikalas thought. They stepped inside the room, and Vicham softly closed the doors. Once again, he found himself awestruck at the sight before him. The main floor of his parent's home was barely bigger than the room Hervott resided in. It seemed ludicrous. Hervott wasted no time in walking up to his favorite window and looking out at the view, almost slipping into a trance. He stood perfectly still without muttering a word for almost a whole minute before finally turning around.

"I don't know how best to say what it is I need to say," Hervott paused as he searched for the words. "Getting home…back to your world…is not going to be possible."

"What do you mean *not possible*?" Nikalas cried. Vicham softly placed his hand on his shoulder as if to remind him that he was indeed still in the room. To comfort or to threaten?

"The device that was used to bring you into this world; I don't have possession of one. The Tobin is the only means of Otherworld travel. We had one in Terria many years ago, but it was stolen. Most likely by the Akordans that brought you back with them."

"And there are no others?" Nikalas questioned. With each passing moment he could feel a rage building up. The desire to hit something was growing exponentially. Hervott simply shook his head and took a deep breath.

"I don't believe you were meant to leave Furlasia. I think you're here for a reason," he explained as he gave a subtle nod toward Vicham. Clearly there had been some prior conversation regarding this moment because Vicham replied to the nod by grabbing a book off the nightstand. He carried the book over to Hervott's desk and set it down. Nikalas curiously glanced down at the title: *Accounts of Furlasia*.

"What's this? A bedtime story?" Nikalas huffed.

"This book is the complete history, well excuse me the *mostly* complete history of the land of Furlasia. Some parts are missing, most of them before there were people willing to spend their time documenting things. It's an extremely important book. There's one chapter, in particular, I find to be extra important. I'd like to share it with you, if you'd allow me," Hervott answered as he motioned for Nikalas to take a seat.

Nikalas hesitated for a moment, glancing momentarily at Vicham expecting a gesture indicating what he should do; however, he received nothing. Shrugging, he decided to take the offer, and sat down. The instant he did, Hervott began flipping through the pages, there was a musty smell to the book that was noticeable at this distance. At last, he arrived at the start of a new chapter and ceased his page turning. *Agavordis, Necromancer of Furlasia,* the page read. The title sounded ominous.

"Agavordis was once a noble wizard, but there was something in him. A drive for more. The Order of Wizards should've seen this overzealous quality in him from the beginning—it could've spared a lot of pain. He was a brilliant student, trained by one of the most famous wizards in Furlasia. Sometime during his studies, he disappeared. For a time, he was feared dead, until he returned with a terrifying new skill. He could manipulate deceased tissue, and bring it back to life."

Nikalas rolled his eyes as he listened to the far-fetched story. It really did sound like a bedtime story. Actually, it sounded a *lot* like a story he had been told when he was younger. Hervott's story continued for what felt like an hour. This version was much more detailed than his father's version. *This would make a great movie,* Nikalas thought, amused.

When the man with magic arrives, the return of the Necromancer will be imminent.

Hervott pointed to the words, and the story was finally over. He looked across at Nikalas, a drink in one hand, the other dragging across the table. The silence continued for a moment before Nikalas finally cracked a smile.

"Oh, so that's me?" He laughed. Hervott looked over at Vicham, confused.

"The signs are all there. The wheels have already started spinning. The Akordans that grabbed you were carrying one of the talismans. If the talismans are being located, that means there is someone interested in using them. A necromancer, or at least someone who *wants* to be. If this is true, then your arrival can't be a coincidence. Someone seeks to gather the talismans and at the same time, you arrive. I admit that I might be reaching a bit, but I'd rather have the man who wrote the prophecy look you over just to make sure," Hervott replied.

"What will looking me over prove?" Nikalas skeptically asked.

"Nikalas," Vicham said finally deciding to break his silence. "All wizards have a connection with a godly realm called The Echo."

"Who picked that name?" Nikalas interrupted.

"It's an old name, I don't know. It doesn't matter to the context of what I'm saying. The Echo is a realm left behind by the Gods; most don't know it exists. There are a few select people, however, who are pure enough to have access to this realm. In doing so, that person is gifted with a bit of the realm's uncertain amount of power. If it turns out you are one of those people, it would put more merit in the King's theory," Vicham explained.

"Listen, we don't have a Tobin, so for now you're not going to be heading back to Earth. You might as well let us have the wizard look you over. He alone will know if you are the one he predicted would arrive," Hervott proclaimed. A draft blew in, fluttering one of the curtains. It brought a welcome cool into the stuffy room. In the distance, the sound of twigs cracking and birds chirping somehow provided some small comfort, made the outlook of being stuck here not seem as bad.

"Who's the wizard?" Nikalas finally asked as he shrugged his acceptance.

"His name is Kunklestick," Hervott cheerfully replied.
"Hey! I've heard of him."

Emlin waved her hands about as she tried her best to offer a proper tour. Nasleigh Keep was so familiar to her that it was hard to decide what was noteworthy, which things would he find interesting. Did they have castles in Michigan? Maybe she was wasting her time; perhaps the castles in Michigan were grander than this. As she pushed open the large doors that hid the dining hall the look of awe that spread across Nikalas' face assured her perhaps she wasn't wasting her time. It was nearly dinner time, and the old maids had begun setting glassware on top of a table covered with a beautiful white lace cloth. The smell of slowly cooked meat was dashing its way into the hall—its scent was enough to make the stomach growl even in someone who wasn't hungry. How long had it been since Nikalas had eaten a proper meal? *Perhaps father will invite him to dine with us.*

Next on the tour was the Grand Hallway, so named because of the portraits and paintings. All along the hallway almost every inch of wall was filled with art. Many of them were painted by Emlin's deceased mother. One painting showed a large moon; unlike the moon on Earth, this one looked blue. A little further down the hall was a painted portrait of a group of men all standing in a line next to each other. In the center there was a man with frosted brown hair, holding a rather large stick next to him.

"That is the Order of Wizards. Most of them perished in the battle with the necromancer. All except him," she pointed to the man who stood dead center.

"Is that Kunklestick?" Nikalas asked.

"Why, yes, it is," she replied taken back at his familiarity with the name. On the opposite side of the hall hung paintings of Terria's Kings. Most of them looked very stern and elderly; there had been eight Kings in Terria before Hervott had taken the throne. His picture seemed mysteriously absent—a fact Nikalas found to be a curious one. His eyes navigated the paintings, thinking perhaps he had missed it, but it simply wasn't there.

"My father hasn't been painted yet," Emlin explained as though reading his mind.

"Oh, I see. Why not?" Nikalas questioned.

"Because Kings are not painted until after their demise. Once they cease to exist and pass into legend, then a painting is hung to memorialize them," she carefully explained.

"Well that seems stupid. I don't know much about painting, but it seems it would be easier to do it with a live subject," he looked her sternly in the eyes. She couldn't help but crack a smile and let out a cute giggle.

"Nikalas, Terrians can recall every detail about anyone they've ever met. We don't need to see someone to remember how they looked," she explained. His cheeks reddened as she continued to smile at him, her dimples adding to her already adorable appearance.

"Shall we continue?" She gestured. He quietly nodded and onwards she went.

Standing in the darkness of his quarters was a normal routine for Hervott. In darkness, the rest of the world could be tuned out. For a King with the fate of thousands of lives on his shoulders, such a feeling was not lonely but comforting. This night, however, he was not alone. Sitting atop his desk on a small stand sat a glass orb. A *Shewglomus,* an ancient device used for communications across great distances. Only certain important figures had been allowed to obtain them. On top of the gift of communication, it also afforded those with the right touch the gift of foresight.

"I told you twenty years ago, and I will tell you again, the talismans are all extremely well hidden," a voice said, the man who sounded older in age was speaking through the glass orb. Each word that emitted from the Shewglomus was accompanied by a flicker of the light within. It was an impressive effect to behold, any outside the castle looking in would think it to be nothing more than a candle flickering in the night.

"I'm telling you the Akordans have one, they found a Tobin and made it to Earth realm and recovered it," Hervott refuted.

"Who told you this?" The voice asked.

"A boy from Earth named Nikalas. I believe he is the one from the vision. The one who is meant to stop the return of the Necromancer," Hervott replied.

"That's quite a leap Dwennon. I've never known you to be brash in your judgments," the voice replied.

"I'm not, this is real I assure you—" An abrupt knock on his door provoked him to startle. "I have to go, someone's here. Please take this seriously. Find out if the Tobin has been recovered. So much rides on your haste," Hervott whispered. Quickly, he picked up the ball and began placing it back in his desk drawer.

"Wait—" the voice said, but it was too late, the Shewglomous had already been sealed away. With his heart still racing, and his mind still wandering he approached the door and slowly pulled it open. Outside looking frustrated stood Vicham.

"I waited for you in the gardens. Where have you been?" He asked. His ears twitched as he caught what sounded like a muffled voice. He looked at Hervott with confusion before shrugging off the strange sound.

"Shall we?" Hervott asked, motioning towards the door. Vicham nodded, and together they made their way towards the gardens.

With the setting of the sun, the garden was transformed from beautiful paradise to peaceful abyss. Each breeze circulating the wonderful scent emitted by the exotic flowers, each deep breath within this oasis could clear even the most troubled mind. Every table within the garden was graced with elegantly designed candles, each of them lit, providing an orange dimness to the atmosphere. All of this was done at the King's request. These gardens were a frequented spot for King Hervott; he had gotten into the habit of visiting them each and every night either before dinner or just before bed. Generally, this was reserved for just him, a place of solace and quiet but there was still the occasion where he invited Vicham to join. Tonight was such a night.

"Must be something. Coming here, to a land so different, so foreign. I often contemplate traveling to a different realm. Heck, even a different city," Vicham said as he sat on a wooden bench and looked up towards the night sky, as his eyes took in the sights he let out a deep sigh, reflection taking over his thoughts.

"Why? Why leave the familiar for the unknown? Myself, I feel content where I am," Hervott replied, sitting next to his friend and placing a gentle hand on his shoulder. "You're a good friend Vicham. I couldn't run this place without you."

"Dwennon you don't give yourself enough credit. Things aren't perfect, but for the most part Terria is a smoothly run city. That's your doing, I merely offer a supportive shoulder to lean on." An older woman began approaching them, she was wearing a white apron and had her hair hidden in a scarf.

"Your Highness? Dinner is about ready to be served," the servant said, bowing her head as she spoke.

"All right, Florence. We will be there shortly," Hervott replied. She nodded and turned around to leave. As she disappeared from sight, Hervott turned to look at Vicham. "Shall we?" He asked.

Vicham nodded his response, and they stood up from the bench. Hervott trailed behind as Vicham led them to the garden entrance, navigating past the various displays of exotic plants. As Vicham pulled the door open, he stepped aside, allowing space for the King to enter. Pre-dinner excitement was in the air; servants were frantically moving about, making last minute preparations. Guests, dressed in fancy formal wear, were slowly trickling in through the main entrance. It was customary for some of Terria's higher society to be invited for dinner at least once a week. Some of them had important roles to play, be they council members, clergymen, or decorated soldiers. As they continued wandering toward the dining hall, Hervott would occasionally shake a hand or pretend to listen to a brief story, whatever kept the people happy. He truly detested having to suck up to the socialites, but they were a necessity so he did his best to play the game.

Hervott took a deep breath as the smell of meat and fresh bread ran toward them, forcing its way into their senses. A couple of nearby guards pulled open the doors revealing the dining room. In its center stood an exorbitant table. It was twenty feet long and hand carved, its golden polish glistened under the light from the chandelier. The socialites were already sitting in their spots enjoying some pre-dinner drinks. Maids and servants were running back and forth trying to keep up with the flood of orders. Hervott rolled his eyes and approached his seat at the head of the table. Quickly, a servant ran up and pulled his chair out and carefully pushed it back in as Hervott took his seat. Emlin sat to his left and Vicham to his right, but where was Nikalas?

"Where is our guest, Emlin?" Hervott asked as he picked up a glass and took a sip from it.

"He's a guest now?" Emlin retorted.

"Yes, of course, dear. I had to be cautious; you cannot fault me for that," he waved to a nearby servant. A humble man with bronze colored skin walked up and politely bowed. "Please find our guest and ask him to join us."

"I'll go, it would be better if he sees someone that doesn't look like they plan on arresting him again," Emlin said as she quickly pushed her chair back and stood. She looked toward Hervott for a moment expecting some objection or a snide comeback. He simply sipped his drink and looked blankly at nothing. *I'll take that as a yes.* She nodded and hastily ran toward the exit.

Chapter 7

Deep in thought, Nikalas sat gazing out his window toward the picturesque night sky. There was a subtle hint of blue to the moon that made it look just different enough to remind him he was not on Earth. Apart from the teal moon, the night sky was remarkably familiar. Millions of stars glistened in the distance, and he couldn't help but wonder if one of them was Earth. Was his home so close yet so far?

His guest room wasn't anything special; it certainly didn't remind him of anything *royal*, but still it was a vast improvement over the places he had gotten used to occupying. The bed was generic, and the blanket looked itchy and old, there was a dusty smell to it that reminded him of something a grandma would dig out of storage for the rare guest. Along the wall next to the window was a mostly empty bookshelf, he had already looked through it. Most of it was uninteresting, but one book had caught his eyes if only for a moment. *Grimworts: Creatures of The Echo* it was called. Inside were some impressively drawn pictures of a small pointy eared creature that looked like something he had seen in a cartoon. His peaceful solitude came to an abrupt end with the sound of a knock on his door.

"Yeah?" He called out.

"Nikalas, it's Emlin. May I come in?" She asked through the wood. Her voice was muffled, but still sounded as lovely as he remembered.

"It's your castle," he replied as he quickly spun around and started running his fingers through his messy hair.

The door flung open before he could even finish, his hair remained a tangled eyesore. In a panic, he quickly put his hands behind his back and cracked a grin. He looked like the cat that ate the canary, full of guilt and surrounded by suspicion. She dubiously looked him over as she stepped into the room.

"Why do you look as though you've just been caught with your hands down your pants?" She smiled, he took a deep breath as she edged closer continuing to eye him with cynicism. "Are you hiding something Nikalas?" His grin widened, and he held out his hands, palms up and open, they were empty.

"Do you always look so suspicious?" Emlin asked.

"Only when I'm around a beautiful girl," he replied as he rested his hands at his side. Emlin blushed and looked to the floor.

"My father would like it if you joined us for dinner. Surely you must be hungry after the day you've had," she continued to look at the stone floor, studying every detail. Her bashfulness was inspiring—could this mean she found him attractive? He could only hope.

"I'm starving, but why should I dine with someone who had me thrown into a dungeon? He's not the most gracious host I've ever met," he replied. She finally found the strength to look him in the eye. Her father was loutish, but if she didn't stand up for him what would that make her?

"I know it felt wrong, but he was only doing what he felt was right. I hope in time you can see that," she answered.

"I thought you were upset with him for doing that?" He asked, confused. She nodded.

"Yes, at first, I was. But dark times have made trust a difficult thing to come by, Nikalas. The line between friend and ally is becoming harder by the day to distinguish." It was true. Outside the walls, there were Akordans and even the occasional bandits from outlying villages, but there were also signs pointing to enemies of the crown being just outside the wall waiting to strike. He nodded in acceptance. Was it her beauty that made him agree or logic? It was hard to tell at this moment.

"Okay, I'll come to dinner. Should I change into something more formal?" He looked down at himself. His clothes looked even worse than normal, dirt was smudged on his knees, and there was a rip in his shirt. He certainly didn't feel worthy of a royal dinner. Emlin quickly looked him over and shook her head.

"That'll do just fine, it might offend some of the higher socialites, but that sounds like fun doesn't it?" She turned toward the door. "Follow me."

The halls were mostly vacant. Normally, there were servants and guards making their rounds, but during dinner, all were given the right to have a break. Golden light from hundreds of candles filled the halls; shadows danced against the patterns drawn into the low pile red carpets. Every few feet, a shelf was mounted to the wall, and on each shelf was a vase with a black flower that threw out a rather potent scent. It was intrusive to the senses yet oddly pleasant.

Dinner had already begun as they stepped into the dining hall. A dozen waiters carried silver platters overflowing with food to the tables while others cleared empty cups or offered refills. Hervott's eyes grew wide with relief as he noticed Nikalas following Emlin.

"Ah, Nikalas my boy, please sit down. There's a plate of food already awaiting you," he motioned to the spot to his left, the spot normally reserved for Emlin; she gawked in surprise but decided to shrug it off. He felt out of place, but he casually sat down as a servant pulled the chair out. Next to him, Emlin took a seat.

"Who is your guest?" A finely dressed gentleman with a gray handlebar mustache asked.

"Detrict, this is Nikalas Noise. He's visiting from out of town," Hervott replied as he placed a hand proudly on Nikalas' shoulder. Detrict Thissle, was foul and uptight, but he was also rich. Richer than the crown, in fact. He controlled most of the money in Terria. Therefore, he had bought himself a permanent spot at the dining table. Hervott hated the man, but his money was important. Without him, Terria would be broke, so he had to play nice. Next to him was his mistress Eliiana; she wasn't much better. In fact, arguments could be made that she was worse; she was a prominent voice in the council, so like her master, she had made herself valuable.

Dinner was uneventful—for the most part. The socialites took turns questioning Nikalas about where he came from and how he knew Hervott. Somehow, he always managed to be taking a drink or chewing some food. After an hour of dodging questions, Emlin stood up and dismissed herself as she dragged Nikalas by the arm. Hervott looked to Vicham, and the two exchanged a look of curiosity. Was she interested in Nikalas already or just being playful? *Still*, Hervott thought, *better Nikalas than that monstrous Septus.*

"Time for some dessert and a smoke," Hervott announced. His voice began to fade as Emlin led Nikalas to the exit and the door closed behind them.

"How was that? Better or worse than you thought?" Emlin playfully asked as they walked into the main hall.

"If I say worse, does that make me sound ungrateful?" He replied. Emlin shook her head. "Worse, definitely worse. Do you really have to listen to those uptight yuppies every day?"

"Only once a week. What is a yuppie, might I ask?" They came to a stop in front of the stairs to the throne and Emlin took a seat on the bottom step.

"It's a word we use back home for rich people who think they're better than everyone else," he replied. Emlin turned her head and pondered for a moment before cracking a smile.

"I like it, yuppie. I'll have to try to remember that," she laughed. Voices started to echo from the hall toward the dining hall cuing that her father and the others were headed to the smoke room to socialize. She promptly stood up and brushed her dress off.

"Well, I should get to sleep. It's been a long day, for both of us. Perhaps we could meet here tomorrow and I can show you around the city."

"That would be nice, this place is weird so far," Nikalas replied. Emlin laughed and turned toward the stairs.

"Until tomorrow then," she bowed ever so slightly and made her way up the stairs. Nikalas watched with fascination as she disappeared from sight. She was an interesting girl. Not twelve hours ago, she was killing Akordans with a sword and now here, in the palace, she seemed like what he would expect from a Princess. The voices continued to travel down the hall, getting louder by the second. He quickly made his way up the stairs and headed toward his guest room.

He managed to find his way back surprisingly well considering he had only been in the room just one time. Once he got inside, he opened up the window to let a breeze in. The air was chilly, but the perfect temperature for sleeping. Of course he couldn't sleep in his stuffy clothes, he quickly stripped down to his underwear and climbed into the bed; the blanket was as itchy as he imagined it would be. Something felt off, uncomfortable, a lump of some kind underneath him. He let out a slight sigh as he reached behind him, there was something hard placed just where his back would lay. His fingers gripped it, and he pulled it out from under the sheet. It was a small book.

"Who put this here?" He asked out loud as he opened it up. Inside was black inked handwriting that looked to belong to a woman — the writing was much too neat for a man.

He looks at me every day, a fierce desire in his eyes. At first, I thought it was my imagination, but in time, it became clear he had his eyes on me. But why? I'm not nearly as pretty as his past wives. I'm nothing but a lowly housekeeper. Should I try to talk to him about it? He is gorgeous but intimidating. What if I'm wrong? If I say something, and I've been mistaken I would be mortified. Perhaps I will wait and see what he does, no sense in being hasty.

He had barely made it through a single page before he passed out. The day's events had left him weary, and his body was overdue for sleep. The reading would have to wait.

Chapter 8

Conversations coming from the halls jolted Nikalas from his slumber. Bright light was shining through the window filling the room with a golden hue. It was already mid-morning—he had slept longer than he planned. Terria was alive and brimming with movement. He could hear the sound of hammers and the laughs of children coming in with the breeze. Promptly, he sat up, and looked around the room. Someone had been inside—and while he was sleeping no less. On the desk across from his bed, there was a small brown box and a note laid next to it. He stepped onto the cold floor and slowly approached the note. The handwriting was poor, and the ink was smudged.

Take care and guard it with your life- With regards, K.S.

Glancing the note over didn't seem to provide any more insight. Who was K.S.? And what was in the box? His hands trembled as he reached for the lid, gently, he flipped open the folds and peered inside. It was an egg, a very large egg, the size of a football. *Screw that,* he thought to himself as he quickly closed the lid and pushed the box to the back of the desk. Perhaps he had seen one too many dinosaur flicks. The sheer size of the egg sent a chill down his spine.

Outside his room, the halls had gone silent. *Now's as good a time as any.* He tiptoed toward the door and slowly pulled it open, just enough to peek out.

"Good morning, sir!" A voice exclaimed. His head nearly struck the door frame as he jolted at the overly cheerful voice. Emerging from the far end of the hallway was a lowly looking servant with gray hair and glasses nearly as large as his face, his eyes appeared colossal behind the thick lenses. He approached carrying a tray with breakfast and a glass of red wine.

"I've brought you some food, sir. Best to start the day with a warm meal," Richardson said as he held out the tray. "May I fetch you some clothes to put on?" Glancing down at himself, Nikalas quickly placed his hands in front of his crotch; he was covered by nothing but his boxers. Richardson continued to hold out the tray until Nikalas sighed and grabbed it, ruining his attempt to hide himself.

"I sleep like this. Sorry," he said as he awkwardly stood in front of the goofy looking servant. "Besides, I have some clothes."

"Nonsense, sir. Those clothes will not do for a guest of King Hervott. I'll fetch you an outfit worthy of your status and bring them to your room for you," Richardson replied. He did a slight bow and turned away, making his way back down the halls. Quickly, Nikalas shut the door and started to laugh to himself. *At least it wasn't Emlin*, he thought to himself.

Whatever the bowl of mush was, it was unexpectedly tasty, he gobbled it down far faster than he had expected. The glass of wine, however, he decided to ignore, clearly things were different here and as curious as he had always been to try drinking, it somehow felt wrong. As promised, Richardson had left a pile of clothes outside his door.

After he finished getting dressed he looked himself over in a nearby mirror. The dark orange tunic back home would've gotten him weird looks and laughs; here, however such an outfit was a sign of nobility. Going from the rags of a street urchin to the garbs of royalty? He was literally living a rags to riches story.

Stepping out into the hall, he slowly looked around, toward one side stood a couple of guards and toward the other was Richardson, who had a pleased grin as he took notice of his guest. He subtly rolled his eyes and made his way toward the servant. The outfit felt strange; he couldn't help but repeatedly adjust it.

"You look astonishing Master Nikalas, truly remarkable," Richardson smiled as Nikalas drew closer. For reasons unknown, there was some kind of charm to this servant. Certainly his overtly happy personality had every reason to annoy him and yet somehow the look of uninterrupted joy on Richardson's face did nothing but bring him a smile.

"Thanks mister—" He paused as he realized he had no clue what the servant's name was.

"The name's Richardson, sir," the servant replied.

"That's the most normal name I've heard since I've been here," Nikalas remarked. The servant smiled and bowed, Nikalas did the same, then continued down the halls.

Standing in the main hall just in front of the throne was Emlin. On her shoulder, a small brown bag was slung that looked to be packed to the brim. *A picnic perhaps?* Making his way down the steps, he couldn't help but feel a little self-conscious. After all, clothes like this were very strange for him. Emlin looked up the stairs as Nikalas made his descent, a look of elation in her eyes.

"Richardson did a good job," Emlin commented as she adjusted a flipped up collar on Nikalas.

"What's with the pack?" He asked, his neck was tightened as Emlin continued to fidget with his tunic. She stepped back as she finished and looked down at the pack.

"We are going on an adventure," she blissfully replied. "Shall we?" Nikalas nodded in agreement and away they went.

Terria's streets were alive and well—aggressively so. It was hardly midday and already the roads were crowded with people. Children ran around laughing, parents behind yelling as they tried to keep up. In each store, there was nothing but smiling faces, each shop owner prepared to woo their customers in whatever way necessary. Everyone seemed so exultant; the effect was chilling. Everything was kept in pristine condition, the roads seemed like they had been washed just hours before, there wasn't so much as a fingerprint on any of the shop windows. They continued making their way through the bustling streets, taking a turn here and another there.

After a few minutes of travel, Emlin came to an abrupt stop and quickly dashed to the far side of the road. Ahead, a group of Terrians donning white robes made their way down the center of the streets. *How bizarre.* It was hardly just Emlin, anyone near the streets or in the streets, horseback or not, all moved to the side as if the group had an infection.

"What's going on?" Nikalas whispered.

"The High Mother's *March of Absolution*," she kept her gaze fixed on the ground as the crowd continued to pass. The March of Absolution was hardly a rare event—in fact, it was done twice a day. For all those doing well in Terria, there was an equal number of people suffering; the starving, the homeless, the hopeless, all benefited from the uplifting presence of the High Mother. Nikalas continued to watch the sea of white as it continued to flow past. Toward the back of the crowd, he finally caught a glimpse of her. High Mother; her attire was atrocious, but effective. No one could mistake her for one of the commoners. A tall golden hat with red rubies along the top sat proudly atop her head; her red satin robes were so long they dragged on the ground behind her. Golden bangles hung from each wrist as she walked with her arms up and her hands palms down. Nikalas felt like he could almost sense disdain coming from her — as if she resented having to expose herself to the commoners. That couldn't be right, though. The spectacle continued for a few more moments until at last, the streets had been cleared.

With the roads now cleared Emlin continued to lead Nikalas down the streets. All along the way there was a noticeable drop in appearance to the roads and businesses. Eventually, they arrived in a part of Terria that smelled like trash and burnt metal. Stains from spilled garbage covered the pathways and avenues, and the buildings had an undesirable quality to them. *The slums of Terria,* Nikalas thought. Clearly this area was in dire need of High Mother's presence, but alas, even she wouldn't make the trip to this part of the city. Arriving at *Falker's Anvil,* clearly whatever hard time had hit the city this business took one of the hardest hits of all. The very sign for the business dangled by one hook and there was a long crack running from the bottom of the door to the top. Despite its rugged appearance, as they came to a stop in front of the building the nearly broken door was pulled open and out stepped Falker, looking worn but not defeated.

"Good afternoon, Emlin. What brings you by on thish lovely day?" Falker said, with his usual lisp. There was a mask on his face, a mask of cheerfulness, Nikalas could spot the façade a mile away, it was the very same mask he had worn each day since his parent's disappearance.

"Falker you know my day is not complete unless I get to see your handsome face." The old man did little to hide his blush; it was true. Emlin had visited every day the past year. At one point they had gone out together in search of Septus, but it had been many months since Falker had lost all hope. True to her word, though, she continued to visit every day with updates on her searches.

"You're not dragging thish young man out on search are you Emlin?" Falker asked as he lifted his shaking arm to point toward Nikalas. *Stastic Fever* they called it, a common affliction among those who work around fires and metals. Once it took hold there was only one way it ended. Emlin smiled and turned towards Nikalas.

"Falker, this is Nikalas. He's visiting from out of town." The old man's hand continued to shake as he extended it out in greeting. *I don't wanna touch him.* The shaky hand was unsettling to behold. Emlin glared at him and Nikalas finally gave in.

"Nice to meet you, *Nikalash*," Falker smiled as he continued his unusually long handshake. Nikalas remained silent; what could he say after all? This poor man looked to be having a terrible time, what could his words possibly do to change that?

"I'm just giving him a quick tour, there's so much that's different about this side of Furlasia," Emlin added. Nikalas took a few steps back until he was once again behind Emlin, his tongue remained tied.

"Ahh and a more perfect guide yoush could not ask for. *Yoush* lucky, *Nikalash*. Many young men like yourshelf would kill to get a tour from Her Highness." The old man's lisp was harsh and distracting; Nikalas could barely make out what he was trying to say. Attempting to be polite, he simply nodded and smiled.

The pleasantries continued for a few more awkward minutes until finally Emlin and Falker said their goodbyes for the day and they continued on their way. *Finally*, Nikalas thought. *How does she know that sad old man?*

"Who was that exactly?" Nikalas asked, they turned a corner and began heading back into the suburbs of Terria.

"Falker? At one point he was one of the most important and skilled blacksmiths in all of Terria. After Septus vanished, he went down a dark path and his health has been declining ever since," Emlin explained. After another few turns she came to a stop on a long street containing nothing but small outdoor shops, all containing different handmade objects up for barter.

"So he's your friend's father, then?" Nikalas asked, still unsatisfied with her explanation. Emlin started walking down the street, shouts from salesman filling the air. Everyone wanted a sale, and deals could be made with almost every shop.

"He's his adoptive father. Listen, do you mind if we don't talk about Septus? It's not an easy subject to discuss," Emlin blurted out. *She loves him*, Nikalas thought. He continued to follow her down the hectic street filled with cacophony and mayhem. It was fascinating to see how similar these merchants reminded him of flea markets back home. Terria so far was nearly a doppelganger of Detroit. The road ended with a horse stable, a quaint little one that had only four horses, each one groomed into tip-top shape. A familiar face sat next to the stable reading a leather bound book. Broli, the large brute he had met the previous day.

"Ah Nikalas how goes it?" Broli exclaimed as he jumped from his seat and set the book down. He promptly gave Nikalas a firm slap on the back as a gesture of friendship. The large brute surely meant well, but his gesture left more pain than feelings of joy.

"Nikalas and I are just out on a tour of the land," Emlin chimed in; a shadow at her feet caught her eyes. Already the sun had reached its midpoint in the sky. Only a few hours of daylight remained, and they had a lot of ground to cover.

"A more perfect guide there could not be," Broli smiled, his teeth were stained and a couple were even missing. There was a touch of decay in his breath. *I wonder if they brush their teeth here.*

"Can we get a couple of horses? I'd like to take him outside the walls," Emlin asked as she glanced towards her usual horse. Becca, a beautiful steed with brown fur, down the middle of her back ran a long white line; her face was freckled with white blemishes. *Riding a horse?*

"I've never ridden one of those," Nikalas interrupted just as Broli had begun to grab a couple of bridles.

"If the boy has never ridden before, perhaps it's best he just rides with you Emmy," Broli interjected. Emlin nodded in agreement and Broli released his grip on the second set of reins. Carefully, he began to untie Becca; once the knot was free, he slowly led the horse around the back and handed the reins to Emlin. She nodded with thanks and began to pull herself up onto the back of the horse. Nikalas gulped as he watched; Becca was a very large horse. Emlin extended her hand out toward Nikalas, who stood, dumbfounded.

"Are you coming?" She asked, cracking a cute smile. *Gotta shake it, can't look like a wimp.* He grabbed her hand, and she began to pull him up, suddenly he felt a pair of large hands grab his buttocks and push him up.

"Easy does it now," Broli coached as Nikalas finally seated himself atop Becca. "Try to take it easier than you normally do Emmy; you're carrying a rookie." Emlin laughed.

"He'll just have to hold on extra tight," she replied. *Finally, a silver lining,* Nikalas thought.

"You'll be fine Nikalas, she'll take care of you," Broli said, attempting to offer some comfort; a smirk crawled across Nikalas' face as he wrapped his arms around Emlin. She smelled wonderful; her scent reminded him of lavender.

"Ha!" Emlin exclaimed, giving Becca a firm kick. They took off so fast Nikalas nearly fell off. *Better hold on tighter.* He smiled. Through the streets they rode, much faster than seemed safe. Despite the massively crowded streets, people seemed more than capable of clearing the way, luckily. As they reached the main gates, Emlin yanked on the reins and Becca came to an abrupt stop.

"Going somewhere Princess?" Harold, one of the guards, asked.

"Open the gates, Harold. We are going to the lake," she explained.

"Mind your tone Emlin, I was only doing my job," Harold retorted. Huffing in annoyance he nodded towards his partner and they began to pull the gates open. "You have three hours, and then the gates stay closed."

"Ha!" Emlin exclaimed yet again. This time, the speed was even more intense; Nikalas tightened his grip and pulled himself close. There was some discomfort from all the bouncing, mostly in his crotch and some in his thighs, but he tried his best to put the slight pain out of his mind. Trees rushed by so blending all together like an oil painting.

The path was scabrous, large pot holes and broken branches hindered the path. It was riddled with tree branches that hung out over the trail — they came by so quickly that it became a game of *dodge the branch*. And yet, despite all the discomforts brought on by the bumps and frequent obstacles that tried to knock him silly, he had never felt freer. In many ways, he found this sensation more relaxing than simply riding in a car. In a car you had the glass that separated you from the world, you were encased in a man made piece of equipment. Here, he was one with nature. Here he could take in the scents, feel the breeze. It was a marvelous feeling; he was submerged in the terrain in a way he had never felt. After riding nearly twenty minutes, Emlin began to softly tug on the reins. As she did, Becca slowed her pace. Ahead of them was a clearing. With it, came a familiar scent.

Becca slowly sauntered onto the grassy clearing, ahead Nikalas could finally make out the lake Emlin had mentioned. The clearing was beautiful, the scent, which had felt familiar finally made sense; there were hundreds of lavender plants scattered all around. They filled the air with their scent, the aroma fighting to pierce his senses. Nikalas couldn't help but think it strange to see the plants here of all places. Furlasia felt so foreign, and yet there were oddly still things that existed here that also did on Earth.

"Whoa," Emlin whispered signaling Becca to come to a full stop.

"Go ahead and climb down," she instructed. Nikalas briefly scouted the area. What he sought even he didn't know. Once he felt confident they were truly alone, he carefully climbed down, his balance uneven until his feet landed firmly on the ground.

There was a humorous smile creeping across Emlin's face as she watched Nikalas dismount. It was always enjoyable taking a rookie out for a ride, they were always so nervous. Those very nerves were, in fact, being the biggest problem. Riding a horse was a breeze — it was the rider that made it more.

"It takes some getting used to," she explained. She gently rubbed the back of Becca's ears and grabbed hold of the reins, leading her loyal friend to a nearby tree. Once the knot had been tied, she strolled toward the lake and sat down in the cushy juniper grass.

"What are we doing here?" Nikalas asked, taking a seat next to her.

"Taking in the sights, I wanted to show you this place. It's a place I reserve just for me, a personal sanctuary, a place for me to come when my head is in need of clearing," she glanced toward him with a subtle nod.

Ah, so that's what this is about, he thought. *She's worried about me.*

"When I was little, my mother and I used to come here." A smirk climbed across her face as she began to reminisce aloud.

"We would bring a picnic, read books, roll in the flowers; she even taught me how to skip rocks across the water. This place was her oasis long before I was born. After she died, for the longest time I couldn't bring myself to come back here. Eventually, though, I did. When I got here, she was waiting for me." Nikalas furrowed his brow in confusion.

"What do you mean she was waiting for you?" He asked.

"Her spirit. I got off my horse and came and sat by the water just as we used to. Across the water I saw something, a faint figure; it was hard to make out, so I ran around to investigate. I paused at first, the figure seemed familiar. Something about it was unsettling, yet it called to me. It was *her*," Emlin's gazed remained fixed on the spot she described. Nikalas followed her eyes across the lake and scoffed in doubt.

"Did she say anything?" He asked, attempting to play along. The notion of a ghost seemed farfetched, but also gave him a pause of hope. If Emlin had seen her deceased mother, could he perhaps be so lucky as to see his parents? Nothing would be more comforting than being afforded one last conversation with them. It was only yesterday he learned of a necromancer bringing the dead back to life. If that was possible, perhaps Emlin's ghost story was as well.

"She told me I had a role in this world more important than I could ever imagine." She reached into her pack and pulled out a cylindrical shaped wooden bottle with two small cups. Next came two small loaves of golden brown bread. Setting the cups onto the grass, she began to pour. A fruity red wine filled the cups, all the way to the brim.

"That's it?" Nikalas asked. He reached down and carefully picked up one of the mugs, spilling a tad bit onto the grass. Emlin nodded and took a sip from the leftover cup.

"What do you think she meant?" He asked as he finally took a sip. *Wine?* He tried to hide the shock; it was bitter and not very sweet. *This is what I've been missing out on?* Emlin continued to stare towards the spot across the lake. A calm breeze began to blow; her hair started to flutter ever so slightly. In the sky the sun had begun its journey towards the horizon; dusk would be arriving in just a few hours. She took one last swig and set the empty cup on the grass. A glossy look crept into her eyes; the wine had a kick that much was clear.

"I've fulfilled my role. Finding you was my destiny. If the legends are right, you are going to be the only one capable of stopping the uprising of the necromancer."

"Way to play yourself second fiddle. You're really reducing your destiny to finding the savior? Surely if you have a destiny, it would be more elaborate than that. I've seen you in action. You're more than just the one who discovers the savior," Nikalas replied. "I mean no disrespect. I just don't think you're thinking your purpose out very well."

"To discover the prophet who will lead the charge in the final battle for Furlasia. That is no small role, it's a crucial one," she looked towards him with a look of determination. "Will you rise to the challenge? Are you that prophet?"

"Emlin, this all sounds ridiculous. They make movies about this kind of fantasy where I come from. That's all it is, fantasy," he replied.

"Perhaps in your world, here it is very real. Magic is very real," Emlin tossed the cup and bottle back into the pack and stood up.

"Why did you bring me here?" Nikalas demanded.

"Follow me," Emlin replied. She smiled as she extended her hand and pulled him up.

She led Becca by her reins and continued to walk alongside the lake. *Now where are we going?* With an air of annoyance, he continued to follow. They spoke no words — there was nothing to say. There was only walking. A splash in the water caught his eyes; it was a fish, a large one at that. *Must've been trying to catch something on the surface.* From the skies, a loud shriek filled the area. His gaze was wrenched upward in amazement; there was something dark plummeting toward the waters. A bird—a large one—its wingspan looked to be four feet, as it got closer to the water, it was engulfed in a fiery blaze before disappearing under the dark water.

"What was that?" Nikalas exclaimed. Emlin paused and looked towards the water with a smirk. The water went still, together they stood watching. Time itself seemed to pause to focus on the moment. The loud shriek filled the air once again as the bird emerged from the water, still engulfed in flames. High into the skies, it soared until it was no longer visible.

"It's something, isn't it?" Emlin asked as she smiled and looked towards Nikalas. "Perhaps this world is more magical than you give it credit."

"What was that?" Nikalas breathtakingly asked.

"A Phoenix. One of the many mystical and magical things about Furlasia. Come on, let's keep moving." She continued to lead Becca and Nikalas around the lake. The sky was beginning to look like a portrait; pink clouds danced across the blue skies like feathers. Soon it was clear where they were heading. She was leading him to the spot where she had apparently seen the figure.

Emlin came to a stop as they reached the clearing. A nearby tree looked like as good a spot as any to secure Becca. She gently pulled on the reins and led the horse toward the branches, knotting the reins around a limb. Nikalas stood next to the lake staring at the skies. Emlin began walking down the slight slope toward the lake.

"This was the spot, huh?" Nikalas asked, looking around.

"Yes, this was the spot," she replied. The pink feathers in the sky had begun to darken. Dusk was nearly here. She pursed her lips together and let out a low whistle. But for what? Nikalas looked around confused. Something was coming off from the grass, a mist. It continued to rise; he jumped back moving closer to Emlin. It wasn't mist; it was a figure—a *woman*.

"No way," Nikalas whispered. The woman hovered above the grass; she looked very much like Emlin, the same hair, the same eyes, the same smile. A near spitting image.

"Hello, Mother," Emlin said calmly. The figure continued to hover, turning its gaze towards Nikalas she smiled.

"You've *found* him," the woman said.

"Yes," Emlin replied.

Chapter 9

It was time, time to make good on his word. Finding the remains of Herratia was now his primary concern. Uncertainty awaited him as he plunged down into the cold waters of Neveraus. The cold water seared his nerves; before long he no longer felt the sting, all sensations of pain had faded. His body had numbed, but his movements so far remained unimpaired. Behind him, his Akordan escorts navigated the water with ease. They tried their best to slow their pace, but at long last they no longer could stoop to his primitive skills. He was alone now; his escorts had disappeared in the darkness of the waters. Fear set in, Arlen Bog was known for its unusual and unpleasant creatures. With his escorts far ahead he was vulnerable. Up top was the promise of air; air he so desperately needed. Even with his oxygen mask, he only had enough air stored to swim five minutes at best before he would need to surface.

His escorts sat on the rocky shores of the Ecglides talking, laughing, and whispering. *About me? How dare they?* Septus slowly crawled from the bog and fell to the ground. Did this define him? How could he possibly be the greatest wizard to walk the land if water could defeat him? On his back, he lay catching his breath. Each passing moment he could feel his muscles gaining strength. They called to him, told him to stand, *rise,* they said. His mask kept him alive, a protective mesh with a fine filter kept the poisonous air out of his lungs. The protective eyewear made it so his eyes did not lose their sight. The time had come. He had shown weakness—perhaps at the cost of authority. He stood up and looked toward his escorts; his vision fogged by his breath.

"You find it funny to leave me behind like that?" Septus bellowed. The Akordans fell silent as they looked towards a weakened Septus. "Pray I don't find an opportunity to even the score. The next one of you to cross me will get a taste of my new powers." His convoy said no words; there was nothing to be said. Akordans were quite skilled in combat, but none of them were willing to test those skills against dark magic. Most had seen the terrible power firsthand; it had humbled them, left them intimidated. Shaking his head, he began to march past his escorts leaving them speechless where they sat.

There was nothing but silence as they continued their way through the Ecglides. Septus didn't mind the silent treatment, in fact, he preferred it. The task at hand required their obedience, not their friendship. In the distance was *Berloth Forest*, and with each step closer to the forest the air became less poisonous. How ironic that he would find comfort in a forest that most wanted to avoid. Compared to the Ecglides, Berloth looked like an oasis. Its trees towered high into the air, but the sun was nowhere to be seen. It was a forlorn region, forsaken by joy and embraced in misery. *I'll take it*, Septus thought, *at least here I can breathe.*

One could all too easily get lost in the labyrinth that was Berloth. Providentially, he had become rather familiar with this particular maze. His time away from Terria had broadened his mind; he was a better navigator and a wiser traveler. There were of course still secrets to be discovered, a forest this size would take a lifetime to master. One region, in particular, piqued his interest. It was in the far south of Berloth, the fortress of Solarian.

Once the stronghold of his father, now just another relic of an ancient war. It was said to be abandoned yet each day smoke still rose from the direction of the fortress. Septus had been tempted many times to seek out the source, but Krytus urged against it. *Best to gain your full powers before you go digging in that graveyard,* he had said. So far Septus had heeded this advice, but for how much longer?

The Akordans might have had the advantage in the swamps of the Ecglides but here it was the elves and men that reigned supreme. For once *he* held the cards, he was in control. His pawns followed him obediently, still refusing to speak. There were four in total; Vixar, Roman, Sef and Drango. They were chosen, not for their skill, but their obedience. Too many of the other candidates would've been tempted to kill Septus rather than follow his orders. These four were hanging on by a thread, one mistake away from banishment. Still, even the weakest and least capable Akordan was still dangerous. Septus had to maintain his control over them with the threat of his newly acquired magic.

"How far is this place?" Sef asked finally breaking the silence. He was one of the most war-ravaged Akordans in Neveraus. A missing eye and many missing teeth kept people from crossing him too often. He was stupid, even for Akordan standards. War was his only skill.

"We will follow this path for twenty days at least. When the air starts to smell foul we will know we are getting close," Septus replied.

"The air already smells foul," Drango retorted. Drango suffered from Vogolis, a disease more and more common amongst Akordans, as a result, his skin had lost its green color in favor of gray and he had many patches where normally tough exterior had given way to soft, vulnerable skin.

"You're just used to the smell of filth and poison," Septus replied rolling his eyes. As they continued along their path, the sun began to set. To the left, a trail caught his attention. Branches and tall grass attempted to hide it from sight, but the traces of it were still just visible enough. Septus squinted towards the trail and began walking toward it. It was unclear where it led. He began pushing his way through, letting the branches fly back toward his escorts. Deeper into the woods they went until at last there was a clearing. A bare patch of grass with an old fire pit in the middle. Dishes littered the ground and logs cut in half had been used as seating.

"What are we doing here?" Drango asked.

"We need to make camp. We aren't marching through these woods in the dark. Too many dangerous creatures." Septus gestured to a spot on the ground for them to lay out their belongings.

"We need firewood. You two fetch some." Septus' fingers pointed at Vixar and Roman, who scoffed at the order before turning around and heading out to find some. *That's all it takes huh? Projecting confidence in my authority and they'll listen.* A smile crept across his face as he began to unpack his belongings. A small roll out pad provided him a dry place to relax. Digging down into this pack, he pulled out a large book and began slowing flipping its pages.

Her story was fascinating; he had read it a dozen times already, and yet he still felt like he learned a little more about her every time. Herratia, Witch of the Hills. Would she live up to the hype? A part of him feared to wake her; he wanted to be the greatest wizard in the land and if she was better that would be an awkward complication. That being said she could be a useful tool. *She could give me an army.* The tomb's location had been lost to time, but if you paid close attention to the details, there were clear clues. Mountains; there were only so many of them. Nearby villages; there were only a handful of villages posted near mountains. Even if he could find her, she would remain dead until he got the remaining talismans. *If the Akordans truly value the return of their queen they had better do their best to find them.* His hands ran along the grooves in the talisman; there was an undeniable comfort to holding it. He could almost feel his father's presence.

    His focus was interrupted as a bundle of wood crashed to the ground. Vixar hovered above with a complacent look decorating his reptilian face. Septus shot him a glare of dissatisfaction, and then continued flipping through the pages. Quickly, Vixar began arranging the wood in the fire pit and began rubbing a couple of sticks together hoping to start a fire. Roman laughed at his efforts and grabbed sticks of his own and tried as well. Nothing happened; the wood was too damp. Moments had passed, arguments had started and still no fire danced in the air. Septus set the book down and sighed. *It's worth a shot isn't it?* Focus was key; he held his hands above the wood and focused on his goal. *Fire, I want fire.* His eyes remained fixed on the small pile of wood. A wave of his hand and flames began to rise, much to his surprise. He had barely practiced demonstrating his new powers; this was either luck or perhaps a sign of true skill. Neither mattered at the moment, as the flames began to stretch into the air he satisfactorily folded his arms.

"That's useful," Roman remarked as he sat back in awe. The Akordans sat mesmerized by the flames as if witnessing a new sight. Darkness covered them like a warm blanket, but the flames provided plenty of light. The creatures of the night had begun taking control of their domain; it was their turn to own the forest. Bats darted through the skies so quickly it was hard to tell what you were seeing. Dortledees danced around providing light shows and attracting the occasional prey. As a few Dortledees started hovering close, Drango began annoyingly swatting them away.

"It's bad luck to swat at those," Septus said as he stared deadpanned into the flames.

"Why?" Drango snickered, ignoring the remark and continuing his futile attack.

"Dortledees are apparently spies of Undr. He used them to keep tabs on Furlasia. They spoke to him. If that is indeed true than swatting at them is a sure way to upset him. They are said to be under the protection of a terrible beast," Septus explained. In the flames, an image of the apparent beast appeared and began running in place.

"Superstitions. That's the biggest load of ordure I've ever heard. Stupid Terrians." Drango laughed.

"Suit yourself," Septus replied, the beast in the flames disappeared.

"I'm bloody starving!" Drango blurted out. "We need food."

"You're always hungry. Didn't you bring enough snacks with you?" Roman asked.

"I ate those ages ago. I'm gonna search for grub. Who wants to join me?" Looking around the fire, it was clear he was alone.

"Fine, but don't expect to me to share with the likes of any of you," Drango barked; he grabbed his sword and headed out into the darkness. Septus sat mesmerized, watching the flames continue their dance, a ballet before his eyes. *What was this place? Who had settled here before?* A howl in the distance ended the reticence; footsteps came crashing toward the camp. Twigs broke, leaves rustled and finally Drango emerged sword in hand and no fresh kill.

"Ha! Seems you're as crummy a hunter as you are a warrior?" Roman jeered.

"Watch yourself, Roman. I am more than capable of killing you where you stand." Drango sneered before plopping firmly to the ground.

"It sounded like you were running? What were you running from?" Septus smiled. "A beast perhaps?"

"Don't be ridiculous," Drango retorted.

Septus continued to observe the blaze, opting to tune out the remainder of the night's pointless banter. Akordans degrading each other could only entertain one for so long before it just became vexatious. The flames were hypnotic, pulling him into their trance and soothing him, whispering to him a soft lullaby. *Dreamchild, leave this place, sleep now,* they whispered. Before long the effect had left him weary, the day had been long and stressful, his eyes grew heavy. Darkness awaited him like an old friend.

Rangmor Mountain was a treacherous climb; each successful step up the steep rocks was a small victory. His arms were starting to grow sore as he continued pulling himself up. Blisters covered his palms; powder from the rocks coated his fingertips. As he neared a ledge, he turned his head and gulped, the ground had abandoned him, or rather he had abandoned the ground. It seemed angry; it wanted him back, as quickly as possible. *You're not getting me.* Arm over arm, he pulled his way further and further up the mountain.

Life seemed more fragile than ever, and death tried to grab him at every turn. Grabbing onto a loose rock proved a mistake. By a stroke of luck, he was able to catch his grip; his heart throbbed so hard it seemed like it was trying to vacate him. His hands were bloody, his anxiety was high, but he had to continue, too much rode on him successfully reaching the top. Higher and higher he continued to climb; the air was thin and cold.

It had taken nearly three hours, but at last, he had reached the opening. The pain and soreness from the climb seemed to fade as he pulled himself up inside.

The way was dark and filled with dreariness. *This is the place*, Krytus had said. *I'm sure of it.* Undr's hidden temple; there was something mythical about this cave. The smell of incense filled the air and in the distance light flickered. *Walk toward the light.* It was massive, much deeper and vaster than he could believe. As he finally reached the source of the light, he found himself in the middle of a large temple. The walls glistened with gold, and large pillars lined the distance. Each wall was painted with ancient symbols and pictures. Slowly he walked toward the front of the temple gazing over each detail. It was methodical; the attention to detail was impressive.

As he neared the front of the temple, he finally saw it, the podium containing the Tobin. It was encased in a blue bubble. Next to the podium stood two statues, one on either side. Each statue was armed with a sword and a stern look. Behind the podium was a statue of Undr himself. As he got closer to the statue he came to a pause; there was someone kneeling in front of it. The mysterious figure was shrouded in a golden cloak that made it impossible to see who it was.

"You have no right to be here, Septus. You are not worthy of *his* presence," the figure whispered.

"Who are you? How do you know my name?" Septus called out warily.

"I know all that happens in Furlasia. I've been watching you your whole life. I am his tool, his paladin. I am Vigil," the voice was soft. Slowly, the figure turned around to unveil a young woman. As she glared with glowing blue eyes, she pulled down the hood to reveal hair as white as snow and skin as dark as the night. She was beautiful yet terrifying, he felt frozen in place as she slowly walked toward him.

"You live up here?" Septus asked, still unable to move.

"I am bound to this place, and this place is bound to me. I have never allowed any who has entered here to leave with their life. So tell me, Septus Crane, why should I let you live?" Vigil asked.

"I've come for the Tobin," Septus replied.

"So you admit you're here to steal from *him*," Vigil remarked.

"Yes," Septus retorted. *Why did I say that?*

"Why? Why do you want the Tobin?" Vigil asked.

"I seek a means to recover that which was stolen from me." Vigil stopped in front of Septus and placed a hand on his cheek; her touch was cold — ice cold in fact. He flinched in discomfort as he continued to watch her, mesmerized.

"The talisman. You think that you can right a wrong by gaining your father's gifts. Agavordis was a man consumed with anger. He was unstable at best, and his powers made him dangerous. His death was important and necessary. Why should his son be any better? I've seen into your heart, and I know what you want. You would be just like him," Vigil walked around him softly touching his neck.

"Your hands are like ice," Septus said.

"My touch is cold," she paused. "But my body is warm." Swiftly she grabbed his hand and pressed it against her inner thigh.

"Are you going to kill me?" Septus asked, pulling his hand back flustered.

"No, I'm going to let you live. And I will even let you take the Tobin," Vigil replied.

"What's the catch?" Septus skeptically asked.

"There will come a time where I will need a favor and when it does I will come to you," She walked towards the podium and gazed at the Tobin, Septus finally able to move followed.

"What kind of favor?" Smiling, she turned and paused. There was something in her eyes, a *fire*, electricity. He had seen that look before, but never this strong. There was nothing he could do to stop it; she pressed her lips against his. This wasn't like any kiss he had shared with Emlin; there was something different about this kiss, something desperate, something *forbidden.* Despite his urge to pull away, he couldn't, his body wouldn't let him. Something grew inside him. Her fire had spread to him, that desperate energy to keep it going. With each passing moment, she softly moaned, and he could feel the fire continuing to grow. He couldn't bear the thought of it ending, there was something about her. She understood him; she saw his darkness and was attracted to it. Vigil was the one; the one he was destined to be with, he was sure of it.

"I love you," he whispered.

A forceful push sent him crashing into the hard ground. *What the hell?* Despite the pain and inevitable bruising, he wanted more. He wanted to taste her warm lips just a little bit longer, she was nowhere to be seen.

"Leave this place," Vigil exclaimed, her voice echoed throughout the temple like the voice of a god. Septus continued to look around trying to find where she had gone. Wherever she was, she had hidden well. Slowly he pulled himself to his feet. In front of him, the Tobin sat suspended in the blue sphere, waiting to be taken. The descriptions had been mostly accurate; it was cylindrical and made of crystal, and at the center was a small red jewel.

"What do I do? How do I retrieve the Tobin?" Septus asked aloud.

"It's not enough that I allow you to take it, now you want me to tell you how? Do not test my generosity," Vigil replied. Still no sign of her; where was she hiding? *What game is she playing?* His glare remained fixed on his goal. Nothing but the mysterious sphere stood in his way. *Just grab it? It can't be that easy.* Perhaps it was—perhaps it was *exactly* that easy. With a gulp, he lifted his hand and slowly started edging it closer and closer.

"Enough of this," He whispered to himself. To hell with caution, he had braved a treacherous climb that would've killed most men. This tool was meant to be his. A couple of deep breaths later, he thrust his hand inside, grabbing the Tobin with a forceful grip. His eyes began to water. He had made a terrible mistake. Searing pain coursed through his arm as his skin began to burn and sizzle.

"What is this!" Septus roared in anguish. *Don't let go of it, don't let go of it.* Terror and pain held him in its terrible grasp. Frailty shook his legs until he could stand no more. Falling to the ground in horrible pain, he had managed to maintain his grip on the Tobin. A splash of rogue liquid followed him to the ground clipping his face and landing on the stones. His cries of pain were so loud anyone within a mile of the mountain could no doubt hear. Local villages would probably assume a demon had been awakened, superstitious folks that they were. Slowly, Vigil approached Septus. His breathing had slowed, and he was near the point of blacking out.

"It is done. Look for my sign and you will know it is time to make good on your end," Vigil whispered. On a tile next to his head, she traced three circles, each growing smaller and a line running vertically through all of them. Her icy touch allowed the sign to stand out as if drawn with a neon pen. Moving was painful, he could find no words, but he managed to turn his head just enough to see the symbol. All went dark.

Septus shot up in his bed, awakened by the sound of Vixar relieving himself on the fire pit, with each splash the embers sizzled and hissed. He grunted in disgust, shielding his sight as he began to gather his things.

"Best not to leave a trace we were here," Vixar explained. "Your kind is always hunting us." *They are not my kind,* Septus thought to himself. They wouldn't understand; their brains were incapable of understanding anything besides fighting. Perhaps it was the Terrians that caused this terrible trait. White smoke rose, and the wood sizzled as the flames began to die down. As Septus finished gathering his things he looked around, the sun was not quite to the middle of the sky. They still had plenty of time to travel. The dream had left him sweating and flushed. It was something he would not soon forget. Always he kept his eyes open looking for the sign. One day she would come, but when? *When will she stop torturing me?*

"Alright you nasty savages, let's get moving," Septus ordered. Drango shot Roman a look of fury before shrugging and falling into line. *I'd rather not drag this out any longer than I need to.*

Chapter 10

Golden light filled the throne room of Nasleigh Keep. At its center, Nikalas stood admiring the fine details of the intricately assembled royal cathedral. Today was the day; the beginning of his journey to meet Kunklestick. He had taken extra care earlier that morning to pack all the essentials. Extra clothes, some snacks, the diary—and, of course, the egg, which he had learned had been sent to him by none other than Kunklestick himself. Vicham, the King's right hand and best friend had volunteered to escort him to a city called Cristol which was the rumored whereabouts of the elderly wizard. Emlin had expressed a desire to accompany Nikalas, but Hervott would have no part of that plan; she had no business taking such a risky journey as far as he was concerned. *Your place is in the kingdom not out on the dangerous road,* he had said. After the inevitable argument that followed, Emlin agreed to remain behind.

From the upper footway, Hervott and Vicham began to slowly descend the stairs. They whispered to each other just quiet enough to mask what they discussed. Vicham looked like he had prepared for a battle—on his hip hung a sword in a golden sheath. Above the throne room, Emlin looked down watching Nikalas with concern. Their time together had been brief, but she already considered him a friend. They were bonded by a secret, and both of them had agreed not to discuss what the spirit had divulged.

"Stay safe, Nikalas," she whispered quietly.

"You have the look of a man ready to grab his destiny by the horns," Hervott smiled.

"I'm still not sure I believe in that," Nikalas mused.

"It's not an easy concept to accept. Hopefully, Kunklestick helps you realize your true potential," Hervott replied. "You packed the egg? He was very specific about that."

Nikalas nodded.

"Excellent. Now take special care to listen to every command Vicham gives you. He's done this journey many times, and he knows how to get there safely. So long as you follow his lead, you'll be safe. Understand?" Hervott rested his hands on Nikalas' shoulders and gave him a firm look. Once again Nikalas nodded in agreement. Hervott bowed in satisfaction and turned to Vicham.

"Travel safe my friend. I will be eager for your return."

"The journey should not take too long, I expect to return by the next full moon," Vicham replied. A remorseful look spread across Hervott's face. He swiftly grabbed Vicham and pulled him close, embracing him in a firm hug.

Life was just as present as ever as they navigated their way through the masses of residents. A feeling of homesickness was slowly brewing inside him, not for Michigan, but for the comforts of the castle. With each step he took further away from Nasleigh Keep, he felt like he was losing his connection to Emlin. How could she mean so much to him after so little time? As they cleared the city gates, the loud click of the lock imprinted the truth in his mind. Terria was now officially behind them. His next path was an uncertain one, and while there was something exciting in that thought, it was mostly terrifying.

Vicham was prompt with his directions; they would need to obtain horses if they were to make the journey in a reasonable amount of time. Waiting conveniently just outside the city walls was a small stable run by an old man with unkempt gray hair and a dirt smudged face.

"Good day to you. I'm on official King's business and am in need of a couple of horses," Vicham firmly stated as he set a rather full coin purse down in front of the old man. The old man picked up the purse and shook his head.

"This is too much coin," he said with a weak voice.

"I can't guarantee their return," Vicham replied.

"Oh, I see." The old man replied. He began to clumsily feel his way around the desk, bumping into it several times until he came to a stop just inches from Nikalas. His eyes were glossy and hollow, emotionless and dead; it had been many years since his sight had been stolen. His vacant eyes brought some discomfort to Nikalas as he looked towards the ground.

"I've got the perfect horse for you," the old man said looking at Nikalas' chin. He navigated the stable surprisingly well for a blind man, he quite precisely led them into the stables and approached a large white horse with black spots surrounding its eyes. As he came to a stop in front of the horse, he began to rub its head with one hand and waved Nikalas over with the other. Nikalas gulped as he approached the large stallion.

"Don't be scared," Vicham said, hoping to sway the clear discomfort plastered across Nikalas' face, his words did little to help, however.

"I've never ridden one of these, not by myself anyways," Nikalas said, shaking with nervousness.

"There's nothing to it. You simply climb on and hang onto the saddle. Use the reigns to steer where you want her to go. She's named *Wildfire* but don't worry; she won't throw you off." Nikalas could feel the pit in his stomach growing as he pulled himself into the saddle. Wildfire was considerably taller than the horse he had ridden with Emlin, and he been intimated by that one. This horse was terrifying; putting your life into the hands of a creature that you had so little control over was a gut-wrenching concept.

Once they had both secured themselves, Vicham began to guide them away from the stables.

"Good luck to you, Nikalas," the old groom called out as they began to fade into the distance. *How does he know my name?* He thought to turn around and offer a wave. *He wouldn't see it,* he realized.

"Hold on tight, Nikalas. We are about to start trotting," Vicham warned, keeping his eye on Nikalas he gave his horse a light kick. "Ha!"

Landscapes came and went as they continued their brisk pace through the enormous Tordenth Forest. The only constant was the heat—there seemed to be no escaping it. Vicham did indeed seem an expert on this particular journey, though. If there was a shortcut, he was keen to take it. He seemed just as eager to get to their destination as Nikalas.

Breaks were few and far between. Vicham insisted they keep moving to make good time. At night, they had nothing to separate them from the wilderness. A pad and pillow were all they were afforded. It wouldn't have been so bad if the forest hadn't been so ripe with the cries and shrieks of unknown creatures. A tent wouldn't do much to offer protection, but it would have at least hidden them. Vicham shrugged off Nikalas' constant plea for shelter.

"Time is not on our side. No tents," he replied. Tents were not an option but that didn't mean he didn't take precautions. At each campsite they made, he stuck a long metal stick into the ground, at its top was a glowing orb he had promised would keep away undesirable creatures.

During the day it seemed they were being followed, not by people but by Oekies. High in the trees they swung about cackling to each other, always their gaze fixed on them. Nikalas had attempted to point out the strangeness of the behavior, but Vicham merely accused him of paranoia. In truth, Vicham knew full well about the animals, and yes, they were indeed following them. Insurance from King Hervott to help keep tabs on their safety.

Seven days had passed since leaving Terria. Their constant speed and lack of breaks had paid off. The journey which normally would've taken nearly two weeks had been cut in half. As they exited the forest, they were greeted by a large plain filled with nothing but field grass and the occasional hills. *Jordoon*, this place was called. A dirt road suddenly appeared; the tracks of former travelers still freshly visible. The plains were vast and utterly mundane. Vicham continued to lead the way. There was a smell in the air that seemed familiar, a brief hint of salt.

As the dirt road turned to limestone, their destination could finally be seen. Ahead was a large wall made entirely of crystal, it shimmered under the sun creating a prism effect.

"That's it?" Nikalas asked as they slowly approached the colossal wall.

"You were expecting more?" Vicham questioned.

"No. I mean, it's amazing," Nikalas defended. There were few wonders he could've seen back home that would've wowed quite to this extent. Cristol, home of the Arnouts, perhaps the closest beings to divinity to walk the lands of Furlasia. There was something over-the-top yet elegant about the wall the Arnouts had chosen to build. In the center of it all was a pair of double doors, the only way in or out of Cristol. All visitors had to pass through these doors. An ancient mystical power made it impossible for anyone to sneak in by going over the walls. Penetration was nearly impossible. Two guards stood outside of the doors looking quite prepared to defend the city at any cost.

"How do we do this?" Nikalas pondered.

"They will either grant us access or kill us where we stand. And believe me they are more than capable of it," Vicham replied.

"Kill us? Are you sure about this?" Nikalas exclaimed.

"Silence," Vicham quietly scolded as they came to a stop in front of the doors.

"What pray tell brings you to the mighty city of Cristol, Terrian?" The guard on the left spoke soft yet stern. His expression was blank and free of emotion. Both guards seemed to have oddly pale skin considering that the sun was beating relentlessly on the city.

"We have traveled a long way for a meeting with someone who claimed to be residing within these walls," Vicham replied.

"Who?" The guard sternly asked.

"Kunklestick," Vicham replied. Both guards exchanged a look of confusion.

"Kunklestick? Here, in Cristol? That's not possible. This is the only way in and out of the city, and we have not seen any sign of him," the left guard stated, he sounded offended at the implication.

"He informed King Hervott he was most definitely here. Says he can't stay away from the ale you guys brew." The guards exchanged a brief smile amongst each other.

"Well, that does certainly sound like him. That man drinks more of it than any of us. Regardless, though, he can't possibly be here." Vicham took a step closer and cocked his head.

"Are you trying to tell me there is no way Kunklestick, a man who is very skilled in magic couldn't get past you?" Vicham questioned as he cracked a smile.

"Well umm, I mean." A gigantic form of a face appeared in the glass wall behind them. It was a woman with pale skin, piercing blue eyes and stunning black hair. *High Lord Fae.*

"Is this interrogation nearly over? I was expecting them to show up yesterday" Lord Fae probed.

"You were expecting them, Your Highness?"

"But of course. Hervott informed me of their arrival days ago. Pardon me, it must've slipped my mind. I should've informed your commanding officer to alert you. The fault is mine. Now please, let them pass," Lord Fae commanded. Her demeanor seemed rather calm, even when issuing commands. She appeared to genuinely respect the guards. Where she could've spoken with disdain and annoyance, she maintained a polite manner. Something King Hervott was sadly missing. Behind the two guards, the glass doors started to slowly pull back, revealing the heart of Cristol.

Vicham offered a courtly nod and waved Nikalas to follow.

Cristol was almost the exact opposite of Terria. Where Terria was crowded and at times messy, Cristol seemed orderly. What few residents filled the sidewalks were all silent. It was almost eerie. Horse drawn carriages navigated the limestone roadways. Under the beaming sun, the roads glistened and sparkled. Vicham continued to lead them down the streets until a carriage came to a stop in front of them.

"You look like you could use a ride," a friendly voice said. The carriage door flung open to reveal Pip, Lord Fae's only son. Nikalas shot Vicham a look of concern.

"We'd love a ride," Vicham replied giddily.

"Are you sure, I mean today is *Belish*. There's sure to be plenty of excitement in the streets," Pip added.

"Scoot over," Vicham commanded.

"Yes, sir," Pip replied smiling. Vicham stepped into the carriage and positioned himself across from Pip. The two shot each other a smile before looking out towards Nikalas.

"So you're gonna take the scenic route then?" Pip asked. Nikalas sighed, then stepped inside. He was clueless, and that was what troubled him. Once again, he was meeting a new stranger and being forced to trust them. The feeling was hard to get used to.

"We're ready," Pip yelled out to the carriage driver. A jolt later and the carriage was navigating the pristine streets. Each new tile of limestone causing a bump against the wooden wheels.

"So he's the one huh? He's here to meet Kunklestick?" Pip asked, looking toward Nikalas.

"You know you can just address *me*," Nikalas blurted out.

"Oh dear, you're right. Where are my manners? I am Pip, son of the giant face you saw on the glass wall. My mother always was a bit dramatic, but hey, she beats the last leader this city had," Pip laughed. The former leader being High Lord Aldon, whose reign came to an abrupt end when he met the sharp end of Lord Fae's blade. *Belish* was a celebration held every year in Cristol to celebrate the death of the former High Lord Aldon. It was the one day a year Lord Fae got to remind everyone that she had saved them all from the grip of a terrible tyrant.

The bumpy ride suddenly seemed to smooth out. Had they stopped? No, the hooves of the horses could still be heard. Their footsteps remained, but the pitch had changed. Nikalas lifted a small shade on the carriage door. There was nothing but water for miles.

"We're almost to the palace," Pip commented, taking notice of the look of concern drawn upon Nikalas' face.

"Are we on a bridge?" Nikalas questioned.

"Well, yeah, that's the only way to cross water. It's pretty neat actually. The entire bridge is made up of the very same crystal as the wall. It floats above the water due to an enchantment. We call it Rasolis, named it after the first Arnout to learn how to manipulate glass. The guy was a visionary. Shame he cut his own head off, one too many ales I suspect," Pip explained.

"Oh. We're here," Pip exclaimed as the sound of hooves stopped. *This guy is weird,* Nikalas thought. The carriage door was pulled open, a tall dutiful servant dressed in a tacky colored uniform bowed as Pip stepped out.

"Your Highness," Gregory greeted. Behind Pip followed Nikalas and Vicham. Nikalas gulped as he looked around. The palace was in the middle of a large lake; the water glimmered under the sunlight.

"Crystal, the whole lake looks like crystal," Nikalas noted.

"Hence the name, young sir," Gregory stated.

"Be nice Gregory, he's not from around here," Pip scolded.

"Ready for the tour?" He asked, gesturing toward Nikalas, while smiling at Vicham.

"Sure, I guess." Nikalas replied. Pip nodded toward Gregory, who bowed and walked toward the palace doors. Nikalas glanced at Vicham with a worrisome look. *Here we go again,* he thought.

"Nikalas, welcome to Eiraf Palace," Pip exclaimed as the door was pushed inward. As they stepped inside one could easily be forgiven if they didn't realize they were inside a building. Plants filled the room from top to bottom offering a resplendent entrance to an already impressive castle. In the center of the room was a subtle yet impressive waterfall that steadily flowed from the top of the ceiling down into a small pond.

Palace guards were placed strategically throughout the main entrance, each one dressed in long ruby colored frocks and wearing golden helmets. Large pillars made of limestone lined the main hall; each pillar had decorative symbols carved into them. Birds chirped as they flew around, some occasionally landing in the pond. Hovering just above the pond, small insects glowed, dancing around the water.

Nikalas curiously wandered over toward the pond. As he got closer, he could see that something was in the water, its image distorted by the impact of the falls. *What is that?* Leaning in closer he could just start to make it out; it looked like a head. *What the hell?* His stare remained focused. It was a head, indeed. It lay underneath the water like a stone, it was creepy and unsettling, yet he couldn't take his gaze from it. His eyes remained fixed on the lonely face until the eyes suddenly shot open. His panic sent him to the ground with a thud.

"Don't be frightened, Nikalas. He can see you, but he poses no danger," a voice echoed. Looking up from the floor, he could see a figure was floating down toward him. A woman garbed in a long violet dress with a cape to match slowly touched to the ground just in front of him. *High Lord Fae.* Her pale skin and soft smile seemed to provide a comfort to mask over the horror he had just witnessed. Nikalas continued to lie on the floor, feeling almost frozen by her presence.

"Whose head is that?" Nikalas asked. Lord Fae smiled slightly before offering her hand, she pulled him up and slowly guided him back to the pond.

"Meet Lord Aldon, former High Lord and tyrannical leader of Cristol. I've since relieved him of his duties. He's been much easier to deal with since his decapitation," she said coldly.

"Mother can be dramatic," Pip added. Nikalas continued to look in horror at the face under the water. Lord Aldon's eyes met with his; there was desperation behind them, innocence.

"Vicham, it has been too long," Lord Fae said, turning to greet her new guest.

"Indeed, it has," Vicham replied gripping her hand and offering a slight kiss.

"So you've brought me a new house guest," Lord Fae commented as she looked toward Nikalas. For his part, he remained standing in front of the pond, still entranced by the ghastly sight.

"King Hervott never ceases to impress. Finding the boy from the prophecy; what a remarkable time we are living in. Although his arrival surely isn't a good sign, I suppose," Lord Fae sighed and grabbed Nikalas by the arm, pulling him away from the pond. "That's enough Aldon," she shouted towards the water.

"Decidedly not. If you believe in such things," Vicham replied.

"You've arrived here at the perfect time. We are to have an enormous feast tonight. It would be an honor if you would join us," Lord Fae offered. Vicham bowed in acceptance and shot Pip a quick smile, who returned the gesture. Fae looked toward Nikalas, who still looked to be dazed.

"Pip, dear," Lord Fae softly said.

"Yes, mother?"

"Do help our guest shake this gloom. We can't have him so dreary at dinner." Lord Fae smiled once again toward Vicham, and began to float back up to the upper level.

Chapter 11

The forest was sultry, each step a chore, an exercise in persistence. Luckily, persistence was something Septus had in excess. His Akordan escorts, on the other hand, had grown restless and agitated with each passing day. The journey was proving far longer and more tiring than they had thought. With no opportunities to procure any horses they were forced to walk each day, the distance taking its toll. Settlements in Berloth were few and far between, mostly all anyone could find were traces of where someone had camped, settlements were a rarity. His legs grew weary, his stomach growled. It had been hours since their last break.

"We have to take a break. We need food," Septus said, breaking the long dreadful silence that had engulfed them the past couple hours.

"He speaks!" Drango exclaimed. "And with good sense."

"I'm glad you agree because I'm appointing you the task of bringing us some," Septus smiled. They continued to walk for a few moments further until they reached a clearing just off the road.

"Don't take too long," Septus commanded as he looked towards Drango. *Hunting? Now there was a task worth doing.* Even with his annoyance at being told what to do by a pipsqueak like Septus, Drango couldn't pass up this opportunity. After all, it was in the very DNA of Akordans to enjoy killing things. With a grin stretching from cheek to cheek, he lifted his sword and headed into the woods. Septus watched with grim satisfaction as the Akordan disappeared from sight. Tossing his pack to the ground, he knelt down next to it and began rummaging through it. *Where is it? It has to be here.* Finally, he found what he was looking for. As he withdrew his hand, he clutched a water skin, it was nearly empty. Each drop was sublime but gone too soon. Holding the container upside down, it was clear they would need to find fresh water and soon.

Thirst gripped him in its loving arms, holding him tight like a mother to her child. Each passing moment in Berloth threatened to be his last. *Keep pushing on,* he told himself. *Your reward will come soon enough.* Did he truly believe his thoughts? Or was he simply trying to comfort himself? Something in the distance grabbed his attention. In a tall patch of grass, something moved around, an animal perhaps? Quickly, he hopped to his feet, his gaze focused on the grass. With each step closer, he could feel his heart race. He was no more than a couple of steps away when something darted out from the grass and took off toward the forest. It wasn't an animal; it was a small person. A gnome.

Septus had heard tales of their existence. Their skills and technology were rumored to be the driving force behind the Beacons and much of the up and coming steam power in Morlay. Still, though, their existence seemed like a fairy tale at best.

"Don't run," Septus called out. "I mean you no harm." His Akordan escorts exchanged a look of confusion as Septus darted from the camp.

The pursuit was short; the gnome surprisingly spry considering the short stature. There was no sign of the creature. It had disappeared.

"What were you up to?" Septus asked, whispering more to himself than to anyone else. A gamy essence permeated the air arousing his stomach and nearly causing salivation. It was coming from up ahead; smoke rose in the distance. Wandering like a dog to the kill, he finally managed to track down the scent. A small village lay ahead. Delopar were plentiful as he crouched down getting a closer look. Frand, one of the most prominent settlements of the Delopar. Inca, whom he knew through Emlin had once told stories of this place. Clearly she had embellished them; Frand was no more than a small settlement at best. Nowhere near as impressive as he had imagined. In the center of the village, a boar sat above flames, juice dripping and sizzling. Standing idly and patiently by, a large Delopar with white and black fur stood carefully rotating the beast above the fire pit. He was outnumbered, terribly so. Best to back away carefully before he got spotted.

By the time he found his traveling companions they all sat around a fire, rubbing their bellies and letting out the occasional burp.

"Where have you been?" Vixar asked, using a small bone to pick his teeth clean. "You've been gone so long we nearly ate your share."

"That would've been a mistake," Septus replied as he took a seat next to his pack and picked up a large leaf with bits of meat on it.

"How long was I gone?" Septus inquired.

"Had to be at least a couple hours," Sef replied. *A couple of hours? But how?*

"So where were you?" Roman asked. Septus piled some of the leftover meat into his mouth and began to chew. The flavor was foul. What had they fed him? He quickly spat it out and wiped his tongue.

"Excuse me? Is there a problem?" Drango asked, offended.

"What in the name of the gods is this?" Septus barked tossing the remaining meat into the fire pit.

"Hey!" Drango exclaimed. "I would've eaten that." Septus shook his head and gathered his pack.

"Let's move. There is a Delopar settlement just up ahead. It stands between us and the mountains. We need to get by, hopefully unnoticed. No killing unless necessary," Septus commanded. Drango mumbled something under his breath as they gathered their things. It was hard to make out, but Septus could certainly guess. The feud between Akordans and Delopar was quite long standing. Most likely the hatred toward the Delopar stemmed from jealousy. Jealousy that they were so easily accepted while Akordans were cast out and treated like vermin.

As the last Akordan gathered their supplies the journey pressed on. Septus remained steadfast in his goal of sneaking by unnoticed. Each step taken toward the settlement set his heart on edge. Even with their considerable skill in combat, Akordans weren't a match against Delopar. And Frand held dozens. Closer and closer they neared the settlement. The pathway lay ahead, but Septus had elected to stay under the cover of the trees. *We're so close.*

Something ahead caught his eyes, in the trees. A figure. A lookout. Septus quickly held up his hand ordering the party to freeze.

"Stay here," Septus whispered. "I'm gonna get a closer look." He moved slowly, his footsteps muffled. The tree was large; the Delopar sat perched high up looking over Frand. They were in luck; his gaze appeared to be directed in the opposite direction.

"Quietly," he whispered to the party. Vixar took a deep breath and motioned the others to keep moving. Things looked optimistic, but that was exactly when things took a turn. The loud snap of a tree branch ended the silence, grabbing the lookouts gaze.

"Intruders!" The lookout bellowed.

"Ah, shit," Septus sighed. It was only a mere few seconds before almost the entire village was lined up facing them with determined looks.

"Now that's a proper challenge," Drango laughed as he looked toward the wall of Delopar.

"Stay back, Septus. We'll handle this," Roman instructed. *You don't have to tell me twice,* Septus thought. From behind the line of Delopar a large one emerged, wearing a makeshift crown of feathers and sporting a medallion on his chest.

"You creatures have no business here," the Chief raucously roared.

"We mean no harm. We only hoped to pass by unnoticed," Septus called out. The Chief confusingly glared at Septus.

"What is a Terrian doing among such foul beasts?" The Chief questioned.

"Did he just call us foul?" Sef asked aloud. Septus raised his hand to silence him.

"We are on a journey to the Hark Mountains," he replied. The Chief turned his gaze towards one of the other Delopar with concern.

"What business have you in the Hark Mountains?" The Chief asked.

"Our business is our own," Septus replied. The Chief turned and whispered to the Delopar to his left. Their conversation was faint, as they spoke they shot glances towards Septus. *Come on, come on. Don't be stupid.* Septus bit his lip.

"You shall pass no further. We control the path. The Hark Mountains are forbidden," the Chief commanded.

"You think you can tell us what to do?" Drango laughed spitting on the ground. "Feline scum."

"Terrian, tell your pet to watch his tongue if he wishes to keep it," the Chief yelled pointing at Drango.

"Let's just kill them, Septus," Drango croaked.

"Septus?" A voice called out from behind the crowd. Inca stepped forward with a look of dismay.

"Inca?" Septus replied.

"You know this Terrian?" The Chief asked, turning toward Inca.

"Yes, he's an old friend," she replied.

"Your friend appears to be a traitor," the Chief remarked. Sef began to show his teeth in frustration.

"I've had enough of this," Sef called out.

"As have I," Drango seconded. The two looked toward each other and drew their weapons prompting the others to follow their lead.

"Guys, wait!" Septus yelled out. It was too late; Drango let out a loud roar and began to lead a charge straight for the line of Delopar. Four Akordans versus a dozen Delopar — the odds were certainly stacked against them.

"Prepare yourselves!" The Chief yelled out as he drew his sword. From above, the sound of air swooshing could be heard. The lookout landed in the front of the pack and quickly drew his sword. The Delopar had armed them—including Inca. The roar of the Akordans was intimidating, enough to make even the toughest Delopar nervous. Septus stepped back, biting his lip as he watched the impending doom. Part of him contemplated making a run for it. There was no way this would end well.

Swords clashed against shields as the Akordans thrust themselves into the line of defense. Using their brute strength, they were able to shove the Delopar back, even managing to knock a few to the ground. Drango and Sef quickly shoved their swords into the downed targets and let out a victorious laugh.

Inca rolled toward Vixar and clashed her sword against his shield. He let out an amused grunt and knocked her back. Unlike her fellow peers, she managed to do a back flip and landed back on her feet ready to fight. She dropped to the ground and began spinning in the dirt, knocking Vixar down.

Elsewhere, the Delopar and Akordans were locked in a heated battle. Warm blood trickled slowly from the many wounds, but there were no tears, no cries of pain. War was a tricky business; there was no room for gentleness. Clink after clink, clank after clank the conflict raged on. The Delopar moved like acrobats, their moves calculated and precise. Akordans, on the other hand, were primal in their techniques. Try to hit something; that was the most thought they could muster up. Septus continued to stand by idly; there was no place in this confrontation for him. Swordplay was not his strong suit.

Inca remained dedicated in her spar with Vixar. The sight of Septus in the distance was distracting, but she had to focus—her life depended on it. *What was he doing with them?* A firm backhand from Vixar sent her crashing to the ground, stars filling her eyes. Septus twitched in discomfort. He had no desire to see Inca brought to harm, but at this moment she did represent his enemy.

Sef dropped his sword and grabbed the Chief by his throat as he ran. With all his might and strength, he slammed him into a nearby tree and pinned him, his hands gripped tightly around the Chief's throat.

"Your kind has hunted us too long," Sef yelled, thick clumps of saliva projected from his mouth splashing on the Chief's face. His grip was firm; with each second in his grasp, the Chief could feel his throat beginning to crush. He thought to beg for mercy, but no words could escape his lips. His eyes turned blood red, with each passing moment they continued to bulge outwards, threatening to eject from their sockets. All was growing blurry. All hope fading away like a mist in the wind.

"Ahh," Sef let out a piercing scream as Inca's blade pierced his chest. As he looked down the tip of a sword glistened under what little sun there was, it almost appeared to wink at him. His grip on the Chief softened, and slowly he fell to his knees.

Anger and humiliation filled the Delopar Chief as he landed on his feet. His glare fixed on his attacker, looking down, he spotted a discarded blade from a deceased comrade. Animosity flooded inside him, coursing through his veins like a poison, with one swift movement he swung the blade, the Akordan's howls of pain faded, his head coming to a stop at

Inca's feet. Septus grimaced in disgust as Inca quickly kicked the head from her sight. Only three of his escorts remained. Now was the time—if he didn't act soon, they would all likely perish. The battlefield grew more hostile, more aggressive and filled with roars of anger as the remaining Akordans took notice of their fallen brother.

The moans of pain from the Akordans would be heard for miles. There was no consoling the loss, no undoing the pain. The three remaining Akordans charged at Inca and the Chief. With the Akordans on the warpath, Septus was left undefended, and it did not go unnoticed. A fierce looking Delopar began charging at him with a blood lust in his eyes. *What do I do?* Panicked and full of terror, he drew his sword and held it out.

As the attacker's blade met his, he quickly found himself unarmed and looking up toward the sky. The Delopar's blade was quickly thrust down toward him. Acute thinking kept him alive as he promptly rolled to the side, dodging the attack. He had to do something—he had no sword and no help. *Focus Septus, focus,* the voice in his head was so clear it seemed like someone had actually said it. Something inside him called to him. A rush of power and anger filled him. He hastily stood up and eyed his attacker. In the distance, the remaining Akordans remained locked in a duel with the Chief and Inca.

"It's now or never," Septus whispered. He grabbed onto his focus as if he was holding the reigns of a horse. The power of the talisman grabbed hold of him, squeezing his hand and guiding him. It was suddenly clear what he had to do. With a wave of his arm, he swiftly lifted the Delopar into the air. His target remained suspended midair, unable to move. In one fell swoop, he thrust his arm forward sending the Delopar crashing into a group of his comrades. All combat abruptly stopped, and every eye turned toward Septus, who stood blank faced with glowing red eyes.

"Septus?" Inca called out confused, her old friend offered no reply, his posture remained the same, his face emotionless and empty. The discarded swords littering the ground suddenly rose into the air. Each began moving slowly toward the remaining Delopar. Drango began to laugh with satisfaction as he and the others slowly moved away. Septus' gaze remained fixed on his targets, his eyes still red, vacant of a soul. Without warning, the blades shot toward the remaining Delopar. Inca quickly dropped to the ground, narrowly dodging the attack. Using impulse and the will to survive, she quickly chucked a loose rock, hitting Septus square in the head and knocking him to the ground, unconscious.

All was lost, her friends had been slain, she was outnumbered and alone. She quickly jumped towards the nearest tree, her claws digging into the trunk, and began climbing. As she made her ascent up the tree, a nearby Oekie took off swinging, shrieking in panic.

"Get that feline vermin," Drango cried out. It was no use. She was too high in the trees. They angrily watched as the last Delopar in Frand escaped into the world above. There was nothing to be done.

"It's no use," Roman said. "Let her run. She's gone. This has been a victory. Let her warn the others to stay the hell away from our kind." Their attention turned toward Septus, who was rubbing his head and slowly sitting up.

"What happened?" Septus asked his head throbbing and red.

"You killed them," Roman replied. "You killed them all."
Septus looked around. A dozen slain Delopar littered the
ground, each of them with a blade protruding from their chest.
He gulped. It was all a blur. He didn't remember anything. He
shivered at the sight and slowly rose to his feet.

Chapter 12

He wiped his forehead as the sweat continued to gather. It had been a couple of days since his black out and yet still he felt troubled. There was a tingle in his eyes, and with each step closer to the mountains, the effect grew stronger. In the sky the sun had begun its inevitable descent, creating an orange sky with hints of fuschia. The faint trickle of water filled the air. *At last. Fresh water.* He had taken what he could carry from Frand, but he had used the last of that water hours ago. The thirst had returned, haziness was kicking in. Septus continued to lead the remainder of his party toward the sound of the water. Surely even the Akordans would be feeling the effects of the heat by this point.

The journey had been mostly silent since the battle in Frand. Drango, Roman, and Vixar had become too filled with anger to continue their normal banter. Sef had been killed and his death left a hole in their hearts. This effect took Septus by surprise, initially. Akordans never seemed to show attachment toward each other and yet these three seemed to. Or was it just the burning desire to avenge one of their own? *Inca, what have you done?* The village Chief may have been the one to decapitate Sef, but it was Inca's blade that had brought him down. With her being the sole survivor left in the village the remaining Akordans had turned their hatred exclusively toward her.

"What is that smell?" Roman asked as they continued toward the sound of the stream. Suddenly Septus was hit with a realization. The air had a burning effect; it tickled the throat and caused discomfort to his eyes. This was no water they were approaching; it was *ricter*. Fresh water had once again become a fantasy, a delusion.

"Damnit," Septus sighed. "I had thought we were nearing fresh water."

"That is no water," Drango muttered. "That's ricter. I knew that nearly a mile back."

"Why didn't you speak up?" Septus questioned.

"Excuse me, but I was under the impression you knew what the hell you were doing," Drango snapped.

"We should change course. We must be nearing a large amount of it. The closer we get, the more likely it is to burn our insides," Vixar added. Septus nodded in agreement. He had made a mistake; Drango was right. He didn't know what he was doing. Since the blackout, his mind had been pulled in too many directions. Focusing on the task at hand had become too much of a chore. *A good night's sleep should help, he thought.* They began to turn and head south, toward the mountains. As they continued on, the air became easier to breathe. *This is a good spot,* Septus thought.

"We'll set up camp here. We leave first thing in the morning," Septus ordered. Drango let out a deep sigh and dropped his supplies onto the ground.

"I'm starving," Vixar complained.

"That's your own doing. You know what we have to eat," Drango replied.

"I'm sorry, Drango, but I can't just eat a friend. There must be something around here we can hunt," Vixar replied, dropping his pack and plopping down into the dirt. A queasy feeling crept into Septus' stomach. The image of Drango removing the legs and arms from Sef and tucking them into bags for later consumption had made him hurl on the spot. It was so barbaric, and yet he understood the need.

Drango and Roman wasted no time in setting up camp. As soon as the packs had been laid, a fire was started and poor Sef was once again reheated, it was the second day in a row he had provided them with sustenance. Septus and Vixar however, did not indulge, the very thought too repulsive for either of them. It was only thirty minutes or so after Drango had begun picking his teeth that Vixar showed up with two small rabbits. Drango began drooling as Vixar carefully placed them over the flames.

"Are you going to eat all of that?" Drango asked.

"This is for Septus and myself. You've already gorged yourself on our friend," Vixar exclaimed. Drango sat back in disappointment.

"No good scumbag," Vixar quietly muttered.

"What was that?" Drango asked. Vixar shook his head, ignoring the question. The flames had started to die down, and the deafening snoring of the Akordans was filling the air, alerting all sorts of vicious creatures to their presence. Septus had thought it fortunate that so far their nights hadn't been interrupted by an attack. As he lay on his pack looking up at the sky, he found himself unable to sleep. Flashes of the battle in Frand still haunted him.

"Septus," a voice whispered. He quickly shot up and looked around; there was no one to be seen. In the woods, he heard movement.

"Who's there?" He whispered. Cautiously moving toward the sound, his question was shortly answered. There he was again; the gnome he had seen a couple of days prior. Once

Septus had locked eyes with him, the gnome took off, letting out a mischievous laugh as he fled deeper into the woods. The chase continued further into the forest until the gnome unexpectedly stopped, he turned to face Septus with a twinkle in his eyes. He was standing in the middle of a circle of black sand. Slowly Septus edged towards it, his gaze fixed on the petite man before him.

"I wouldn't do that if I were you," the gnome cautioned. This gnome looked different than the ones he had seen in illustrations. His skin looked decrepit and discolored, a green pigment made him appear sickly. The top of his head was littered with tangled curly black hair, and his smile was hideous, most of his teeth were rotted; those that remained were crooked. He wore rags and had a small hat placed atop his head. The hat was the nicest part of his appearance. A small purple gem at its center.

"Who are you?" Septus asked.

"I've been called many names. Murderer, traitor, demon, prince. My given name was Epard the Wise," he replied with a sinister sneer. Septus stopped just outside the circle and knelt down.

"What do you want from me? Why have you been following me?" Septus probed.

"I'd like to help you," Epard responded.

"Who says I need help?" Septus questioned. Epard began laughing, moving closer to the circle's edge.

"Is that supposed to be a joke? I saw you in the village. You haven't the faintest idea how to use your powers," Epard replied.

"And you do?" Septus skeptically asked. Epard raised his hand and revealed a glowing ball of light.

"I'd say I have more of an idea than you. More importantly, it was I who trained your father. I who helped him discover his true potential and escape the shadow of that wretched old fool.

"Kunklestick?" Septus asked.

"The man has no imagination. No vision, and certainly doesn't have what it takes to be a great wizard. All of those dupes tainted the very title they clung to. I found your father and recognized his potential. I brought him to greatness," Epard explained.

"Why do you want to help me? What's in it for you?" Septus grilled.

"I have my reasons. Perhaps one day I'll explain them to you, but not this night. If you want to truly unlock your power, you'll need my help." Epard stepped outside the circle and reached into his pocket, pulling out a small blank card. With a grin of satisfaction, he handed it to Septus who cautiously accepted it.

"When you're ready to truly learn your powers use this card to contact me," Epard instructed. He quickly turned around and started walking toward the forest.

"This is blank," Septus called out. Epard continued on his way, ignoring the observation as he made his way toward the trees. Septus examined the card in confusion, what was he meant to do with an empty blank card? He headed toward the forest line, hoping to spot Epard, but it was futile, the gnome had vanished.

The following morning arrived too soon. Noise and grumbles from the Akordans gathering their things awakened him in a sweat. Had the previous night been real? He quickly rummaged through his pack and pockets until he found the blank card. Epard's intentions and motivations were unclear at best, but he couldn't help but let out a sigh of relief upon finding it. *I'm not crazy after all.*

"We are near the mountains. We had best get a move on," Roman stated as he extended a hand to Septus.

"Yes, let's." Septus replied, accepting the assistance. He promptly gathered his things and looked towards the mountains.

As they neared the foothills, it became clear this place had been touched by darkness. The whole place was bathed in an ominous tone. Dark clouds covered the skies and a frigid breeze swept through the air. The very concept of sound seemed to have vacated the area long ago — not even the howl of the wind could be heard, just its bitter sting remained. *So the rumors were true.* Septus mused as they continued up the pathway. Even the Akordans were lost for words; what could be said about a place so horrible? If his theory was correct, these mountains were where Herratia's remains would be found. All signs pointed to this being the spot, from the hostile attack of the Delopar to the deadness of the air around them. She was here; he was sure of it. What evil had been unleashed when she was slain? How did her powers continue even after death? Septus had always thought his father was the most powerful wizard in the land, but this place brought him doubt. *Her influence was so strong it continues to exist after her death.*

Darkness continued to spread the further up the trail they sauntered. The ground was ash covered; no tracks were left, not even where they had previously walked. *The mountains that were once brimming with life had now become dead as the night.* No truer words could be uttered. Septus could recall the shiver that crept over him when he first read the phrase. After lighting a torch, Septus took a deep breath. Nervousness had made wimps of them all—even the Akordans looked pale and scared, not a normal emotion, nor one they would acknowledge.

"Don't be scared. If this is indeed the resting place of your mother, then this place poses no danger to you," Septus said, trying his best to offer comfort.

"How can you be sure?" Vixar shakily probed.

"Just trust me," he replied. He turned and looked at the path ahead. "Keep moving."

Chapter 13

A fantastic feast covered an equally exotic table. There were desserts a plenty and greens overflowing from their decorative serving bowls. A large boar cooked to perfection sat in the middle of the table, steam rising into the air and with it a tantalizing smell. The dining hall was lined with banners of gold and gray; each banner demonstrated a picture of Lord Fae's rise to power. Nikalas sat among dozens of winged beings straight from the pages of his favorite fantasy stories. Next to Nikalas sat Vicham, and directly across from Vicham was Pip. His place was generally reserved at his mother's side, but today he opted to avoid the location for a more direct view of Vicham.

Dinner was awkward; Pip spent most of the time sending amorous glances toward Vicham, while spending an equal amount of time bashing his mother and demonstrating his childish behavior. He resented her for her position. Her recognition came from being a murderer. More than that, she organized a festival every year to celebrate her accomplishments. Pip just missed the normal life they had once had.

As the feast wrapped up and the desserts had all but been consumed, Nikalas was dismissed and shown to his quarters. Fresh air flowed through his carelessly maintained hair as he followed a majestic woman wearing a nearly transparent nightgown. Her soft tone offered him a comfort as she did her best to offer a tour. Eiriaf Palace was designed to create the feeling of being outdoors. Before arriving in Furlasia, Arnouts lived in a magical land known as Tandorne. *The Great Plague* had driven them from their home, and as they fled their ships crashed upon the shores of Furlasia. Quickly they became the center of attention; all in Furlasia were enamored by these mysterious beings. Their gift of flight and their various powers had helped them maintain the status of being divine. As his guide described Tandorne it was clear she missed their homeland. It had apparently been an entire kingdom within an enchanted forest, built just for them by a goddess named *Pomari*.

"I'd give anything to go back," she added as she stopped in front of a door lined with silver and hazy crystal. She pushed it open and bowed slightly as Nikalas stepped inside.

The room overlooked the glistening waters of Lake Cristol, the prism effect that was present in the light of the sun continued the effect as well under the grace of the moonlight. The slightly blue beams reflected against the waters, making the whole lake look like a sapphire. Plopping himself down onto his bed, he could feel himself begin to sink. The linens felt soft to the touch and had the aura of fresh flowers. As he looked out to the night sky, he found himself wondering, *Where are the bad parts of Furlasia?* Everything he'd seen so far had been remarkable. Surely there must be some undesirable places. His attention turned to his pack which had been carefully set onto the floor in front of the bed. Walking on the tip of his toes so as not to be heard, he picked up the pack and began searching its contents. The egg sat nestled, still sealed, still safe. In the front pouch was the diary. Its author remained a mystery.

"Back home, I mocked television shows about the inner feelings of young ladies; here I am captivated by the secret words of some hopeless maid. Life does have a sense of humor," he whispered to himself.

Vicham stood fixated on the flowing of the waterfall. His gaze was fixed on the face in the water. He had seen it many times, but it never got easier.

"What are you doing?" Pip asked as he entered the room.

"It's hard to take your eyes off it," Vicham responded.

"That's the idea. She wants to make some kind of sick point," Pip replied, stopping next to Vicham and looking down into the water, the ripples continued to obscure the face. Pip touched his finger to the water, and the ripples moved to the side, allowing the face to be clearly visible.

"It's sick, isn't it?" Pip asked.

"Perhaps, but it's effective. It reminds everyone what she is capable of," Vicham replied. He turned and looked toward Pip.

"And what are you capable of, Vicham Vilhamie?" Pip smiled. Vicham took a step closer and looked Pip in the eyes.

"I know how to handle little boys who think they know best," Vicham leaned in for a kiss, but Pip pulled away.

"Not here. My mother doesn't know," Pip whispered.

"I've traveled all this way to see you," Vicham argued grabbing Pip's hand.

"You mean you're not here because you believe Nikalas is the one from the prophecy?" Pip sarcastically asked.

"Maybe he is, maybe he isn't. Anyone could've escorted him here. I came here for *you*," Vicham replied, cracking a smile.

"That's sweet. All right then, Mr. Vilhamie. Follow me," Pip ordered. He carefully released his grip on Vicham's hand and began to stroll across the foyer toward an open door leading to a balcony. The balcony was positioned against the left side of the castle and faced directly toward the moonlight. As they stepped onto the balcony, Pip slowly closed the door. With the clicking of the latch, he put his arms around Vicham and gripped him tightly.

"What are we doing?" Vicham asked. Pip remained silent with a grin pushing the question aside; instead he began subtly fluttering his wings until at last the two of them began to rise slowly into the air. Vicham gulped and tightened his grip. Each passing moment the balcony became more and more distant until it was barely visible.

The calm breeze felt wonderful, warm, yet slightly cool Vicham found himself envious of this ability. Being able to take flight whenever one wishes, there could be no freer feeling. On the shoreline outside of Cristol sat a gazebo, well-lit and abandoned. Pip slowly set them down onto the ground, as he did Vicham let out a sigh of relief. Flying was enjoyable enough, but not being the one in control made flight a nerve wracking affair.

"Were you worried?" Pip asked. His arms were still wrapped around Vicham.

"Of course not. I knew you wouldn't drop me," Vicham replied coyly. Pip moseyed toward the gazebo and placed himself onto the bench positioned within.

"This place is beautiful," Vicham commented as he drew a deep breath.

"It's my favorite place in the kingdom. A place to get away from the judgmental gaze of that cruel woman," Pip replied.

"She isn't that bad, is she?" Vicham asked, his fingers slowly finding their way to Pip's.

"I'm a colossal failure. A disappointment, an embarrassment to the kingdom. That's what she's always telling me," Pip replied. "She's harsh and brutal, yet she's my mother, so I love her."

"Have you told her that recently?" Vicham asked.

"Heavens no," Pip laughed. "We should just leave, run away. Find a place more peaceful than this. A place where we can be together."

"That sounds great. But we both know that isn't realistic. Not yet anyway," Vicham leaned toward Pip and gave him a soft kiss on the lips.

"I've missed those lips," Pip whispered.

"I as well," Vicham responded. He leaned in for another soft kiss. "I could sit here, under the moonlight with you for the rest of our lives. Leave it all behind. Maybe Nikalas will be the key to making that finally happen."

"Do you believe the necromancer is really going to return?" Pip asked.

"Hervott does. I've always trusted his instincts," Vicham replied. He slowly stood up and walked toward the water.

"Well, hopefully, Kunklestick is up for the chore," Pip approached behind Vicham and put his arms around him. "If he can crawl out of his bottle that is."

Nikalas lay on his back, mouth wide open, drool oozing from within. Bright sunlight filled the room trying to wake him. A knock on his door finally ended his slumber, doing the job the sun could not.

"My lord?" the soft voice said from through the door.

"What is it?" Nikalas called out, wiping the drool away.

"There is food prepared in the dining hall." Nikalas shot up, bumping the diary to the ground.

"All right, I'll be right there," Nikalas replied.

The breeze in the foyer was beguiling; each pass against his skin was rejuvenating. He couldn't remember where the dining hall was, the scent acted as his guide. As he reached the entrance, he pushed aside the linen entry way revealing the festivities. A massive feast of fruits, meats, and fresh bread, all of it looked untouched as if the whole thing was put together just for him.

At the head of the table, a plate sat assembled especially for him by one of the waiters. Looking around, he couldn't help but wonder if this was a normal ordeal or just a continuation of the *Belish* Festival from the prior day. The first bite of meat was succulent and juicy, a flavorful herb present in each taste.

From outside the rear door that led to the kitchen, he heard the roar of a smoker's cough and the banging of pots and pans. Without warning, the door flung open, revealing an old man, tall and slender and wearing a robe that was wide open revealing his drawers. His hair was sloppy and was all pointing upwards in a messy point. The elderly fellow looked toward Nikalas and let out a sigh as he slowly approached the table. Nikalas continued to watch with curiosity as the elderly man took a seat and poured a tall glass of red wine. Reaching into the large pocket of his robe he pulled out an old, warped wooden plate and began to slowly pile on fruit and bread. He glanced toward the plate of sliced meat; it was positioned rather far from him.

"Excuse me," the old man said, wiping some drool from his chin. "Would it trouble you?" He nodded toward the sliced meat; Nikalas quietly stood up and reached for the plate, carefully setting it down in front of the elderly man. The old geezer looked down in confusion as Nikalas returned to his seat.

"Do you mind?" He asked as he held up his plate. Nikalas took a deep breath and forked a couple of slices onto the plate.

"Thank you," he replied, setting it down and stuffing an entire slice into his mouth. "Delicious." Nikalas continued to watch, enamored, unable to turn his gaze from the filthy looking doyen. With each bite, he littered the table with crumbs and bits of meat. Each sip of wine squandered on his chin and drawers. His table etiquette was ghastly, like that of a poorly taught child. He belched without remorse, drooled without consequence and continued to disgust with each second he sat at the table. *Thank God, no one else is here to witness this old fool,* Nikalas thought to himself. When his cup had emptied, he held it out as though expecting a servant to come to his beck and call.

"Could I trouble you?" He asked. Nikalas looked around confused. *Is he kidding me?* It became clear he wasn't. His arm remained extended; the cup still waiting patiently. Groaning with annoyance, he poured some wine into the empty cup. The old man quickly chugged the cup and held it out again. Once again Nikalas filled the cup, this time to its brim. Again the old man downed the whole cup, spilling half down his face.

"That was most delicious," the old man said, he let out a loud burp and wiped his face clean using the white linens covering the table.

"Who are you?" Nikalas finally blurted out.

"They call me Kunklestick," he replied.

Chapter 14

Silence surrounded Hervott as he sat in his quarters looking over an old photo album. A smile spread across his face as he looked at pictures of his first love, Herratia. Their bond had seemed so deep—he had always imagined they would grow old together. Sadly, that hadn't worked out. He regretted his decision to have her arrested—it was harsh. Unfortunately, grief and anger outweighed his logic. *I should've tried harder to talk to her. Why did I allow grief to ruin our marriage?*

Outside his window, life was stirring. *I should pay more attention to the people. The council has been riding my back.* Crime had been rising; poverty was at an all-time high, and yet none of it hindered his thoughts. His every waking moment was filled with thoughts of a greater terror. Which form would the necromancer take? Who would it be?

His focus was interrupted as Zewop appeared at the window, urgently knocking. Hervott quickly tossed the photo album onto his bed and flung open the window. Zewop jumped to the floor, panting and waving his arms erratically about.

"What is it, my friend? What happened?" Hervott asked. Zewop started howling and grunting, waving his hands frantically while occasionally shrieking.

"An attack in Frand? Who was it?" Zewop continued his primitive communication, Hervott's eyes widened as he continued to listen.

"The Akordans? In Frand? How strange! I wonder what led them there?" Hervott pondered. As he began to zone out trying to fathom the reasoning, Zewop started a deep growling howl; Hervott paused with a look of dread coming over him.

"Septus?" He asked. A weakness came over him. His worst fears had been realized. Sluggishly, he wandered toward his bed, sitting and resting his head in his hands. Memories of past conversations flowed copiously through his mind. Vicham's warning seemed more real than ever. "He was right. I have brought about the very darkness I feared."

Commotion rang through the streets as Inca leaped over Terria's bordering wall. The two guards placed in charge drew their weapons and took aim before realizing her familiarity. She seemed distressed, her breathing heavy and from her left side, a small amount of blood was oozing. Inca eyed the guards with ferocity, prepared to fight yet hoping not to. As they lowered their weapons her eyes rolled into her head, and she passed out, hitting the hard street with a thud. Quickly the guards rushed over to her unconscious body and tried to wake her. As they noticed the wound, they quickly waved over a citizen passing by.

"Get some help! This woman needs the infirmary." One of the guards ordered.

Emlin raced down the halls of Nasleigh Keep, each step sending echoes against the walls. Rushing past various servants carrying linens and guards carrying Beacons she ignored all, dodging anything that hindered her path. Inca had been spotted and worse she was injured. From the opposite side of the catwalk, Hervott was scrambling as well. They both descended the stairs, stopping in front of the throne and looking at each other.

"Where are you going?" Emlin asked as she tried to catch her breath.

"To the infirmary," Hervott replied.

"Me too," Emlin said. Together they descended the last flight of steps into the foyer and ran toward the entrance. As they neared the door, the stationed guards promptly pulled it open. The drawbridge had already been lowered—it was typical to remain dropped during the waking hours. Their footsteps resounded against the wooden bridge; they continued to dash toward the infirmary as if competing in a foot race.

Emlin pushed the door of the infirmary open, revealing a room full of beds, most of them empty and a nurse named Alma. As they both stepped inside, Alma quickly jumped to her feet to greet them.

"Your Highness! This is most unexpected. What can I do for you?" Alma asked, bowing before Hervott.

"I need to see the injured Delopar that was brought in here," Hervott commanded.

"Uh, she's in rough shape and is not conscious. I'm afraid any conversation will not be possible at this point," Alma replied. Emlin stepped forward, nudging her father to the side.

"She is my best friend. I will wait by her side," Emlin said, leaving little room for debate. Alma stepped aside and Emlin decidedly brushed past her, putting the elderly nurse's concerns aside. There were only two residents filling beds, so Inca was easy to spot. Just as Alma had asserted, Inca lay wrapped snugly in a blanket and unconscious, her breathing shallow. Emlin gently grabbed a nearby chair and pulled it next to her friend's bed.

"What do you hope to accomplish?" Hervott questioned as he stepped behind her.

"I'm going to find out what happened," Emlin responded.

"Perhaps it's best you don't pester her with questions as soon as she wakes up. She's going to need rest," Hervott cautioned.

"She's going to need *vengeance*," Emlin replied. "And I intend to see that she gets it." Hervott looked toward Alma, hoping for a hand in convincing his stubborn daughter to vacate the infirmary. Septus was alive and well and joined with the Akordans, the talisman Zewop had described was unmistakable. Septus was indeed attempting to follow in his father's footsteps. He would need to be dealt with quickly and quietly. He did not look forward to explaining to Septus that it was he who had banished him in the first place, few conversations seemed more unpleasant.

"Your father is right your highness. Your friend is in no position to be answering your questions. Best you come back tomorrow, give her time to rest today," Alma interjected. Emlin let out a huff and stood up, shooting her father a displeased look before storming out of the infirmary.

"Do not let her come back in here," Hervott whispered. "I can't have her getting any crazy ideas." Hervott looked down toward Inca, who was still engulfed in a deep slumber despite the commotion.

"How do I wake her?" Hervott asked. Alma gazed at him with dismay, the King's words perplexing her simple mind.

"Your Highness? You just said you agreed she shouldn't be pestered," Alma replied.

"That was to get Emlin to leave. Wake her up. I need to speak to her," Hervott ordered. Alma sighed and walked over to a dresser and pulled open the upper drawer. Reaching inside, she pulled out a syringe and walked over to Inca. She glanced at Hervott one last time in hopes he would change his mind. His deadpanned look dismissed any notion of that. Slowly she inserted the needle into Inca's arm and pushed the contents inside. Almost instantly Inca's eyes shot open, her breathing rapid and loud.

"Remain calm child," Alma comforted. "The King would like to have a word with you," she gently nodded to Hervott who wore an all too pleased look upon his face.

"Leave us," Hervott commanded. She respectfully bowed and made her way toward the exit. A simple nurse was in no position to debate with a King. Once the door had closed, Hervott sat in the chair and looked at Inca.

"Tell me everything," he directed.

Emlin wandered the streets purposefully. Broli, surely Broli would be interested to hear about Inca's arrival. What had happened? And why was her father acting so mysteriously? Wandering around aimlessly seemed as good a plan as any, Broli was a fan of ale so there was always the likelihood he was near one of the taverns.

After checking a few of the local spots he was known for frequenting, she began to feel it was time to give up. Perhaps she could sneak into the infirmary and see Inca. Surely Alma had to step away at some point. Something was being hidden from her, she was sure of it.

As she neared the infirmary, she spotted Alma. The old nurse *had* stepped away, and she was walking down the streets in haste with a handbag and a pep in her step. *Now's my chance.* Quickly Emlin darted toward the infirmary and flung open the door. Inca shot up in surprise, causing her to grunt in pain.

"Really, Emlin, is that how you enter a room full of sick and injured people?" Inca quipped.

"Sorry. I had to sneak in. That old lady didn't want me talking to you," Emlin replied strolling to Inca's bedside. Without asking for permission, Emlin pulled back the blanket to reveal the bandage covering Inca's wound; it was still attached but blood-soaked and in need of changing.

"Nor did your father," Inca added. She tried to pull herself up, but the pain was too intense.

"What do you mean?" Emlin asked.

"He made me promise not to tell you we spoke," Inca added. "Unfortunately for him, he doesn't know we don't keep secrets from each other." Emlin let out a sigh of relief. Since they had been little, they had always had a very open and honest relationship. Delopar were naturally very blunt, and Emlin's moral compass always steered her clear of telling lies. To avoid getting around the occasional need to do this, she simply avoided situations that could lead to a lie. So far her moral compass remained untainted, which was impressive for the daughter of a King.

"What did he want?" Emlin questioned.

"He didn't want me to tell you who did this," Inca replied. "Emlin the identity of my attacker and the one who attacked Frand will likely upset you." Emlin shook her head, confused.

"It was Septus. He's the one who did this," Inca confessed. Emlin paused in disbelief, her heart beginning to race. Septus had been missing for just over a year. In that time, she hadn't heard a peep from him. No sightings, no traces of him, as if he had vanished from existence. *Now this?*

"What do you mean it was Septus?" Emlin queried. Inca attempted once again to sit upright, pain be damned, this conversation was too important to have while lying down.

"Emlin, I know this isn't easy to hear, but Septus did this. He has allied himself with the Akordans, and together they attacked the village," She fell silent as the horrible moment ran through her mind. That dark look in his eyes, that power, the instant demise of those she held close to her heart. Tears formed in her eyes as she looked at her distressed friend, feeling remorseful at having to bear such bad news.

"That's not all Emlin," Inca said quietly, the lump in her throat growing so big the words could barely find room to squeeze through. "He did something, something terrible."

"What did he do?" She asked, concern masking her face, the look in Inca's eyes spelled doom.

"Well, go on, spit it out!" Emlin demanded.

"He killed them; he slaughtered everyone in the village like they were nothing but wild animals. He used a magic like nothing I've ever heard of. Emlin, I think Septus is the one from the prophecy. He is the necromancer." The words hit hard, each syllable bringing Emlin offense — she would have no part of these delirious accusations. Inca was tired, her wound was taking its toll. Clearly, she was mistaken. She had to be, right?

"You're wrong," Emlin shoved the chair back and stood up. "It's impossible."

He knew just what to do, the next course of action was clear. Sure, he could wait on Kunklestick to rendezvous with Nikalas and train him in the art of magic, but by then it would surely be too late. No, this required immediate attention. Septus needed to be stopped, sooner rather than later. And what of his transgressions? He couldn't allow Emlin to discover the truth about Septus' disappearance. The sooner he was taken care of, the better the odds Emlin would never find out. Matters such as these required a delicate but firm touch, and there was one man in Terria who could provide just that: *Thadeus Thundt.*

The day was growing long, and the sun was getting tired. It was at its tail end, having already reached the middle of the sky; it had begun its slow descent into darkness. Still, though, the heat was intense, that would not give way for at least a few hours. It seemed days since the last rainfall, and Terria's plants grew thirsty. Not just the plants but everyone was waiting for the rain—the heat and humidity were drastically reduced after a storm. Each passing moment walking the streets in his overblown royal garbs was a chore. If only the Vanguard barracks were closer.

Thadeus was the General of the Vanguard Army. Appointed just over three years ago, he had already made remarkable progress with his training of the troops. He had an attention to detail that the previous General had lacked. The chatter of the troops and the sound of target practice filled the air as he neared the barracks. Each step closer bringing with it the usual cacophony. Thadeus' office was clearly marked and easily discernable. Approaching the perfectly stained wooden door, he gave a slight knock.

"Who is it?" A voice barked from the other side.

"It's me, Dwennon," Hervott replied. Through the door, Hervott could hear the commotion of Thadeus promptly shuffling about, no doubt attempting to make his normally disastrous office presentable.

"Come on in," Thadeus called out. Wasting no time, he carefully pushed the door open. There sat General Thadeus Thundt, hands folded above a stack of paperwork. Underneath the stack was a map of Furlasia with a pathway drawn in red pencil.

"This isn't a bad time is it?" Hervott asked, closing the door behind him. On the backside of the door was an expertly drawn family portrait.

"Of course not. I was merely going over some plans for the next batch of recruits. What can I do for you?" Thadeus asked, motioning toward a chair for his guest.

"This is a sensitive matter. One that must absolutely stays between the two of us," Hervott cautioned.

"Of course," Thadeus replied.

"I need your help. I need *Stiletto*," Hervott cautiously whispered.

"I don't do that anymore, Dwennon. I came to Terria to get away from that lifestyle," Thadeus retorted. Before his days as the General of the Vanguard, Thadeus had once gone by the name Stiletto, and his work had been *legendary*. He had been an assassin of the highest class, but the toll of the job had grown tiresome, and he had migrated to Terria with the hope of tossing away his old identity. Hervott abruptly stood up tossing the chair back a bit.

"This is serious, Thadeus. The prophecy was real. The necromancer is returning." He carefully pulled out a bag of gold coins and tossed them onto the general's desk. Coin, it was the one language all men like Thadeus understood. As the coin purse came to a rest, the General eyed it with curiosity. His addiction to wealth was a quality long gone — at least he had hoped it was. It just so happened however that he was feeling the sting of poverty, at least by his standards. His normal lavish lifestyle had been replaced with a humble one. Perhaps now was the time to make an exception.

"I've heard the stories about what happened. Sounds like Agavordis was quite the bad ass in his day," Thadeus replied, he curiously undid the small rope that kept the coin bag closed and peered inside. There was a lot, enough to make sure he didn't struggle with money ever again.

"He was the most dangerous man alive. Now his son seeks to take his place. Septus, the boy who was spared, must now be eliminated, before he gains full use of his father's power," Hervott explained. "If we don't stop him now, we may not be able to later."

Thadeus stood up and began walking around his office. In the far corner, there was a large chest made of auburn wood and lined with gold trim. He inserted a key and gave it a quick turn before lifting the lid. Inside was a pair of daggers made from *Herilium,* a rare metal not found anywhere in Furlasia.

"Are you sure about this Dwennon? He's only a boy. If he dies, it's on you. Can you live with that?" Thadeus asked, stepping towards Hervott.

"I can. If you were here, if you'd seen the things I'd seen. You would understand," he explained. Thadeus nodded in acceptance and offered his hand.

"I'll do it, but not because of the coin. I uprooted my family and brought them all the way to Furlasia to keep them safe, to escape the insanities from whence we came. If this boy truly is the danger you claim him to be then I've failed in that task," Thadeus explained, the handshake was firm. It served as a binding contract; it was the only form of agreement he had ever required.

"How do I find him?"

"He was last seen near Frand, just outside the Hark Mountains," Hervott answered. *The Hark Mountains? Now there was a place which preceded its own legend.* Nothing good could come from anyone wandering near those parts. Before migrating to Furlasia, Thadeus willingly wandered to many places most considered to be undesirable. But that was many years ago. Now he tended to avoid places like the Hark Mountains.

Thadeus walked back over to his desk and pushed aside the stack of papers clearing room for the map of Furlasia. Following the paths with his index finger, he finally located the mountains.

"That'll take at least a week to get to. I'll need to bring a few of the Vanguard with me to help with the Akordans he's traveling with," Thadeus pondered aloud to himself. "This will put me behind schedule with the new recruits," he added. Hervott stood silently observing as the General came up with a plan.

"I'll leave in a few hours," Thadeus said, reaching a decision.

"Bring me the talisman when you've finished the job. It'll need to be hidden again," Hervott instructed.

"Yeah, yeah. One dead kid and one piece of jewelry coming right up," he chuckled. The King, however, appeared slightly less amused. This wasn't easy for him. It was not to be taken lightly. This wasn't for fun; it was for the safety of those who called Furlasia home.

Chapter 15

With each passing moment the climb became more and more treacherous. Icy winds stung the skin and brought with it the dust that had settled on the ground. It had to be close, if the stories were correct, the cave that Herratia had holed up in was somewhere on this mountain pass. Septus looked toward the sky; the clandestine sun made it impossible to determine what the hour was. Certainly they had to be on the right track.

The tales of the witch had effectively turned these mountains into a forsaken wasteland. No one dared come near this place, despite tales of her death. If anything, the condition of the mountains after her death further fueled the horror, keeping the mountains jilted. There were traces of the first Akordans all along the path. Claw marks carved into the rocky walls acted as a guide; the cave was near.

"We've been wandering up this mountain for hours now. Just admit it, you've duped us. You haven't a clue where you're going," Drango yelled.

"Look at the marks you fool, this is the right path," Roman lectured motioning towards the claw marks lining the mountain pass. Drango looked at the marks with interest. The first Akordans had to be quite stout to make such engravings with just their claws.

Septus brushed off the banter and pressed on. Ahead of them was a tree, one that had a lean to its point and no leaves. It grew in the shape of a hook, and even for Furlasia it was an oddity. As he looked it over he recalled such a tree being described within the text, it was said to be very close to the entrance of the cave.

"I wonder," Septus whispered to himself. Slowly he wandered towards the mountain wall and began to run his hand across its coarse surface. *This has to be it,* he thought. His attention turned toward the hook-shaped tree, and he could see there were tiny stubs all along it.

"I have to climb up," Septus said aloud. He made his way toward the tree and looked up. Just above the top of the tree were grooves carved into the mountain. Grooves just big enough to be held onto. *What an odd coincidence. Who did this?* Aiming his gaze up the mountain wall, he followed the grooves to a dark spot in the mountain—a spot reminiscent of a cave.

"It's there," he said, pointing to the opening above.

"By Herratia, he's right. He's actually done it," Roman praised with as much of a smile as Akordans could muster.

"That's great. How do we get up there?" Drango asked skeptically. Their claws made it obviously an impossible feat; he would have to continue this part alone.

"This part is up to me," Septus replied.

"And if you find her, how do you get her down?" Vixar asked.

"We will need rope, enough of it for me to lower her safely," Septus replied. Roman excitedly opened his pack and pulled out a long spool of braided tree bark.

"You mean something like this?" He asked as he happily handed it to Septus.

"Perhaps you creatures aren't as stupid as the Terrians say after all," Septus remarked, grabbing the robe and flinging it over his shoulder. Drango growled at the remark, every instinct telling him to slap some sense into the cocky kid. But alas, they needed him to do the climb.

"We don't have time to waste," Septus nervously said. Carefully, he began to climb the small branches up the hooked tree. This was the easy part; it was as if it were designed to be climbed. Once he reached the top, it took cunning balance to maintain his footing. The first groove into the mountain was large; he would have to jump towards it. He glanced to the ground, he wasn't too far off from it, if he failed with this jump the fall wouldn't be fatal. Still, though, he didn't feel like wasting time climbing the tree again.

A deep breath and carefully planned maneuver later, and he had begun his climb up the mountain. *Why does everyone always hide inside mountains?* Perhaps there was something to these awkward locations. He silently pondered getting his own cave lair as he carefully ascended the lonely cliff.

The cave was small; there wasn't much to it. There were clear signs of experiments, vials and beakers were scattered throughout. A fire-pit where she had kept warm, skeletons of animals that had been consumed. Claw marks on the walls, just as they had been along the mountain path. He lit a torch using a couple of rocks and proceeded into the depths of the cave. His journey was short; his goal lay in front of him. Laid carefully on a podium of stone was a cocoon the size of a person.

Placed in the center of her protective shell was a blade. The blade that killed the witch of the hills. He found himself surprised it had been left behind. Surely it would have some value. The cocoon was rock hard to the touch. If she were inside, she would be quite well preserved. *What could've done this?* He wondered. A skeleton in the corner of the room caught his attention; the body was small like that of a child. The stories appeared to be true—Herratia had stolen the remains of her daughter. This place had an eerie and unpleasant feel to it. He wasted no time grabbing the cocoon and freeing it from the podium.

The legends said she was indeed a very powerful witch, so powerful that even the wizards had been dumbfounded by the skills she had. Her very demise froze the Hark Mountains in time, leaving no trace of life. Many expeditions had been attempted to study the remains, but none could gain access to the mountain pass. It was too well guarded by the Delopar, or, at least, it used to be.

Once the rope had been secured tightly around the remains he began to slowly lower the body down the side of the mountain. After Herratia had reached the bottom it was Septus' turn. The climb down went fairly well—after all, this wasn't his first time scaling into a hidden cave. As he descended the mountain wall, he couldn't help but think of the last time he had done this and the strange woman he had met. *Vigil.* She had mentioned coming to him one day seeking a favor. When would she come? Even now she enamored him. The feeling she had given him. *Vigil, where are you? Why do you make me wait?*

Drango, Roman, and Vixar all stood around the remains enamored and skeptical.

"I want to see her," Vixar said.

"She must be kept in her preserved state. We don't know how long it will take Septus to bring her back. She's safest like this," Roman countered. Septus approached the group and looked down at the remains.

"Are you sure it's her?" Drango asked.

"It's her, I feel an energy emanating from her," he said. He slowly reached down and placed his hand on the cocoon. Flashes of a wolf being torn to shreds jarred him and sent him falling back.

"What happened?" Vixar probed.

"It was nothing," he replied.

Chapter 16

Kunklestick? Nikalas abruptly stood up in outrage. This man *had* to be lying. There was no way he traveled all this way to be trained by this oaf.

"You're Kunklestick?" Nikalas questioned.

"Whoa, whoa, whoa, kid. You're throwing a lot of loud dialogue my way. Bring it down a notch or two. My head is killing me," the old man replied as he took a tall sip of his wine.

"You're Kunklestick? The legendary wizard who defeated the necromancer? The one who fought the leader of the giants?" Nikalas questioned. *This can't be Kunklestick. It simply can't be.* The elderly man continued to nibble on his food, shaking head in response.

"You can't be. You're nothing more than a common drunk," Nikalas accused.

"Hey, don't be rude. I have no problem with turning you into a chair," Kunklestick threatened. With a quick motion, he waved a wand above his plate and a juicy, sizzling steak appeared. Blood oozed from the succulent steak as he began to cut into it. Medium rare, the only way true gentlemen would take it.

"That's phenomenal. Best steak I've ever made," he moaned as he took a bite.

"You are him aren't you?" Nikalas asked awestruck. The wizard nodded as he continued to gorge on the hearty steak set before him.

"It's a bit bloody in the middle. But that's the only way to truly enjoy it," he explained, cutting off another slice. His chewing was loud and abhorrent, his lack of table manners seemed appropriate, however, given his disheveled appearance.

"Are you just going to stand there and watch me eat this delicious steak or are you going to sit down and join me?" Kunklestick asked. Nikalas remained still, unsure what to do. On one hand, the steak looked amazing, but on the other hand this man was unpleasant and drunken. Each moment spent in his presence seemed an exercise in futility. How could this be the legendary Kunklestick? His thoughts came to an abrupt end as Kunklestick slowly stood up and grabbed Nikalas' empty plate.

"Fine then," he yelled as he chucked the plate across the room. The elegant glassware made a disastrous mess as it crashed against the wall and shattered, raining pieces of glass all over. Nikalas' heart raced at the scene he'd just witnessed. The fool was even crazier than he'd imagined. A maid promptly darted into the room and looked at the mess. As she saw the shattered glass she gave him a displeased stare.

"If you do not enjoy the meal that is one thing, but disrespecting the High Lord's favorite glassware is entirely inappropriate. I have half a mind to drag you before Lord Fae and have you explain yourself," the old maid yelled.

"I didn't throw that," Nikalas defended. "It was that old fool." He replied as he pointed toward the table. *Where was he?* There was no sign of Kunklestick; not even a trace of the plate where he had eaten.

"He was just there. I swear it, it was Kunklestick." The maid followed Nikalas' gesture toward the empty table and shook her head.

"Young man, if you were not an honored guest of the High Lord, I can assure you there would be a punishment for this callous behavior. If Master Kunklestick were in Cristol, I would be one of the first to know," she replied. "Now, leave this room at once!"

He continued to stare toward the table. *Where had he gone?* Behind him, the displeased throat clearing of the maid served as a reminder of her demands. Silently, he exited the room, being mindful not to look in her direction. As he entered the main foyer, the sight of Vicham and Pip walking into the room from one of the balconies grabbed his focus. Hastily he approached Vicham, his nerves still shot from being reamed by the kitchen maid.

"Where have you been?" Nikalas demanded. Vicham looked towards Pip, who offered naught but a shrug.

"Uh, good morning to you, too, Nikalas. What seems to be the problem?" Vicham asked.

"The *great* wizard, you brought me here to meet," Nikalas used a quotation mark gesture with the word great not realizing the gesture would have no significance to Vicham. "Kunklestick. He's no more than a drunken fool!" Nikalas exclaimed. Pip started to laugh, further infuriating young Nikalas.

"Nikalas that's one of the oldest stories in Furlasia," Pip smirked. "Kunklestick has been a reclusive drunk for years now. He only usually surfaces when he needs to restock his ale. Didn't anyone tell you what happened?"

Nikalas paused and shook his head.

"He lost everyone, every wizard he knew, including his brother all died during the war. Since then, he hasn't been the same. It broke him, the grief. He blamed himself," Pip explained.

"Why?" Nikalas asked finally beginning to calm down.

"The story is that he had an opportunity to destroy Agavordis, well before he amassed his army, but he refused to do it. He cared too much for him," Pip replied. "But that's just the story. No one knows the truth except him."

"Nikalas, despite what you see on the surface there is always more to a person. Don't ever be too quick to judge someone," Vicham cautioned. "You experienced this first hand when you arrived in Terria. The King unfairly judged you because of how you look on the outside. You are proof that there is always more to someone than what you see on the surface."

Nikalas stood silently pondering Vicham's words. They were wise indeed, but he was still angry.

"You've been handed an incredible opportunity here. To be trained by Kunklestick? There is no greater honor I can think of. Perhaps the broken part of you can empathize with Kunklestick. Maybe together, the two of you can help fix the torment that resides inside you. Providence, Nikalas. It is far-fetched, but it may just be real. Give this a chance. I have a feeling you won't regret it," Vicham smiled and looked towards Pip.

"Leaps of faith are most rewarding when the leap is big," he added. Pip smirked and looked towards Nikalas, nodding in agreement.

The following day the journey had begun. Kunklestick finally made his presence known at the previous evening's dinner and had privately apologized to Nikalas for his unusual behavior earlier that day. Vicham's words had stuck with him. *Don't be too quick to judge someone.* Such an easy thing to do, and yet it could be so costly. Nikalas had decided to take the leap of faith after all. If he didn't like what the old man had to offer, he could always run away.

On the back of his horse, he felt more comfortable than he could've imagined. A bond seemed to be formed between him and Wildfire. An understanding about who the other truly was. Strapped to his back was his pack which contained a few extra clothes that had been given to him by Pip and, of course, the strange egg. Kunklestick carried nothing with him other than a cloth bag filled with bottles of wine from one of the taverns in Cristol and his famous staff. *Hopefully, he doesn't get drunk again,* Nikalas thought as they continued their journey.

Two days later, they began to near the city of *Morlay*. Steam rose from behind the walls, filling the air with the smell of sulfur and oil. It certainly didn't have the beauty appeal that Cristol did. No, this certainly seemed like an industrial city. Nikalas continued to watch the great wall surrounding the city with eagerness only to be surprised when they didn't stop. Instead, they continued west toward *The Hills of Edmere.*

It wasn't long before he saw the shape of a building in the distance. Kunklestick let out a sigh of relief as they neared their destination. Nikalas stared at the building with shock and awe. It was a quaint building made of wooden logs that looked extremely weathered.

"This is the Hall of Wizards?" Nikalas asked as they approached.

"Yes, it is," Kunklestick smiled. "It's something, isn't it?" Nikalas continued to stare in confusion. Throughout, the journey Kunklestick had told stories about how grand this place was. How the greatest wizards ever to be born all lived within this marvelous fortress. Staring at the log cabin in front of him, Nikalas couldn't help but feel let down.

Kunklestick secured both of their horses to a post in the stable and led his new apprentice toward the entrance. There was a rusty lock that had been crookedly installed into the dirty wooden door. He began to fiddle clumsily inside his pockets, looking for the key. It was a large key, hard to lose and yet he frequently did.

"Where is that thing?" He mumbled to himself. "Aha!" He pulled from his pocket an old copper key and placed it into the lock, it took a bit of jiggling, but eventually the key inserted and the door clicked open.

"Welcome Nikalas, to The Hall of Wizards," Kunklestick smiled. With a grand gesture, he pushed the door open as though revealing some sort of marvelous prize.

Nikalas' jaw dropped in shock as he stepped inside. The place was far more elegant and massive than the outside appearance made it seem. Seven chairs made of white stone sat atop a small flight of stairs at the front of the main hall. Behind them, a statue of a man stood, dressed in robes and wearing a pointed hat. The walls were made of white bricks, the tables dressed in silver clothes, the floors tiled with sapphire. Chandeliers floated high in the ceiling with no chains to secure them, each chandelier filled with a couple of dozen candles each all perfectly burning a white flame.

Kunklestick let Nikalas take in the sights for a few moments and then led him down a passageway made up of a dozen black doors with a pair of red double doors down at the far end. He stopped in front of the third door on the left and pushed it open.

"So this is you," Kunklestick pointed inside the room. "We'll have dinner in a bit. In the meantime, I suggest you unpack and make yourself at home. We'll be turning in early tonight. It's been a long journey, and I'm tired. Plus, you'll need your rest. Tomorrow your training begins."

Chapter 17

She looked at him and smiled. Her long brown hair was blowing ever so slightly in the wind. Her face was blurred, but he knew who she was. This was hardly the first time he'd dreamed of her since he had arrived in Furlasia. Only one thing seemed different about the dream this time. Her face; it had never been obscured before. *What did it mean?* She led him down a boardwalk, his father walking next to her gripping onto her hand. They took turns looking back and smiling. Their smiles were so pure, so *lively*. This was one of his favorite memories from their time together. Along the boardwalk the ocean splashed, seagulls flew high in the skies, the laughter of children running past them, the thump of feet against the boards. It was music to his ears. After so many years together his parents had gone from tangible beings that he could see and touch, to images in his mind. Each day he awoke thinking their disappearance was the dream; that they were still, in fact, in his life. But the more time went by, the easier the truth had become to accept.

The obnoxious thud against his door shook him from his mental oasis. Once again he awoke in this strange land. Today was to be the day he began his training with Kunklestick, the very wizard he had idolized from his childhood stories. It was hard at times to not dismiss all that had happened lately as fantasy, everything about this seemed like fiction and yet here he awoke, in the *Hall of Wizards*.

"Time for breakfast," Kunklestick croaked through the wooden door. Nikalas slowly sat up, looking around at the sights. Sunlight peered its way past the curtains like a spy trying to remain hidden. His eyes still heavy, he set his one foot at a time onto the cold stone floor. On his vanity sat the strange egg, a candle next to it flickering and waving about. *I don't remember doing that,* he thought to himself. *It had to be Kunklestick.* But how had he done it so silently? Everything about the man seemed bumbling and clumsy. Against the far right wall stood a large wardrobe. Using caution, as if to expect a startling surprise, he pulled the doors open, inside was a barrage of outfits all appearing to be his size. They were odd—certainly not the type of clothing he would ever choose to wear. Most of them were simple and gray, reminiscent of a uniform, there were also a couple of wizard robes and finally some oddly colored pants and shirts. He shrugged at the strange selection and pushed the doors shut.

Kunklestick sat with a cup of steaming tea and a slice of overcooked toast as Nikalas entered the main hall. Light shone proudly through the stained glass windows casting colors galore across the floor and walls. As Nikalas neared the table, Kunklestick set his toast down and glanced him over.

"Do you feel well rested?" Kunklestick asked, taking a sip of his tea.

"Yeah, I think so," Nikalas replied, pulling out a chair and sitting down. Scanning the table, he noticed there was no plate made for him. "Where's my food?"

Kunklestick set his cup down and glared at Nikalas.

"Your food? Which food would that be?" He asked.

"You said it was time for breakfast," Nikalas replied. Kunklestick smiled and finished off the last bite of his toast.

"That's correct. However, I never specified that I had prepared your meal," Kunklestick explained with a grin. "Do I look like your royal servant?" Nikalas sat dumbfounded.

"Well, I just assumed," he stammered.

"Your first mistake of the day. Never assume. Assuming can be a deadly mistake when it comes to magic," Kunklestick lectured. "Here's the deal. I will feed you and provide you shelter, but you must earn your keep. You'll need to pitch in with things around here. I won't just hand you things." Nikalas remained silent, holding in his urge to yell.

"Deal," he replied, his lip subtly quivering with frustration. Kunklestick nodded in satisfaction and pointed toward a door to the left.

"Through that door is the kitchen. Your plate is all fixed up. Do drink all of the tea in your cup. When you're done, change into one of the uniforms in your wardrobe and meet me back here. Let's say, in a half hour?" Kunklestick commanded.

Nikalas stood and wandered toward the door. As promised next to a cast iron wood stove sat a plate of food and next to that a cup of piping hot tea. He quickly grabbed the items and headed back out into the main hall. His mentor had apparently decided not to stick around. *At least I'll get peace and quiet*, he thought.

There was a strange, foul taste to the so-called *Tea* Kunklestick had asked him to finish. For a moment he debated dumping it out. But he couldn't escape the paranoid feeling that the old geyser somehow lurked about, waiting to pounce on his every mistake. Holding his nose, he quickly sipped the unpalatable beverage and scarfed down the toast and eggs.

It wasn't the best food he'd had since arriving in Furlasia, certainly nothing compared to the food at Cristol. He had an overwhelming suspicion that the days of elegant feasts were long past. At least not until he learned some of Kunklestick's clever tricks. His plate had been emptied; his tea drank. As he neared his room, he heard a strange racket from inside. *Kunklestick?*

"Now what's he doing?" He muttered to himself as he pushed the door open. There was no sign of the wizard anywhere. His attention quickly turned to the vanity where the egg had been placed; it was cracked, and pieces had been tossed about.

"Oh shit," he whispered. With his heart beginning to race, he scanned the room. *What kind of creature could've been in that shell?* Whatever it was, he hoped it was friendly. His search began with the wardrobe; there was nothing. Under the blankets on his bed? Nothing there, either. In the vanity drawers? Still nothing. With trembling hands, he knelt down on all fours. Crawling around like a canine he continued his search. Underneath the bed, something seized his attention—a pair of tiny glowing eyes. Taking in this terrifying sight, his heart rate increased dramatically, trying to leave his chest like a prisoner ripe to escape. Slowly, he dragged his knees against the rough tiles, keeping his movements short and slow. The two eyes remained stagnant, doing nothing except blinking occasionally.

Finally, he had gotten too close for comfort. The creature, let out a small squeak and darted backward. The unexpectedness of the high pitch squeal caused him equal panic, his head nearly hitting the bed frame as he pushed himself back. Flying through the air was a small turquoise creature with large pointed ears and tiny wings, its flight unorganized, mostly consisting of bouncing from wall to wall. It took all his bravery not to scream as he watched the creepy little creature panic. The fear was decidedly mutual.

"Ah, I see your egg has hatched. *Finally*," Nikalas let out a high pitched scream as Kunklestick entered the room unexpectedly, the tone freaking out the creature as well. Rather than apologize for causing him panic, Kunklestick merely laughed. Each note of his chuckle deeper than the note before.

"Do you always startle so easily?" He asked, continuing his obscene cackle.

"What the hell is that thing?" Nikalas pointed.

"Why, that's your Grimwort, of course," Kunklestick replied. The small creature flew toward Nikalas and landed on his left shoulder. Panic flowed through him as he attempted to watch the strange beast with his peripherals.

"What is a Grimwort? And why did you have me carrying this freaky thing all around?" Nikalas demanded.

"A Grimwort is a creature that bonds itself to those who have magical potential. The very fact that it has hatched — and taken a liking to you — at least confirms King Hervott's theory about you. If only just a little," Kunklestick replied. Grinning from cheek to cheek, he slowly approached Nikalas, and began to carefully rub the creature's ears, smiling.

"He's very cute. Congratulations," he said.

"Hold out your finger, it's time you introduce yourself to your new companion," Kunklestick advised. Continuing to tremble, Nikalas followed the advice holding out his left index finger. The Grimwort chirped and happily climbed aboard the finger, his tiny feet gripping firmly. The sensation was uncomfortable, but he opted not to show it. As he brought the creature in front of his face, a smile began to form. From this view the creature wasn't scary, he was rather adorable.

"What will you name him?" Kunklestick asked. Nikalas began to think back to his life at home, remembering the cockatiel his mother had gotten him, he was always quite fond of the little bugger. Fawn, that was the name he had given it, perhaps the name would suit this little creature as well. After all, it was just born moments ago, like a baby deer, it was nothing more than a fawn.

"Fawn. His name is Fawn," Nikalas replied, rubbing the creature's ears. Kunklestick cheerfully smiled as he watched the two begin to bond.

"Well, you've taken your first step toward becoming a wizard. Are you ready to take the next step?" He asked. His skepticism had begun to fade as he continued to watch his new pet. Kunklestick's crappy attitude had changed; the old man was smiling and actually talking like a normal, polite person. Maybe he could give this a shot. Besides, he still wanted to be able to conjure a steak out of thin air, so he didn't have to eat any more of those foul eggs. Grinning with satisfaction, Nikalas turned to face his new master.

"I'm ready," he replied.

Chapter 18

Splashes of water continued to rain down, creating puddles in the streets. Emlin did her best to avoid them, to keep her feet dry. At this point, it seemed like a nearly impossible chore, however. Her clothing was already quite wet—despite her attempts to remain on the sidewalks and under the protective awnings offered by some of the shops. Inca's words rang through her head like a migraine, and each time she relived the conversation, she felt herself grow angry. How could she say such an awful thing about Septus? After so many efforts and searches to find him she had turned up empty handed. Her father knew something about his disappearance; she was sure of it.

With Inca held up in the infirmary—not to mention delusional—and Draxton being on hiatus, her only option was Broli. He had always been a loyal and caring friend. A virtue that apparently was in short supply. Dark smoke rose into the air, casting murky blemishes into the already darkened skies. Terria felt lonely tonight; most had taken shelter—many at home, and some in the local taverns. That's where she had planned on finding Broli. As nice of a guy as he was, he was hopelessly addicted to the tavern life. Not just the drinking, but the ambiance—the people, the *music*. He had considered himself to be quite talented at singing, and never shied away from the opportunity to show it off.

Broli's apartment was in the slums of Terria, a destination she normally would never consider venturing to at this late hour, but she was in need of company, so it was worth the risk. The further into the slums she traveled, the stranger the people got. Many were dirty, covered in soot or oil from the factories. All of them giving her suspicious looks. What was she doing in a place like this? She had done her best to duplicate the appearance of a peasant, but she had forgotten one key thing. A filthy face mixed with the air of desperation.

The scent of rotten food was a good sign; it meant she was near the city trash dump. Broli's favorite tavern *The Hardy Place* was located only a couple blocks from this giant pile of stink. She had been to the tavern only once, the stink and its location didn't exactly make it a hot destination. Clogged street drains had caused the streets to flood around the dump and the tavern. Emlin looked ahead at the rancid water and contemplated turning back; it was heinous and smelly. Bits of trash and leftover food floated in the puddles and avoiding them wasn't an option.

"For Septus," she whispered to herself. With that, she trudged through the puddles until at last she came to a stop in front of *The Hardy Place*. Already the sound of laughter, drunkards, and music could be heard through the doors. Peering through the window, she could see Broli sitting with a group at the back of the tavern. She started to reach for the door when it was thrust open and a couple of ladies walked out, laughing.

"Watch where you walk, you fastidious cow," one of the drunken ladies slurred.

"Yeah, what she said," the other laughed. Emlin looked at the two ladies with humiliation and shrugged off their heinous remarks. Stepping inside the tavern, the wood at the front entrance was soft and mushy, a result of the frequent flooding of the sewage drains in the streets.

Cheerful laughs and clumsy singing filled the air. The layout was fairly simple. Down the middle of the tavern sat three circular tables with chairs for larger groups. Lining the left and right walls were rectangular tables for smaller groups. Broli sat at the one furthest back. She gulped and began weaving past the drunks and wenches, keeping Broli in her line of sight. As she neared his table, Broli was preparing to take a large gulp of ale, foam frothing over the top and filling his beard with its tasty white caps.

"Emmy?" Broli exclaimed, setting his mug down and clumsily trying to stand, his large belly bumping the table and spilling his mug along with everyone else's. The petite woman to his left laughed as she lifted her equally large cup to her mouth and took a sip.

"What are you doing in a heap like this?" Broli asked as he grabbed Emlin's hand and gave it a gentle kiss.

"I was hoping to speak with you," Emlin responded. Broli quickly grabbed a spare chair and set it at the far end of the table for her.

"Please have a seat. I've just been telling these fools the tale about how I defeated a Worthriar with my bare hands," Broli explained.

"He's a bloody liar," one of the guys sitting across from Broli yelled.

"Emmy, settle this. Tell them the truth; you were there. You saw the whole thing," Broli pleaded. All eyes at the table suddenly turned toward her. Shyness taking its toll left her mute, the best she could do was a nod. It was apparently enough for as soon as she did the table gawkers all burst out in laughter as she confirmed the great oaf's story. Disbelief replaced by wonderment.

"By Undr, I knew you were strong, Broli, but that's damn impressive," his drunken comrade laughed. Emlin sat down and Broli followed her lead after pushing her chair toward the table. For a brutish man, he was not short on manners, that much was clear. The music in the tavern came to a pause, offering Emlin her first chance to feel her sanity since she stepped into the messy establishment. Shelly, the dingy wench who ran the night shift approached the table. Her hair was brown like the color of dirt and riddled with knots and split ends, her uniform was smudged, wet and stunk of ale yet most guys in the tavern couldn't resist flirting with her.

"What can I get you, sweetie?" Shelly asked as she stopped in front of Emlin.

"She'll take a pint of your finest ale," Broli injected before Emlin had a chance to respond. Shelly nodded and headed off towards the bar.

"So what's this about, Emmy? What was so important you wandered all the way to the slums?" Broli asked. Emlin opened her mouth, about to speak when a sad-looking woman took the small stage and started singing while the band behind her played their instruments loud enough to mask the footsteps of a giant.

"It's about Septus—he's been spotted in Frand," Emlin yelled. Broli continued to smile as he looked at her, totally oblivious to what she had said.

"Ah, I love this song!" Broli exclaimed. He grabbed his tankard and turned his attention toward the stage, bobbing his head with joy. *This is no use,* Emlin thought. *He's far too drunk for conversation.* Shelly the Wench finally brought a tall ale and set the tankard down in front of Emlin, offering a wink and a smile. Emlin lifted the cup and took a small sip before quickly setting it down. It was foul and smelled like monkey piss. *Why do so many people crave this?* She wondered. Broli turned his attention from the stage and looked at Emlin sitting behind the large tankard of ale. The cup was so big it nearly hid her from his view. With a cheerful grin, he raised his cup, offering a toast.

"To friends, health, and getting drunk!" Broli exclaimed, he waited for the others at the table to raise their mugs, as they did, he crashed his cup against theirs spilling ale across the table. He turned to Emlin and cracked a huge grin.

"Emmy?" He asked nodding his head toward her tankard. Emlin let out a sigh and lifted it up crashing it into his. Broli let out a tremendous laugh and quaffed down the remainder of his ale.

"So how do you know the Princess?" One of the drunks asked. Emlin shot the man a look of shock. *He knows who I am?*

"Old Emmy and I have been friends for a couple years now. She's the reason I had to fight the Worthriar. She was out hunting one day, and for some reason decided to pick a fight with one of the toughest creatures in Tordenth. Needless to say, we've been friends ever since," Broli laughed as he explained.

"So *that's* when you killed the beast. Now it all makes sense," the petite woman commented.

Another hour had passed, and Broli seemed no more ready to leave than he had been when she had first entered the tavern. At this point, even Emlin was feeling the effects of the ale. Her vision was foggy, and she was feeling rather warm. She couldn't resist smiling at all the wild antics she saw happening around her. Taverns really were an interesting place; so many different types of people to see and meet. *Perhaps that's what he likes so much about them,* Emlin thought. Broli stood up and wandered towards the stage and began discussing a song choice with the band.

"What's he doing?" Emlin asked to no one in particular.

"You'll see," one of Broli's friends replied. Emlin turned her attention back towards Broli as he turned to face the crowd. *By Undr he's going to sing.* Broli let out a thunderously loud throat clear which silenced most in the bar. Emlin watched with anticipation and nervousness, a smile decorating her rosy cheeks.

Before the city of a thousand lies a man came by to knock in the night, he tried with all his might to knock my door out of sight

Before the city of a thousand lies a man came by and we had a fight, we punched and we fought until I knocked that man clean out

Before the city of a thousand lies I beat up a man who wanted my life, and the town threw me out, their minds were filled with doubt

Before the city of a thousand lies I rode on my horse into the night, more lonely I had not felt, as I rode on my horse and dwelt

Before the city of a thousand lies my horse got sick and fell on its hind, it crushed me by my spine, and took off and left me behind

Now I lay dying in the night all because I got in a fight, the wolf comes to take me out, and I let out a shout

But no one hears me... in the city...of a thousand...Lies

"What a depressing song," Emlin exclaimed. The band began playing random tunes and Broli slowly wandered away from the stage. "I thought taverns were supposed to have cheerful songs."

"Taverns are also one of the best places to let out a few bottled up tears. Songs like that help just as much as cheerful songs do," one of the friends replied.

"What is the city of a thousand lies? Who is the man in the song?" Emlin questioned. Broli stumblingly sat down and grabbed his fresh ale, taking a considerably smaller sip than the ones he had been taken earlier in the night.

"Barox Thorn," Broli replied. "The poor fool was banished from Morlay after he beat a man half to death—and rightfully so at that. The man planned to rob him and leave him for dead. Anyways, he knew the right people, and instead of being imprisoned, he got away scot-free. Poor Barox was tossed out and ended up being attacked by a wolf. Everyone in that city heard his screams and pretended they didn't. Bunch of liars, all of them. They say he haunts the lands around Morlay, traveling with the very wolf that killed him, searching for anyone even remotely related to the ones who lied and cast him out."

Emlin shuddered at the story and looked towards the others at the table. All their faces were blank, free of the smiles that had previously occupied them. Broli stood up and pulled out a bag of coins and began rummaging through them. Trying to maintain his composure, he carefully set down six coins.

"Well, I suppose I should walk Emmy home," Broli announced as he looked towards her, his face pale and sweaty. All at the table laughed at the idea; he was clearly too drunk to be escorting anyone—it was more likely she would be escorting *him*.

Emlin kept her arm around Broli as they walked through the mostly dry streets. The rain had ceased, and the slow drains had finally started doing their job. Broli's apartment was conveniently close to the tavern—right across the street, in fact. Another reason it was his favorite hangout spot. He fumbled with his door for a moment and finally got inside. Emlin helped him hobble to his bed and he collapsed backward so quickly she half expected the frame to break.

"You wanted to talk," he slurred as he tried to keep eye contact.

"I'm going out on another search for Septus. He was spotted near Frand. I was hoping you would come with me," Emlin replied.

"Emmy," Broli sighed. "It's been over a year. Don't you think if he wanted to be found, he would have by now? He left. He left *all of us* without any explanation."

"I don't believe that, Broli. He loved me. He would've done *anything* to be with me. There's something else going on here. My father is hiding something; I know it," Emlin explained. "I'm going with or without you. I plan to leave at daybreak tomorrow. Can I count you in?"

"Yes, of course. I'm not going to let you go you into Tordenth alone. What of Inca and Draxton?" Broli sighed.

"Inca's the one who claims to have spotted him. She's injured and in the infirmary. I have to see for myself. I have to see if he's who she claims him to be. She claims he's taken a dark path. An *evil* path," she explained.

"And if he is? Then what?" Broli asked.

"I'll cross that road when the time comes," Emlin replied. "Get some rest. I'll come fetch you in the morning."

Chapter 19

Nikalas followed Kunklestick with an eager anticipation; perched securely on his right shoulder was Fawn. Together they followed Kunklestick through the main hall and out into the front pasture. It was somewhat of a relief to be in the midst of pure fresh air, no factories, no fires, nothing to distract from the natural aura of the wilderness. In the far distance were the Hills of Edmere, a mountain pass rumored to be the secret home of the gnomes, but no one was certain of this.

"Now that you have your Grimwort, it's time you understand the reason every wizard has one," Kunklestick explained coming to a stop. Reaching into his baggy, brown robe he pulled out a wand. As he grabbed both ends of the wand, he began to pull on each side. A small bright white light began to radiate from the wand—so bright Nikalas had to shield his eyes. Moments later, the light had faded. As he opened his eyes the wand was gone, Kunklestick instead holding onto a tall, crooked staff that looked like no more than a fallen tree branch.

"How did you do that?" Nikalas questioned, glancing at the poor excuse for a staff.

"That's for another lesson," Kunklestick replied, waving off the question. "Grimworts are creatures that bind themselves to those who have magical potential. They act as a magician detector so to speak. More than this a Grimwort is our only way of accessing *The Echo*."

"What is *The Echo*?" Nikalas asked.

"I can explain, but I think it best to show you. Grab onto my shoulder," Kunklestick instructed.

Nikalas followed the prompt, ignoring the voice in his head that constantly preached disobedience. It had done him little good in life acknowledging its existence. With his hand rested on his mentor's shoulders, he let out an exasperated breath. Kunklestick mumbled something as he drove his staff into the dirt. When he did, something unexplainable happened — the sky darkened for no seemingly obvious reason. What had once been a sunny field was now drenched in gloominess. There was an odd mist that flowed all around, its movements unpredictable and irrational, it seemed almost alive — if such a thing was possible. It was everywhere, taking up every square inch of the land except for the air immediately surrounding them. As the mist neared them, it diverted its path. Nikalas quietly scanned the expanse with consternation. It looked like a *nightmare*.

"What happened?" He asked as he waved his arm around the mist, it still refused to touch him.

"Welcome to *The Echo*," Kunklestick grinningly said.

"It looks like the same place we already were," Nikalas replied. "There's the hall just over there." He pointed towards the quaint building from which they had just emerged.

"*The Echo* is not a different world so much as it is a different plane of existence. It is always around, its energy always felt, but never seen. It's a realm that stands between ours and the realm of the gods," Kunklestick explained.

"Grimworts like the one on your shoulder are native to *The Echo*; they were born here. Until the first wizard brought them to Furlasia, this was the only place they existed. The energy that this place gives off is what gives a wizard his power. If you are not capable of tapping into that energy, you'll never be a wizard. Grimworts can sense when they are near someone who is capable of using this energy. When they are near such a person, they are drawn to them in the same way they are drawn to this place."

"For this reason, all potential candidates who seek to be trained in magic are sent an egg containing a Grimwort. If a candidate is meant to be trained, the egg will hatch. If not, the egg will remain closed. Yours hatched, so you like me can tap into the energy of The Echo."

"I still don't understand why we are here; there's nothing to see. It's just a creepy version of where we just came from. What the hell is the point of this?" Nikalas impatiently asked.

"Nikalas, in order to truly understand how to use your power, you must first understand where it comes from. Furthermore, there are tactical advantages to being able to access this realm," Kunklestick retorted.

"How so?" Nikalas asked? His last word had hardly landed when the beating sound of wind seized his focus. It sounded like wings, wings belonging to something fairly large. His eyes looked toward the overcast skyline, scanning for an answer to the strange pitch. Each moment the sound grew louder, he continued to spin around, searching for an answer. His eyes darted back and forth, but still the source eluded him. He had just considered giving up when something caught his eye. His eyes grew wide, and his jaw fell open. Soaring toward them at breakneck speed was a large turquoise creature with white stripes. Jagged wings emanating from its posterior. Its wings caused a powerful roar of wind with each new thrash. As it neared, it let out a howl.

"Is that a—"

"Yup," Kunklestick said with a confident smirk. The Grimwort hit the ground with a thud, kicking up bits of dirt and grass as its hooves dug into the soil. He smiled as the creature cackled and bowed its head. Grimworts being affectionate beings, they thrived off of simple physical contact with their masters. Kunklestick slowly approached and began rubbing its ears, it let out a satisfactory sound that was almost a horse's neigh and shook its head.

"This is Yogurn, my oldest and most loyal friend," he moved his hands toward her neck and continued to rub. "Come closer and say hello. She won't bite. There is no species that exists that is more loving and loyal than a Grimwort."

He couldn't help but feel hesitant at the offer, so many times back home people had given him assurance that they had a friendly dog, only to have him end up pulling his hand away quickly as they went in for a bite. But the old man seemed right; Yogurn seemed calm, collected, and well trained. He began to approach slowly, avoiding sudden movements. Good manners for any animal, despite their temperament. Her reactions were minimal to none; she hardly paid him any mind. At last, he found himself close enough to extend a hand and touch her. There was a very thin layer of soft, downy hair lining the skin. As he rubbed her neck, it felt as though he was touching a peach.

"Why is she so big?" Nikalas asked as he continued to caress Yogurn's neck.

"Yogurn is full grown. She is very old, seventy-two years old to be precise. She's just as peppy as she was the day she hatched, though. Wonderful creatures, Grimworts. It is truly a gift to be blessed with their bond. In time, Fawn will reach this size as well."

Kunklestick grinned.

"Are you ready for a tour of *The Echo*?" He asked.

"You mean on this thing?" Nikalas nervously asked. "I don't know. Riding a horse is one thing—"

"And riding a Grimwort is no different, other than its way more fun and quite a bit faster," Kunklestick interrupted. It seemed the matter wasn't truly open for discussion, without awaiting a response Kunklestick climbed aboard Yogurn's back. Once he had made himself comfortable atop the saddle, he held out his hand, offering assistance to his nervous companion. Nikalas hesitated, thoughts of falling filling his mind. There was something in the old man's eyes that indicated this was happening no matter what Nikalas thought of it. He sighed and accepted the offer.

"Don't be frightened. It's quite safe—if an elderly man with poor balance like I can handle it, a fit young guy like you should have no problems," Kunklestick laughed. "Oh, but do hang on, take off can be a little bumpy," he cautioned. "Just grab onto me and all will be fine."

Fawn chirped happily. He was very new to this world, but he already knew Yogurn was somehow connected to him. Hearing the little bugger gave Nikalas a thought.

"What do I do with Fawn?" Nikalas questioned. "He can't just stay on my shoulder."

"Just place him in your front pouch—it's plenty roomy. He'll be fine," Kunklestick replied. Nikalas nodded in agreement and held his finger up to Fawn, he seemed all too eager to jump aboard. Once he had Fawn properly balanced on his finger, he brought it down to his waist and opened the pouch. Kunklestick was right, it was roomy. Still, though, if he pressed too snug against the old man he would surely crush the poor creature. *I'll just have to be careful*, he thought to himself. Fawn happily climbed inside and curled into a ball.

With his grip secured on the ball of the saddle, Kunklestick whistled and gave Yogurn a light kick. She let out a satisfied neigh and dashed toward the mountain pass. As she sped up so did the beating of her wings until moments later, they were airborne.

Nikalas looked toward the ground as it grew smaller and smaller, breath taken yet terrified. The higher they climbed the smaller everything looked. Eventually it got to the point where The Hall of Wizards was so small it looked like a speck against a sea of emeralds. The chilled wind passed through his hair, clouds passed by in a blur of white and gray and his nerves that were previously on edge began to feel serene. No moment in his life had ever had such a gratuitous feeling as this one.

"Woohoo!" Nikalas cried out. Kunklestick turned his head and began to chuckle.

"Hang on tight," Kunklestick warned. With another light kick, Yogurn began to climb higher, spinning all the way up. When she reached her limit, which was rather high, she neighed and began to dive. Kunklestick laughed, but Nikalas tightened his grip and Yogurn howled in satisfaction. As Yogurn leveled out, Nikalas began to survey the area. The familiar sights were all there, Morlay looked exactly as before—except it was missing the billowing smoke and foul stench. Something else caught his eyes, just outside the border of Morlay, little yellow orbs hovered around, moving in very determined motions.

"What are those lights?" Nikalas asked, yelling over the wind.

"People," Kunklestick replied. "Those are the traces of people in Furlasia. We can see their spirits; we just can't see their forms because they are not allowed here."

Nikalas nodded in satisfaction, continuing to watch the scenery. Yogurn navigated the skies with grace and dexterity. She knew what she was doing; her wings continued to create the powerful whooshing sound he had heard earlier. Their path took them over the swamps of Neveraus and beyond the forest of Roo. In the far off distance lay a city. From this scope it looked like nothing more than a mirage; a mirage of an elegant city of white bricks. Nikalas carefully leaned around his mentor, hoping for a better view. Closer they approached, until the mirage faded, leaving nothing but the remains of a ruined city.

Kunklestick gently patted Yogurn's neck, signaling it was time to land. She bobbed her head and began to dive rapidly toward the ruins. Nikalas tightened his grip. Wind howled in his ears, and swooped around his glasses into his eyes. He quickly shut them to avoid letting them dry out. Darkness engulfed him in its warm embrace. There was nothing but the sounds to lead his way. Kunklestick's elderly chuckle, continued until the whooshing of the wind ceased, ending with a firm thud, and then silence.

"What is this place?" Nikalas asked, rubbing his eyes.

"This is Rangmar. Once, it was a great city of the Delopar. Now, it's nothing but a tomb," Kunklestick replied. "Climb on down."

As he glanced down embarrassment set in, his arms were wrapped rather snugly around Kunklestick, he quickly let go and shrugged it off. As his feet hit the ground, he scanned the area, something about this place seemed off, a nefarious presence poisoned every inch of the once great city.

Yogurn generously knelt to the ground, offering her master a less harsh departure. Kunklestick gratefully accepted the assistance, he grunted and groaned, but eventually his feet found the soil, he sighed with relief and gave Yogurn another rub. Silence surrounded them; nothing but the silent hum of the wind and the swaying of the grass could be heard. Suddenly, there *was* something — very faint but definitely noticeable. Nikalas began to look around, there was a small muffled chirp trying to be heard, but no sign of a source. Then it clicked, *Fawn*. Fawn was still in his pocket.

"Oh, yeah," he said carefully pulling open his pocket. There sat Fawn, curled into ball patiently awaiting release. As the light reached his eyes, Fawn quickly sat up and flew out, hovering just in front of his master's gaze.

"Well, go on," Nikalas smiled. "Get on my shoulder." The tiny Grimwort quickly did as told, perching its tiny feet securely atop his master.

"So why are we here?" Nikalas asked, looking around. Rangmar was a battlefield; buildings had been shattered, leaving scattered bricks strewn about. The age of the Delopar had been a long time ago; Rangmar now belonged to Furlasia. Wild grasses, vines and moss all fought for control of the land, and the vines appeared to be winning.

"There's something I wish to show you," Kunklestick replied, without further explanation he began leading them to a large building just ahead. It looked like an important location, and strangely enough was the only building in the area not to have damage. Nikalas followed behind with enthusiasm, something about the city piqued his interest. Fawn happily chirped as they continued to stroll closer to the monstrously large fortress. A loud crunch under his feet brought him pause. *What was that?* Looking down he gasped and jumped back. The crunch had been his foot cracking the remains of a skeletal arm — the rest of the body still connected and just as decayed. Kunklestick promptly turned around upon hearing Nikalas' shriek, as he noticed the remains he turned and approached his shaken apprentice.

"One of the slain Delopar," Kunklestick explained.

"They don't get a burial?" Nikalas asked.

"In war, sometimes honor and respect for the fallen is a lost quality," he replied.

"Seems wrong to just leave them to rot under the sun," Nikalas retorted. Kunklestick pondered, cocking his head in thought.

"It is wrong, Nikalas. But the people responsible for this atrocity aren't the type of people who care about honor. Evil does not follow the path of honor; honor requires self-sacrifice and compassion. Those who are evil only sacrifice others and lack all compassion," Kunklestick explained. "We can be better than them Nikalas. We *have* to be."

"Come," he abruptly turned around and continued heading toward the building.

Stepping inside the stronghold, it was clear the Delopar had at one point been far more civilized than they currently were. The interior of the stronghold was reminiscent of ancient Egyptian architecture. Stencil art covered the walls — each picture telling a tale about a life long forgotten.

"Delopar are the oldest species in Furlasia, some say they were the first ones to settle in this region. It was them that opened the doors to us, after the war their numbers dwindled. They are now nearly extinct," Kunklestick lectured as he pointed out the wall paintings.

Light trickled into the halls through cleverly placed skylights. Torches mounted every few feet served as a replacement for the hours when the sun decided to rest. Dried animal hides hung in each doorway, providing separation from the hall and a small measure of privacy.

Kunklestick continued to play tour guide and once they reached the upper floor, he paused in front of a door. Red markings indicated this was no normal room. Of all the rooms they had passed, this was the only one with a proper door, but why? He pulled the handle open and stepped inside; the room was mostly dark, torches lining the walls burned diligently, casting shadows from one wall to the next. There was a peculiar smell, musty, like something old. A podium at the front of the room sat mysteriously shrouded in darkness. A lantern was perched on each end; two in total, each lantern had a unique green flame. In between them, something lay on the podium, wrapped in darkness.

"What is that smell?" Nikalas asked covering his mouth. His mentor remained silent in observation. Curiosity took over, and Nikalas quickly found himself approaching the podium. His heart raced with each step; he dreaded what he might find, yet he knew he had to see it. He stopped as he reached his destination and looked down. He didn't scream—every part of him wanted him to but he couldn't—his heart had already warned him what he would find. There was no surprise to be found. A skeleton lay on the table, its hands folded over its ribs, draped from its neck a golden chain and an inscribed medallion. The eyes were hollow, decayed long ago and yet there was something entrancing in their hollow darkness.

You shouldn't have come, boy. The fires come for you. The flames will rise high in the sky, and there is nothing you can do to stop them. Nikalas Noise, you will perish.

Images of war soared throughout his mind. Terria in ruins; gates knocked down, corpses in the streets. Nasliegh Keep smashed to rubble, a mob of people sobbing and huddled in a circle. Nikalas pushed past them. Their faces were blank—no eyes, mouth, or nose. They glared at him with empty faces as he continued to move them aside. In the center of the mob were the bleeding remains of Princess Emlin. Blood poured from her neck creating a scarlet river that flowed through the cracks in the street and came to a stop in front of a temple.

"Nikalas," Kunklestick burst out. There was no response. Nikalas continued to stare down at the remains, his eyes vacant, his pupils gone.

You will never see them alive again. Their corpses will be your only reward.

"Nikalas, snap out of it!" Kunklestick exclaimed, grabbing a hold of him and shaking him.

Kill yourself, and I might be convinced to let them go. Your sacrifice is to be your only redemption.

Kunklestick slapped Nikalas as hard as he could.

"What the hell, man?" Nikalas yelled rubbing his cheek as tenderness began to settle in.

"What happened?" Kunklestick urgently questioned pulling Nikalas away from the podium.

"There was a voice in my head—an angry one. It knew my name. It told me to kill myself. Said I would never see them alive again," he replied. His cheek continued to throb as he rubbed it. "Do you know what it was talking about? Who am I never gonna see again?"

"I haven't the faintest idea," Kunklestick replied as he scratched his chin.

"There's something else," Nikalas added. "I saw a vision. It wasn't good. Terria was in shambles, and Emlin was dead."

"I see," Kunklestick replied. He turned and headed toward the room's exit.

"Whose body is this?" Nikalas called out. Kunklestick stopped in his tracks and slowly turned around.

"Drachen Crane; more commonly known as Agavordis." There was a tremble in his voice, a fear that Nikalas hadn't thought him capable of.

"How can he speak to me? How can he show me things? He's dead," Nikalas said, approaching his teacher, the old man seemed more shaken than he even was.

"Evil doesn't die," Kunklestick replied.

Chapter 20

Septus led the way as they continued their journey back to Neveraus. It had been a day since they'd acquired the remains of Herratia, since then he had the displeasure of listening to his escorts argue over who had to carry her. Right now, Vixar had the chore. One would think that carrying the remains of your ancestor would be an honor, but it was not so, apparently. These three fought over who got *stuck* with the burden. He tried his best to tune out the nonsense. He couldn't wait until they reached Neveraus and he could be rid of these fools. There was only one thing on his mind, the talisman. Two more remained, and he intended to find them. The bargain with the Akordans was for them to help with that—hopefully they had made headway.

The village of Frand lay ahead, and the air still smelled foul. As they neared it, various animals scurried into the woods. Septus stopped when he came to the pile of carnage that they had left behind. The Uboroxs and Worthiars had been busy, there wasn't much left. There, in the coldness of the ground laid the remains of the Chief, his face was missing but the rest of him was intact. It was here that Sef had had died. Here where he had faced his old friend Inca. The look she had given him still haunted him. It was disgust, betrayal, anger, and fear. What happened was regrettable, but inevitable. Septus knew that.

"Perhaps we should stop for a bit," Drango said. "Surely we could use some food." Septus looked around at the carnage and grimaced. He shook his head in disgust.

"I'm not eating dead Delopar that have been sitting out for days, but you guys are welcome to," Septus replied. Vixar set the remains down and approached Drango, who stood over the Chief licking his lips.

"This one still looks tasty," Drango grinned. Septus shook his head and wandered toward the village. It was primitive; the Delopar lived like savages. What happened to the once great species he had heard about? Their huts were basic, made of animal hide. He approached one and opened up a flap, inside was a small cot, made of scrap wood and a small fire pit. Dishes were strewn about, but overall, the place looked like a dreadful place to live.

"How did Inca put up with this?" He whispered to himself. He was determined to live a grand life. Abissal Keep would be his, his father's legacy restored to its former glory. Walking back out into the main section of the village something seemed off; the forest was never this silent. Up in the trees, there was an Oekie, and something about this one was familiar. He had seen it before. Suddenly it clicked; this was the very same Oekie that he had seen in the trees after they had attacked Frand the first time. It watched him with determination; a paranoid feeling suddenly crept over him. For reasons he couldn't quite explain without sounding crazy, he was quite sure that Oekie was spying on him.

He quickly ran back toward the Akordans. The Chief had all but been demolished, only his midsection remained.

"You ate him raw?" Septus asked in shock.

"Too hungry to waste time with a fire," Drango replied. Septus glanced around in disgust, Vixar had a leg hanging from his mouth and Roman sat with an arm in his hand.

"Well hurry up, something is wrong. We're being watched," Septus cautioned. The Akordans continued to demolish the remains of the Chief in the most savage way they could until there was nothing left. Rather than packing their things up like Septus had urged, they laid down and rubbed their bellies.

"Did you idiots not hear what I said? I said we are being watched. We need to move. Get off your asses and get moving!" Septus yelled. Drango quickly stood up and approached Septus, anger in his eyes.

"This has gone on long enough. You've had your fun, playing the leader. We do what I say now. Or did you not notice? You're greatly outnumbered," Drango threatened with a sneer. Septus gulped, but held firm, he grabbed the talisman.

"You think we're scared of your jewelry?" Drango asked. Septus and Drango continued to stare each other down, both ready at a moment's notice to attack the other. The tension was palpable. In a physical match, Septus held no chance, and he knew it, his only hope was that he could use the talisman to summon some power. Suddenly, something broke the tension—the tree behind them sizzled and smoked, a tiny hole had been burned. Septus gulped, his fears had been realized. They had been found.

"Beacon!" Septus yelled out. Drango stepped back and looked around. From the distance, the sound of Beacon blasters filled the air; small beams of ultra-heated light came flying towards them. Septus dropped to the ground, the Akordans following suit and began crawling toward the forest. As they continued their cautious crawl, Vixar paused. *Herratia,* he thought. Keeping low, he carefully crawled to where he had set the cocoon. As he reached the remains, he gripped them firmly, dragging them behind him. The screeching sounds of the lasers howled through the air as they continued their crawl.

Once they reached a line of trees, Septus slowly rose to his feet and lined himself perfectly against one. Vixar kept low as he carefully set the remains into a pile of brush, tossing loose branches and leaves to mask its existence. The screech halted, and the air went silent.

"Are they gone?" Drango whispered. Septus shook his head in response and gave the signal to be silent.

Thadeus stood in front of his band of Vanguard soldiers with a pleased look plastering his face.

"Sir, they've fled the area," one of the soldiers said. Thadeus turned and smiled.

"They can't have gone far," he replied. He slowly reached to his waist and withdrew his two daggers. With a confident swagger be began marching forwards, his soldiers following behind. Their footsteps nearly silent as they approached the area with their Beacon blasters raised and ready.

"We know you're here, boy," Thadeus called out to the empty air. "Those creatures you're traveling with make far too much noise for you to have a chance of being sneaky." He turned and smiled towards his second in command, Colonel Sabasio Vanduest. The colonel nodded and gestured to his men to fan out. As silently as they could, the soldiers split into two groups and took off in opposite directions.

"I'm just here to talk to you. King Hervott has some concerns he'd like to address," Thadeus continued his approach, keeping his soldiers in his sight line. The silence continued as he edged his way closer to the tree line. He could feel his heart racing, adrenaline filling him with an excited energy.

The sudden scream of a soldier ended the peaceful silence. There was a loud crunch as one of the soldiers was thrown against a tree. He fell to the ground crying in agony, unable to move. It began, screeching filled the air once again as the soldiers quickly fired their Beacons. The thunderous growls of the Akordans were terrifying enough to bring nervousness to any man. Not Thadeus however, he lived for the thrill of combat.

Thadeus stood peering into the distance as he watched his soldiers engaging the enemy Akordans. Large swords swung through the air, cries of pain echoed and blood splashed about as the Akordans continued their attack. Beacons were a very powerful weapon; the heated lasers they emitted could pierce metal if used properly. That being said, to get the true advantage of them one had to hold the trigger. Doing this caused a focused beam that would burn right through a target if held long enough. In the midst of combat like this, though, it was the small laser bursts that one was most likely given the opportunity to use.

Cries of agony continued as the Akordans continued wiping out soldiers. They seemed to laugh at the tickle created by the small lasers. Thadeus ran into the combat, daggers drawn and ready for blood. Drango lifted his sword and swung it down, his blade met with the head of a soldier making it all the way down to his chest before stopping. He laughed and kicked the soldier to the ground while simultaneously freeing his blade. His laughter came to an abrupt end as he turned just in time to see Thadeus charging at him.

As Thadeus made contact, he drove his shoulder in the Akordan sending him crashing back. Drango quickly jumped to his feet, attempting to catch his breath. His breathing staggered by the impact to his chest. Thadeus stood across from him, grinning and holding a blade in each hand.

"You're not like the others," Drango observed, his words dragged out due to his breathing. "You don't use their weapon."

"Nah, I've always found Beacons to be more trouble than they are worth. No, I prefer to make my kills with Gertrude and Fiona," Thadeus nodded at his daggers as he said their names.

"Very honorable, but very foolish," Drango exclaimed as he swung his blade toward Thadeus. Thadeus quickly dropped to the ground and brought his legs around, knocking Drango to his feet. Like a gymnast he quickly hopped to his feet, glancing toward Drango and offering a wink, with a cocky smile he tossed Gertrude toward the sky.

"Goodbye, my love," he whispered. Drango attempted to stand, but before he could move an inch Fiona dashed toward him, pinning his tail to the ground, rendering him temporarily immobile. Moments later, Gertrude came back to the party in spectacular fashion; she opted to greet Drango from a much less friendly approach. The dagger unapologetically pierced the top of Drango's skull, wiping the smile clear from his face as he fell to the ground in disgrace. Blood slowly oozed from the wound as his eyes went blank.

"Thank you, dear," Thadeus whispered as he reacquired his favorite ladies.

Septus carefully navigated around the carnage; five Vanguard soldiers had already been slain. There was only a handful left, but, unfortunately, the Akordans numbered only two. He would have to help if he was to survive this attack. Picking up an abandoned Beacon, he took aim and started firing at the soldiers. Their armor was designed to repel hits from the Beacons so this regrettably didn't work. Instead, the blast he had fired bounced back towards him, he quickly dove to the ground narrowly missing the searing beam.

Colonel Sabasio crouched to the ground, his gaze fixed on Roman, who was currently engaged by a couple of the remaining soldiers. He carefully lifted his Beacon and steadied it on his knee. Just as Roman was about to swing his sword, he squeezed the trigger and held it firm. A focused beam of light darted toward the aloof Akordan. An unsuspecting soldier who was standing nearby accidently turned and walked into the beam. His body fell to the ground in two halves, his cries of agony filled the field but no help came. Colonel Sabasio kept his finger tight on the trigger — it felt as though time had slowed down.

With his sword above his head, Roman paused, a familiar odor entering his senses. His belly started to growl with hunger pangs as he realized what it was — the smell of juicy fresh meat being heated up. *Yum,* he thought as he licked his lips. His thoughts of joy were quickly replaced for sharp pain emanating from his side. As he dropped his sword, he looked down to see a beam of light making a fool out of him. He cried out in anguish as his gut continued to sizzle. When the pain became overbearing, he fell to his knees. As he did, the beam moved its way up his body until it exited from the top of his head. His upper torso fell into two halves, and he slumped to the ground in a piping hot mess.

"Take that, you gnarly beast," Sabasio whispered with a grin.

Thadeus scanned the battlefield for a sign of his prey. He had lost many soldiers, a good eight lay dead, and a couple more lay dying. His head cocked in confusion as he caught a glimpse of a soldier who had been halved, the wound clearly came from one of the Beacons. Looking around, he saw Sabasio rising from a crouched position, as he did, he looked toward Thadeus and shrugged.

"In war, people must die," Thadeus whispered to himself. His focus returned to the battlefield, and he grinned as he located Septus. This was not personal, he had no feelings one way or the other about whether or not the boy should live or die, but he had been paid a fat sum of money. He had to see it through. In the background, he heard the cries of pain as the last Akordan, Vixar, fell to the ground riddled with steaming holes of doom.

Septus was all who remained. He quickly jumped to his feet, still holding the Beacon, his fingers trembling. He thought to run, but there were too many. He would never escape, and he knew it. As Thadeus began his approach, Septus opened fire.

"Leave him to me," Thadeus said as he began zig-zagging and dodging the beams. His soldiers stood down as told and simply watched. The blasts from the Beacon continued to hurl toward him while he dodged them with insane precision. As he closed in on Septus, he grabbed Gertrude and threw her straight ahead.

Septus continued firing the Beacon, trying desperately to hit his mark, but Thadeus moved too fast and his aim was too shaky. A fiery feeling filled his chest—the impact from Gertrude sent him crashing back a few feet. He was down, on his back and looking toward the sky, his breathing beginning to shallow.

"You've made powerful people very nervous," Thadeus explained as he casually approached Septus. "Personally, you don't seem like you're that dangerous." With tears in his eyes, Septus locked eyes with his attacker, the pain intensely radiating as he tried to tilt his head.

"You always just do as you're told?" Septus coughed, tears slowly pouring down his cheeks.

"Hey, it's not personal. I'm a mercenary. I work for a paycheck. For the right amount of coin, I'll kill whoever needs to be killed," Thadeus replied. Septus began spitting up blood as he tried to laugh.

"And you think I'm dangerous?" Septus laughed.

"I don't. King Hervott does. He thinks you're some badass wizard. Clearly he's wrong—you didn't use a single spell during this whole fight. You're nothing but a kid," Thadeus explained.

Septus shook his head in frustration, blood continuing to pour from his wound, the throbbing spreading throughout his whole body. Thadeus grabbed Fiona and knelt down next to Septus, redness filling his eyes, a single tear finally formed making its way down his cheek.

"You got a raw deal here, kid," Thadeus whispered as he wiped the tear from his cheek. He took a deep breath and lifted Fiona above his head.

"Wait!" Septus called out. Thadeus stopped, his arms still raised.

"Tell Emlin I still love her."

"All right, I will," Thadeus replied. At that moment, he quickly plunged Fiona into his throat before quickly withdrawing her. Septus began coughing, his screams of pain muffled by the blood filling his throat. Shaking his head in anger, Thadeus wiped Fiona and Gertrude on his leg and returned them to their rightful place in his sheath.

"Come on, let's get a move on." He commanded. Sabasio and the remaining soldiers nodded and followed the general away from the battlefield.

"That was an atrocious waste of manpower," Thadeus said as he approached Sabasio. "That kid was no more a threat than my wife." Further and further they continued to wander away. A flash of light in the distance halted the procession. It was bright; bright enough to be seen even from this distance. Thadeus stopped, turning his attention toward the tree line. The light faded almost as quickly as it had appeared. He shrugged, dismissing the anomaly, and continued his way.

"What do you think that was?" Sabasio asked.

"I really don't give a shit," Thadeus replied.

<u>Part 2</u>

Chapter 21

It was a bleak day in Tordenth Forest; the air was particularly humid leaving a sticky coating on the skin. Emlin stood at the edge of a river, desperate for a fish to swim by. The Jordoon River was generally an alluring river filled with crystal clear water. Today, however, that was not the case, and it was dark, almost black. This was making the prospect of catching any fish seem less likely. Still, though, she persisted, patiently waiting for an unsuspecting fish to swim by. The water was darkened, but Terrians had particularly good eyesight.

In her hand was a makeshift spear she had assembled by taking a sharp rock and patiently grinding a point into a fallen tree branch. Fishing had never been a talent, but all shortcomings were just opportunities that hadn't yet been realized. Her patience seemed to be paying off, a large fish with ruffled fins slowly approached. Holding her breath, she waited for the right moment. *Splash!* Her attempt made all kinds of ruckus, but did little else. The target fish had quickly taken off. Frustration setting in, she decided she'd had enough. Grabbing her bow from her back, she quickly loaded an arrow and fired it blindly into the water.

"Are you really trying to fish with a bow and arrow?" Broli exclaimed as he emerged from over a hill. She paused as she looked at him. Her expression was one of guilt—as if she'd just been caught misbehaving. He began to laugh as he made his way down the hill toward the river.

"Emmy, I know I've taught you better than that." He said. As he reached the shoreline, he came to a stop by her side and glanced at the dark waters. She quietly rolled her eyes, walking out into the river and retrieving the arrow. Stuck on the end was a large, dead fish.

"You were saying?" She laughed.

"You got lucky," he retorted.

"Perhaps. Or perhaps you aren't the foremost expert on hunting you think you are," she replied, just then an aroma made its way into her nose. A smoky scent with undertones of salt and fresh meat. She glanced over the hill at the rising smoke coming from their camp.

"What's that smell?" She asked.

"Oh, that's the boar I caught earlier while you were down here pretending to fish," Broli exclaimed. Emlin tossed her fish into the water and promptly marched from the water.

"Damnit Broli," she huffed, giving him a playful shove.

"There's plenty for both of us, if you like, that is," he added as she marched past him. "Oh, Emmy I was just playing with you. Don't act like that. You know I hate the silent treatment."

He chased her up the hill as fast as his overly plump body would allow for. By the time he reached the top and back to camp Emlin had already begun cutting some of the meat for herself.

"Good kill," she said, her blade slowly sliding back and forth until at last she had a decent slice. Broli approached and grabbed a small bowl and his blade. As he turned to approach the boar, Emlin tossed the piece she had just cut into his bowl.

"Thank you, Emmy," he smiled. A nearby boulder provided the closest thing he'd seen to a chair since leaving Terria. Once they had both been served, Emlin found a reasonably clear spot in the dirt and sat down. She began shoving the meat down her throat with haste. It had been a couple of days since their last meal, and she had all but given up hope they would find anything nearly as good as this boar.

"So I thought we might make our way toward the Hark Mountains," she mumbled, her mouth full of food. It was certainly not Princess-like behavior, but then she never had considered herself very lady-like.

"Why in the name of all things would you want to go there?" Broli asked.

"Just a feeling. The mountains are near Frand, which is the last place he was seen," Emlin explained. "I just have a feeling he's been there."

"Look, Emmy, We've been out here for weeks looking for him," Broli retorted.

"But we haven't been *there*," Emlin fired back.

"We were just outside of it and found no signs." He took one last bite of boar and tossed his bowl to the dirt. "Haven't you come to realize the truth yet?"

"Don't say it," Emlin demanded.

"He doesn't want to be found. He's left you. He's left all of us. If he were ever truly our friend, he wouldn't have done that. Inca is a very loyal and trusting friend. It's not in the nature of Delopar to fabricate. If she says that Septus attacked Frand, and he was traveling with Akordans, then I believe her," Broli slowly pulled himself up from his boulder, his legs popping until the moment he was upright.

"And what about the other part? The other thing she claimed," Emlin asked, there was darkness in her eyes, the likes of which Broli had yet to witness.

"The dark magic?" Broli nodded. "It's troubling to imagine. He always seemed like a good kid. I never knew he had an interest in sorcery. But perhaps that's what he wanted us to think. You know of the prophecy. The necromancer will return. Perhaps Septus is the vessel by which that will be made possible."

Emlin quickly stood up. It didn't make sense; she had known Septus so well. *Intimately* so. Was it truly possible for someone to hide so much about themselves from someone they loved? Perhaps. But she decided she wouldn't be satisfied until she saw for herself. She owed him that much at least.

"Broli, I understand what you're saying. It probably even makes sense. But, I don't know. Do you comprehend love? I love him. And when you're in love with someone, you want to believe the best. It might be ignorant; I could be terribly wrong. But it's my duty to find out. Love demands that you fight for it," Emlin approached Broli and rest a hand upon his cheek.

"All right, Emmy," Broli sighed. "We'll head toward the Hark Mountains."

Once the camp had been torn down and what meat they could salvage from the boar had been stored they began once again on the path toward the Hark Mountains. It would be two days' journey on horseback. The smartest course of action seemed to make it as far as Frand and set up camp in one of the huts. Broli had at least managed to convince her to follow his lead even if she was the one picking the destination.

As he rode atop his steed, his mind raced in a thousand different directions. There would be consequences for what he had done—escorting the Princess away from home for this long would not be met by a positive response. Emlin had assured him that this was her doing and that he was merely a supportive friend. King Hervott could blame nobody but his daughter. Or at least, that's what Broli was hoping.

The village of Frand lay just ahead, the air smelled different than the last time they had journeyed here. It reeked of death. Broli drew his weapon as the horse slowly neared the main village. As before, the village was deserted, no one in sight. He quickly dismounted from his steed and surveyed the area. Something was off he could feel it. Emlin followed suit, pulling out her bow. She quickly led the horses to a post and tied them before joining Broli in the village center. He glanced at her with concern and put his finger to his lips signaling for her to be silent.

The smell seemed to be coming from the backside of the village. One cautious step at a time they made their way past the huts and into the rear of Frand. The remains of the slain Delopar lay baking in the heat; blood and guts were strewn about. A queasy feeling crept into Emlin's gut as she looked around. This scene of horror confirmed at least one part of Inca's story. There had been a battle, but whether or not Septus was involved was a different matter entirely.

Broli continued to trek deeper into the woods, his eyes fixed toward the ground as he followed what looked like the shuffling of feet. A blaster mark in a tree caught his eye. *Beacons,* he thought. *There is more going on here than what we thought.* He pointed the burn out to Emlin, who nodded and continued to follow. The tracks continued deeper into the forest.

As they reached a clearing, Broli paused. His jaw fell open, and his ax fell into the dirt. It was a massacre, the likes of which neither of them had ever seen. Scattered all around the ground were the remains of Vanguard soldiers and three slain Akordans. Emlin dropped to her knees, tears filling her eyes as the realization finally hit her. If Septus had been here, with the Akordans as Inca had said, he had surely been slain.

"I'm sorry, Emmy," Broli tried to offer comfort in the best way he could. He continued to wander the carnage, looking for a sign of Septus, there was plenty of blood, plenty of guts but no sign of him. That's when he spotted it; there was a patch of dirt drenched in a pool of blood, but no sign of a body. Someone had died here; he was sure of it. But what had happened to the body? Emlin slowly approached behind, tears pouring down her face. As she saw the puddle, she began to sob aloud. Broli quickly turned to embrace her in his arms.

"We don't know that he was here," he whispered. She continued to cry in his arms as a calm breeze passed through, stirring up the leaves and the odor of death. In the trees above, an Oekie sat watching. She glanced up with curiosity, as she did the creature took off, swinging from branch to branch. *Strange,* she thought.

They didn't spend much time lingering in the carnage; there wasn't anything to see except death. It was bad enough that Septus had likely perished there, but why weren't the dead brought back to be buried. She would have more than a few words for whoever was in charge of this atrocity. She had decided they were best not to make camp in Frand for the night. The odor of the deceased corpses was sure to attract some of the forests more inimical beasts, so they continued their path north until the sun had begun to set.

"This seems like a good place," Broli said, pointing out a grass patch free of rocks and mostly free of twigs. There was no time to waste; one didn't want to be exposed without shelter in the forest at night. He quickly began to assemble their tent; time would not allow for him to assemble two. They would have to bunk together this evening.

Creatures of the night sang to each other, whispering mating calls and whatever else nature chooses to discuss. It was of no concern to them. As she lay there, all Emlin could think about was the idea of Septus being dead. Her heart told her it was true—it made sense. The Akordans he was rumored to be traveling with had all been slain. He had to have been there. His body had likely pulled away—some vicious animal looking to feed a family. That's what he was now, a meal for a family of carnivores. Tears filled her eyes, but she would not allow herself to make a peep. Broli had been burdened enough by this fool's quest; he deserved a sound night's sleep.

They wasted no time the following morning tearing the camp down and getting on their way. Their horses grew weary, water was in short supply and it had been quite some time since they had a drink. The plan was to take the path to the Jordoon Lake and once they restocked on water proceed north back to Terria. Emlin dreaded the inevitable conversation she would have to engage in with her father—he would want an explanation.

The day was at its most intense, the heat and humidity sweltering, Broli found himself constantly wiping his face clear of sweat. His vision was becoming blurrier by the second.

"This isn't good, Emmy," Broli said, his breathing heavy and weak. "We need water."

"What did you say?" Emlin asked. The heat had begun to take its toll on her as well. They didn't have much time. If they didn't reach the lake soon, they would both pass out. And what of the horses? They had to be nearing death's doorstep. Onward they pressed, desperately trying to maintain a hasty speed. Being caught in Tordenth in midday without water was a grave mistake. A *deadly* one.

At last, Emlin could hold on no more. The heat had taken its toll, without so much as a word of warning, she fell from her horse onto the ground.

"Emlin!" Broli cried out, jumping from his horse as fast as he could. The forest was blurry; Emlin was becoming harder to make out with each step he took. As he looked to the ground, it had become so difficult to see that everything around him looked smudged, like a pastel painting. Emlin lay on the ground in an unconscious heap; Broli quickly dropped to his knees and shook her.

"Emmy," He desperately tried to wake her, but she was out, her dreams held her focus now. *Is she dead?*

"Emmy!" Broli cried out desperately rocking her back and forth. No response. Guilt took over, filling him like a glass of water, not half full but overflowing. Obscurity called out to him, begging him for his company. He shook his head, urgently trying to fight the urge to sleep.

"Emmy!" He cried out once more. His energy had faded; it was time to rest. Carefully, he lay down on his back and looked up to the bright sky. The light tried its best to steal his sight. *No,* he thought to himself as he closed his eyes, letting the darkness have its way. He was faced with obscurity, nothingness. All that remained was the guilt. *Emmy!* He called out, but it was only in his mind.

Whispers filled her mind like a poisonous fog, the voice was a female. *Mother? No, not her. Someone else.*

"Who is that?" Emlin mumbled, her head pounded like after a night of too much wine.

"Ah, she's awake," the woman said. There was the voice of another woman as well. They both sounded old, maybe in their sixties, but unfamiliar. Perhaps it was the dehydration.

"Where am I?" Emlin whispered, her mouth seemed dry. "Do you have any water?" The mysterious woman quickly brought a water skin to her lips and opened its lid.

"Careful now, don't take too much," the woman said. The water filled her mouth slowly; she swallowed as much as she could before she began to choke. Lying down was not the best position for consuming a liquid; unfortunately, she was too exhausted to sit up.

"Where am I?" Emlin whispered.

"You're on your way back to Terria. Your father sent for you. He's been most worried about you" the woman said.

"Where's Broli?" Emlin mumbled.

"Your kidnapper? He is in a different cart. He will be dealt with in due time," the woman scornfully replied.

"He is my *friend*," Emlin muttered.

"Rest now dear, all will be taken care of. You're safe now."

Chapter 22

A cool breeze flowed in through the window, ruffling the lace curtains and bringing with it the smell of freshly baked bread and the laughter of children. As Emlin sat up, she looked around; she was in her bedroom. *But how?* On her nightstand sat a vase with freshly picked lavender, and next to that a crystal glass filled with water. Her head pounded like a thousand drums as she slowly made her way towards the nightstand and picked up the glass of water. Next to the glass was a small vial that read, *drink me* — likely from the royal apothecary. Her hands trembled as she carefully opened the small lid. Lifting it to her nose it had a strange odor reminiscent of mint mixed with sesame.

It tasted about as bad as it smelled, but the effects seemed quite instant, the drums in her mind began to fade slowly, leaving room for clear thoughts. The massacre at Frand. The slain Akordans. The mysterious pool of blood with no corpse. It all came rushing back like a flood of frigid water, stinging the nerves and raising her pulse.

Her wardrobe had been restocked with freshly cleaned clothes including a couple of new dresses she had yet to wear. She shook her head as she looked them over; they were quite feminine, elegant and soft. Perhaps it was the strain of her body and mind, but something about the orange dress called to her. As she pulled it out from the closet, she looked it over, orange satin with red lace and flower patterns all the way down.

The halls seemed particularly empty this morning; even the usual guards posted in her hall were absent. No sign of the servants, no signs of the maids. It was as if she was the only one in the castle. She knew this to be an impossible notion, so an investigation seemed in order. Her father's quarters seemed a good first destination. They had much to discuss; he had been keeping secrets for far too long.

As she gracefully made her way down the stark halls of Nasleigh Keep a thunderous groan could be heard — it was deep and resonated in the walls like drums. The closer to the main foyer she got, the louder the sound grew, until at last it became clear that it wasn't thunder. It was voices, hundreds of voices, all speaking at once. Standing on the catwalk above the foyer, she looked down to witness about two hundred people huddled together, standing in front of the stairs to the throne. Her father sat in his chair, and next to him stood Thadeus, their faces were decorated with concern and equal parts annoyance.

The crowd was diverse — noblemen toward the back, and directly behind them the Diastons and the High Mother. The front of the crowd was led by the impoverished citizens, and standing directly in front of them facing the whole audience was a line of Vanguard soldiers, all with weapons drawn and ready to fire. Currently, there was no good way to determine what the gathering was about; the whole room was just a mess of voices all speaking over each other like an angry mob. Thadeus stood calmly next to the King, whispering something in his ears.

"Nice to see you awake," a voice said from behind her. Emlin hurriedly turned around to see Inca up and moving, looking far better than she had last seen her.

"I could say the same to you," Emlin exclaimed, jumping into her friend's arms. They embraced each other in a brief hug before pulling apart.

"What is going on here?" Emlin asked, nodding towards the mass gathering.

"Your father sent a squad of soldiers in secret out on a mission, needless to say, none returned except for General Thadeus and Colonel Sabasio. The people are demanding answers," Inca explained. "Also, since you've been gone, the Akordan presence in the area has been greatly increasing, and people are nervous. They're starting to wonder if your father has what it takes to handle the situation."

Looking down to the crowd, King Hervott had risen from his throne and was raising his arms, attempting to silence the audience. After a few moments with no success, General Thadeus approached one of the soldiers grabbing his Beacon. Without warning, he began firing the weapon toward the ceiling and entrance. The crowd grew silent, fear gripping them.

"He certainly has a flare for the dramatic," Emlin remarked. Inca smiled as they continued to observe.

"If this crowd doesn't want to behave in a controlled manner, my soldiers are going to start shooting!" Thadeus yelled out. "Unless anyone in this room fancies themselves a burned hole where their brain ought to be, I suggest silence."

Hervott gave Thadeus a scornful look. He shrugged in return and handed the Beacon back.

"This has been an outrage," Hervott exclaimed. "In all my time as King, I have never seen such callous behavior."

"Then answer the bloody questions," a voice called out from somewhere amongst the crowd.

"Step forward, sir. Identify yourself," Hervott replied. From the middle of the audience emerged Wort, formerly the city drunk now a devout follower of the Diastons and the High Mother.

"Wort?" Hervott asked with surprise.

"Hanrae Elenor. That's my given name, and I'd much appreciate being addressed by it," Wort replied.

"Of course Hanrae," Hervott nodded. Hanrae took a few steps closer until he was only inches from the Vanguard soldiers.

"Why the secrecy with this soldier skirmish?" Hanrae asked. "Why the lies?"

Inca leaned in toward Emlin.

"He has been making big waves lately; since he was reformed by the High Mother he has been going around the city stirring up debates, trying to turn the tide against your father.

"I was only gone a month," Emlin whispered. "How could I have missed so much?"

"The kingdom is under no obligation to explain military tactics to the civilians of Terria. These questions are highly inappropriate. What happened to those soldiers was unfortunate; the Akordans are becoming a problem—that much is clear. The council and I have doubled our meetings as we try to solve this. When a solution has been presented, the people of Terria will be the first to know," Hervott explained.

"And what if the people of Terria no longer believe in your leadership?" Hanrae asked, the room fell silent—Hervott himself was even taken aback by the question. He was the King by birth yes; the issue had never come up before. The laws of Terria allowed for a King to be removed from his position, but in the history of Terria, that clause had never been used.

Emlin turned toward Inca worried and distraught.

"Don't worry. It won't happen," Inca said as if reading Emlin's mind. Across the catwalk, on the far side opposite of them stood Vicham. He looked down at the audience with a look of concern and shock.

Two hours later the castle had been cleared of the mob, and King Hervott sat at the far end of a wooden table, candles sitting in the middle every few inches, and wine glasses filled to the brim at each place setting. This was not the dinner hall, but a private room that Hervott had designated as council chambers. The nine members of the Council sat around the table, each with a cigar and a glass of wine. The room stank from the odor of cigars, and the air was cloudy — each moment spent in the chambers irritated the eyes, but such was the custom.

"You're losing the faith of the people, Your Highness," Eillana said as she puffed on a much more ladylike version of a cigar, it was long and narrow and didn't quite have the same odor.

"This is troubling," she added.

"What is this true meaning of this business with the soldiers? What really happened?" Detrict asked. Detrict Thissle, once a rarely seen or heard member of the Council, he had recently decided to make his move to Terria permanent, much to the joy of King Hervott.

"I authorized General Thadeus to take some soldiers with him and hunt down a man who was traveling with the Akordans. A man capable of dark magic," Hervott replied. Whispers erupted around the table; Hervott glanced towards Vicham, who nodded in approval.

"The prophecy?" The High Mother asked. At the far end opposite from the King sat the High Mother of the Diastons. Her place on the Council had been secured due to her extreme influence with the citizens of Terria. Diastonism had, in the last few years, become the prominent religion in Terria, moving Lavaridies to second.

The Council fell silent; all eyes turned to the King.

"Yes, the necromancer. I found his new vessel and sent a team to dispose of him," Hervott replied.

"Who was it?" Lord Danston asked as he took a sip of his wine.

"It doesn't matter. What matters is, the prophecy has been prevented. The necromancer shall not return," Vicham added.

"It wasn't an easy call, but it had to be done. History could not have been allowed to repeat itself," Hervott explained. Most at the table seemed satisfied with his response. He had a point; the time of the necromancer nearly destroyed all of Furlasia. No one was interested in letting that happen again. Still, though, there was a certain questionable factor to the King's actions. Had he overstepped his bounds in ordering an assassination? Why hadn't the Council been previously notified of this theory?

"How do you know this person was the vessel?" High Mother asked, she lifted up her teacup and took a sip. "What evidence have you that you didn't condemn an innocent man?"

Proof. Hervott looked toward Thadeus, suddenly remembering he had requested the talisman be brought back. At this moment, with eyes locked onto each other, the stern general realized his mistake.

"There was a talisman. One of the three hidden by the wizard Kunklestick," Thadeus spoke up.

"Well, where is it?" The High Mother asked.

"I apologize," Thadeus said, "but it was lost during the conflict."

The High Mother took another sip of her tea and carefully set down her cup. "Pity," she replied with a grin.

Hervott stood in front of his window looking out towards the forest, the sun beginning to set painting the sky elegant streaks of pink and orange. There was comfort in the skies, a comfort that his heart needed desperately. *How had it come to this?* It seemed no matter how good or honorable his intentions, he was being met with criticism at every turn. His peace and solitude was short lived as the door to his room was thrust open and Emlin barged in like an angry storm.

"We need to talk," she demanded. A couple of guards began to run hastily toward the room in protest, but before they could reach her, the door had been shut.

"You're hiding something. You *know* something about Septus. Tell me now or so help me, I will leave this city and never return," Emlin demanded. Hervott slowly turned around. His heart was racing, and he had butterflies in his stomach and throat.

"You're right, I am. I've been keeping something from you for years. I was trying to protect you, but I see now the error in my ways," he slowly approached her. His eyes red, remorseful as ever. The burst of anger she felt when she stormed into the room seemed to fade; she hadn't expected to see her father this way. He seemed human for the first time in a long time.

"Septus didn't just leave on his own. I exiled him, there is far more to him than you could ever know," his words soft, his tone anomalous. Emlin quickly scanned the room. She spotted the royal bed and perched herself atop its luscious quilts and drew a deep breath.

"What are you talking about?" She sounded exasperated. A year of endless searching for him and her father had known all along what happened. The notion nearly made her sick. Glancing toward a sword on the wall her mind began to wander.

"Septus is the only child of the necromancer Agavordis. After the war, Kunklestick had brought him to me. I spared him, but always lived in fear of him. I feared the same darkness that dwelled within his father might dwell within him," Hervott explained.

"Once I saw how close you had become with him I panicked. Exiling him was admittedly rash, but I have lost too many who were close to my heart to risk losing you. I made a decision knowing full well what it might cost." Emlin jumped from the bed and shoved him, nearly knocking him to the floor as he bumped into a chair.

"You colossal fool!" Emlin yelled.

"Sweetie, I did it for you. To *protect* you," he countered.

"You were prepared to risk my love for you and our relationship on a hunch. On your ridiculous paranoia?" She continued to yell.

"I've lost *everyone* I've ever loved!" Hervott exclaimed. "My first born daughter Tamlin, Herratia, your mother, almost everyone I hold dear has perished into darkness." He walked over to the window and flung it open.

"Do you see that? This city and you are all that matter to me. I will protect you and it with my life," Hervott explained as he pointed toward the city center.

"At the expense of your honor? At the expense of any quality that makes you worth loving?" The words hit like a hammer on concrete, and like concrete, Hervott began to feel the cracking. It was clear his actions had in fact caused all his fears to be realized. He was the bringer of destruction. He questioned his very fabric, everything about him seemed false. The cracks continued to spread with each passing moment, Emlin's hateful glare causing them to further consume him. *How can love steer a man so wrong?*

"You had him killed didn't you? Broli and I found the massacre; we saw the carnage your soldiers left behind," Emlin's demands, her resentful tone had become too much. Each passing moment he could feel his vision blurring, his daughter beginning to becloud before him. He could find no words to respond, just a nod. A nod of admittance, an admittance of guilt, of murder.

"Well, congratulations, Dwennon. Your actions may have just cost you the last two things you hold dear," she declared. *May have?* He thought to himself.

"Oh, don't mistake, you've lost *me*. That much you surely knew. But on top of that. You may very well lose the city you hold so close to your heart. How appropriate it would be. For your paranoia to finally leave you with nothing."

With that, she stormed toward the door. The cracks had spread too far; the cloudiness had become too thick. He hit the floor with a thud, the impact to his head nearly knocking him unconscious. Emlin stopped and looked toward her father, who lay on the floor in a slump.

"Pathetic," she whispered. With that, she opened the door and stormed out, slamming it behind her.

Chapter 23

Nikalas lingered behind his elderly teacher as they followed a jagged path along the river. The current was strong, its sounds relaxing. Still, though, he could feel exhaustion setting in. His legs demanded a rest. Fawn sat perched on his shoulders, enjoying the free ride and chirping every so often. *Must be nice,* he thought. The further along the path they continued, the louder the sound of the current got until it was clear they were nearing a waterfall. No longer flat, the trail had become a hill — and a steep one at that, filled with loose rocks, each one hoping to trip you. Kunklestick kept his weight pressed against his staff as he climbed his way up the perilous path. The rushing of the water and the splash of the waterfall filled the air with its static-like roar. It wasn't a pleasant sound, at least not to Nikalas' ears.

Kunklestick came to a stop as he reached the top of the hill and looked down toward Nikalas, who still struggled with each passing step. He smiled and shook his head as he patiently waited.

"I won't say anything," Kunklestick smiled as Nikalas finally reached the top.

"Shut up," Nikalas replied. "We don't exactly have a lot of waterfalls where I come from."

"Oh, certainly," Kunklestick chuckled. "You clearly are just out of practice."

"Yeah," Nikalas replied. "So what are we doing up here?"

Kunklestick pushed the question aside and began walking towards the river. Running conveniently just across the near edge of the waterfall was a narrow rock, just wide enough to walk on. The water passed around it rather than over it. Nikalas could feel his heart racing, concern filling him as his old teacher navigated onto the rocky surface. He turned and motioned for Nikalas to follow, he hesitated at the idea, everything about this seeming like a bad idea.

"Don't be a coward," Kunklestick taunted. Nikalas shrugged and slowly made his way across the rock path.

"Why are we standing on the edge of a waterfall?" Nikalas asked as he looked over the edge. "A very *large* waterfall," he added.

Kunklestick compressed his staff into wand form and placed it carefully inside his robe. There was a small slot made just for holding wands located on the left side of the inner robe.

"We're going to jump off," Kunklestick replied.

"Have you lost your mind? You're quite old, so I wouldn't put it past you," Nikalas laughed. His mentor did not share in this merriment. His face remained serious.

"You're *not* joking are you?" He added.

"No," his mentor replied. "Training is no time for comedy."

Nikalas looked over the edge once again, this time taking in the sights. The river was precarious—sharp rocks littered the riverbed, some of them even emerging out of the water. The current was strong and ferocious. Surely, if the rocks didn't kill you, the current would.

"I'm not jumping off this waterfall. If the fall doesn't kill us, the rocks surely will," Nikalas argued.

"You're not going to touch the water or the rocks," Kunklestick replied. "Using some of the energy from *The Echo*, you are going to create a temporary stasis bubble around yourself, one that will give you shelter and protection just long enough to save your life."

"How do I do that?" Nikalas questioned.

"It's quite simple. You just need to clear your head and focus on your goal. That is the trick; clearing your mind in the face of danger, using your focus to access your energy. It's the single most important thing you could learn. Once you learn to harness some of that energy for yourself, there is no telling what feats you might be capable of," he replied.

"Close your eyes," Kunklestick instructed. Nikalas sighed and did as told, the world became dark. Nothing but the static of the waterfall remained.

"You're alone in your thoughts. There is nothing except you and the water. There is no necromancer; there are no rocks, no threat of death lingering over you. Take a deep breath and hold." Nikalas followed the instructions as best as he could. There was something very tranquil about the exercise. The stress did seem to fade away with each passing breath.

"Is your mind clear?" Kunklestick asked. Nikalas continued to hold his eyes shut while nodding. "Good. Now jump as high as you can and imagine being submerged in a bubble."

With his eyes shut, he did as he was told, skepticism filling his thoughts. To his surprise, his feet didn't land on the ground as he expected. He promptly opened his eyes.

"Holy shit! I'm doing it!" Nikalas laughed as he continued to hover ever so slightly above the rock ledge.

"Very good, Nikalas. Very good. See? I told you. With focus and connection to *The Echo* there is no telling what you can do."

Suspended in midair Nikalas looked around, toward the sky, toward the trees. There was something, a *feeling*. Like he could hear the words whispered by the winds, hear the trees begging for rain, eavesdrop on the birds making plans for the day. His focus remained steadfast, his stasis lasting longer than even Kunklestick imagined — three minutes in total, before he landed softly back onto the rock.

"Excellent, Nikalas. In all my years of training, I've never seen any student pick that up so quickly. That is very encouraging indeed. Now comes the real test, can you maintain that level of connection under duress? Can you tune out fear and distraction?" Kunklestick peered over the edge of the waterfall.

"Let it all go. Don't grab fear's hand. If you do, you'll struggle to shake free of its grip. When fear tries to offer you its embrace, turn it away. Do you understand?" Kunklestick explained.

"I think so," Nikalas replied, his tone sounding about as confident as his words. Without a moment's notice, Kunklestick jumped forthwith from the safety of the ledge, down he plunged, toward the recess of the hungry waterfall. Nikalas gasped at the suddenness of his mentor's actions. There was no splash, just the continual static of the waterfall.

"He expects me to do that, huh?" Nikalas muttered to himself. Stretching his arms and cracking his knuckles he continued to look over the ledge.

"You probably shouldn't be here for this part," he said, looking at Fawn. As he held up his finger, Fawn chirped and stepped aboard. "Wait for me by the river," Nikalas instructed as he tossed his pet into the air. The tiny Grimwort began rapidly flapping its wings as it headed back down the steep hill. As the creature disappeared from view, he turned his focus once again to the task at hand.

"Can I trust this old fool?" He said aloud. "*Should* I trust him?" He leaned his neck toward the right; there was a slight popping sound, and he repeated the action on the left side.

"Here goes nothing!" Nikalas yelled, and at that moment he lunged from the safety of the ledge. The wind rushed through his hair, splashes of water littered his uniform. He reached for his focus, attempting to grab onto the connection he had just had with the world around him. Images from the necromancer rushed into his mind, his words filling his mental cavity with fear and terror. In his mind, a large hand crept toward him, its index finger waving toward him, *summoning* him. He pushed it away. Emlin's river of blood flowed toward the temple. Nasliegh Keep crumbled to the ground, the rubble crushing the skulls of the slain. The hand returned, this time grabbing him in its grip. His mind screamed and his body remained imprisoned in its grip.

The water was piercingly cold; the impact sent a shockwave into his mind. He had gotten lucky and avoided the numerous sharp rocks, but still the current had gripped him.

"Help!" He cried out. Each moment in the water, his nerves felt seared. He trembled, the bitterness having its way with him. Just as he considered giving up, letting the current emerge victorious, he felt himself lifting from the icy water. On the shoreline stood Kunklestick, his eyes closed and staff in hand. Under his breath, he was whispering, a streak of white energy emerging from the top of the staff and making its way toward him. The stasis bubble continued to carry him to safety, as it reached the shore it hovered in front of Kunklestick, the elderly man shook his head and released his control of the bubble. Nikalas fell to the ground, shivering, drenched and humiliated.

"Do not fret, I didn't expect you to pull it off your first try," Kunklestick said as he offered Nikalas a hand.

"You let me nearly kill myself," Nikalas exclaimed. "Are you insane? What good am I going to be to anyone if I crack my skull open against a rock?"

"What happened? Why did you lose your focus?" Kunklestick asked.

"It was him; he's been haunting my mind since you brought me to that awful place. His words hold onto me and won't let go," Nikalas replied. Kunklestick nodded in understanding. Indeed, he had noticed the restless nights, the cries of terror and dark circles forming under his student's eyes. Something needed to be done. If Nikalas didn't learn to purge the darkness from his mind, he would surely be consumed by it.

"I apologize, Nikalas, to be fair, though, your life was never in any danger. I wouldn't allow you to risk your life," Kunklestick replied. "Let us return to the hall and continue our lessons there."

Nikalas groaned and did little to hide his antipathy toward his mentor as he pulled himself together. Kunklestick took notice of the expression, paying it no mind — there was little to be accomplished from an argument. There was no time to waste. Disagreements and anger were a luxury they didn't have time for. Leaning on his staff, he began the journey back toward the Hall of Wizards. Nikalas pursed his lips and did his best to whistle. It was weak, but got the point across. Fawn chirped and quickly fluttered his wings until at last he had perched himself atop his master. With Fawn in place, Nikalas trailed behind his mentor, cursing under his breath as he looked back toward the river that had nearly consumed him.

Chapter 24

Vicham maintained a safe distance—twenty paces back—as he trailed the scoundrel known as Wort through the streets of Terria. King Hervott himself had requested that a watchful eye be kept on this meddlesome instigator. There had to be an agenda to Wort's actions, his sudden turn from village drunk to insurgent seemed too random, something else was going on, that much was clear. The goal of today's pursuit was to determine whether or not Wort was working alone. There were plenty of citizens populating the streets to make pursuing Wort that much easier. Anytime he felt the slightest chance he might get caught, he would approach a crowd and pretend to be engaged in conversation.

It wasn't too long before they had migrated all the way to the shopping district of Terria. Here, one could find tailors, bakers, butchers and trinket makers. His gaze remained fixed as he quickly sat on a bench between two strangers. Wort had paused in his tracks and turned, paranoid or just surveying the area he had come quite close to catching a glimpse of his stalker. Once Wort continued on his way, Vicham quickly jumped to his feet and resumed his pursuit.

Cornlee's Bakery lay ahead, just on the far right side of the street next to the largest bank in Terria. Cornlee's was one of the more modest bakeries in Terria, it was rarely ever crowded, but it did have a following—once they managed to attract a new customer they usually had them hooked. Wort pulled open the door to the bakery and stepped inside. Through the glass window, Vicham continued to observe. Wort seemed disinterested in any of the baked goods; he merely wandered around in circles until a man draped in a black hood emerged from behind a curtain and summoned him.

"Now, what's that all about?" Vicham whispered to himself. He wasted no time in barging into the bakery, a small bell rung to alert the staff to his presence. Fresh meats and cheeses filled the air with a smoky, earthy smell. Sweet rolls fresh from the ovens added a touch of sweetness. It was all he could do to keep his stomach from growling as the aromas fought their way into his senses.

"Can I help you, sir?" An elderly woman asked from behind the counter.

"Yes, I'm on official business from the King, he's taken an interest in certain shops throughout the city, there have been sanitary concerns with several places, an alarming number of people have been turning up in the infirmary. I wonder if it wouldn't be too much trouble if I check on the condition of your back room. Just as a caution. I'm sure everything is fine — once I take a quick peek, I'll cross this place off my list of possible offenders and be on my way," Vicham replied. *Not bad,* he thought to himself. The entire story had of course been false, but he needed to get behind that curtain, Wort was up to something, he was positive.

"Well, generally speaking, we don't let customers back there," the old woman paused. "But seeing as you're on official King's business, I see no problem. All should be in order. I run a pretty tight ship."

"I expect as much," Vicham replied as he made his way toward the curtain. "May I?" He asked, gesturing one last time toward the back. The elderly woman nodded and started wiping down the counter.

There wasn't much of interest to be seen behind the curtain. Nothing but a large table covered in flour. An outsized stove, extremely hot and covered with pots of boiling water. A hefty tub stacked with dishes waiting to be scrubbed, and ropes upon ropes of dried meats. Everything looked to be in order—except for the fact that Wort was missing. There was no sign of him, nor the hooded figure. Vicham scanned the room, opening cupboards, peeking under the table. No sign of Wort.

There was a wooden door next to the pantry that led to the alleyway behind the shops. He hurried and pulled it open. Trying his best to be sneaky he poked his head just ever so slightly out from inside the doorway. The alley was empty apart from some trash and a couple of small children digging through it. Closing the door behind him, he started aimlessly wandering the alleys, with no particular goal or sense of direction. Wort had played a trick; he was sneaky. As he wandered the alley, he began to tug on the handles to random doors. Most were locked, but near the end of the alley just before it became a street again, he discovered a door that was unlocked, in fact, it wasn't even sealed shut.

"Here goes nothing," he whispered as he pushed the door open. He found himself in yet another back room, this one belonging to a tailor. There were several young ladies sitting at tables, all with fabric and needles in front of them. As he stepped into the room, a couple of them ceased their stitching. Most, however, paid him no mind whatsoever.

"Don't mind me, ladies," he said as he began curiously exploring the back room. In the distance, he could hear a pair of voices, one he was unfamiliar with but the other was most certainly Wort. Both voices were muffled, as if behind a door. He wandered towards the front of the shop; there was a well-dressed man standing behind a counter, he was positively pulchritudinous, with his slick hair and perfect posture. Once again, there was no sign of his mark, though; Wort was nowhere to be seen.

"What are you doing back there?" The man suspiciously asked.

"Is there another room back here? I'm on official King's business. I am tracking a criminal, and I believe they came into this shop," Vicham replied.

"There is nothing back there but what you see," the man replied. "Where is your identification? How do I know you're with the King?" Vicham gawked at the man with confusion. It honestly came as a shock that he still had to defend his position in the kingdom. He was the King's oldest friend and most trusted advisor; he was by his side at nearly every public occasion. For someone not to realize who he was, was truly puzzling.

Vicham ignored the question and returned to the back room. He had no time to be explaining himself. A large cabinet grabbed his attention. *Could it be?* It was heavy and cumbersome, but he managed to slide it aside, his suspicions seemed founded, standing in the darkness of the secret room was Wort, all by himself, though, no hooded figure in sight.

"Ah, Vicham, the King's royal dog. What brings you here?" Wort asked. He wore a guilty expression despite his attempt to play cool.

"Who were you talking to Wort?" Vicham asked as he stepped into the room. There was almost nothing to the room; there were a few stools and some drawings on a desk and the wall behind it. Wort stood just in front of them, distorting his view.

"Hanrae," Wort corrected. "And I haven't been talking to anyone. I'm merely back here working on some of my private studies. I'm hoping to become an official representative of the Diastons, but first, I must pass a very meticulous test. This back room, volunteered by my good friend Roger has been rather useful in having a private place to study and focus."

Vicham took a few steps closer to Wort.

"I saw you with a man," Vicham replied. "A man hidden by a dark hood." Wort skeptically shook his head.

"You must be seeing things then," he coyly replied with a grin.

"Sir?" A voice suddenly said from behind. "You are not permitted in this area. I have asked you for identification, and you've provided me none. Now I'm going to have to ask you to leave," Roger, the man from the front demanded. Behind him stood the women who had been previously sewing. They had since replaced their sewing needles with daggers. Vicham took a deep breath as he looked around. *What is going on?*

There was nothing he could do, but graciously bow and make his way past Roger and his armed seamstresses. Roger shot him a threatening glance as he passed by, the ladies all did the same. He gulped as he cleared the doorway and darted straight for the main exit.

"Dobus dulu crum," Wort whispered, his words were faint but Vicham could just make them out. He paused for a moment in front of the door, hoping to hear a bit more, but Wort had gone silent. As Roger came around the corner, Vicham quickly thrust open the door and darted into the streets.

Colonel Sabasio stood dressed in his best uniform in front of a mirror. His hair slicked to the side and his face freshly shaved. Today was the day; it was time to begin training the new recruits. Training was always stimulating to him — bringing in young minds and teaching them the tricks of the trade was a rewarding experience. Their job was important, Vanguards protected not just Terria. Together with the other armies, they helped protect Furlasia. They had been fortunate to have pleasant relationships with the two other armies. There was a time, many years ago when the three kings fought for control of the land, but that battle had since ended. They had Agavordis to thank for that.

Recruitment for the Vanguards was generally once a year, however, with rising Akordan attacks — not to mention the recent skirmish that ended in bloodshed — the Council had voted to add an extra recruitment phase to please the people.

The selection process was pretty straightforward, as a boy hit the age of fourteen he was eligible to volunteer. There was no draft; there was never any need for it. The army was mostly well stocked. There hadn't been a war in twenty years, and at this point, the soldier's main purpose was to police the city and the surrounding area.

Training happened in three phases. Phase one: mental manipulation by use of extreme force or torment. This was the phase that weeded out the ones meant to be warriors from the boys. Phase two: physical conditioning and combat training. It was this phase where their body was built to take pain, punishment, and abuse. Here, they also learned how to use the Beacons. Phase three was a newer part of the program; the recruits would take a journey and meet at a designated battleground in Morlay. There they would spar against the new Iron Soldiers of Morlay. Sabasio was only in charge of the first two phases. After that, General Thadeus took over. He got to have all the fun.

The sun was at its peak as he exited his office and made his way down the halls of the barracks. King Hervott had spared no expense when it came to Terria's armed forces; the barracks were enormous, capable of housing five thousand men if need be. The Vanguard army was not quite that size, however. In fact, it was nearly half that amount. But perhaps they would finally fill that quota. He pushed open the squeaky door to the main yard to be greeted by the familiar sight of one hundred boys, all in uniform and eager to learn. As the breeze hit his lips, he took a deep breath and sighed. *I live for this.*

"Your mother is dead, your father is dead, your siblings are dead. You have nothing; you have no one except the man standing next to you. You can forget ever having a family of your own. Vanguard soldiers are the most important people in Terria. They swear away everything that a person could want or desire in life in service of protecting this great city. You love no one; you protect *everyone.* When you are finished with phase one, you will either be a soulless soldier who will fall on a sword if I ask him to, or you will be back in your mother's arms, crying about how you're a failure," Sabasio preached with the most disheartening tone that he could. It seemed to work. His words had certainly got more than a few drops of sweat out of the recruits.

"As long as you're under my training, I will consider you to be my enemy who wants to do me harm. If you do anything I don't like, there is a fair chance I could take it as an act of aggression, and I will end you in self-defense. I will tell your families they raised useless piles of shit, and that you died in a cowardly way. Are we all clear about what I want?" Sabasio demanded.

"Sir! Yes, sir," they chanted together. One however, did not. Instead, he let tears roll down his cheeks. *Big mistake.* Sabasio swiftly approached and looked him over with a smug look of dissatisfaction.

"Why don't you get the hell off my field?" He nodded toward the back gate that led to the city. "Does this look like a nursery? We don't have space for babies in the Vanguard army." The boy was young—clearly the minimum age. Acne had taken over his skin; as the tears passed over the numerous red blemishes they turned blood red. It was repulsive. It was all Sabasio could do to keep from vomiting in disgust.

"I said get the hell off my field!" Sabasio yelled. The boy remained steadfast, keeping his posture while still tearing up. *My first successful recruit,* he thought to himself. Crying was not a sign of weakness—at least not in his eyes. A recruit that cried showed vulnerability and compassion, which is something any fair and balanced authority figure needed. The very fact that he remained standing in the face of all the insults implied strength and determination. He was the perfect recruit, despite his hideous acne.

"All right, our first exercise is called face slaps, and yes, it's exactly what it sounds like. Pair up," he ordered. Quickly the recruits broke their formation and got into pairs. All but the acne infested boy had a partner; there were an odd number of applicants this time around. He would have to be paired with Sabasio.

"Who knows how this exercise works?" He asked aloud. A single hand rose into the air, likely related to another Vanguard soldier. "Speak."

"Sir, the object of this exercise is to get your partner to cry and surrender. Anyone on the field caught crying, or those who give up, go home failures," a square-jawedyoung boy answered.

"I couldn't have put it better myself," Sabasio replied. He began to march in between the groups of boys, eyeing each one of them with skepticism.

"You there, pimple boy," he called out. The acne-infested crier looked toward him, his cheeks red with humiliation. "There are an uneven number of recruits here, and you have no partner. You'll have to be with me." The boy gulped. Sabasio grinned and approached, coming to a stop directly across from him.

Without as much as a word, he slapped the boy across the face as hard as he could — the thud could be heard across the whole crowd. The boy remained firm, barely even flinching.

"Begin," he called out. Within seconds the field was filled with the sounds of a hundred slaps, all echoing together and creating a hurricane of chaotic sound. *Music to my ears.*

Thadeus sat in his excellently crafted and overly decorated desk chair as he sat across listening to Vicham. The man was annoying, a bore and a boy lover yet for some reason he was in the King's good graces, so here he sat listening to him when he'd rather be doing almost anything.

"So you found him in a back room whispering to himself?" Thadeus asked, he felt tempted to roll his eyes, but was concerned the gesture would become a big ordeal. It was best to hold it in.

"He wasn't alone; I don't know where the other person went, but there was someone else with him. I'm sure of it," Vicham explained. Thadeus sighed and grabbed a piece of paper and began to scribble some thoughts down with his quill.

"So after the tailor and all the women threatened you with daggers you waltzed out. That was it?" Thadeus asked. If he sounded sarcastic, it was by intention. This wasn't of any interest to him. Wort was nothing more than a drunk; he was hardly a threat. It would likely be only a matter of days before he was back in the dungeon for public drunkenness again.

"Dobus dulu crum," Vicham replied. Thadeus ceased his scribbling and looked up. His interest was mildly piqued.

"What did you say?" He asked.

"Dobus dulu crum," Vicham repeated. "Wort whispered that just as I was leaving." Thadeus scribbled the words down and looked up with a smile.

"Do you know what it means?"

"It sounds like garbage," Thadeus replied. "But I'll look into it." A knock on the door broke the tension. "Come in!" He called out. The door flung open and in the doorway stood Colonel Sabasio, his cheeks red and a smile on his face.

"You look like you've been pissing off the ladies at the brothel again," Thadeus laughed.

"There were an uneven number of recruits," Sabasio explained. "I'm not interrupting am I?"

"Oh no, I think we're done here," Thadeus replied. "We are done here, right Vicham?" Vicham nodded and stood from his chair.

"Let me know what you find out. I'll continue to look into things on my end," Vicham said, nodding slightly.

"Hey, no problem, we are in this together," Thadeus smiled as Vicham exited the room. Once the door had closed, he let out a sigh of relief.

"I *hate* that guy."

Chapter 25

The day was early, and the sun was doing its best to greet the day with beauty. Its light painted the sky with shades of tangerine and fuschia. Nikalas and Kunklestick stood side by side looking down into a large quarry. The quarry was massive; its depth nearing half a mile. At its bottom sat a small lake, the water dark as tar. Morning dew filled the air with beads of water that fell to the ground. Time appeared to be moving slower, and as the sun hit the beads they lit up creating hundreds of miniature specs of light.

"What is this?" Nikalas asked as he waved his hand curiously amongst the beads, with each pass his palms getting moist.

"It's just dew," Kunklestick replied.

"I've never seen dew look like that before," Nikalas retorted.

"Well, normally it doesn't. There's something about the quarry that causes time to move slower for the area surrounding it. It's a spectacular effect, and a blessing most in Furlasia will never witness. One of the many reasons to get your day started early. It's impossible to see this and not feel an immediate rush of relaxation, it does wonders for clearing the mind of stress or whatever else weighs your mind down," Kunklestick explained.

"Ah, so that's the point of all this," Nikalas realized. "You're trying to help me clear my mind."

"Uh, yeah, you're right," Kunklestick coyly replied. "You caught me." The simple truth was he rather enjoyed the view. His mind was just as weighed down by stress as Nikalas'.

Coming here in the mornings was *his* private therapy. No, for the issue of Nikalas' focus he had a much more interesting plan.

They continued to observe the prodigious effect for a few more minutes, both of them remained silent, captured in the moment like a portrait. As the sun continued its ascent into the sky, the effect finally faded. The morning dew had dried under the delicate morning rays.

"How do you feel?" Kunklestick asked, glancing toward Nikalas. His pupil still seemed to be captured in the euphoric feeling brought on by the marvel of the dew.

"I feel good, I'm ready," he replied.

"Excellent," Kunklestick replied. In his hands, he carried a large, cream colored burlap sack. He plunged his arms inside and began to rummage around; *tings* and *tangs* could be heard from the numerous contents bumping into each other. Eventually, he withdrew his hand. In it, he held a small gray ball, reminiscent of a rock. He smiled as he looked it over and then held it up towards Nikalas.

"Any idea what this is?" He asked.

"Looks like a rock," Nikalas replied, as he reached out to touch the object Kunklestick quickly pulled back.

"This is no rock, my boy," he retorted, almost sounding offended. "This is an *Elephas*."

"What's an *Elephas*?" Nikalas asked.

"This my friend is how we are going to help you learn to use magic under duress. This is used in focus training. It's highly effective. As you recall, the reason you failed your waterfall jump was because the moment you were in free fall, dark thoughts came to you and you couldn't focus. If you can't focus, you can't access your powers. A wizard who can't use his powers in extreme circumstances isn't much of a wizard. Enter the *Elephas*. It's been used for hundreds of years to train young wizards like yourself," Kunklestick explained.

"How does it work?" Nikalas asked, continuing to glare at the strange object.

"Once I activate it, the *Elephas* is going to come after you, trying to hit you. Using the same focus I asked you to demonstrate at the waterfall, you are going to repel this away from you," Nikalas gulped, the idea didn't sound like the most pleasant. It sounded rather painful.

"So, stand over there. Let's give this a try." Nikalas sighed and did as he was told. There were now at least fifty feet between him and his mentor.

With his arm outstretched Kunklestick whispered something and let go of the *Elephas*. The object remained hovering in the air.

"Ready your wand," he instructed. Taking yet another deep breath, he reached inside his uniform and pulled out a small black wand, he had been given it a few days ago and had yet to be asked to use it; this was the first time. With his hands shaking, he lifted the wand and aimed it toward the *Elephas*.

"Remember. Clear your mind, focus on your objective — stopping the *Elephas*. Nothing else matters," his focus on Nikalas remained steadfast.

"Zimmen semo," Kunklestick proclaimed.

At that moment, the *Elephas* darted toward Nikalas with alarming speed. It hit him square in the chest, knocking him to the ground. Nikalas hollered in pain and began to cough — the impact had knocked the wind right out of him. In the dirt he lay, chest throbbing, filled with anger. Kunklestick held out his hand and the *Elephas* promptly returned to his grip.

"Again," he instructed. Nikalas slowly climbed to his feet, eyes red with anger.

"That fricken hurt!" He yelled.

"All the more reason to not let it hit you," Kunklestick mercilessly replied. Nikalas returned to his starting position, his wand raised again. This time, his anger would be his tool.

"Zimmen semo," Kunklestick called out. As before, the *Elephas* briskly darted towards him. This time, it was aiming not for his chest but his legs. Before he could react, Nikalas found himself on the ground looking up toward the sky, a throbbing sensation in his left leg. *At least the sky looks nice,* he thought to himself.

"What is going on Nikalas?" Kunklestick questioned. "I thought you had cleared your mind."

"It moves too fast," he retorted.

"The speed of the *Elephas* is irrelevant. If you are focused, tuned into your powers you will be able to stop any object, regardless of speed." He returned the Elephas to the burlap sack and approached his pupil who still lay in the dirt looking pathetic as ever.

"Perhaps I made the wrong assumption about you," he said looking down at Nikalas. "Maybe you aren't the one I prophesied about."

"Yeah, maybe not," Nikalas retorted.

"Very well then. Let's not waste anymore of the other's time. If I indeed did make a mistake, then I've already lost valuable time. I'll need to begin searching for the proper student at once." With that, he stormed toward the hall.

Nikalas sat up and watched as the figure of the old man continued to shrink in the horizon until at last he was alone with naught but his thoughts and Fawn. As he climbed to his feet, he looked around. In the distance, he could see smoke rising from Morlay, clouds lingering around the Hills of Edmere and a calm breeze blowing through the blades of grass.

Slowly he limped his way back to the hall, each step came with a sharp burst of pain. *This is ridiculous,* he thought to himself. *I should never have come here.* As he stepped into the hall, he peeked around. Kunklestick was nowhere in sight. He was in no position to begin his journey back to Terria; for starters, he had no idea how to get back. He dreaded the awkward conversation of explaining to Emlin that he'd had to give up. And then there was the matter of getting back to his own world. There was apparently no possibility of that happening anytime soon.

His room was just as he had left it, cluttered and scattered with grimy undergarments. Light was trying to sneak its way around the small curtain, in its rays all the dust in the room could be seen delicately floating like insects. He pulled the curtain shut, blocking out the light and eliminating his floating companions. Fawn climbed onto his makeshift bed and nestled up for a nap. As he tossed himself into bed, Nikalas looked to the ceiling and began to drift.

Kunklestick sat in a large red armchair with a pipe in one hand and a glass of wine in another. His focus was fixed on a painting that hung on a wall next to his bookshelf. In the painting, he stood with his arm around a younger man, whose hair was blond and skin was pale. They both wore ear to ear smiles in front of a backdrop of rolling hills. As he continued to stare at the painting, a single tear rolled down his cheek. He took a large gulp and finished the last of the wine. With his head tilted toward the ceiling, he found himself staring at a cup that was bone dry. On the stand next to him was a bottle, he grabbed it and refilled his glass to the near brim.

Just as he began to bring the cup to his lips, he noticed his shewglomus blinking, its light casting a shadow on the ceiling.

"Kunklestick are you there?" A voice asked. It was King Hervott of Terria; he sounded distressed. He carefully sat the glass down and approached the dresser.

"What is it?" He asked, standing just over the shewglomus.

"How is the training going? How is Nikalas doing?" Hervott asked. Kunklestick let out a sigh.

"The boy won't focus. I've seen no evidence so far that he is the one I am meant to train," he replied.

"He *is* the one Kunklestick. I know it," Hervott replied.

"How?"

"You and I both know he is. Learning to focus is the hardest step in learning magic. You know that better than most." There was truth to his words, after the war. After the death of his friends, Kunklestick had become so overridden with grief he had lost his ability to use his powers. His mind wouldn't let him, be it the fact that he chased his pains away with wine or the fact that his mind was overly clouded; it had taken him a long while to gain back his powers.

"Things are getting rocky in Terria. Big changes may soon be approaching."

"What do you mean?" Kunklestick asked. "Why do you sound distressed?"

The sound of a knock at the door disrupted the conversation, it came from the shewglomus.

"I have to go," Hervott abruptly said. The light in the shewglomus faded, Kunklestick stood dumbfounded with his focus still fixed on the small glass orb.

"You can't defeat me, boy. You'll never be rid of me," the shadow figure said. Nikalas stood on the edge of a cliff, his back facing a treacherous drop and in front of him stood the shadow of Agavordis. His eyes glowed red and in his hands he held a mace covered in spikes nearly two inches long. Nikalas stood armed with his staff; its top glowed blue, and around him there was an aura of blue light.

"You don't scare me. You were beaten once; you'll be beaten again. This time, not even your memory will survive," Nikalas retorted. The shadow growled and charged at Nikalas with a furious rage. Nikalas quickly lifted the staff and brought it across the face of the shadow. The impact sounded like thunder and sparks flew about. The shadow cried in pain before stumbling to the edge of the mountain, feet barely secured to the ground.

"Your time is near, your death is inevitable," the shadow threatened.

"We'll see about that," Nikalas replied. With that, he thrust the top of the staff into the necromancer. Once again sparks flew about, and a thunderous clap filled the air. The shadow was sent flying from the edge. It screamed all the way down until it crashed into the rocks below. An explosion rippled into the air. The darkness that had filled his mind began to clear. Sunlight and green grass pushed back the shadows and the sharp rocks.

He shot up in his bed, still catching his breath. It had felt so real, and perhaps it was. He felt a new burst of energy, one he hadn't felt since the nightmares started. He had driven Agavordis from his dreams, defeated him with magic. It had to be real; it sure felt like it. Quickly, he jumped from his bed, his feet hitting the cold floor.

"Kunklestick," he exclaimed to Fawn, who sat up and cocked his head.

"I have to tell Kunklestick. I beat him. My mind is clear."

His joy was hard to contain as he darted from his room and down the hall toward the red double doors. He grabbed the handle and gave it a lift. The lock clicked as the handle was lifted. On the floor lay Kunklestick. Next to him a broken glass and a small puddle of spilled wine. He quickly ran inside and began to frantically shake the old man.

"Kunklestick, wake up," Nikalas pleaded. His gentle shaking became more aggressive with each lack of response. The old man groaned and whimpered, but his eyes remained shut.

"What's wrong?" Nikalas asked as he continued to rock his mentor back and forth. There was no use; he wouldn't wake. Nikalas exasperatedly began to gather up the pieces of loose glass, once he discarded of them, he turned his focus to cleaning up the spilled wine. Kunklestick continued to lie there, his whimpering unrelenting. For all the confidence and sanguine charm Kunklestick tried to display, at this particular moment he looked like no more than one of the many drunk bums littering the street of Detroit. Pip had tried mentioning that Kunklestick was living with heavy grief. He hadn't expected to see if for himself, perhaps it was inappropriate for him to have let himself into his mentor's quarters. He grabbed a blanket from atop of the bed and lay it down across his drunken mentor.

"Tomorrow's a new day," he told himself. "Tomorrow's a new day."

Chapter 26

Pip sat on an outdoor bench with a book in his hand. Its pages were blank; it was not a book to read, but rather a book to write in, a journal. In his hand, he gripped a magical device that Arnouts had come up with to make it so that they never ran out of ink. In his diary, he wrote his thoughts, his dreams, his regrets, his ambitions, his love for Vicham. It was all within the pages, as soon as he was not the one touching its cover; the letters all faded leaving a book with nothing but blank pages. One of the many enchantments he had placed on his possessions.

It had been nearly a month since he last seen his Vicham. Each day felt so long, each day *hurt*. The pain of loneliness was not able to be filled by activities; there was no activity he could find that would replace the need for love. For so long he had tried to remain positive about the situation. There wasn't much that could be done after all. They lived in two different worlds; they were two different *species* even. They both had heavy burdens placed upon their heads. He was heir to the throne of Cristol and Vicham was arguably one of the most influential people in Terria.

He sighed as he continued to scribble his notes, the cool breeze flowing from the water felt good, it blew his hair around ever so slightly. It was midday; the sun was perched just above Eiraf Palace, the small rainbows floated through the air, a result of the prismatic quality of the water. It would soon be time for him to meet with his mother for tea. It was the same time each day, and each day he dreaded it. All she ever wanted to talk about was everything he was doing wrong. If she had anything nice to say it was quickly countered by a negative; there couldn't just be a positive conversation. Pip knew she loved him, that was clear even if her words didn't always show it, but still he couldn't help but hold resentment against her.

As he scribbled down the last of his thoughts, he looked at the pages, giving them a quick once over and then closed the diary. His focus turned to the water. In the distance, he could just make out the spot where he and Vicham had spent their last night together. *Mother can wait,* he thought to himself. His wings began to flutter and before long he was airborne and darting straight for the gazebo. He felt free; free of his troubles, free of his mother. Nothing could weigh him down. This was *their* place, and no one could take that away. *Vicham might not always be with me, but we will always have this place.*

As if his positive thoughts offended the gods a blaze started in the gazebo. Flames climbed higher and higher and within seconds, the whole thing was engulfed in a fiery blaze.

"What in the name of Julon!" Pip yelled out. His pace quickened, quickly he dropped to the ground, tears filling his eyes as he watched his one memory of Vicham disappear in the flames.

"It hurts, doesn't it?" A low voice said from behind the flaming gazebo. Pip abruptly looked up, from behind the flames a figure emerged wearing black robes, there was no face, it was masked by a hood.

"Watching the things you care about fall apart before your eyes?"

"Why did you do this?" Pip asked. His wings flapped and carried him to his feet, gently setting him down.

"You have something I want. And you're going to give it to me or I'm gonna do this same thing to your beloved palace," the voice replied.

"Who are you?" Pip yelled out. The figure slowly pulled back the hood, not enough to uncover the face, but the eyes. They glowed red; there was darkness in them. "You," Pip said, understanding dawning like a bolt of lightning.

"You have the talisman," the figure declared. Pip scrunched his nose in confusion.

"No, I don't," he retorted. "Why would they give it to me? I'm the last person they'd give it to."

"True, you are a fool—an ignorant boy child with no potential or ambition. You're selfish, and your mind only is concerned with your well-being. That's why having you keep it was a perfect idea. You'd guard it with your life," the figure explained.

"What are you talking about? I don't have the talisman!" Pip yelled. In that instant the figure was directly in front of him now, it grabbed him by the throat and began lifting him off the ground. Pip began coughing; the grip was strong, and he could feel each finger digging deeper and deeper into his muscles.

"Wait," Pip begged. "I'll tell you where it is."

"No need," the figure replied. At that moment, his grip around Pip's neck tightened and quickly turned. There was a loud snap and then nothing, Pip struggled no more. The figure dropped the body to the ground and ripped open his garments. There was a lump just in the middle of Pip's chest.

"Poor fool," the figure whispered. Pulling a knife from his robe he began cutting around the lump until the flesh had been pulled aside. There, covered in blood, was a silver talisman, inscriptions carved into its front plate.

The figure held up the talisman and looked at it under the bright sunlight. His eyes continued to glow red, and a grin spread across his face. He pulled off his hood. Septus, or Agavordis, as he was now calling himself carefully wiped the bloodstained talisman against his robes before placing it over his neck. He now was in possession of two; one gold and one silver. He laughed as he looked down toward the body of the slain Pip.

Chapter 27

Beads of sweat poured down his face as he darted through the fields of grass, the Elephas hot on his tail. Kunklestick was playing dirty; he had already managed to block the attack of one Elephas. After a few successful attempts, Kunklestick had decided to throw out a second. In the air behind him, there was a familiar whistle — the Elephas was near. A sudden growl in the forest grabbed his attention, his alertness of the Elephas now faded as he scanned the area for the source of the growl. Suddenly, he yelped in surprise as one of the Elephas hit him right in between his buttocks.

"Hey," Nikalas called out in surprise. Ahead of him, the second Elephas approached, it whistled through the air as it persistently made its way toward him. Nikalas raised his wand and brought it up.

"Protectus," he whispered. Around him, a bubble arose creating a bulwark of safety. As the Elephas neared, it crashed against the shield before falling to the ground.

"Beat you," Nikalas grinned as he lowered his wand. He looked down toward the inactive Elephas and reached to pick it up. That's when he heard it; there was another whistle.

"Another one?" Nikalas asked aloud. He quickly put the two inactive Elephas' into his pouch and began looking around. There was nothing in front of him, nor toward the sides. A grin spread across his face as the realization hit him. Slowly he turned around and there it was. Not one Elephas but two more in fact. They approached fast; as they neared they began zipping back and forth, an obvious attempt to confuse the student. *I wonder,*

Nikalas pondered. He quickly extended his wand into staff form and spun it in circles before driving it down into the ground. A powerful shockwave shook the area; it howled like a wolf and darted toward the two pursuing Elephas'. They were instantly pulverized and turned into rubble as the shockwave passed by.

"Damn," Nikalas whispered to himself. He approached the piles of dust and pushed his foot through them. It was difficult to resist the urge to feel smug as he looked around the area, tree bark had been ripped off, the leaves had been blown about, the whole area looked like it had been leaf blown.

"Very impressive, Nikalas," Kunklestick said as he slowly approached the area. He was leaning on his staff pretty heavily today; his steps seemed dicey as he neared.

"That was a very powerful spell you just used. Do you even know the name of it?"

Nikalas shrugged.

"*Cyliamo Sensio*, the vortex shockwave. That's not a spell taught to students; only grand master wizards use it. Interesting that you were able to conjure it so early in your training."

Nikalas nodded in satisfaction before reaching into his pockets and withdrawing the two inactive Elephas'.

"You've done very well today, Nikalas. I must say I am happily surprised," Kunklestick accepted the Elephas' and placed them back in his burlap sack.

"I notice that you turned your wand into a staff. I think it's time we discuss that. It will often be very important to know when to use which form. For each form has its advantages. For example, a spell done with a wand is typically less powerful than one done with a staff. The reason is simple, a wand is a smaller item, it can't draw as much energy. A staff can be cumbersome and inconvenient, but it can hold more energy. Do you understand?"

"So I should mostly keep it as a staff then?" Nikalas asked.

"It's more complicated than that. There are certain spells that can only be done with a wand and vice versa. I will teach you to the best of my abilities which spell is best for which form," Kunklestick replied.

"Come now; I feel now is a good time to break for lunch. You look exhausted."

"Speak for yourself," Nikalas smiled.

"Okay, *I'm* exhausted. I'm in need of some rubble juice and some food."

They began making their way back toward the hall. It wasn't far, the forest lay directly behind the hall. As they continued their walk, Nikalas stayed a few steps behind and observed—his mentor's movements still seemed shaky. *Was it his age or something else?* Memories of the night before played throughout his mind, he had found Kunklestick drunk on the floor and totally out of it. He wouldn't respond, and when questioned about it today, he had no recollection of the event.

What caused his pain? What happened to make the once great wizard from children's stories nothing more than a reclusive drunk? There was pain there, Nikalas could see it, his mentor wore the same expression that he often did. Guilt, regret, fear, Nikalas knew these words all too well. It seemed Kunklestick did too.

Once they were inside the hall, Kunklestick hobbled his way back to the kitchen. Nikalas took a seat at a table. Fawn walked back and forth from one side of the table to the other chirping and dancing. For a creature with so little going on in his life, he sure did seem chipper. *Maybe that's the key,* he thought. *Toss away your responsibilities and just live.*

It had been nearly fifteen minutes since Kunklestick disappeared to the kitchen to fetch their lunch and he had still not returned.

"You wait here," Nikalas instructed Fawn. He climbed to his feet and made his way back to the kitchen. There sat Kunklestick; he wasn't drinking, he wasn't eating, he was just looking out of a window, silent in his thoughts. As he heard Nikalas enter the room, he turned.

"Sorry Nikalas, I got distracted," he explained. Nikalas shook his head.

"No need to explain. What are you looking at?" As he neared Kunklestick, the view of the quarry came into play.

"The quarry?" Nikalas asked. Kunklestick silently nodded and continued to stare.

"Did something happen there?" He asked. Kunklestick let out a deep sigh and stood up.

"What do you say we get that lunch you were promised?" Kunklestick retorted.

"Don't change the subject," Nikalas commanded. "I found you drunk on the floor and totally unable to answer me. What happened at the quarry?"

"My boy, that quarry is where it all went wrong," Kunklestick explained. He set his staff down and began gathering up some meats and cheeses; there was also a basket of dinner rolls. Nikalas grabbed what he could, Kunklestick grabbed a goblet and a pitcher and carried it out into the main hall. As he emerged through the doorway, he nearly stepped on

Fawn, who had ignored his master's commands and was patiently waiting just outside the door.

"Get back over there," Nikalas demanded. Fawn lowered his head and let out a sigh before flying back to the table where he had been instructed to wait. As they set all the food and drinks down Nikalas began to dispense the food at two different places. Kunklestick plopped down into the head chair and poured himself a drink.

Together they ate, mostly in silence except for the occasional grunts of Kunklestick and the chirps of Fawn.

"What is rubble juice?" Nikalas asked finally breaking the silence.

"It's from a plant up in the hills. It's rare, but the juice has good benefits for old people like me," Kunklestick explained. As they finished their meal they both took part in clearing the table, this time, Kunklestick appeared to be walking a lot better.

"What do you say we head out into the town and celebrate? You've done very well today. You made this old man proud," Kunklestick gave Nikalas a cheerful pat on the back.

"Sounds awesome," Nikalas smiled. At that moment, he realized the term probably seemed odd to his mentor. "It means exciting."

"Yeah," Kunklestick replied. "I got that."

The sun had started its descent in the sky; they didn't have much light left to travel with. Luckily Morlay was only a short ride away, not to mention a very bright city. They would just need to follow the bright light in the distance, and it would be fine. Still though, the goal was to leave while still having sunlight. Kunklestick carried his staff in his hand as he walked over toward the stables to untie the horses. Nikalas took notice of the fact that he was carrying it rather than leaning on it. *Must be the rubble juice,* he thought.

Once the horses were untied Kunklestick handed Nikalas a set of reins, and they both mounted. He had never expected to feel so comfortable aboard an animal, and yet here he was, feeling like a natural. He rode on *Wildfire,* the very same horse he acquired outside of Terria. Kunklestick rode *Leddi,* an elderly gray horse that looked like she had seen a lot of action. Together, they rode the trails leading toward Morlay, mostly silent, although there was one conversation about mermaids and how they didn't exist. Nikalas shrugged in disappointment as they continued their journey.

Morlay was just ahead, its large wall loomed in the distance, it was lined with enormous torches that were placed every few feet. As they neared the entrance, a couple of guards approached and lifted their hands.

"There is no passage into Morlay tonight, "one of the guards said.

"Good gracious why? Don't you know who I am?" Kunklestick retorted.

"Of course we know who you are," the guard replied. "Doesn't matter who you are tonight. No one is getting inside of Morlay. The city is on lockdown following the tragic passing of our fair King."

"Robin? King Robin Ucertine? Dead? How? I demand you tell me at once!" Kunklestick shrieked.

"An illness took him in the night. It spread very fast. There was nothing that could be done. The city will remain sealed until Prince Linuk is sworn in."

Kunklestick quietly nodded, a disheartened look masking his face.

"There's a tavern just up that way. *Mother Margary's*, just follow the path into the forest. It's a small little place, but you can't miss it."

They quietly pulled their horses away from the gates and continued along the path as instructed. It was dark now, the air had a breeze and with it a chill. The forest was unsettling. It seemed stark — who knew what creatures lay hidden in the dark. Luckily, the ride would be short. Up ahead as promised was a small tavern with a crooked sign announcing *Mother Margary's*. Music and laughter could be heard coming from inside, happy faces moved about in the windows. Kunklestick jumped from the horse and tied both Leddi and Wildfire up. Staff in hand, he pulled open the tavern door and let the ambiance rush over him for a moment before pushing the door shut.

It was a quaint little place, very few tables, and a rather small bar. There was a grill that was smoking; on it a couple of rabbits were being flipped again and again. Seating was pretty limited, but toward the front of the tavern was a perfect small table. A red haired waitress led them to the table and set down a couple of tankards overflowing with ale. Kunklestick happily nodded before taking his seat.

He lifted the tankard to his lips and let out a big sigh before taking a large gulp.

"You knew him, huh?" Nikalas asked.

"Robin and I were friends for many years. Thirty to be precise. He was a good man and a great friend. I wish I would've known he was ill. I know a spell or two that has been known to help," he replied. Nikalas looked at the tankard of beer and shrugged. The first taste was bitter, but after a few more gulps he began to see the appeal. It was rather refreshing.

It wasn't long before they were both in need of a refill. The waitress returned to the table once again and brought the replacement tankards as she cleared away the empty ones.

"So his son will take over now, then?" Nikalas asked. Kunklestick nodded as he took a sip.

"In this instance, yes. Morlay doesn't follow the same policy of having a King's child take the throne. There is an election and a vote. I'm not surprised Prince Linuk was voted in; he has been by his father's side all his life. He knows the ins and outs of Morlay intimately," Kunklestick explained. He looked around the tavern, there were very few sad faces. Most seemed ecstatic as ever, how could everyone be so cheerful when the King had just passed?

"I heard you talking about the Prince," the red-haired waitress said as she approached the table. She was thick but not fat, pale, but not pure white, her eyes were blue like water and lips plump and red. She was young, far younger than normal bar maids back home. Her name was Zanna, and she was more than just a mere wench, she was the owner of the tavern. As such, she was prone to hearing all kinds of gossip.

"What have you heard?" Kunklestick asked. Zanna grabbed a seat and sat across from him.

"For starters, the King died four days ago. Prince Linuk has already been sworn in. That's not why the city is on lock down," Zanna explained.

"What do you mean?" Kunklestick asked.

"The city is on lockdown while an investigation is pending. The King's death was suspicious. There are questions being asked. Poison is suspected," she replied.

"How do you know all this? Who are you?"

"My name is Zanna. My brother is High Leech inside the city; he's the one who inspected the body. He said it was the most gruesome death he'd seen. There was literally a hole in the body where the heart used to be. It exploded, sometime after he ate his dinner."

She began to look around the tavern before leaning in to whisper.

"My brother was the only one to escape the city before the lockdown."

"Why? Why did he run?" Kunklestick asked, his fascination distracting him from his drink. Nikalas sat silently by observing the conversation.

"He told me just after the King passed, he saw something. Something that scared him to his core. Something *evil*," she explained, with each passing second her skin grew paler.

"What did he see?" Kunklestick asked. Precipitously something in the window behind Kunklestick grabbed her attention. It was a shadowy figure with glowing red eyes; the figure was masked in darkness.

"That," she said as she stood and pointed toward the window. A look of horror spread across her face. Kunklestick abruptly stood, hurling his chair back. His eyes fixated on the eyes in the window. Smoke started to rise slowly from the floor; the smell of burning embers crept into his senses. The flames crept from under the window. The tavern had been set ablaze.

Chapter 28

Emlin stood next to Inca outside of the entrance to the barracks. It was here where the underground dungeon was kept, here where they would find Broli. Broli had been a resident of the dungeon since returning to Terria after he and Emlin had gone on a search for Septus. Since then, she had learned the terrible truth of her father's wrongdoing and the murder of her dear friend. The time had come to free Broli; he would not spend another night in the dungeon—she would be sure of it.

The door to the barracks slowly pushed open and out stepped Thadeus, strolling slowly with not a care in the world. Emlin huffed as he approached and looked toward Inca, who simply shrugged.

"What can I do for you, Princess?" Thadeus asked. "Sabasio told me this was urgent."

"You are to free the prisoner known as Broli at once. He has done nothing wrong, and he does not belong in the dungeons," Emlin demanded. Inca looked at her consternation, in all her time knowing Emlin she had never been this forthwith.

"Easy there, Princess. You might talk to your Daddy like that, but you are not going to talk to me like that," Thadeus firmly locked eyes with Emlin. They stood engaged in a little game of intimidation until finally Emlin broke eye contact and looked to the ground. *I win,* Thadeus smiled.

"You're not in charge of determining guilt. Your father was the one who had him imprisoned. Only he can have him freed. Now if you want to drop the dramatic attitude, I can allow you to go and visit with him. In terms of just freeing him this very instant, you'll have to talk to your father." Emlin looked toward Inca, who nodded in agreement. Thadeus was brash and unpleasant; they would not accomplish much with him unless the King got involved. At the very least they could let Broli know his freedom was on its way.

"Good. I'll have Colonel Sabasio show you down there. If that's all you needed I have other work to do," he nodded and turned to walk away.

"Jeez, Emlin. When did you get so feisty?" Inca laughed. "You sound like me."

"I will take crap from no man; they've had their fun running my life. *I'm* in charge now," Emlin replied as she wiped some dust from her shoulder. Inca smiled and nodded in satisfaction. For so long Inca had always been the one to fight Emlin's personal battles. It seemed that would no longer be necessary. But if she didn't fulfill that role what good was she? Colonel Sabasio emerged from the barracks looking frustrated and impatient.

"This way to the dungeons," he said.

Thadeus sat at his desk looking over a couple of old textbooks. *Dobus dulu crum.* The words rang in his head like a migraine. Since his conversation with Vicham, he had been tirelessly reading through old texts trying to find the origin of the phrase, but so far he had learned nothing. There was something ominous to the words, he was sure of it. He had spent so many hours flipping through the pages that the words had begun to blend together, it was becoming more difficult to identify individual words, each page looked like it was simply filled with a black blob.

He wasn't alone in his venture; he had agreed to figure this mystery out in conjuncture with Vicham. Despite his personal feelings for the man, he couldn't deny his intelligence. The King was wise to keep him by his side. So far, his best guess was that it was something to do with Undr and Diastonism. Wort, after all claiming to be reformed, perhaps it was a prayer of some kind. But why the bad taste in his mouth when he uttered the words aloud?

His focus was short lived; there was panic in the streets just outside the barracks. Something was awry. He quickly slammed the book shut and grabbed his two favorite daggers and placed them in his holster. Darting down the hallway he flung open the exit and emerged onto the field. As he glanced to the right, he could see a crowd of people swarming toward the city gates.

"What now?" He whispered to himself. Like a sheep in the herd he followed the mass panic, people continued to bump into him, disregarding him. He was just a part of the flock. His uniform seemed pointless; no one bothered to acknowledge it. The city gates were wide open and a crowd had formed a circle. As he neared the edge of the circle, he began pushing his way past the citizens. In the center of the circle, lying on the ground was the remains of two bodies that looked to have been mauled by Akordans. One of them was Draxton, the blond haired friend of Emlin's. The other was a younger man, brunette and looking to be in his early twenties.

Both bodies were littered with claw marks, and each had a gash in the stomach. Intestines poured from each wound. There was panic in the streets as everyone stared at the carnage before them.

"All right everyone, standing around here is not helping anything. It's only further complicating an already stressful situation. Get back to your lives and leave this to the Vanguards," Thadeus looked around as he finished his last word. No one appeared to be moving.

"NOW!" He yelled. That did it; within seconds the crowd had begun shuffling about, within minutes the streets were back to their normal appearance. There in front of the city gates, he stood looking down at a horrible massacre. This would not play well for the King. A few minutes later a few soldiers ran to the scene, each one carrying a stretcher. The bodies were loaded, covered and would be brought to the city morgue. With the streets clear and the bodies removed Thadeus froze in deep thought. He had a bad feeling, one he couldn't explain.

"Blimey Emmy, what are you doing down here? This is no place for a Princess," Broli exclaimed as he noticed his two friends standing outside his cell.

"This is no place for an innocent man, either," Emlin responded. "How are you holding up?" Broli dubiously looked around before standing up and approaching the bars.

"Food could be better; there's no ale down here either. But not too bad besides that. Have you spoken to your father? When is this getting cleared up?" He whispered in his best whisper—which was still loud enough to be heard at the opposite end of the dungeon.

"You'll be out of here soon big guy," Inca chimed in. "I'm surprised you didn't just break these bars down and walk out." The three of them shared a chuckle; it was the first time in a long while since any of them had seen humor in the world.

"I didn't want to make the other prisoners jealous," Broli explained. "Emmy, there's a lot of prisoners down here who have been held far longer than they should be. Your father's fears of crimes are going to cause him trouble one day. It's not right how people are being treated."

"Of that, we agree. In fact, the climate out there is changing. It's looking more and more like a coup could be possible," Emlin replied.

"Really?" Broli shockingly asked. "It's gotten that bad?"

"The news is out about the massacre of the soldiers. People are not happy," Emlin explained. "There's something else," she paused for a moment, looking to the floor. She could feel the tears welling up in her eyes already.

"What is it Emmy?" Broli asked. Nothing hurt him more than seeing a woman cry; nothing got his rage flowing like the tears of a lady.

"It's Septus. My father is the reason he disappeared. He had him exiled because he and I were growing closer, and that made him nervous," she explained.

"Why?"

"Because he's the only child of Agavordis," Inca interrupted. Her feelings on the matter were decidedly different than Emlin's. Where Emlin saw a victim, Inca saw a monster. She was glad he had been killed. The world would be safer without him.

"I see; it all makes sense now. I always knew something was different about him. He seemed weighted down by something. Now we know," Broli replied.

"*What* do we know?" Emlin retorted with frustration. She quickly wiped away a few rogue tears and looked Broli in the eyes. She needed to see his eyes when he said it. She needed to see his eyes when he tried to keep a straight face and defend her father's callous actions.

"That he was dangerous. That there was *darkness* in him. One that would've led him to follow in his father's footsteps. Evil like that is a sickness. And like any disease, it's passed down through the blood. I feel bad for him; he was doomed from birth. He was a good friend, and I know you loved him. But if he had lived — with what we heard about the attack in Frand — who knows what would've happened next?" Broli let out a sigh and returned to his makeshift chair which was simply two crates stacked on each other.

Emlin stood in shock, unable to respond, unable to defend her position nor attack his. If Septus and Nikalas were indeed both parts of the prophecy, what did it mean for Nikalas now that Septus was eliminated? Was the threat over? Can fate really just be changed like that? She wiped away a few more tears and took a deep breath.

"We will get you out of here soon Broli, that much I promise," Emlin said. She nodded toward Inca, who had a look of concern on her face. A difficult emotion to pick up on in Delopar, and yet here it was clear as day. They turned as they prepared to leave.

"I'm sorry, Emmy. I really am. You know I was always happy for the two of you. Wherever he is now, I hope he's at peace. He deserves that much," Broli added. Emlin nodded and continued on her way. It was time to speak with her father. She didn't want to, she hadn't *planned* to, but Broli's freedom depended on it. Furthermore, she was having regrets about their last conversation. Inca and Broli had gotten into her mind. She was starting to believe they were right about the outcome with Septus. Did that make her any worse than her father? Where does one draw the line between defense of someone you love and cold-blooded murder? This seemed right on the border, but she seemed to be the only one to think so.

As they climbed the ladder from the dungeons, they caught a glimpse of a mob of people that had begun to disperse. Inca turned to Emlin.

"I wonder what that was about?" Inca asked. Emlin shrugged, her energy for mystery had been spent. Whatever the crowd had gathered for she felt confident she would know soon enough.

Chapter 29

King Hervott and Vicham sat in the King's quarters flipping through old textbooks they had borrowed from the library. The goal, find the meaning behind that strange phrase. So far they couldn't find any mentions of that exact phrase, but Vicham felt confident the answer would soon be upon them. How hard could it be to decipher a foreign language after all?

Two hours into reading and they still had turned up nothing. The answer, it seemed, was more difficult to come up with than either of them could've imagined. Hervott could feel the strain from all the reading taking its toll on his eyes.

"Let's take a break," he said, breaking the silence. Vicham looked up from his reading, glasses on his face and smiled.

"Excellent idea, sir," Vicham replied. It was at that moment that a knock on the door interrupted their plans. Hervott glanced to Vicham, who nodded in response and then jumped up. His face was plain, and his eyes were tired, as he pulled open the door he was greeted by Thadeus.

"Thadeus? What brings you to the King's chambers?" Vicham asked. Thadeus ignored the question and instead stepped inside.

"Your Highness, there is a matter that requires your urgent attention," he said. He turned toward Vicham and gave him a slight nod. The nod said, *I acknowledge your presence but choose not to address you*. It was his best attempt at an apology, and a poor one at that, but for Thadeus, apologies didn't happen often.

Instant dread filled the King as he slowly rose from his desk. Lately, good news had been in short supply; he had doubts this situation would be any different.

"What is it, Thadeus?" Hervott asked, a bead of sweat already forming at the top of his forehead.

"I request that you escort me to the morgue," Thadeus replied.

"What is it?" Hervott asked.

"It's best you see for yourself," Thadeus replied. There wasn't much sense in debating. Obviously, the matter was serious, the look on the stone cold general was enough to indicate that much. As quickly as they could they all darted from the room and made their way down the catwalk. Nearing the steps to the throne, he could see that there was a visitor waiting for him. It was the High Mother, and she looked to have an urgent need to speak.

They quickly made their way down the stairs. As they reached the bottom, the High Mother raised her hand as if to speak, but before she could utter a single word, Hervott held up his hand in protest.

"I apologize, Fernalda, I do, but there is urgent business I must take care of. Is it possible to meet later?" He politely asked. She gave him a sour scowl and nodded.

"I'll come to the chapel and meet with you at your office, I promise," Hervott called as they exited the foyer. The fresh air felt good as they stepped onto the drawbridge. The bakers had been busy; the air smelled of sweet cakes and rolls. As they cleared the bridge, it was plainly obvious that something was awry, most of the citizens had heavy looks to their expressions. All seemed scared of Thadeus as he led them through the streets toward the morgue. The morgue, as it turned out, was a couple of blocks from the infirmary; this location choice had always been odd. Nurse Alma had frequently complained of having to travel so far to dispose of the dead, but alas, nothing had been done.

The morgue was a small derelict looking building assembled from red bricks and containing no windows. On the roof were the vents which provided the only means of obtaining fresh air. Needless to say, the poor coroner was quite accustomed to having to rub mint extract underneath his nose every hour just to keep from gagging on the rancid smell of decaying corpses.

Thadeus pulled open the door and immediately plugged his nose. The smell was horrendous, the air smelled of rotten meat and feces. As they stepped inside the coroner quickly approached and offered everyone mint extract to rub underneath their noses. They all gracefully accepted and then followed the grizzly little man to the back of the building. Lying on a table were the two corpses that had been brought in earlier, blood oozed on the floor underneath them, and bits of flesh dangled from each torso. Hervott gasped at the sight; he wasted no time in covering his mouth and slowly approached the table.

"Animal attack? A bear perhaps?" Vicham asked as he examined the bodies.

"No, sir," the coroner replied. "Look at these claw patterns. The lines are far too sharply cut and jagged to be a bear. And here," he added as he pointed. "Look at this gash across the chest."

Vicham leaned closer and examined the wounds. As his eyes observed more, he came to the realization this was an attack by none other than an Akordan.

"So these two were outside the wall and must've got ambushed by a couple Akordans," Vicham concluded. Thadeus quietly grinned in the corner as he observed the conversation; his grin did not go unnoticed.

"What is it?" Vicham asked, his eyes fixed on Thadeus.

"I beg your pardon, sir. It's very easy to understand why you would believe the Akordans did this. This looks very much like their handiwork. But if you pay close attention you will notice this was not the work of any animal or beast at all. It was done by a man," the coroner explained.

"Excuse me?" Hervott asked, finally removing his hand from his mouth. "This was an Akordan attack, just look at the chest and claws."

"No, Your Highness, this is a frame job. Meant to look like an Akordan attacked these two. These two were killed by a man. But who would do such a horrible thing is the real question," the coroner covered the bodies with sheets.

"Who saw these bodies?" Vicham asked.

"Everyone," Thadeus replied. There was the kicker; the reason he had acted so mysteriously, the reason this was so urgent. If Terria's citizens had seen this carnage, there was sure to be another outburst of anger. The people would begin blaming the King, accusing him of not being capable of protecting the kingdom. It was at that moment that Vicham came to a realization; something in his gut told him he knew exactly who did this. It had to be Wort; he had been acting so mysterious the other day, it somehow just made sense.

"It was Wort," Vicham said. "He's behind this. Think about it, Dwennon. He has it out for you, for some reason or another. And he is working with someone. I think he is trying to get you removed from the throne. And after this tragedy? It doesn't look good. We must begin planning a countermove immediately; we need to gather the Council. Assure them that we are handling the situation. It's them who will be able to keep things from getting out of hand."

Hervott could not believe his ears. It was a serious accusation, but it made perfect sense. After all, it was Wort who was being the most vocal at the riot the other day.

"Wort needs to be found. He must be brought to me. Can you handle this?" Hervott asked, looking toward Thadeus.

"Yeah," Thadeus replied. "I can find that dirty little sleazeball. In the meantime, Vicham is right. Call a Council meeting as soon as possible."

Inca stood in front of the palace window and looked out to the streets of Terria. Behind her sat Emlin, who was sitting on her bed and running through a speech in her head.

"Do you have it figured out yet?" Inca asked.

"I think so. I'm going to start with apologizing for our last conversation. Then I will politely explain how the whole trip was my idea, and Broli only came along to keep me safe. If he loves me as he says, he should be grateful for him, not locking him up," Emlin replied.

"Well that's good, because it looks like he's on his way back to the palace," Inca said nodding toward the window. Emlin quickly jumped up and followed her friend's gaze. Sure enough, there was her father, next to him was Vicham. There was something in their expressions. Like something awful had just happened.

"He looks like he's seen a ghost," Inca commented.

"Yes, he does look troubled. Perhaps now isn't the best time to speak to him."

"Or, it's the perfect time," Inca retorted. Emlin continued to stare out the window as her father neared the drawbridge.

"You might be right," Emlin added. The King and Vicham both disappeared from sight as they entered the castle; out in the streets, something interesting caught her eyes. Walking casually down the streets was the High Mother and next to her the former bumbling drunk Wort. She seemed to be doing all the talking, all he did was nod. At least, that's how it seemed from this view.

"What do you think that's about?" Emlin as she pointed out the odd pair.

"Beats me. He's claiming to be a born-again Diaston. She's probably just having him help with all her charitable activities around the city to prove his loyalty," Inca replied. Emlin continued to watch the two until they had faded from sight. It had looked like they were heading toward the *Rajlomor Cathedral*, the High Mother's personal church, and office. She couldn't explain it, but something about seeing the two of them together made her skin tingle. Wort had never been a man of faith; in fact, he had frequently professed he was a non-believer. And now she was apparently supposed to believe he not only switched his views but also became a devoted follower of the High Mother? It didn't add up.

She remained in a daze momentarily as her mind ran through various ideas, each more preposterous than the next.

Her silence became an awkward, unwanted guest. Inca grew restless as she waited for her friend to snap out of it.

"Emlin," she said, her voice cut through the silence like a machete, Emlin jumped from shock then turned her attention to Inca.

"Shouldn't you speak with your father?" Her mind was still somewhere else, but she nodded in agreement, yes, it was time to speak with her father. The feud had to be put aside, Broli's freedom depended on it.

Emlin wasted no time in marching down the halls, her focus fixed on the direction of her father's quarters. The plan seemed as good as any — appeal to whatever compassionate side of him remained. If that didn't work, the next step would be belittling him until he gave in. She had used this technique on him many times before; one of the methods would surely be successful.

She paused for a moment as she approached her father's door. There were voices inside — two, it seemed. One was her father's; the other sounded elderly. She knocked on the door to alert him of her arrival, a courtesy she was not accustomed to giving, but it all seemed relevant.

After waiting a couple of seconds, she decided to invite herself inside. Hervott stood next to his desk; a strange glass globe sat on top, it had a light that went dim just as she entered.

"What is that thing?" Emlin asked.

"It's a shewglomus," Hervott replied as he tossed the orb back into his desk drawer. "I thought you didn't want to speak to me anymore. What brings you here?"

"Father," Emlin sighed as she took a seat on his bed. "I'm sorry for how harshly I reacted to what you told me. To be fair, I was in love with Septus. He meant everything to me. I wanted to spend the rest of my life with him."

Hearing those words sent a shiver down Hervott's spine; one he did a poor job of masking. If Emlin hadn't been looking toward the floor, she would have surely noticed.

"I understand that the war was terrible. I understand your fears of evil being a trait that is passed on. But that's where we disagree. People aren't born evil; they are taught it. It's nurtured. I don't think he would've been the man you imagined."

"Then explain the massacre in Frand," Hervott interrupted. "If he wasn't following in his father's footsteps what was he doing using dark magic? He had one of the very talismans that contained his father's powers. And what did he do with it? He murdered a dozen Delopar. No Emlin, he had evil in him. There is no doubt about it."

"Perhaps it was an evil put there not by his father, but by *you*." Hervott opened his mouth to speak, then paused, the very words she said froze him. It was indeed an idea that had come to him once before. He had often wondered if he were to blame. Vicham's words to him from a year ago playing through his mind. *What if doing this causes the boy to snap? What if you're forcing him to become the very monster you fear?* Those words had haunted his thoughts since he learned of the attack in Frand. Could something as simple as banishing him have caused this? What does losing the love of your life do to a man? That's when he realized, he knew exactly the answer.

Losing a loved one is exactly what made him so paranoid and mistrusting; it turned him into a man of compromised morals. He knew it; he knew when he was doing all those corrupt actions that it was wrong, but he couldn't stop himself. The damage had been done, his mind had been broken. He had been molded into a monster. Not so very different from Septus.

"You see it now, don't you?" Emlin asked. She stood from the bed and approached Hervott, placing a soft hand on his cheek.

"It's my fault, all of it. I did this," Hervott whispered.

"The question is, what can you do to redeem yourself? You've done horrible things, but in your heart, you're a good person. Are you ready to prove it?" Emlin asked. A few tears formed in his eyes as he shook his head in compliance.

"You need to release Broli from the dungeons. He did nothing except try to protect me."

"You're right. He should be *commended* for his service, not punished. I'll have him released immediately," Hervott replied. Emlin nodded in appreciation and turned to exit his room.

"Is it too late for me, Emlin? Can I fix this?" She stopped in her tracks, turning to face her father.

"It will never hurt to try." Hervott offered his best attempt at a smile as she opened the door and exited. Standing just on the other side of the door was Vicham. *How long had he been standing there? What had he heard?* He had a rather pleased look to his face as Emlin passed by. He quickly stepped inside and softly closed the doors.

"What is it?" Hervott asked, wiping his face clear of his tears.

"The Council will assemble tonight," Vicham replied.

"Ah, so you managed to summon them."

"Actually, sir, they've summoned *you*," Vicham replied.

Chapter 30

Kunklestick continued to stare at the figure in the window as the flames began to slowly rise. It was as if they were peering into each other's soul. Each of them trying to read the other. It wasn't long before the presence of the flames caused a panic. Patrons began to scream and run about, grabbing their things as the flames continued to climb. Kunklestick still remained peaceful as he continued to look at the figure in the darkness. It was Nikalas, who finally shook him of his tranquil state.

"Kunklestick we have to go!" Nikalas exclaimed as he frantically shook his mentor. His desperate attempt to alert his mentor to the situation seemed to have worked. Without so much as another word, Kunklestick darted out the front door, quickly grabbing his staff before he cleared the building. Nikalas looked around; the flames had gotten quite immense by now; half of the building was engulfed; the whole roof had a fiery blaze dancing across the rafters.

Nikalas began to follow Kunklestick when he took notice of the waitress Zanna; she was behind the bar frantically gathering up coins and tossing them into a bag. Nikalas quickly ran up and tugged on her arm.

"We have to go!" He exclaimed.

"Not without my earnings. This money is all I have," Zanna replied as she continued to madly empty her various tills. The flames in the rafters continued to eat slowly away at the support system. It wouldn't be long before rafters were falling from the ceiling and crashing down to the floor, sending hot embers flying through the air like a meteor shower. Letting out a deep sigh of annoyance, Nikalas decided to stick around. He swiftly helped her empty the last couple tills until she finally nodded in satisfaction and darted for the exit. The building was totally engulfed in flames by the time they made their exit.

Outside the tavern, a crowd of patrons stood, all staring at the spectacle before them with wonderment and confusion. As he looked around, he could see Kunklestick was nowhere to be found. *The back of the building,* he thought. He wasted no time in running around the flaming monstrosity, sure enough, there stood Kunklestick, panting and looking confused.

"He's gone, Nikalas," Kunklestick exclaimed. "Vanished." He looked angry as he began to scan the surrounding area for clues. *Who was the mysterious figure, and how had he or she so quickly lit the fire? And most importantly, why?* He had just about given up looking for any clues when he heard the sound of twigs snapping in the distance. Kunklestick quickly looked toward Nikalas then took off into the depths of the forest, faster than he had ever seen the old man move.

"Should I come with you?" Nikalas called out. He got no response. He stood for a moment pondering his next move, the heat from the flaming tavern beginning to warm his skin. "Screw it," he whispered to himself. Throwing caution to the wind, he reached into his uniform and pulled out his wand, quickly he extended it into staff form and took off after his mentor.

The stark darkness of the forest provided no comfort; there was only fear to be had. It was silent—too silent—as if all wildlife had just up and left. All he could hear were the footsteps of Kunklestick trampling in the distance. How had the old man found so much haste?

Kunklestick continued to chase after the sound of rustling leaves and sinister laughter. As he stepped into a clearing, he noticed the figure standing across from him; maybe twenty-five feet separated them. The eyes of the mysterious stranger were no longer glowing; they looked like the eyes of any mere mortal. Kunklestick stood patiently still as he studied the stranger before him.

"They said you were nothing but a drunk. They said you had lost your touch. I must say I'm impressed for someone of your age to be able to move so swiftly," the figure said.

"I'm full of surprises, Septus," Kunklestick replied. At that moment, Septus removed the hood and revealed himself.

"That's not my name anymore. I don't go by that. You can call me Agavordis," Septus replied.

"That's not very original. That was the name your father used. Couldn't you have come up with something better? Something that belongs to only you."

"Kunklestick you're a fool, and you will rue the day you ever decided to cross me!"

At that moment, a ball of energy, red as blood began to surround Agavordis. As the ball took its shape around him, it began to spin—slowly at first, then it continued to pick up speed. It came with a gale so strong it tore apart the forest surrounding it, tree bark was peeled off, leaves and rocks were whipped around. He was the eye of the hurricane, a vortex of terrible power.

Kunklestick gripped his staff with both hands and drove it into the dirt. Just as with Agavordis, from the top of his staff, a ball of white light began to form. His vortex spun as well, the two wizards stood firm, hiding behind their power as the forest continued to take the brunt of the damage. He clenched his teeth as he continued his focus; it had been a long time since he used his magic in a duel. It was certainly taking its toll. Beads of sweat formed on his brow, his muscles quivered. But his focus remained steady. His vortex kept on spinning; the contest was in full swing.

As Nikalas finally caught up to his mentor; he froze in place; he had never seen anything like it. His sense of awe and wow was masked only by his sense of dread. The wind pulled his hair in every which direction, debris darted past him, occasionally even hitting him. Kunklestick turned his head as he took notice, panic took over. Nikalas was in the worst possible position he could be in; he was right in harm's way. Using a slight telekinetic grab, he pulled Nikalas from harm's way and into the protective vortex.

"You shouldn't be here," Kunklestick said as he continued to quiver. Inside the vortex they continued to stand, each passing moment meant destruction for the surrounding forest. Nikalas had never felt so helpless. Here he stood at the mercy of his mentor, cowering behind his awesome power.

After a few moments, Agavordis decided to drop his spell. The vortex shattered into a million little pieces, sending bits of red light flying around like a meteor shower. The red glow of his eyes began to return as he lifted his hand and aimed it toward Kunklestick. From within his very palm, a green ball of light began to form. Smaller specks of light could be seen pulling toward his palm, as though the very power was manifested from the air around them.

As the energy struck against Kunklestick's vortex, it began to crack, hundreds of tiny lines began to spread across the white ball of energy. Kunklestick quickly shoved Nikalas from the vortex, using a bit of telekinesis to get him further from danger. As the vortex shattered, he quickly lifted his staff and caught the end of the green energy with the top of it. He grunted and groaned as he struggled to move the staff back and forth. He wrestled with the attack for a few moments, trying desperately to pull firm enough to tire Agavordis. After a brief tug of war, Agavordis brought his hand to his mouth and whispered something before throwing a wall of green energy towards Kunklestick. It traveled through the air at an incredible speed before being shattered to pieces by a fist made of light that emerged from the elderly wizard's staff. On the sidelines, Nikalas excitedly did a celebratory fist pump. The stories didn't do him justice; seeing Kunklestick in action was truly an honor. Kunklestick looked toward the tree line, still panting, trying to catch his breath. Agavordis was nowhere to be found; they were alone.

"Where'd he go?" Nikalas asked, standing up and approaching his teacher.

"Back to the shadows, with his tail between his legs," Kunklestick replied as he put his weight on his staff, using it once again as support for his weakened body.

"Who was that?"

"That was Septus, son of Agavordis, who is now going by that very name. It's truly a shame to see a good person go bad. Is everyone back there okay? Did they all get out?" He asked.

"Yes, although the waitress seemed hell bent on dying in the fire just for some money," Nikalas replied with a shrug.

Together they wandered back toward the tavern; the rising black smoke made it all too easy to spot. Nikalas found himself wondering about their horses; hopefully someone had moved them away from the destruction. The sounds of nature had finally returned—crickets and birds chirped. Oekies swung in the trees and wolves howled in the distance. As they neared the ruined tavern there was the ever so slight sound of someone sniffling, perhaps crying? The tavern was in ruins, there wasn't much left. With all the alcohol not to mention the older wood it hadn't taken long for the flames to do their work. Zanna knelt to the ground, her sack of money next to her, tears pouring down her face as she watched the last of the glowing embers finish the task.

"You have your safety and your life, be grateful you at least have that child," Kunklestick harangued as he slowly approached her side. Her rosy cheeks had managed to become even flusher than they naturally were. With tears still weeping from her eyes, she looked up.

"This place was everything to me. It was the one memory of my mother that still existed. Now I have nothing. Her last possession destroyed in a blaze of horror," Zanna explained.

"I'm sorry. I didn't know," Kunklestick replied.

"It sucks losing a parent," Nikalas chimed in. "I lost both of mine, they vanished without a trace. No bodies, no evidence. *Vanished.* Each day I hold onto this, to keep them in my thoughts." He reached into his pocket and pulled out a small pocket watch. It was a gift from his mother to his father. Generally, he carried it with him each day, but on the day they disappeared, he had oddly decided to leave it behind. When they had not come home, and the realization that something had happened kicked in, he took it for himself. As a keepsake and reminder of the love he had for them.

Zanna wiped her cheeks and held out her hand. She examined the watch with curiosity. There was an engraving on the back side.

So long as you carry this, time will always be on your side.

"It's beautiful, what is it?" She asked as she handed it back.

"A pocket watch. Where I come from, it's used to keep track of what time it is in the day. My point is that I know what you're feeling," Nikalas handed the watch back to her.

"I can't keep this," Zanna remarked.

"I want you to have it. I've made peace with my situation. In time, you will too. Perhaps this will help you," Nikalas smiled.

"That's overly kind. You don't even know me," Zanna replied.

"I know what you're feeling. That's enough."

Kunklestick grinned, as he hobbled over to the horses. They had indeed been moved and tied to a couple of branches away from the flames. It was odd that everyone had left; all the patrons had simply darted away into the night, leaving poor Zanna alone with her thoughts. What carelessness — what selfishness.

"Where will you go?" Kunklestick asked.

"I don't know. Perhaps an inn in the city," she replied before casually bumping her palm to her forehead. The city was sealed; there would be no entry tonight.

"You can stay with us," Nikalas suggested.

"An excellent suggestion. We have plenty of room, and we could use some extra company around the place. A lady's company is always appreciated," Kunklestick replied. He carefully pulled himself atop his horse; it was harder this time than it was when they had initially left. The rubble juice had clearly had an effect, one that was sorely missing now. Nikalas walked toward his horse and carefully undid the knot — it took a minute to figure it out.

Once he had mounted his horse, Nikalas carefully steered Wildfire toward Zanna. He tugged on the reins as he neared her and held out his hand.

"Are you coming?" Nikalas asked. Zanna blushed as she approached. Indecisiveness filling her mind, she knew nothing about either of these two. What reason did she have to trust them? The watch could quite easily have been a way to gain her trust. Morlay was filled with strange and mistrusting people. Most of the criminals in Furlasia resided behind those very walls. But there was something genuine about them, something familiar, especially about the old man.

"Zanna, trust me your mother wouldn't want you out here alone. Especially in times like these," Kunklestick added. He gazed at her, his eyes filled with veneration. It finally hit her as she peered into his eyes. She knew him, or she had met him.

"You knew my mother?" Zanna asked.

"Indeed, I did. Margary was a dear friend. You probably don't remember, but you've met me once before. Long ago, when you were still quite young." The memories began to pour in as she continued to stare at him. It *had* been many years. Her mother was once a devoted priestess of the Penecoth religion. She had used it to help pull the lost souls of Morlay into a greater cause, helped give them something to strive for. It was Kunklestick who had been there for her, who helped her get her feet off the ground and bring in followers. He who was there for her after the illness took hold. How could she have not remembered?

Zanna accepted Nikalas' hand, he carefully pulled her up, she quickly situated herself, letting her sack full of money rest between her and Nikalas.

"You guys better not live like slobs. I hate messy people," Zanna smiled as she wrapped her arms around Nikalas.

"Don't worry, Nikalas keeps the place pretty tidy," Kunklestick winked and gave his horse a kick. "Ha!"

Leddi took off with furious speed, darting quickly past tree after tree. Nikalas did his best to keep up. Wildfire was fast, but not as graceful—it took all he had just to stay on. He did, after all, have two lives in the balance this time. Morlay looked the same as they quickly darted past, the two guards still stood patiently by, armed and ready for business. The blue moonlight casts its silver light, across the ground, creating shadows and glitter on the frosted grass. The journey was short, neither Morlay nor the tavern was far out. After a fairly uneventful and mostly silent jaunt, they arrived in the clearing that surrounded the Hall of Wizards. Under the silver light it looked neither impressive nor mediocre, at least not in Zanna's eyes. She was used to locations of far less class than this quaint little cabin.

Nikalas, acting unusually chivalrous, carefully dismounted before reaching up to offer Zanna a hand. He even went so far as to offer the same treatment to Kunklestick. *What the heck,* he figured. *The old man had done all right for the night.*

After the horses had been tied off and fed, Kunklestick fumblingly searched his oversized pockets for the key.

"Aha," he happily said as he felt the cold copper against his elderly fingers.

"He does that every time," Nikalas remarked as he grinned at Zanna. She smiled, he was a charming boy. Something about him was different than most of the men she knew in Morlay; he was certainly more polite.

Her jaw fell wide open as she stepped into the hall behind Nikalas. The Hall of Wizards lived up to its reputation after all. It was elegant—impressive but not over the top.

"So this is the famous *Hall of Wizards*," she remarked with a grin.

"In all its glory," Kunklestick replied. He limped against his staff as he headed toward the kitchen. "I don't know about you two, but I've worked up quite the appetite."

"Can either of you two even cook?" Zanna asked. She quickly started following after Kunklestick, who paused and turned.

"I've been known to whip up a pretty good steak," he replied. Nikalas smiled as memories of their first encounter started running through his mind. He had been positive the old man was literally insane; he had certainly acted like it. As it turned out, he had just had a little bit too much fun the night before. All in all, Kunklestick wasn't so bad.

Zanna dismissively shook her head and darted toward the kitchen, passing Kunklestick as though it were a race. By the time he finally caught up to her she had already begun grabbing different meats and vegetables to put together a stew.

"Why can't you do *that,* Nikalas?" Kunklestick smiled as he sat down and watched her work. Nikalas shrugged off the remark with a chuckle, and they both sat in awe as if the concept of intense cooking was foreign.

An hour or so later and a few trips back for seconds—and thirds—Nikalas pushed his bowl ahead of him and let out a happy sigh. He hadn't eaten this well since coming here. Perhaps Zanna would be a nice presence after all.

"Don't get used to it. I'm not that kind of lady. But I'm grateful for the company and the shelter," Zanna blurted. It was honestly as if she had read his mind.

"Well, we are happy to have a new face around here. Nikalas, would you show her to one of the spare rooms? I need to rest," he stood slowly, grabbing his staff and began to hobble away from the table.

"I bid you goodnight," he added. Silence filled the air as he vanished from sight. The table was a mess, empty bowls and crumbs littering the polished tabletop.

"We can take care of this tomorrow," Nikalas said, ending the silence as he pulled himself from his chair. "Ready for bed?"

Zanna nodded in compliance. Nikalas quickly led them toward the hall of dormitories; he turned the handles for a couple doors. As it turned out, the one door unlocked was just across the hall from his own room.

"I guess this is for you," he said as he pushed it open. Zanna smiled and stepped inside. It was homey, the linens were fresh and finely pressed, a vase with lavender sat on a vanity cabinet next to a hand mirror and a couple of books. She turned and looked at him with confusion.

"Why does this look like it was meant for me?" She asked.

"He's good like that," Nikalas replied. "Good night, Zanna." He bowed slightly and pulled her door shut.

Chapter 31

Emlin walked toward him with a delicate smile, her hair blowing softly in the wind, her yellow dress doing the same. She motioned to him with her finger. Slowly he stood from his bed and walked toward her. His feet felt heavy; the ground was too soft. He was sinking, each attempt to get closer only proving more futile. But still she kept waving, her smile constant, forgiving and dangerous. The softness of the ground suddenly gave way to quicksand—now he was *really* sinking. Emlin smiled as he sunk down to his chest. Suddenly, the ground solidified, and he sunk no more. He was stuck, unable to budge. Emlin casually walked up toward him, her grin as graceful as always, but there was something in her eyes.

"I can't move," Nikalas said. She continued to approach, as she neared him she put her hand on his cheek, slowly she leaned in and licked his forehead.

"What are you doing?" He asked.

"Silly Nikalas, did you really think I could love you over him?" Emlin asked.

"Who?" Nikalas questioned.

"Septus. He's more man than you'll ever be. You'll never be anything but an orphan. It's time for you to join your parents." Emlin reached up underneath her dress and pulled out a small, glass dagger. Nikalas gulped as she held it in front of him, teasing him with the inevitable. She quickly raised the dagger above his head, letting out a terrifying scream she started to thrust the blade down.

"Nooo!" Nikalas cried out; he sat up in his bed, sweat beading on his forehead, his sheets moist and sticky. Fawn jumped from his bed and flew to his side, chirping, his breathing heavy. *It was just a dream.*

"It's okay, little guy," Nikalas softly rubbed the backside of his young pet's ears. "I'm fine." Fawn flew towards his face and hovered in place, slowly he licked his master's cheeks, his tongue felt coarse, it tickled.

"Okay, okay that's enough," Nikalas turned his feet off the bed and looked around his room. Daylight was just barely starting to sneak past the curtains. On the nightstand next to his bed sat the diary he had found in Terria and his wand. He hopped off the bed and approached his wardrobe. A shower was in order—the unpleasant nightmare hadn't done him any favors. He *stank*. He couldn't allow Zanna to see him like this. Quickly, he grabbed a spare uniform from his closet and carefully opened his bedroom door. The hall was empty, now was his chance. He quickly darted down the hall—the bathroom was near the very end, just before Kunklestick's door. As he stopped in front of the door, he pulled on the handle, but it was latched shut. His efforts to get inside didn't go unnoticed.

"Just a minute," Zanna called out through the door. Nikalas quickly turned around and darted down the hall. He had nearly reached his room when the bathroom door flung open, out stepped Zanna, wrapped in a robe, her hair wet.

"I'm done now," she said as she timidly made her way down the halls. Nikalas turned red with embarrassment. His hair was a mess, his breath a disaster, and his armpits reeked of old sweat. Not a good presentation. As she neared her door, she stopped in front of him.

"I wanted to thank you for inviting me to stay here," she said.

"It was nothing, I know what it's like to be homeless," Nikalas blushed, her robe was open just a tad bit at the top, he could nearly make out the top of her bosom.

"Still, it was nice. You don't even know me. I could be a murderer, a thief, a spy." She edged closer to him, his breath grew heavy, his cheeks continuing to flush.

"Are you one of those things?" He nervously asked. Gingerly she leaned in and gave him a light kiss on the cheek.

"Wouldn't you like to know?" She turned and pulled open her door. As she closed it shut, Nikalas let out a deep sigh and proceeded down the hall to the bathroom.

It wasn't much, nothing like the facilities at Nasleigh Keep. The water wasn't heated; the shower wasn't elegant. There was a simple metal basin in the middle of the room and just above it a pipe that ran down into the floor. At the base of the pipe was a handle that was used to pump water from the well into the pipe. From there you were treated to a fairly cold shower, it was all the more incentive not to waste the water. The less it touched your skin, the better. A basket sat next to the basin with homemade soap, in the bottom of the basin was a drain that sent the water into a separate pipe that emerged from the side of the building and emptied outside.

Feeling fresh, clean and rejuvenated Nikalas made his way down the hall. As he neared Zanna's door, he blushed, memories of their last encounter fresh on his mind. What had made her act so casual? Kunklestick and Zanna sat at the main dining room table, each of them sipping on a cup of warm tea as he regaled her with stories of the good old days and of her mother.

"Ah, Nikalas. So good of you to finally join us. What took you so long?" Kunklestick asked. Nikalas pulled out a chair and grabbed a finely crafted, white teapot from the center of the table and a spare cup.

"I had to freshen up," he replied as he poured himself a cup of piping hot tea.

They sat in silence for a few moments as each of them enjoyed their tea as well as a couple of small slices of bread. It tasted stale. For the life of him Nikalas couldn't understand why Kunklestick didn't just use his powers to conjure up elegant food all the time as he had in Cristol. Once their cups were empty, their snacks gone and their bellies full, Kunklestick broke the silence.

"Well Zanna, it's been a pleasure having your company this morning. But I'm afraid it's back to work for Nikalas and I. After last night, I fear we may be running out of time," Kunklestick explained.

"Kunklestick, I was wondering," Nikalas paused. "How come *you* can't just defeat Agavordis? Why does it need to be me?" Kunklestick nodded in agreement.

"Excellent question Nikalas. I don't know that it has to be. I'll certainly give it my best shot next time I run into him. But the vision showed someone else. A *stranger*. It seems likely that I won't be able to. However, that remains to be seen. As I said, I'll certainly try my best," he explained.

"One thing is for sure. He is learning how to use his powers faster than I could've imagined. *Someone* must be teaching him. Who that is remains a mystery, but I do have a hunch. He's acquired his second talisman, but he will find acquiring the third and final to be nearly impossible. This will buy us some time, which we need. If Agavordis truly is behind the death of King Ucertine, then he's clearly getting his pieces ready for the game. If we want to beat him, we had best get on the board," he quickly stood from the table — his balance appeared improved compared to last night. Perhaps he had added a little rubble juice to his morning tea.

Nikalas sat in thought, pondering his position, his relevance to the future. Doubt clouded his mind; he didn't feel like a wizard. Seeing the way the two of them had dueled yesterday, their sheer power, their skill, nothing about him seemed capable of such a feat. He shrugged as he let out a sigh and rose from the table. He nodded toward Zanna, a gesture he had often seen in movies, a sign he believed to be polite, then headed back toward his room without saying a word.

"Where are you going?" Kunklestick asked.

"Well, I can't do magic without my wand," he replied. "Plus, I'm sure Fawn would appreciate some fresh air," Kunklestick said nothing in response. He simply smirked as he turned his attention to Zanna.

"Is he always so moody?" Zanna asked.

"He's a growing boy who has been transported through a portal into another world where he was told he was destined to save it from an evil wizard. I'd say — all things considered — his mood is pretty fitting," Kunklestick explained. There was a time not long ago when he had thought the boy was poorly mannered — brash and ungrateful. But then it dawned on him; he wasn't so very different. Best not to judge him so harshly when he hadn't even sorted out his issues.

"So it's just the two of you? Where are the other wizards?" She asked.

Kunklestick turned toward her with shock. Could she not know? The stories of the war were told over and over again. It was taught in schoolhouses, preached in churches. People young and old were informed of the terrible outcome of the war. Surely a wench from the outskirts of Morlay should be well versed in the tale.

"You mean you really don't know?" He asked, shocked. She shook her head.

"Well then, that my dear is a story for another time."

A door closed in the distance, Nikalas emerged from the dormitory hall, staff in hand and Fawn perched atop his shoulder. His little pet looked all too cheerful as they entered the main foyer. As Fawn caught a glimpse of Zanna, he swiftly abandoned his position and flew happily toward her.

"Hey, little guy," she smiled as Fawn landed atop her finger. She carefully rubbed the backside of his ears. Each delicate rub provoked an even more enthusiastic chirp of enjoyment.

"What is this thing?" She chuckled as Fawn began to lick her fingers delicately.

"His name is Fawn; he's a Grimwort," Nikalas explained.

"He's so cute," she replied.

"Yeah, he is," he replied. He slowly approached Zanna and lowered his hand in front of Fawn. There was a brief hesitation, but after a firm glance, Fawn obediently climbed aboard.

"The Hall is your home, Zanna. Don't be shy, help yourself to anything that catches your fancy. We will be just outside if you need anything," Kunklestick began making his way toward the door with haste.

The sky was overcast, the air heavy with moisture, leaving the grass wet and the mood dreary. It seemed appropriate, however, considering the circumstances. The very reasons for needing to train Nikalas were, in fact, forlorn.

"Stand near the edge of the quarry," Kunklestick instructed. Nikalas hesitated for a moment—it didn't seem like the ideal place to position himself, but then again, perhaps the fear of falling would invoke better results. Kunklestick seemed to be a sink or swim kind of guy. He took his position near the edge, opting to remain a good ten feet away from the actual drop. Kunklestick stood across from him.

"You've trained some with your wand, now it's time to learn the power and advantage of using your staff. When going up against someone as powerful as Agavordis you're going to need access to as much power as you can get. Only in staff form will you be truly powerful enough to match him," Kunklestick explained.

"In our first exercise I will be sending a wall of energy your way, if it strikes you, well, I think you can guess how that will play out. The key here is to focus, as always. Visualize what you want to happen. Last night, you saw me conjure a spell that shattered his Shockwave and kept me safe. The spell is *amendondulano*. Say those words, while visualizing your goal— which is to shatter my shockwave, and you will succeed."

"Are you ready to begin?" Kunklestick firmly asked. Nikalas sighed and nodded his head.

Kunklestick acknowledged the consent and under his breath whispered a spell. From his staff, a small ball of white light began to form. In a motion quicker than would have seemed possible for a man of his age, he swung the staff toward Nikalas. The ball of light quickly became a full wall of light, traveling toward Nikalas with a slow but steady speed.

"Okay, say the words, clear your mind and focus," Nikalas muttered to himself. "I can do this. I can do this. Amendon dulano!" He exclaimed. Suddenly, a blue ball of light formed at the top of his staff. It swirled around pulling bits of blue light toward it. At last, the ball of light began to extend itself into a line, which quickly moved toward the wall of white light Kunklestick had produced. It traveled fast, gaining momentum as it neared, just before hitting the wall of light the blue line transformed, taking the form of a rhinoceros. It let out a howl and ran into the wall of light, breaking it into pieces. It didn't stop there. The spell darted straight for Kunklestick, who had to quickly jump to the side to avoid being hit himself.

Nikalas tossed his staff to the ground and swiftly ran to his mentor's side to offer a hand.

"Excellent job, Nikalas. Truly remarkable." As it turned out he didn't need a hand getting up, he ignored the gesture rather than accepting it.

"I must say, I'm impressed that you could pull that off on your first attempt. You just may be the one from the prophecy after all."

He carefully reached down to the ground and retrieved his discarded staff.

"Let's try it again," Kunklestick instructed. Nikalas nodded and made his way back to his position. He had barely managed to pick up his staff before the second wave of energy darted toward him, this time a bit hastier.

"Amendon dulano," Nikalas bellowed. There was urgency in his voice, the urgency evidently translated to his spell, for it emerged from his staff far more rapidly than it had the last time. As before, once his spell neared the wall, it transformed into a rhino and crashed through it, shattering it into a million little pieces of white light. The stars flew toward him, filling him with satisfaction. *I've got this*, he smiled to himself.

Kunklestick brought his hands together and let out a soft clap, the training was going better than he could've hoped. To think just a few days ago, he had doubted his choice with Nikalas. Now, he began to wonder if there was something just a bit extra special about him. His displays of his power were far more impressive than ought to be for such a new recruit. His connection to *The Echo* was either very strong, or he was very gifted — either answer was encouraging.

"I think I've got that down," Nikalas confidently boasted. "What's next?"

"Oh? Two successful tries and you think yourself a master?" Kunklestick retorted.

"No, I'm not a master, but I think I've got this one down," Nikalas replied.

"Very well," Kunklestick replied. He quickly lifted his staff from the ground while in the same motion compressing it back into wand form. Nikalas did the same with his own. There they stood, across from one another, master and apprentice, both armed and ready to duel.

"This is the dueling spell. The most common attack used in a wizard duel. First, I want you to practice. Pick a tree in the forest, any tree. Any will do. Aim your wand and say Inginimo," he instructed.

"Inginimo?" Nikalas asked. Kunklestick offered no words, just a silent nod of affirmation.

Okay, you've got this. Nikalas took a deep breath and raised his wand. His eyes carefully scanned the tree line, looking for the right target. One tree, in particular, grabbed his attention; it looked vaguely like a person. *That's the one*, he thought.

"Inginimo," he whispered. As the last syllable rolled off his tongue, his arm began to quiver, his wand began to vibrate and a beam of blue light quickly darted from its end. As his spell hit the tree, bits of bark began to be torn off. Flying in every direction. There was a scream in the air that radiated like a siren. It sounded far away and yet so close at the same time. Then he realized where it was coming from — it was the tree itself. It cried out in pain, it *begged* him to stop. Quickly he shook his wand and let go of his focus. The spell was canceled, but the damage had been done, there was a dark black mark where the spell had made contact — it still glowed red from the heat of his blast.

"Why did you stop?" Kunklestick asked. Nikalas stood silent, looking at the tree, trying to make sense of it. How could a tree scream?

"There was a sound when my spell hit the tree," Nikalas softly mumbled.

Kunklestick approached him, concerned. Nikalas seemed in a daze, unaware of his surroundings.

"What sound? Tell me what you heard," Kunklestick commanded.

"I heard a scream, it was the tree," Nikalas explained. He turned toward his mentor, his eyes red with tears. "I'm not crazy. I *know* what I heard." Why did this affect him so? Since his parents had disappeared, all he could think of was screaming, yelling to the sky, flushing his pain. And yet, he couldn't. He couldn't express his anger. He couldn't cry out his sadness. He was numb; instead, he took it out on everyone in his life. But this tree? It had *screamed*. It had called out for help, it had begged him for mercy. Something about it was so affirming, he finally felt it was okay to allow his feelings out. There was no harm in crying, no harm in yelling. It took a tree to help him finally embrace his emotions.

"Shit!" He yelled out, his outburst so unexpected that poor Kunklestick dropped his wand from surprise. Nikalas continued to look toward the sky, tossing his wand to the ground, tears rolling down his cheeks.

"Why!" Nikalas bellowed towards the dreary clouds. "Why did you leave me? Why did you leave me behind?"

Kunklestick gently rested his hand on Nikalas' shoulder, causing him to snap out of it, as he turned toward his mentor, his eyes were red, tears flowing down his cheeks.

"What is it Nikalas?" Kunklestick asked.

"Why did they leave me? Why did my parents just disappear? They could've told me where they were going. Why didn't they tell me?" The emotions finally poured out; there was no stopping them. Kunklestick quickly threw his arms around Nikalas and embraced him in a firm hug.

"Sometimes the ones we love have to keep secrets to keep us safe," Kunklestick explained. "I don't know why your parents left, or what happened. But they loved you. They wanted you to stay safe. Keeping you sheltered from whatever it was they were hiding was their way of protecting you. It's okay to be angry. It's okay to be sad. Losing those we hold closest leaves a wound in our heart, one that never fully heals. One day, there will be a scar left behind, and like all scars it will hurt from time to time, but the worst of the pain will be behind you. What you must do, is keep them in your thoughts. Remember them for who they were. And the love they had for you. If you do that eventually, the scar will stop hurting. And you'll be able to just hold onto the memories. You'll be able to think of them and smile rather than cry. This I promise you."

Together they stood, embraced in each other's arms, tears coming down each of their faces. His words were true, he knew that to be true and yet he had struggled with this very feeling. The impossible anger, the guilt, the remorse. It had driven him into a bottle—he had locked himself up in his own sorrows and refused to open the door. Perhaps in helping Nikalas confront his pain, he would finally be able to confront his.

After a few more moments of tears, Nikalas finally pulled himself away.

"I'm ready," he said. He quickly reached to the ground and retrieved his wand. Kunklestick nodded and returned to his position. Nikalas raised his wand and aimed it toward his mentor.

"Inginimo," he called out. A jagged beam of blue energy emerged from his wand, heading toward Kunklestick with speed. Kunklestick wasted no time in returning the favor; their two spells clashed together with a thunderous boom. In the middle, where the two colors met, a ball of energy had formed. It spun with a furious speed, a loud roar like that of a jet turbine. The ball was blue, indicating that Nikalas had cast the stronger spell. As the ball of energy continued to spin, it edged its way slowly toward Kunklestick. The air was filled with the wailing of the energy as it continued to spin.

Without any notice, the color of the ball suddenly changed, it faded from blue to white as it started edging toward Nikalas. Kunklestick's spell had become the most powerful of the two. Nikalas gritted his teeth, trying his best to focus, but the ball continued to make its way toward him. In the distance, Zanna approached, a look of dismay on her face as she neared them. The energy continued its pursuit toward Nikalas, his teeth continuing to grit, sweat pouring down his forehead. Closer and closer the ball of energy came, its wailing signaling his inevitable defeat.

"No!" Nikalas cried out as he realized he had lost. It was too late, his mind was too flooded, his skills too weak. The energy hit him like a wall, sending him flying into the air. Onwards through the air, he continued to soar, until at last he landed a few sheer inches from the edge of the quarry. On his heels, he landed, chagrin covering his face. It was only mere few seconds before he lost his balance, tumbled over the edge and fell into the quarry. He screamed as he continued his descent, and all went dark.

Chapter 32

King Hervott sat at the head of the Council table, accusatory faces looking back at him. His only two allies in the room were Vicham and Thadeus, everyone else seemed against him. Cups of wine sat at each placemat. In the center of the table sat two large pitchers of wine. It was a serve yourself sort of ordeal, however.

"I've already explained this. The coroner doesn't believe this was the work of Akordans. He thinks it's a frame job," Hervott explained. His words appeared to fall on deaf ears. None but his two friends seemed convinced.

"Your Highness, if what you say is true and the citizen Wort is indeed behind this savage attack, then it's of the utmost importance that he be apprehended. He must be made to confess in front of the citizens," Eliana said.

"If I may, Your Highness," The High Mother piped in from the end of the table. "Why are you so sure it was Mr. Elandor? Terria has many citizens that despise you; any one of them could be behind the frame, if it is indeed a frame."

"We don't. That's why he must be questioned," Hervott replied.

"My men are currently searching Terria looking for him, if he's still here, he will be found," Thadeus added.

"In the meantime, we need to deal with the unrest that is brewing. Terria needs to remain united—now more than ever. If we as a city are to face the lingering threats that hide in the shadows, we simply must be united," Hervott explained. All around the table nodded in agreement. Indeed, it was an important time for Terria to remain united, but it was beginning to become unclear if such unity was possible under the leadership of King Hervott. His failings of late had brought doubt into the minds of many.

The meeting didn't go on too much longer. The High Mother agreed to steer people toward his leadership, defend him and explain why he was the best choice to remain in control. Surely with her amount of influence over the people she could stop the unrest from continuing to rise. Detrict Thissle had offered to help pay for the training of more soldiers and also recommended a thorough sweep of the area surrounding Terria. A good plan seemed to have been formed. The Council members seemed pleased. Once everyone had emptied their glasses, they said their goodbyes and the Council adjourned.

It was time for the streets to be cleared, there was a stark overcast to the sky, and it seemed imminent that a storm was approaching. Since it had been a while since a ricter storm had occurred, most assumed this was one of those storms — intuition, plus the strange smell in the air. Both signaled the inevitable. Ricter storms were native to only a few select areas in Furlasia, Terria being one of them. It was for this reason that each building had been coated with a special protective gel that helped shield them from the acidic effects. Citizens would be ordered to remain in their homes, but there was always a few that would be unfortunate enough to get caught outside when the storm commenced. Nurse Alma had gotten to be quite the expert at treating such wounds.

Vicham lingered behind Hervott as he made his way back toward his quarters, he had time for a quick nap but first they had to have a discussion. There was a political momentum occurring, what was unclear was which way that momentum was flowing. Nasleigh Keep was unusually silent today; their footsteps echoed against the vacant walls. As they stepped inside the King's quarters, Vicham quickly pulled the door shut.

"What do you think my friend? Is this something we can bounce back from?" Hervott asked.

"We have seen worse situations than this and come out on top. I don't see why this would be a problem," Vicham replied.

"I'm concerned about what you told me—about the tailor, about the women with the daggers, the secretive behavior of Wort. He's not working alone; there seems to be a movement happening. How can we contain such a thing when we don't even know whose involved?"

A soft blue light began to radiate from inside the King's desk. It was faint, almost unnoticeable, but to the trained ears, one could also just make out the soft sound of a whistle that accompanied it. Hervott quickly approached his desk and flung open the drawer, there sat the shewglomus, glowing softly. He pulled it from its hiding spot and set it atop his desk.

"Kunklestick is that you?" Hervott asked.

"It's not Kunklestick, you fool. This is Lord Fae of Cristol," she snapped at his question like a dog hungry for a snack. Hervott looked up the desk and toward Vicham, they both shrugged in confusion. She had rarely ever used this technology.

"What can I do for you Lady Fae?" Hervott calmly asked.

"He's dead. My son has been found murdered. The talisman cut from his body, and his body left to rot in the sun," she calmly replied. Vicham turned ghostly white as the words washed over him, his knees grew weak and his stomach grew queasy, he slowly backed toward the bed and sat down, his face flush and sickly.

"What are you talking about?" Hervott questioned.

"The talisman had been kept with Pip for safe keeping. Someone killed him and removed the talisman," Lord Fae replied. Her voice was curiously calm—perhaps Pip had been right. She didn't seem too broken up about his death. She was indeed a cold, heartless woman.

"Why did you do that to him?" Vicham exclaimed. Why did you put his life on the line like that? Did he even know you had done such a cruel thing?"

"Vicham I assume? My son was a wretched brat at the best of times, but I loved him dearly. The talisman was given to him at birth because I knew it was the best place to keep it safe," she explained. "I know about you. I know how you felt about my son. I will have you know that I was very pleased to see the joy you brought to him. I never cared about his fondness for boys. This is hard to hear. I have been a wreck for three days. I finally realized that the time for grieving has passed. If the talisman has been stolen, that means the necromancer is still out there. He has acquired two. One more and we will all be in grave danger."

Hervott looked to his friend, whose eyes were filled with tears. In all the years they had been friends, Vicham hadn't once trusted him with this secret. He had kept it to himself. Now, with the secret out, he finally felt like he knew his friend completely. He was filled with pride rather than anger, but he was also filled with sorrow at the look in Vicham's eyes.

"Septus is dead. I took care of that," Hervott replied.

"Apparently not. Who else would be gathering the talismans? He survived your little assassination attempt and went straight for my son," she snapped. Hervott stood dumbfounded by what he was hearing. If she was indeed right, things were far more perilous than he even imagined. The danger would soon be at his doorstep. If Septus had indeed survived, he had likely developed even more hatred, which would make him far more dangerous. Suddenly, things started to make sense. The hooded figure Vicham had mentioned — what if it *had* been Septus? What if he was somehow leading a coup to get revenge?

"Lord Fae, I'm going to have to get back with you," Hervott calmly said. He quickly tossed the shewglomus back into his desk and rushed to Vicham's side.

"Why didn't you tell me?" He asked. Tears poured down his friend's cheeks. He said no words, his throat too coarse to respond. There was nothing to be said. This was a moment for grieving, not chit chat. A great loss had occurred — one so great its effects were felt all the way in Terria. The time for business could wait; the time for friendship could not.

Emlin stood outside the morgue. Next to her stood Broli and Inca. She had to see if the rumors were true. They certainly seemed to be so far. Draxton hadn't been seen in days, and today she had been greeted with terrible news. The clouds in the sky continued to churn angrily, moving in a circle, like confusion. The air felt stale and still, there was no breeze; it was calm. A storm was approaching. The sirens had already been set off to signal the return of everyone to their homes, but this was important. She had to see for herself.

She finally worked up the courage to push open the door, and they followed inside, covering their faces as the odors rushed to their noses. Broli had been freed just earlier that day. Colonel Sabasio was initially hesitant to listen to her command; a dagger to his throat from Inca had provided some extra incentive. Now here he stood, a free man in the midst of death.

The coroner swiftly approached them, his footsteps silent and chilled. There was a ghost-like air to him, it was unsettling, he was an unpleasant fellow indeed.

"Your Highness, you shouldn't be here," he quietly whispered, shooting Broli a look of concern.

"Step aside, you creep," Inca hissed. He did little to protest; he bowed and hastily returned to the back room.

On the table sat two bodies, covered with a blood soaked sheet.

"Emlin, you don't need to see this. You can wait outside," Broli offered. She shook her head in refusal. Slowly she approached the sheets, the odor in the air was pungent, and the urge to vomit was insatiable. Taking a large gulp, she lifted the first sheet, the body was mutilated, its skin had started to turn gray, the wounds looked dried yet fresh. Inca covered her face as she looked at the damage.

"This was an Akordan for sure, I'd know their attacks anywhere," Inca whispered. The body had been mutilated, but not to the point where it was unidentifiable. It wasn't Draxton, that much was clear. Emlin looked at the final body, her hand hovered just above as she prepared to remove the sheet. Suddenly she turned to Broli.

"I can't do it," she whispered. Broli softly nodded his head and approached the table. He briefly paused as he glanced towards Inca and Emlin, they both watched with determination, anger filling Inca's eyes and dread filling Emlin's. He let out a big sigh and pulled back the sheet. Emlin gasped and covered her mouth, tears pouring down her face. Inca growled, her face twisted with fury as she looked at the remains. It was indeed Draxton — the rumors were true for once.

"They will pay for this," Inca hissed, she quickly stormed from the morgue and darted into the streets. Emlin had turned to follow when Broli softly placed a hand on her shoulder.

"Let her go, Emmy. Let her go," he advised. Emlin nodded as she looked towards her slain friend. His eyes were shut, but she couldn't help but imagine what the last thing he saw was. His last moment filled with horror. *Who was the other person?* She wondered. *Why were they outside the city gates?*

Together they stood as they looked at the remains of their slain friend with heavy hearts. It wasn't long before Emlin had seen enough. She carefully pulled the sheet back over the top of Draxton and promptly made her way to the exit. The fresh air of the city was a welcome transition, being in the morgue for even a few minutes was enough to dull the senses. She took a deep breath as she looked around. The clouds continued to stir, the air remained still. Broli stepped behind her as he finally exited the morgue.

"We best get inside, Emmy," he cautioned. "Smells like a ricter storm."

She nodded in agreement, and that's when the first drop fell. It landed softly on a bit of grass, the grass instantly browned and started to droop. The storm had begun.

Chapter 33

Hervott sat at his desk looking over old letters he had written to his former wife, Herratia. What a time it had been, when they were madly in love. To this day, he couldn't forgive himself for casting her out. She was merely dealing with her grief, but at the time he was too filled with anger to see that. All he saw was the desecration of their daughter's tomb, something he could not stand for. He flinched in pain as he continued to sit at his desk.

"What is that?" He asked himself. He lifted his leg and felt around; he had a small sliver that had dug into his left thigh. "I hate this chair." He jumped to his feet and looked at the chair with disgust. He ran his hand along his thigh until he was able to locate and remove the foreign object. This was hardly the first sliver he had sustained from this chair, but it would be the last. He had tolerated its presence far too long. The High Mother be damned, this chair was as spiteful and cold as she was. He huffed as he approached his door and slowly cracked it open.

"Is anyone out there?" He blindly asked. The sound of footsteps approaching him served as an appropriate answer. One of the royal guards stood in front of him, his hair wavy and brown, his chin was firm and his uniform was spotless.

"Can I help you, Your Highness?" The guard politely asked.

"Yes, you can. I'd like the chair at my desk discarded and a new one brought up," Hervott replied pushing his door open. The young guard nodded and followed the King deep into the quarters where at the desk, the chair waited. As they approached the desk, the guard paused.

"That's the one," Hervott pointed. The guard quietly nodded and proceeded to pick it up. It was cumbersome and awkward to carry, but nothing he couldn't handle. Hervott followed the guard to his door and pushed it shut as he made his way out, hobbling as he carried the chair.

"Good riddance," he muttered as he closed the door. He sauntered over to one of his few windows and rested his arm above it as he peered out at the city. The storm had passed, leaving a sky that looked like a majestic painting. Elegant colors of rose and marigold marbled the sky within the remaining feathery clouds. It seemed almost symbolic. No matter how dark things got, no matter how dreary, there was always beauty waiting just around the corner. He sighed as he took in the sights. How had it gotten to this? He had sat at the throne most of his life and for the first time, he feared losing it. The right incidents were happening all in a short time frame, and doubt was filling the minds of his citizens. In his heart, he knew he was to blame for most of it. His role in this world's suffering was a secret only he a Vicham truly knew. His mistakes, his paranoia, his attempts to be compassionate, always ended up leading to turmoil. In truth, he was a terrible ruler; he knew that now. But was it too late to fix it?

A crowd of people dressed in their best dress clothing made their way down the streets; they had been returning from another one of High Mother's jibber jabber lectures. She had been appointed with the task of trying to point people towards following his leadership. She never seemed to particularly like the King, but she was not a woman to break promises. Her influence over the people was rivaled only by his, and perhaps lately, even surpassed his own influence.

Poor Vicham, he thought as he continued to watch the crowd split, each of them heading their separate ways. He had always suspected his ways lay a bit different than average; there was often a look in his eyes when they spoke. Lord Fae was not a woman to react lightly. With the murder of her son Pip, there was no doubt in his mind, she was assembling an army. *Could her words be true? Had Septus indeed survived?* Thadeus was very good at his job. His work was legendary, as were his results. But he had forgotten to retrieve the talisman as instructed. *Could he be working with Septus?*

The time had come to put aside his feelings about the High Mother and go to her. She had asked him a couple of days ago to speak, and he had blown her off. Now here he stood, needing her influence more than ever. He casually approached his wardrobe and pulled it open, peering inside at its contents. If he were to speak with her, he would need to look his best. He pushed aside one outfit after the other until he finally came to a stop.

"That'll do," he whispered to himself.

Hervott carefully navigated his way down the city streets. It wasn't often he wandered outside Nasleigh Keep without the company of his closest friend, but Vicham was under far too much stress to join him on this journey. Instead, he was followed by the young guard who had discarded the chair for him. His blue cape fluttered in the wind as he continued his journey towards Rajlomor Cathedral. Each step closer to the High Mother he could feel his heart thumping. It was like entering a den of wolves, she wasn't necessarily as vicious, but he sensed she had the same primal urge to destroy him.

After a brief walk filled with a mixture of dirty glances and smiles, he found himself standing at the bottom of a flight of steps that led to the entrance of the cathedral. Two guards stood stationed at the door; each draped in red garments and each equipped with a large sword. These were private security, not Vanguards—as such they didn't have permission or access to the Beacons. Their method of combat was the old primitive iron sword. The guards served their duties diligently, however. As he continued his way to the top of the steps, they kept their gaze firmly fixed on him.

"Your Highness! What brings you to Rajlomor Cathedral?" One of them asked as he stopped at the top of the steps.

"I'm here for a meeting with Fernalda," he replied.

"Is the High Mother expecting you?" The other guard sternly asked. There was anger in his eyes, perhaps his use of her real name was seen as disrespect.

"Yes, she is," Hervott replied.

"We will need to search you," the guard replied. The young royal guard reached toward his sword, preparing to take action when Hervott glanced towards him and softly shook his head. He lifted his arms in cooperation as the guard did a pat down.

"You may proceed," he said as he finished his search. Hervott silently nodded and pushed open the entrance door.

Rajlomor Cathedral was every bit as grand as the stories had said. There were rows and rows of pews, elegant stained glass windows and a red carpet that ran the distance all the way to the altar. There was a strange smell in the air, like a mixture of grass mixed with a familiar chemical he couldn't quite place. Placed just above the altar, high in the midst of the upper walls was a red tinted window. This was the High Mother's office. As he walked down the path, he could feel her eyes watching.

Standing atop the altar, just in front of a side entrance door was yet again another guard, dressed the same as those posted outside, with the exact same look of displeasure covering his face as well. As Hervott approached the door, the guard remained silent, pushing the door open. Hervott met the man's eyes as he proceeded inside, they were filled with resentment.

Just inside the door was a flight of stairs, the further up he ascended, the more vulnerable he felt. His young guard had chosen to remain outside. The Diastons wouldn't allow any foreign guards to come anywhere near the High Mother; she was much too valuable for that. Once he reached the top he saw the door to her office, decorated with scripture and pictures of Undr. Hervott carefully knocked on the door. Without warning, it opened. Standing behind her desk, looking out her one window stood Fernalda Franco, the High Mother.

"Welcome, Your Highness. I'm glad you finally found the time to speak to me in private," she said while keeping her gaze fixed outside the red stained glass window.

"I apologize for it taking this long; there has been much keeping me occupied of late," Hervott responded politely. High Mother turned around. Her hair was hidden by an over the top maroon hat, filled with diamonds. Her skin was a soft white and her lips red and perfectly pursed. She quietly pulled out her desk chair and sat down, motioning for Hervott to take a seat as well.

"What do you think of the cathedral?" She asked. "You've never once stepped foot in here."

"It's impressive. Truly amazing. Diastonism isn't for me Fernalda. It's nothing against you, I just don't follow your beliefs," he carefully explained. She nodded her head and lifted a small cup from a saucer and brought it to her lips. She smiled as the warm tea made its way down her throat.

"Why do you think that is, Your Highness?" She asked curiously.

"I've seen too much grief to believe in deities," he replied.

"Dobus dulu crum," she said gingerly before taking another sip of tea.

"What did you just say?" Hervott asked, his heart beginning to race.

"Down with the King," High Mother replied. A knock at the door jolted the awkwardness. "Yes," she called out. The door slowly pushed open and in stepped Wort, a confident grin on his face.

"What is *he* doing here, Fernalda?" Hervott demanded.

"Hanrae has been staying here for a few weeks now. He was in need of a place to stay, and I'm never one to turn away a devoted follower," she explained.

"Do I make you nervous, Hervott?" Wort asked as he stepped beside him. Hervott sat in silence, his heart thumping through his chest and his gaze fixed on the High Mother.

"What is the meaning of this? You've known where he was this whole time? You *lied* to the council?"

"I was never asked if I knew where he was, not that I would have told you. All you would do is have him tossed in your dungeons where he would be of no use to me," the High Mother continued to smile. "Would you agree when I say that as a King you've been a dismal failure? You have time and time again led the people of this city toward grief and despair. More than that, you are corrupt. Taking matters into your hands, and ignoring the very laws you swore to uphold," she lectured.

"I knew it; you've never liked me. You've looked at me with disdain ever since we were kids," Hervott accused.

"That's because I recognized immediately you were a lousy Prince—full of greed and selfishness," she replied

"Or jealousy. Perhaps you wish you could've been me? Or was it something different? Maybe you were sitting aside secretly wishing it was you sitting on the throne with me. You always treated Herratia with cruelty," Hervott angrily bellowed. He attempted to rise from his seat, but Wort quickly pushed him back down.

"What is this, Fernalda?" He demanded.

"This is justice. This is *peace*. This is the beginning of the end," a voice said from the shadows. Hervott glanced around the room; there was no one, just the High Mother and Wort.

"Who said that?" Hervott demanded.

"Don't you recognize the voice of doom?" From behind the High Mother, a black cloud briefly appeared before fading away to reveal Septus.

"Septus?" Hervott whispered. "So it's true."

"Yes, as a matter of fact, it is. I'm alive, no thanks to you and your whipping boy," Septus replied. "And I don't go by that name anymore. You killed Septus, in that you were successful. I am Agavordis, son of the great necromancer and bringer of death to this corrupt land."

"Are you here to kill me?" Hervott asked.

"No, that's too good a fate for you. I don't want to kill you. I want to destroy you. And oddly enough, you've given me all I needed to do it. Your arrogance, your corruption, and your overprotection of Emlin has given me more fuel to throw on the fire than I ever could've imagined," Agavordis replied.

"Don't you *dare* speak her name," Hervott ordered.

"Does it look like you're in a position to make demands? You're hopelessly outnumbered. For once in your life, your power is gone." Agavordis slowly crept from behind the desk and stood next to Hervott. He nodded slightly to Wort, who promptly turned the chair, bringing Hervott face to face with Agavordis.

"You've aged terribly since I last saw you. You're not handling stress very well," Agavordis smirked.

"Why are you doing this Fernalda? Why help him?" Hervott asked, turning his focus to the High Mother.

"A mother will always protect her son," she replied. Hervott glanced at her with confusion.

"You're not his mother," Hervott said.

"No, but I took it upon myself to look out for him. I knew immediately he would be in for a hard life. I knew he would face hatred."

"She and the blacksmith took care of me, cared for me when no one else would. She gave me hope. Between her, Falker, and Emlin, I was doing pretty well. Despite all the odds that were stacked against me, I was living a mostly happy life. Until *you* took that away from me. It was she that led me to the Akordans, who helped me realize my potential. She that taught me that you could be stopped. That I could be with Emlin and get my vengeance, I need only seize the power that was stolen from my father, and all would be mine. Emlin would be mine," Agavordis explained.

Hervott once again attempted to rise from his seat, his cheeks red with anger, his eyes teary from the error of his ways. Once again Wort stopped him.

"Let him go, there's nothing he can do to stop me now," Agavordis commanded. As Wort released his grip, Hervott swiftly darted for the door.

"Kunklestick will stop you, Septus. Just as he did your father, he will destroy you." With that he flung the door open, making his way down the steps so fast he nearly tripped. His heart continuing to race until he finally reached the exit. His young guard stood just where he had let him.

"Are you okay, Your Highness?" He asked, taking notice of the look of despair masking Hervott's face. He offered no response, darting down the stairs as fast as his feet would take him.

Chapter 34

Air rushed around him, his thoughts scattered. *How did this happen? Am I going to die? No, I can't die. I have to focus.* Each moment he continued his descent into the darkness of the quarry felt slower than the last. As he continued to descend, he attempted his best to clear his mind. Suddenly he saw a face; he was a sickly looking man, his face gaunt, his hair long and gray, and his beard hung to mid chest.

"Help me, Nikalas," the man said. Under his left eye, he bore a strange scar; it resembled a serpent. Nikalas looked at him with confusion. How did he know his name? Who was this mysterious man?

His fall came to an abrupt stop as Yogurn swooped from the skies and grabbed him by the collar. Her wings roared as she gained momentum. As he surrendered control to the Grimwort, he found himself looking down into the darkness that had nearly swallowed him.

Clear of the quarry wall, Yogurn dropped him to the ground and took off into the skies before vanishing into a small tunnel of light. Zanna quickly rushed to his side, as he lay on the ground catching his breath.

"Are you okay?" Zanna exclaimed. "I thought you'd fallen to your death." Nikalas nodded silently as he sat pondering the image he had seen. The man had asked him for help, but he had not the slightest idea who he was. Kunklestick approached much more deftly; his concern seemed far less than Zanna. As he came to a stop above Nikalas, he held out his hand and offered assistance. Nikalas looked up at the gesture with equal parts anger and gratefulness; he wasn't sure which feeling was dominating. He reached up and accepted the hand, Kunklestick gave him a firm pull, and he was back on his feet.

"I wasn't going to let you just fall to your death," he quietly explained. Nikalas nodded, he was angry at the circumstances, but at the same time, he knew his words to be true. Even when he felt all hope was lost and that he would surely perish a part of him knew his mentor wouldn't let it be.

"What happened? Why did your spell weaken? I felt your energy; you could've beaten me, but something detained your thoughts. What was it?" Kunklestick asked.

Nikalas stood silently pondering the question. On the ground to the left, he noticed his wand protruding from the grass. He silently reached down to pick it up, sliding it carefully into his pocket. Fawn sat in the grass near the trees, awaiting his master's call. He pursed his lips and subtly ordered his pet to return to his side. Kunklestick stood patiently awaiting an answer, but it appeared Nikalas was fresh out of those at the moment.

"I saw something as I fell," he said finally. Zanna and Kunklestick both turned, shifting their focus as his words ended the awkward silence.

"I saw an elderly man with long gray hair and an obnoxious beard. He asked me for help," he explained.

"It was likely just an illusion your mind perceived during your panic," Kunklestick replied.

"There was a scar under his left eye that looked like a serpent." The words crashed into him like a freight train. Kunklestick darted quickly towards Nikalas and grabbed him by the shoulders.

"What did you say?" He blurted out.

"He had a scar under his left eye that looked like a snake," Nikalas repeated. Kunklestick darted toward the quarry and peered over its edge. *Could it be possible?*

"What did he say to you?" He asked, his gaze fixed on the darkness below.

"Help me," Nikalas replied. "Do you know who it was?" Kunklestick remained steadfast in his silence as he kept his focus on the quarry.

"Do you always use such dangerous forms of training with your students?" Zanna asked, unapproving. Nikalas looked at her and smiled; it served as a confirmation of her suspicions. Between having him jump from a waterfall and now practicing at the near edge of a deep quarry, it was safe to say his mentor had no objections to throwing his students into harm's way.

"We must continue your training a bit later," Kunklestick said as he turned from the quarry and headed toward them. "I have an urgent matter that needs attention." With no further explanation, he proceeded past them, leaving them with confusion and doubt. Together they stood as they watched the elderly man shrink into the horizon.

"Shall we?" Nikalas asked, nodding toward Zanna.

"Honestly, what was that about?" She asked as they began to follow slowly.

"He's not the most social person you'll ever meet. I don't know what he's thinking half the time I'm with him," Nikalas explained. A sudden burst of energy darted from within the hall, sending the door flying off its hinges and crashing into the dirt. Nikalas looked briefly at Zanna before entering a full sprint and darting as fast as he could toward the hall. Emerging from within the doorway was Agavordis; he was small from this distance—difficult to make out, but that red hair was unmistakable.

Agavordis lifted his hand, sending a streak of green energy darting toward Kunklestick, who had been knocked to the ground. As the energy reached its target, it wrapped itself around Kunklestick's arms and legs, securing him and holding him in place.

"Nice place you have here. Pity you left the door unlocked," Agavordis taunted as he continued his hold on Kunklestick.

"What are you doing here, Septus?" Kunklestick demanded.

"I told you not to call me that! I'm Agavordis!" He shouted, furious.

"You're not Agavordis. He, at least, was a powerful wizard. He, at least, had *courage*. You're nothing but a boy pretending to follow in his father's shadow," Kunklestick mocked.

"You're a dolt, Kunklestick. An old relic of the past whose only quality or unique trait is how much alcohol he can consume and remain standing. You're haunted every day by the mere memory of my father. And soon his will shall be done. He killed your brother; he killed all of those fools. And once I get what I need, I will fulfill his final task."

As Nikalas finally caught up to the action, he withdrew his wand and aimed it at Agavordis.

"Inginimo," he quickly called out. In an instant, a streak of blue energy darted toward Agavordis, knocking him to the ground and canceling his grip on Kunklestick. His mentor fell to the ground. The impact knocked him out, leaving him defenseless. Agavordis rose to his feet, but not by way of his hands or feet. No, some invisible force of energy pulled him to his feet, setting him down softly.

His eyes were filled with anger as he glared at Nikalas.

"The boy from the prophecy, how cute," Agavordis laughed. He quickly sent a beam of energy darting at Nikalas.

"Inginimo," Nikalas quickly called out. His streak of energy clashed against Agavordis' with a deafening roar. As before, in between the two streaks of energy a ball formed, spinning persistently with a neon green glow. The orb continued to edge its way toward Nikalas.

Clear your mind. Remember the Elephas, he thought to himself. Zanna watched with horror at the sight before her as she kept a firm protective grip on Fawn. The orb switched colors and directions; it was now fully blue and heading straight toward Agavordis. Nikalas couldn't help but smile as his spell began to win the duel. *It's working.*

Agavordis wailed in anger as his powers dwindled before his eyes. How could a boy who barely understood the concept of magic be so powerful? It was *impossible.*

The orb changed colors once again, returning to green and moving back towards Nikalas.

Nikalas snarled as he firmly grasped his wand, its constant trembling made it arduous to keep a hold of. He wouldn't give up, though, he *couldn't.* Their lives depended on it. The orb whirled, continuing to career toward him with increasing speed. *No,* Nikalas thought to himself. Each moment the orb edged closer the more failure clouded his mind.

"You can do it, Nikalas," Zanna called out from behind. Her words were faint, hard to hear over the wailing of the spells, but somehow he heard them. How could she believe that? She had only just met him. Her words of encouragement fell into darkness; he couldn't accept them. All he could accept was the sphere persisting toward him.

Memories of the past couple months raced throughout his mind—the boys beating him in the park. The lecture from Mr. Anderson. The portal. The dungeon. Emlin. The spirit, Cristol. So much had happened—so much that had led him to this moment. He wasn't meant to lose. Too much had occurred for losing to be his fate. He had lost his whole life; today he would *win*. He had to. He had to recover what he had lost when his parents left. *Himself.* For too long he had been a prisoner of his mind. The past holding onto him, keeping him secured in his despair, unable to win, unable to thrive, unable to succeed. Enough is enough. It was time for misery to yield.

"I don't need you anymore," he whispered to himself.

He strengthened his focus in a way he never knew possible. The wand ceased to quiver—holding onto its grip was no longer a struggle. The orb returned to blue once again, hurtling rapidly toward Agavordis.

Agavordis thrust his arm to the sky, sending both spells hurtling to the heavens. The quickness of the motion caused Nikalas to lose his grip and drop his wand. Quickly, Agavordis ran to Kunklestick's side, the elderly wizard still unconscious. A cloud of black smoke appeared, surrounding both him and Kunklestick.

Nikalas speedily reached for his staff and aimed it at the black cloud. As it faded away, both Agavordis and Kunklestick were gone.

"Where did they go?" Zanna asked, tears beginning to form in her eyes. Nikalas stood in shock—at a loss for words as he watched the final bits of the black smoke dissolve into the wind.

"Kunklestick?" He asked aloud. In his mind, he knew not to expect a response, but he couldn't help himself. If these very simple words brought him some kind of satisfaction, as if uttering these seemingly pointless words somehow made his master reappear then it would be worth looking foolish. As it turned out, however, there was no response; his master was gone. Vanished as abruptly as he had entered his life. He looked up at the sky in wonderment. *Where did they go?*

Chapter 35

Emlin sat on her bed, her eyes staring into space as she relieved the previous day. It had been one of the worst days she could recall. Seeing Draxton lying on a table, lifeless, bloody, mutilated. He had been such a good man, such a loyal friend and yet she mostly felt like she let him down. There were so many times when she had declined his company for Inca's or Broli's. *I hope he didn't think I disliked him*, she thought. As the sun's bountiful rays crept past her glass panes, she tried her best to crack a smile. It was truly a lovely day. Perhaps the universe was apologizing for the dreadful weather the day before. The ricter storm had appeared swift and harsh, but didn't stay around very long. On a positive note, this was one of the first ricter storms in history not to cause the untimely demise of some poor soul caught off guard. That was at least a small comfort.

Yes, the sun shined proudly in the sky, sharing its rays with all who walked the fair streets of Terria. It was a small consolation, but one she was happy to see. She rose from her bed, taking in the rays and stretching her arms. She hadn't seen Inca since the previous day; she had gotten angry and stormed out of the morgue. Perhaps today she would be more willing to speak. As she opened her wardrobe, she began to browse through her options. She wanted to feel bright like the sky. There might be pain hiding underneath, but she could at least try to look cheerful. The orange dress, with white lace and a ruffled bottom, seemed to fit the bill.

She wandered the halls with determination; there was something odd about today. The guards seemed nervous, the servants and maids all whispering as they navigated the mighty halls of Nasliegh Keep. Down in the foyer, her father was seated on his throne, speaking to one of the townspeople. She appeared to be complaining about the bakery she worked at not paying her a fair wage. This was becoming a more common problem in the city. As times got desperate, as tensions grew shop owners always tended to cut back wages and even staff. People were far less likely to shop when they were scared to leave their homes. No one knew what was coming, but the consensus was that it wasn't good.

Emlin quietly made her way down the stairs, as she reached the final step she nodded silently to her father. His eyes looked puffy; he looked more grieved than was usual lately. What had happened? What put such a vacant look in his eyes? She was trying to understand him a bit more; he was after all her father. His actions were questionable, some just plain cruel, but his heart was always in the right place. Inca had been traumatized after her run in with Septus. It was her reaction plus the final conversation with her father that helped her come to terms with how things played out. It was murder, and to be fair, he shouldn't have been banished in the first place. But those actions couldn't be taken back. She did find herself troubled by how quickly he turned from the charming son of a blacksmith to the young man determined to wield dark magic. Perhaps her father was correct about the darkness within.

"Excuse me," Hervott said, politely interrupting the elderly woman.

"Emlin, where are you off to?" He asked as he rose from his throne.

"I'm off to get some fresh air and visit Inca," she replied.

"Please take a guard with you," he requested. Emlin opened her mouth, preparing to protest, but something in his eyes said he was not going to budge. She quietly nodded and gestured to one of the nearby guards to escort her.

"I'm sorry ma'am. Please continue," Hervott said, returning to his seat.

Emlin looked at the guard and rolled her eyes. He seemed brash and sour. Most of the Vanguards were—joining an army at such a young age tended to do that to a person. Nevertheless, they were good at their job. That much was clear.

They walked through the streets in silence, barely even giving each other a glance. So far his presence seemed redundant; no one had hardly given her a glance, yet alone a threat. There was excitement in the air, but no clear indication why. Most people seemed to be whispering. Occasionally it seemed like people were looking directly at her as they whispered. But perhaps she was merely paranoid.

Inca's temporary residence in Terria was in an apartment building toward the slum district. Her father had put her up as a gesture of good will, mostly because of her close friendship with his daughter. That being said, it seemed too much a task for him to house her in the better part of the city.

Once they had reached the entrance to the apartment, Emlin turned to the guard and gave a firm stare. It said, *Stay here*, while still seeming friendly.

"Your Highness, your father requested that you not be out on your own," the guard fervently replied.

"I'm not out on my own. No harm will come to me in this apartment. This is the home of my friend now kindly wait outside. If I need you, I will summon you," Emlin replied.

Without waiting for a response she pulled open the dingy door, it was once white, but that had been long ago, it now seemed grayer, a byproduct of being so close to the factories. Up the creaky stairs she went, with each step she could feel her feet sinking downwards, the wood was old, water damage had taken its toll.

She carefully pressed her ear against the crooked oak door that belonged to Inca. Inside, she heard someone mumbling and moving around. Taking a deep breath, she firmly pounded on the door.

"Who is it?" Inca yelled.

"It's me," Emlin replied. The door flew open almost instantly. Inca looked exhausted, anger and distress filling her eyes.

"What are you doing here?" She abruptly asked.

"I'm here to see how you're doing; you took off so quickly yesterday. I was worried," Emlin replied.

"I'm fine," Inca snapped.

"Well, can I come inside?" Inca stepped aside and walked toward a poor excuse for a rocking chair and sat down, her tail hung out the backside and swung back and forth.

"You don't seem okay," Emlin said, closing the door behind her.

"Everything is so messed up lately. A year ago things were going smooth. Septus wasn't killing people; Draxton was alive. Broli wasn't being locked up. You weren't constantly sad. Everything's changed," Inca explained.

"What's happening out there? Why is it all falling apart? I lost an entire village of friends to a savage attack from someone who was once our close friend." Emlin nodded in agreement and sat on the dusty floor just in front of the rocking chair.

"You're right. Everything *is* changing. The world is becoming a dark place again. Not since we were kids has it been like this. Draxton was a great friend, he didn't deserve to meet such a cruel end," Emlin stood up and approached the apartments one window. Outside children played, picking up trash as though they were toys. Their faces scuffed and filthy, their hair tangled and dingy.

"So what do we do?" Inca asked. "How do we thrive in a world so polluted with hatred?"

"We persist, we move forward. We fight for what's right, we don't let the darkness win," Emlin replied. Inca skeptically shook her head.

"You make it all sound so easy," Inca replied.

"It's not, but it's necessary," Emlin replied. A loud horn shook the peaceful silence that had filled the street.

"What is that?" Inca asked. Emlin spoke no response. Her eyes instead remained fixed on the streets, entranced by the spectacle. There was a massive crowd beginning to form. Each of them garbed in white robes, a hood pulled over each of their heads. At the back of the crowd were a couple of people holding large brass horns, and next to them another couple holding drums.

Inca jumped to her feet and joined Emlin in observing the strange scene.

"What's going on?" Inca inquired.

"I don't know, but it makes my skin crawl," Emlin replied. The horn-wielding citizens proceeded to blare their instruments with a boisterous roar. With each beat of the drums, the crowd began to march, their footsteps in unison with each other. Emlin turned and darted toward the door.

"Emlin, no!" Inca called out. Emlin paid little attention to the warning. As she reached the door, she hastily flung it open and darted down the steps, Inca following in tow.

"Your Highness, we need to get you back to the palace," the guard nervously said. Emlin shook her head in agreement, together Inca and Emlin tried desperately to remain as close to the guard as possible. They carefully navigated their way around the mob as it continued to move forward, their destination unclear, but Emlin had a pretty decent guess.

They remained silent as they continued to navigate the streets. Under the guidance of the young guard, they had managed to find a path different from the mob, but the blaring of the horns and beating of the drums made it difficult not to feel intimidated. The streets seemed mostly abandoned; most had retreated to the safety of their homes or the nearest open business.

As they approached the entrance to Nasleigh Keep, Hervott stood calmly, arms crossed, next to him Vicham, looking slightly less calm.

"Emlin, hurry. Get up here!" Hervott exclaimed as he noticed his daughter. She wasted no time in obeying his command—not the normal behavior for her, but nothing about this afternoon seemed normal. No, this was highly unusual; the kingdom seemed volatile, on the edge of rebellion. Had the flames of war already been lit? Was it too late?

In the distance a new chant emerged, followed by the rumble of numerous boots—the Vanguard. Under the leadership of Colonel Sabasio and General Thadeus, fifty Vanguard soldiers jogged toward the steps in front of the palace and took up position. Each of them raising their Beacons and aiming them into the street ahead. General Thadeus gave Sabasio a confident pat on his shoulder and proceeded up the steps.

"What's going on, Thadeus?" Hervott asked.

"It appears the Diastons are marching on the keep. My scouts reported around three hundred, all marching this way," Thadeus replied.

"And yet you bring so few soldiers?" Vicham confusingly asked.

"We don't need to worry about the Diastons. They are not going to attack," Thadeus replied with a grin. His overconfident demeanor was one of his least desirable qualities, at least to Vicham. It took all his restraint to keep his mouth shut. *Not in front of Dwennon,* he thought.

Their eyes remained fixed on the streets ahead, the clamor of the marching feet, the horns, and drums all ascending in tone. The procession was close; that much was clear. Emlin gulped as the sound continued to fight its way into her ears. With each obscene blast of the horns, she found it more and more difficult to not grit her teeth, a habit she long had in times of stress. She looked at Inca, concern in her eyes. Inca quickly grabbed her hand and held it firm, their focus returning to the streets ahead.

There was something in the distance; it was hard to make out at first, but with each passing moment it became clearer, more discernable. Two large banners accompanied the crowd, which as Thadeus had reported, numbered nearly three hundred. Hervott squinted as he tried to make out the text covering the banners.

"Dobus dulu crum," the crowd began chanting. Again and again, they chanted until, alas they came to a stop only a few feet away from the line of soldiers. Without warning the chanting stopped, and all eyes turned to the right. In the street ahead the High Mother approached, and next to her was her devoted follower Wort and a couple of her personal guards.

"Fernalda, what is the meaning of this?" An unknown voice asked. She slowly turned her head, being sure not to put too much strain on her neck for fear it would detract from her effort to purse her lips. Walking out of a bank just to the left of the street was Detrict Thistle, fellow Council member, and friend.

"This is not what the Council wanted," he said. "You were to unite people to follow the King, not spark a rebellion. You don't think I recognize the old words?"

She offered no response. After all, she was a highly revered religious figure and he was nothing but a banker — a glorified money man whose only importance was purchased.

"King Hervott, as you can see we have quite a following of people here with us today," Wort called out. His voice carried through the air rather impressively, then again, it had gotten so silent you could nearly hear the King's breath from all the way at the top of the steps.

"And what is the meaning of this gathering, Hanrae? Why do you and your followers appear hostile?" Hervott asked.

"You take our intentions the wrong way, Your Highness. We are not hostile. We want no violence. What we want is simple," Wort explained.

"And that is?" Hervott replied, his demeanor was calm, but inside, his heart pounded like the drums the Diastons had just been beating.

"We are gathered here, at the foot of these steps because we, the people of Terria, no longer have faith in your leadership abilities. Your careless actions and abuse of power have led to the demise of two poor citizens at the hands of Akordans. And it was you who started it. You who cast the first stone. What say you to these accusations?" Wort demanded. All eyes turned to Hervott, who stood in silence, contemplating his response. It was Wort who murdered those two poor souls, but he couldn't prove it. Tossing out accusations in front of the townspeople would likely not end well.

"What you say is true. I made a mistake ordering of the soldier skirmish. I do apologize to those families that were impacted by the weight of my decision. As a King, I am responsible every day for the protection of an entire city; decisions are placed at my feet that are not always easy. Sometimes the wrong call is made," Hervott explained. The crowd was silent, mesmerized by his words. Most in the audience had been swayed by the High Mother; it was her words that had instilled doubt in their minds. That being said, if she were to move forward with this plan, she would need to keep the crowd angry. If they calmed down, she would lose.

"I was visited not long ago, by a few of the widowed wives, whose husbands and sons were killed in this skirmish. They confided in me their pain, and something else. That you had not been to visit them, you had not even attempted to offer them comfort nor compensation for their loss," High Mother called out. The crowd reacted with awe, once again filled with deep frustration. Hervott scanned the audience, his hold was failing quickly, his influence fading before his eyes.

"There have been many issues placed at my feet lately. I have not yet found the time—"

"The time to personally apologize for getting soldiers needlessly murdered?" The High Mother interrupted. "Pardon me, Your Highness, but I find that *unacceptable*."

"Fernalda, enough. This has gone on long enough. You've had your fun," Detrict pleaded. She shot him a solemn glance before raising her hand and striking him across the face. Detrict turned red with humiliation. Those who saw the blow exhaled with dismay. He quickly brought his hand to his face, his cheeks warm and throbbing, and covered the cheek to hide his shame. There was no speaking to her. He gave her once last glance, a look of contempt before slowly backing away.

"Do you claim to know what's best, High Mother?" Hervott questioned. All eyes turned from Hervott and instead focused on High Mother. This was a debate—a public spectacle—not one he asked for, but he had no intention of losing.

"Every day I walk the streets. Every day I see suffering. Crime in the slum districts is out of control, and yet you give people no means to defend themselves, you hog your precious Beacons and save them for your Vanguard soldiers. What right have you to deny the people this right to protection?" She countered.

"You didn't answer my question, Fernalda," Hervott pointed out. "If you wish to discuss your issues with my leadership, I think it would be best to do it in private."

"Oh, it's too late for that, Your Highness. I merely wanted to explain to you why the people have decided to move forward with a vote to remove you from the throne. You've had your fun, and you've ruined plenty of lives in the process. The time has come; your days on the throne are at an end."

Emlin had never really gotten to know too much about the High Mother. She had long sensed the animosity between her and her father. When questioned about this, Hervott merely said that it stemmed from childhood and refused to elaborate further. This action was spiteful; it seemed *personal*. What had her father done to earn the scorn of such an influential woman? And worse, could he beat her? At the moment, she appeared to have more fans than he.

High Mother stood with her arms crossed and her lips pursed, awaiting a response. Her patience was wearing thin as Vicham leaned in to whisper in the King's ear. After a brief exchange between the two, Hervott smiled and calmly raised his hand, settling down the whispers that had spread across the crowd.

"There will be no need for a vote, Fernalda. I have already made a decision to step down as King at the beginning of the next full moon. In order to give my replacement time to be properly trained," Hervott announced.

Shock and awe leaped over the audience, taking all by surprise, including High Mother. She gave Hervott a cold glance and gracefully nodded. *One point to you,* she thought.

"If the people would have it, I have chosen to let my daughter succeed me as ruler of Terria. She is wise, intelligent, fair, balanced and most importantly, compassionate. Qualities I have somewhat lost track of with time. I realize that I am no longer fit to remain a leader, my heart is too heavy, my mind too crowded. I have already begun training her, teaching her the ins and outs. Once the transition is complete I intend to leave Terria and settle down somewhere private, live out the last of my days with a worry free mind, and hopefully find some closure for the mistakes I've made," he explained.

She couldn't believe her ears. *What was he talking about?* He hadn't begun training her; he was lying once again. Was he capable of telling any truth at all? Or was he truly so lost in the midst of his fibs that there was no coming back? Had he dug himself into a hole he couldn't crawl out from? It had always been the plan for her to take over the throne — he had put this in her head at a very young age. And since that age, she had rejected the notion. There was no freedom in being a ruler — it was a punishment, a sentence not much different from a lifetime in the dungeon. No matter how much right you did, there would come a time where most would hate you. She couldn't bear the thought. The fields, the forest, among nature, that's where she belonged.

"I don't want this," she whispered.

"Why not?" Inca asked.

"He has no right to do this to me," Emlin angrily whispered.

"Interesting move, Your Highness. But it's too late for that. The people want the right to choose; we want a vote. Having a corrupt ruler choose his own replacement seems contradictory wouldn't you say?" Wort replied.

"I'm fine with it," a voice called out from the crowd.

"I as well," cried another.

"Princess Emlin will make an excellent ruler. All in favor of allowing her to take over, say aye," a gruff voice from within the crowd yelled. The crowd unanimously voted in favor of Emlin ruling as Queen in Hervott's stead. It was over; the rebellion had been squashed before it could truly get started.

There was a devious grin covering the High Mother's face. She didn't look like someone who had lost a battle. Rather, she looked like someone who had won one.

"It seems the people's will be done, Fernalda," Hervott smiled. He turned to Emlin. Her cheeks flushed with anger, but she had a smile on her face regardless. It was not a smile of joy; it was of necessity. Too many hopeful faces watched her, she had quickly gone from unimportant Princess to savior of the throne in a matter of minutes. There was no going back, it was done. Anger aside, she couldn't deny feeling humbled by the votes of confidence. She had always tried her best to be approachable, and it seemed she had succeeded. She turned toward Inca, whose face was twisted into a position she had never seen a Delopar pull off, it looked remarkably like a smile. It couldn't be.

"Why didn't you tell me?" Inca whispered.

"He never told me," Emlin replied.

The audience erupted in cheers, all those wearing hoods pulling them off as they celebrated the accomplishment. Emlin peered into the crowd and grinned. Standing just behind Wort, clapping while laughing joyfully was Broli.

"It was you," she laughed, her eyes remaining fixed on her friend.

"What?" Inca asked.

"It was Broli who initiated the vote," Emlin replied, pointing into the crowd.

"Is he a Diaston?" Inca asked.

"No. He *hates* them," Emlin laughed.

Dark clouds began to roll in, bringing with it a cool breeze. A powerful crash of thunder ended the cheers as all turned their attention to the skies. The beauty of the day was quickly being overshadowed by the gray clouds moving in from the east.

"Akordan!" A voice exclaimed. "Akordan at the gates!" From the back of the crowd, a young Vanguard soldier ran panicked through the crowd, stopping just in front of Colonel Sabasio.

"Calm down, son. Speak slowly," Sabasio ordered. Thadeus quickly ran down the steps to join them.

"There is an Akordan at the gate named Krytus, who wishes to speak with the King regarding his act of war," the soldier explained as he caught his breath. Thadeus looked up the stairs at Hervott as he slowly made his way down, each step accompanied by a tremble. All had fallen silent, trying to overhear the conversation.

"I'll go to him," Hervott replied, placing a hand on the general's shoulder.

"He's asked for General Thadeus as well, sir," the guard added. Thadeus looked toward the King and nodded.

"You're going to take accountability for your actions?" Wort asked, surprised.

"Yes, Hanrae, I am. Would you care to join us?" Hervott retorted.

"Yes, I would," he replied. "Let's just say the two of you aren't known for being diplomatic."

"Then let's go," Hervott calmly replied.

Chapter 36

King Hervott walked calmly alongside General Thadeus as they followed a trail into the woods, accompanying them was the instigator Wort and a couple of additional Vanguard soldiers who had been sent for extra protection. In fairness, both Hervott and Thadeus knew two soldiers would not be enough to save them should it be a trap.

They reached a clearing in the woods. There awaited a single Akordan as promised. Next to him stood a vicious beast with rugged rust-colored fur and sharp fangs called an Uborox.

"So you came," Krytus noted. "And you brought extra protection. Smart idea."

"Did you?" Thadeus asked.

"I don't trust Terrians as far as I can throw them. Of course I brought backup," Krytus replied.

The forest was dim, darkened by the thundering clouds that lingered above. There was no rain, nor lightning, just swirling clouds and thunder. Unusual weather, even for Furlasia. Wort gulped as he looked at the Uborox, it persistently growled as it licked its lips.

"He's hungry," Krytus replied.

"Show your backup," Thadeus demanded. Krytus nodded with a grin.

"Come on out," he commanded. From behind a large tree stepped a hooded figure, shrouded in darkness. Thadeus froze in place as he saw the face.

"That's a neat trick," Thadeus commented. "How did you survive?"

Agavordis smirked as he slowly approached them, his bare feet pushing aside the dried leaves and discarded twigs from the trees above.

"Let's just say I have an ally with interesting abilities," he replied. He came to a stop just in front of the King and folded his arms in satisfaction.

"Why are you smiling?" Hervott asked. "Your plan failed. Emlin is taking over the throne." Agavordis nodded with satisfaction.

"She'll do far better than you, but then again, that's not too hard. Your incompetence would make even *this* fool look capable," Agavordis gestured to Wort, who scoffed at the insult.

"Oh don't fret, Wort. You've served your purpose quite well. You're a very obedient dog. A master couldn't hope for a better pet."

"Why do you speak to me like this? I have done everything you asked," Wort replied.

"There, there. Yes you have. You've done so well. You're such a good boy," Agavordis laughed.

Filled with anger, Wort reached to his side and withdrew a dagger bringing it quickly toward Agavordis. The blade, however, stopped in its tracks. His arm was frozen in place.

Agavordis smiled as his eyes began to glow red. With a coy smile, he willed Wort's arm to turn around, aiming the knife back toward himself. Slowly, the knife edged closer toward his gut. Wort's eyes filled with terror as he realized there was nothing he could do to stop it.

"Enough of this, Septus!" Hervott demanded. The blade stopped as Agavordis turned his focus towards the King.

"You would spare his life after all the scheming he made against you?" Hervott silently nodded. "Wait. You'll exile me for doing *nothing* at all? You send this murderer to kill me, but you'll spare this drunken moron?" Agavordis roared.

"I'm a changed man, Septus," Hervott replied.

"My name is *Agavordis*," he yelled. His eyes turned blood red, and the blade plunged itself into Wort's gut, blood oozing from around the wound. Wort stood shaking, unable to move. Blood dripped from his lips as Agavordis forced him to twist the blade. With each new twist, more blood drained from the wound. Once the pupils had rolled back in his head, Agavordis released his hold, allowing Wort to fall to the ground in a slump.

"That felt *good*," Agavordis laughed. The Vanguard soldiers raised their weapons, taking aim.

"Just say the word, sir," one of them said.

"Okay," Agavordis replied. With a sinister grin, he forced the two soldiers to aim the weapons at Thadeus, who simply smiled at the gesture.

"You're either gonna kill me, or you're not. But get it over with, I can't look at that ginger hair anymore," Thadeus dictated.

"I'm not going to kill *you*," Agavordis replied. "You're going to kill Hervott. Just as he sent you to kill me, now I am commanding you to kill him."

Hervott turned towards Thadeus. A loud crash of thunder broke the silence, if only for a moment. With eyes locked onto each other, Agavordis and Thadeus stood, each waiting for the other to speak.

"Do it, Thadeus," Hervott finally said. Thadeus turned to him with shock.

"If you don't, he'll just kill us both."

"He might do that anyway," Thadeus countered.

"No, I have no interest in seeing you die. You're going to be useful to me in the coming months. That being said, if you don't kill him. I will kill you. Colonel Sabasio will fit the bill just as well as you," Agavordis threatened.

Thadeus reached for his daggers, which he had placed on his hips when he first heard the beating drums. Slowly, he withdrew one of them and took position in front of Hervott. *This isn't right; there is no honor in this. Even for me, this is low.*

"What are you waiting for? Kill him!" Agavordis demanded.

Thadeus stood, frozen in time. His eyes fixed on Hervott, who stood blank-faced awaiting his death not with fear but with honor. How would he explain this to Emlin? How could he face his troops, knowing he had killed the King?

"Do it now!" Agavordis cried out. Thadeus looked at the King and winked before quickly plunging the knife into his heart. Hervott let out a mighty shriek as the pain seared his chest. He quickly withdrew his blade causing blood to spurt heavily from the wound. It splattered all over not just the ground, some of it even splashing across his face as well. Tears rolled down the King's cheeks as darkness began to take him in its loving grasp. His breathing shallowed as the wound took its toll, draining his strength, causing him to buckle to his knees.

Thadeus quickly dropped down in front of him, catching the King as he started to tip forward. There they knelt, pressed against each other both of them blood-soaked. The King's breathing was becoming raspier and raspier as he looked out to the forest. It was beautiful; it had been so long since he had set foot into the forest. There was so much beauty he had turned his back on. Now at the hour of his death, he finally had a front row view. In the trees above he could hear the sorrowful whimper of an upset Oekie. Each shift in his body weight was excruciating, the pain traveled from his heart down all the way to his legs, yet he had to see. He had to see his fair friend one last time. Looking up into the tree overhead, he could see the sweet Oekie he had once held dear to his heart. Zewop's face was heavy with grief — even he knew what was happening. His friend would soon be no more. He quietly whimpered as he watched in sadness.

After a few agonizing moments passed, the echo of the King's weakened breath faded, leaving nothing but the chirping of the birds and the cries of the insects. Thadeus carefully lay the King's lifeless body in the grass and looked up at Agavordis filled with hatred and anger. He slowly rose to his feet, his hands trembling as he glared at the monster that stood before him. Agavordis remained calm, only offering a sneer of satisfaction as he studied the lifeless corpse. Hervott's eyes remained open, his mouth still wide from drawing his last breath. Agavordis glanced to Thadeus once more, this time smiling, being sure to show each one of his crooked, yellow teeth. His smile was cold enough to burn a hole into your memory. They stood in silence, staring at one another, one filled with anger, the other filled with joy. King Hervott was gone; his spirit had drifted away to the unknown, and in the unknown it would remain.

Glossary

Akordans: Akordans are a race of aggressive yet intelligent reptilian type creatures that are reminiscent of Alligators. They are strong warriors and ill tempered, making them quite dangerous.

Delopar: Delopars are a race of feline type creatures reminiscent of leopards. They are cunning and wise and very calculated when it comes to battle. They are also one of Furlasia's oldest species.

Arnouts: Arnouts are a species that migrated to Furlasia within the past hundred years. They are gifted with wings, which allows them to fly at will. They also have various magical abilities.

Terrian: Terrians are a form of elf that resides in the city known as Terria. They mostly keep to themselves when it comes to regional politics, but amongst each other they are nosey and mischievous.

The Echo: The Echo is a godly realm that exists between Furlasia and the realm of the gods. It is populated only by Grimworts and it contains an energy that can gift those capable of tapping into it with magic.

Ricter: Ricter is an acidic liquid that flows through various rivers throughout Furlasia, eventually emptying into a large body of water near the Hark Mountains. It is dangerous and deadly to all to come into contact with.

Shewglomous: A Shewglomous is yet another ancient device left behind by the god Undr. It is a gift designed to allow communications among great distances. A few select people have even been said to have seen visions of the future within its glass.

Beacon: A beacon is a rare type of weapon that uses focused light to produce a massive amount of concentrated heat. Its blast can either be short quick burst, or long focused burst that burn through almost any material within seconds.

Uborox: An Uborox is a vicious wolf type creature, usually with brown sharp fur. They are quite fast and large enough to ride, the Akordans once had them tamed to serve them but that time has passed. Now they wander the forest as one of Furlasia's many dangers.

Worthiar: A Worthiar is a bear type creature that engulfs itself in flames when it feels threatened. When that happens all nearby best be prepared for a fight to the death.

Oekie: A primitive ape type creature that has red skin and is furless, they are constantly navigating the tree tops searching for food and keeping an eye on travelers.

Grimwort: A Grimwort is a creature that originated within The Echo and was eventually brought into Furlasia as a way of providing access to The Echo and to identify those worthy of using magic. They live quite long and eventually become large enough to travel atop.

Diastonism: One of Furlasia's up and coming religions it mostly exists within Terria. Many have called it radical as its beliefs revolve around a worldwide cleansing being necessary.

Penecoth: The most widely accepted religion in Furlasia that preaches compassion and the importance of being one with nature as a way of getting closer to the gods.

M.P. VanderLoon is a first time author who lives in Rockford, MI with his husband along with their cat and dog. In addition to writing, he also works for the school system as a bus driver. To find out more about M.P. VanderLoon, feel free to visit his twitter at twitter.com/mpvanderloon